BLOOD CANTICLE

BLOOD CANTICLE

THE VAMPIRE CHRONICLES

ANNE RICE

ALFRED A. KNOPF

New York · Toronto

2003

THIS IS A BORZOI BOOK
PUBLISHED BY ALFRED A. KNOPF
AND ALFRED A. KNOPF CANADA

www.aaknopf.com
www.randomhouse.ca

Knopf, Borzoi Books, and the colophon are registered trademarks
of Random House, Inc.

Knopf Canada and colophon are trademarks.

Library of Congress Cataloging-in-Publication Data
Rice, Anne, [date]
Blood canticle / Anne Rice.—1st ed.
p. cm.—(The vampire chronicles)
ISBN 0-375-41200-X
1. Lestat (Fictitious character)—Fiction. 2. Mayfair family
(Fictitious characters)—Fiction. 3. Vampires—Fiction.
4. Witches—Fiction. I. Title.

PS3568.I265 B63 2003
813'.54—dc21
2002192475

National Library of Canada Cataloging in Publication
Rice, Anne,
Blood canticle / Anne Rice.
ISBN 0-676-97597-6
I. Title.
PS3568.I22B63 2003   813'.54   C2003-901782-6

Manufactured in the United States of America
First Edition

For
Stan Rice
1942–2002

—the love of my life.

Rejoice, O young man, in thy youth; and let thy heart cheer thee
in the days of thy youth, and walk in the ways of thine heart,
and in the sight of thine eyes; but know thou, that for
all these *things* God will bring thee to judgment.

ECCLESIASTES 11:9. *King James Version*

BLOOD CANTICLE

1

I WANT to be a saint. I want to save souls by the millions. I want to do good far and wide. I want to fight evil! I want my life-sized statue in every church. I'm talking six feet tall, blond hair, blue eyes—.

Wait a second.

Do you know who I am?

I'm thinking maybe you're a new reader and you've never heard of me.

Well, if that's the case, allow me to introduce myself, which I absolutely crave doing at the beginning of every one of my books.

I'm the Vampire Lestat, the most potent and lovable vampire ever created, a supernatural knockout, two hundred years old but fixed forever in the form of a twenty-year-old male with features and figure you'd die for—and just might. I'm endlessly resourceful, and undeniably charming. Death, disease, time, gravity, they mean nothing to me.

Only two things are my enemy: daylight, because it renders me completely lifeless and vulnerable to the burning rays of the sun, and conscience. In other words, I'm a condemned inhabitant of eternal night and an eternally tormented blood seeker.

Doesn't that make me sound irresistible?

And before I continue with my fantasy let me assure you:

I know damned well how to be a full-fledged, post-Renaissance, post–nineteenth century, post-modern, post-popular writer. I don't deconstruct nothin'. That is, you're going to get a full-dress story here—with a beginning, middle and end. I'm talking plot, characters, suspense, the works.

I'm going to take care of you. So rest easy and read on. You won't be sorry. You think I don't want new readers? My name is thirst, baby. I must have you!

However, since we are taking this little break from my preoccupation with being a saint, let me say a few words to my dedicated following. You new guys follow along. It certainly won't be difficult. Why would I do something that you find difficult? That would be self-defeating, right?

Now, to those of you who worship me. You know, the millions.

You *say* you want to hear from me. You leave yellow roses at my gate in New Orleans, with handwritten notes: "Lestat, speak to us again. Give us a new book. Lestat, we love the Vampire Chronicles. Lestat, why have we not heard from you? Lestat, please come back."

But I ask you, my beloved followers (don't all stumble over yourselves now to answer), what the Hell happened when I gave you *Memnoch the Devil?* Hmmm? That was the last of the Vampire Chronicles written by me in my own words.

Oh, you bought the book, I'm not complaining about that, my beloved readers. Point of fact, *Memnoch* has outsold the other Vampire Chronicles completely; how's that for a vulgar detail? But did you embrace it? Did you understand it? Did you read it twice? Did you believe it?

I'd been to the Court of Almighty God and to the howling depths of Perdition, boys and girls, and I trusted you with my confessions, down to the last quiver of confusion and misery, prevailing on you to understand for me why I'd fled this terrifying opportunity to *really become* a saint, and what did you do? You complained!

"Where was Lestat, the Vampire?" That's what you wanted to know. Where was Lestat in his snappy black frock coat, flashing his tiny fang teeth as he smiles, striding in English boots through the glossy underworld of everybody's sinister and stylish city packed with writhing human victims, the majority of whom deserve the vampiric kiss? That's what you talked about!

Where was Lestat the insatiable blood thief and soul smasher, Lestat the vengeful, Lestat the sly, Lestat the . . . well, actually . . . Lestat, the Magnificent.

Yeah, I like that: Lestat, the Magnificent. That sounds like a good name to me for this book. And I am, when you get right down to it, magnificent. I mean, somebody has to say it. But let's go back to your song and dance over Memnoch.

We don't want this shattered remnant of a shaman! you said. We want our hero. Where's his classic Harley? Let him kick start it and roar through the French Quarter streets and alleys. Let him sing in the wind to the music pumping through his tiny earphones, purple shades down, blond hair blowing free.

Well, cool, yeah, I like that image. Sure. I still have the motorcycle. And yeah, I adore frock coats, I have them made; you're not going to get any arguments from me on that. And the boots, always. Want to know what I'm wearing now?

I'm not going to tell you!

Well, not until further on.

But think it over, what I'm trying to say.

I give you this metaphysical vision of Creation and Eternity here, the whole history (more or less) of Christianity, and meditations galore on the Cosmos Big Time—and what thanks do I get? "What kind of a novel is this?" you asked. "We didn't tell you to go to Heaven and Hell! We want you to be the fancy fiend!"

Mon Dieu! You make me miserable! You really do, I want you to know that. Much as I love you, much as I need you, much as I can't exist without you, you make me miserable!

Go ahead, throw this book away. Spit on me. Revile me. I dare you. Cast me out of your intellectual orbit. Throw me out of your back-pack. Pitch me in the airport trash bin. Leave me on a bench in Central Park!

What do I care?

No. I don't want you to do all that. Don't do that.

DON'T DO IT!

I want you to read every page I write. I want my prose to envelop you. I'd drink your blood if I could and hook you into every memory inside me, every heartbreak, frame of reference, temporary triumph, petty defeat, mystic moment of surrender. And all right, already, I'll dress for the occasion. Do I ever not dress for the occasion? Does anybody look better in rags than me?

Sigh.

I *hate* my vocabulary!

Why is it that no matter how much I read, I end up sounding like an international gutter punk?

Of course one good reason for that is my obsession with producing a report to the mortal world that can be read by just about anyone. I want my books in trailer parks and university libraries. You know what I mean? I'm not, for all my cultural and artistic hunger, an elitist. Have you not guessed?

Sigh again.

I'm too desperate! A psyche permanently set on overdrive, that's the fate of a thinking vampire. I should be out murdering a bad guy, lapping his blood as if he was a Popsicle. Instead I'm writing a book.

That's why no amount of wealth and power can silence me for very long. Desperation is the source of the fount. What if all this is meaningless? What if high-gloss French furniture with ormolu and inlaid leather really doesn't matter in the grand scheme of things? You can shudder with desperation in the rooms of a palace as well as in a crash pad. Not to mention a coffin! But forget the coffin, baby. I'm not what you'd call a coffin vampire anymore. That's nonsense. Not that I didn't like them when I slept in them, however. In a way, there's nothing like it—but what was I saying:

Ah, yeah, we're going to move on, but—.

Please, before we proceed, let me whine about what was done to my mind by my confrontation with Memnoch.

Now, pay attention, all of you, new readers and old:

I was attacked by the divine and sacramental! People talk about the gift of faith, well, I'm telling you it was more like a car crash! It did sheer violence to my psyche. Being a full-fledged vampire is a tough job once you've seen the streets of Heaven and Hell. And you guys should give me some metaphysical space.

Now and then I get these little spells: I DON'T WANT TO BE EVIL ANYMORE!

Don't all respond at once: "We want you to be the bad guy, you promised!"

Gotcha. But you must understand what I suffer. It's only fair.

And I'm so good at being bad, of course, the old slogan. If I haven't put that on a T-shirt, I'm going to. Actually, I really don't want to write anything that can't be put on a T-shirt. Actually, I'd like to write only on T-shirts. Actually, I'd like to write whole novels on T-shirts. So you guys could say, "I'm wearing chapter eight of Lestat's new book, that's my favorite; oh, I see, you're wearing chapter six—."

From time to time I do wear—Oh, stop it!

IS THERE NO WAY OUT OF THIS?

You're always whispering in my ear, aren't you?

I'm shuffling along Pirates' Alley, a bum covered with morally imperative dust, and you slip up beside me and say: "Lestat, wake up," and I pivot, slam bang! like Superman dodging into the all-American phone booth, and voilà! There I stand, full-dress apparitional, in velvet once again, and I've got you by the throat. We're in the vestibule of the Cathedral (where did you think I'd drag you? Don't you want to die on consecrated ground?), and you're begging for it all the way; oops! went too far, meant for this to be the Little Drink, don't say I didn't warn you. Come to think of it. *Did* I warn you?

All right, okay, yeah, forget about it, so what, stop the hand wringing, sure sure, knock it off, cool it, shove it, eh?

I surrender. Of course we're going to revel in pure wickedness here!

And who am I to deny my vocation as a Roman Catholic storyteller par excellence? I mean, the Vampire Chronicles are MY invention, you know, and I am only NOT a monster when I'm addressing you, I mean, that's why I write this, because I need you, I can't breathe without you. I'm helpless without you—.

—And I *am* back, sigh, shudder, cackle, tap dance, and I'm almost ready to pick up the conventional frame of this book and fix its four sides with the infallible super glue of sure-fire storytelling. It's going to all add up, I swear to you on the ghost of my dead father, there's technically, in my world, no such thing as a digression! All roads lead to me.

Quiet.

A beat.

But before we cut to Present Time, let me have my little fantasy. I need it. I am not all flash and dash, boys and girls, don't you see? I can't help myself.

Besides, if you can't really bear to read this, then cut to Chapter Two right now. Go on, get!

And for those of you who really love me, who want to understand every nuance of the tale that lies ahead, I hereby invite you to go with me. Please read on:

I want to be a saint. I want to save souls by the millions. I want to do good everywhere. I want to have my life-sized plaster statue in every church in the world. Me, six feet tall with glass blue eyes, in long purple velvet robes, looking down with gently parted hands on the faithful who pray as they touch my foot.

"Lestat, cure my cancer, find my glasses, help my son get off drugs, make my husband love me."

In Mexico City, the young men come to the seminary doors clutching small statues of me in their hands, while mothers weep before me in the Cathedral: "Lestat, save my little one. Lestat, take away the pain. Lestat, I can walk! Look, the statue is moving, I see tears!"

Drug dealers lay down their guns before me in Bogotá, Colombia. Murderers fall to their knees whispering my name.

In Moscow the patriarch bows before my image with a crippled boy in his arms, and the boy is visibly healed. Thousands return to the Church in France due to my intercession, people whispering as they stand before me, "Lestat, I've made up with my thieving sister. Lestat, I renounced my evil mistress. Lestat, I have exposed the crooked bank, this is the first time I've been to Mass in years. Lestat, I am going into the convent and nothing can stop me."

In Naples, as Mt. Vesuvius erupts, my statue is carried in procession to halt the lava before it destroys the seashore towns. In Kansas City, thousands of students file past my image pledging to have safe sex or none at all. I am invoked at Mass for special intercession throughout Europe and America.

In New York, a gang of scientists announces to the whole world that, thanks to my specific intercession they have managed to make an odorless, tasteless, harmless drug which creates the total high of crack, cocaine and heroin combined, and which is dirt cheap, totally available and completely legal! The drug trade is forever destroyed!

Senators and congressmen sob and embrace when they hear the news. My statue is immediately put into the National Cathedral.

Hymns are written to me everywhere. I am the subject of pious poetry. Copies of my saintly biography (a dozen pages) are vividly illustrated and printed by the billions. People crowd into St. Patrick's Cathedral in New York to leave their handwritten petitions in a basket before my image.

Little duplicates of me stand on dressing tables, countertops, desks, computer stations worldwide. "You haven't heard of him? Pray to him, your husband will be a lamb afterwards, your mother will stop nagging you, your children will come to visit every Sunday; then send your money in thanksgiving to the church."

Where are my remains? I don't have any. My entire body has become relics, scattered all over the world, bits and pieces of dried flesh and bone and hair put into little gold cases called reliquaries, some fragments fitted into the hollowed-out backs of crosses, some in lockets that can be worn on chains around the neck. I can feel all these relics. I can slumber in the awareness of their influence. "Lestat, help me to stop smoking. Lestat, is my gay son going to Hell? (Absolutely not.) Lestat, I am dying. Lestat, nothing's going to bring my father back. Lestat, this pain will never end. Lestat, is there really a God?" (Yes!)

I answer everyone. Peace, the certainty of the sublime, the irresistible joy of faith, the cessation of all pain, the profound abolition of the meaninglessness.

I am relevant. I am vastly and wondrously known. I am unavoidable! I have pierced the current of history! I am written about in the pages of the *New York Times*.

And meantime, I'm in Heaven with God. I am with the Lord in the Light, the Creator, the Divine Source of All Things. The solution to all mysteries is available to me. Why not? I know the answers to positively every question.

God says, You should appear to people. It's the proper work of a great saint. People down there expect this of you.

And so I leave the Light and drift slowly towards the green planet. There is a slight, prudent, loss of Full Understanding as I slip into the earthly atmosphere. No saint can carry the Fullness of Knowledge into the World because the World couldn't grasp it.

I adorn myself with my old human personality, you might say, but I am still a great saint, and I am totally geared for an apparition. And where do I go? Where do you think?

Vatican City is dead quiet, the smallest kingdom on Earth.

I am in the Pope's bedroom. It's like a monk's cell: just a narrow bed, one straight-back chair. So simple.

John Paul II, eighty-two years of age, is suffering, the pain in his bones too much for true sleep, the Parkinson's tremor too strong, the arthritis too widespread, the ravages of old age so mercilessly upon him.

Slowly he opens his eyes. In English he salutes me.

"Saint Lestat," he says. "Why have you come to me? Why not Padre Pio?"

Not a great response.

But! He means no slight. It's a perfectly understandable question. The Pope loves Padre Pio. He has canonized hundreds of saints. Probably he loved them all. But how he loved Padre Pio. As for me, I don't know if he loved me when he canonized me, because I haven't yet written the part of the story in which I get canonized. And as I write this, Padre Pio was canonized last week.

(I watched the whole thing on TV. Vampires love TV.)

Back to the moment.

The frigid stillness of the papal quarters, so austere, despite the palatial dimensions. Candles glow in the Pope's private chapel. The Pope groans in pain.

I lay my healing hands upon him, and I banish his suffering. A quiet penetrates his limbs. He looks at me with one eye, the other squinched closed as is often his manner, and between us there is suddenly an understanding, or rather I come to perceive something about him which the entire world ought to know:

His deep selflessness, his profound spirituality, come not only from his complete love of Christ but from his life lived under Communism. People forget. Communism, for all its hideous abuses and cruelties, is in essence a vaunting spiritual code. And before that great puritanical government shrouded John Paul's young years, the violent paradoxes and horrifying absurdities of the Second World War surrounded him, tutoring him in self-sacrifice and courage. The man has never, ever, in his life lived in anything but a Spiritual World. Deprivation and self-denial are intertwined in his history like the double helix.

It is no wonder that he cannot yield his deep-rooted suspicions of the tumultuous voices of the prosperous capitalist countries. He simply cannot grasp the pure charity that can arise from abundance, the sublime immensity of vision possible from the vantage point of secure excess, the selflessness and sweeping sacrificial ambition that can be born when all needs are luxuriantly met.

Can I broach this subject with him in this quiet moment? Or should I only assure him that he must not worry about the "greed" of the Western World?

Softly I talk to him. I begin to elucidate these points. (Yeah, I know, he's the Pope, and I'm a vampire writing this story; but in this story I'm a great Saint. I cannot be intimidated within the risks of my own work!)

I remind him that the sublime principles of Greek philosophy arose in affluence, and slowly, acceptingly, he nods. He is quite the educated philosopher. A lot of people don't know that about him, either. But I must impress upon him something infinitely more profound.

I see it so beautifully. I see everything.

Our biggest mistake worldwide is our insistence on perceiving every new development as a culmination or a climax. The great "at last" or "inth degree." A constitutional fatalism continuously adjusts itself to the ever changing present. A pervasive alarmism greets every advance. For two thousand years we have been getting "out of hand."

This derives of course from our susceptibility to viewing the "now" as the End Time, an Apocalyptic obsession that has endured since Christ ascended into Heaven. We must stop this! We must perceive that we are at the dawn of a sublime age! Enemies will no longer be conquered. They will be devoured, and transformed.

But here's the point I *really* want to make: Modernism and Materialism—elements that the Church has feared for so long—are in their philosophical and practical infancy! Their sacramental nature is only just being revealed!

Never mind the infantile blunders! The electronic revolution has transmuted the industrial world beyond all predictive thinking of the twentieth century. We're still having birth pangs. Get into it! Work with it. Play it out.

Daily life for millions in the developed countries is not only comfortable but a compilation of wonders that borders on the miraculous. And so new spiritual desires arise which are infinitely more courageous than the missionary goals of the past.

We must bear witness that political atheism has failed totally. Think about it. In the trash, the whole system. Except for the island of Cuba, maybe. But what does Castro prove? And even the most secular power brokers in America exude high virtue as a matter of course. That's why we have corporate scandals! That's why people get so upset! No morals, no scandals. In fact, we may have to re-examine all the areas of society which we have so blithely labeled as "secular." Who is really without profound and unshakable altruistic beliefs?

Judeo-Christianity *is* the religion of the secular West, no matter how many millions claim to disregard it. Its profound tenets have been internalized by the most remote and intellectual agnostics. Its expectations inform Wall Street as well as the common courtesies exchanged on a crowded beach in California or a meeting between the heads of Russia and the United States.

Techno-saints will soon rise—if they have not already—to melt the poverty of millions with torrents of well-distributed goods and services. Communications will annihilate hatred and divisiveness as Internet cafés continue to spring up like flowers throughout the slums of Asia and the Orient. Cable television will bring countless new programs to the vast Arab world. Even North Korea will be penetrated.

Minorities in Europe and America will be thoroughly and fruitfully assimilated through computer literacy. As already described, medical science will find cheap harmless substitutes for cocaine and heroin, thereby eliminating the evil drug trade altogether. All violence will soon give way to a refinement of debate and exchange of knowledge. Effective acts of terrorism will continue to be obscene precisely because of their rarity, until they stop altogether.

As for sexuality, the revolution in this regard is so vast that we of this time cannot begin to comprehend its full ramifications. Short skirts, bobs, car dates, women in the work place, gays in love—we are dizzy with mere beginnings. Our scientific understanding and control of procreation gives us a power undreamt of in former centuries and the immediate impact is but a shadow of things to come. We must respect the immense mysteries of the sperm and the egg, the mysteries of the chemistry of gender and gender choice and attraction. All God's children will thrive from our growing knowledge, but to repeat this is only the beginning. We must have the courage to embrace the beauty of science in the name of the Lord.

The Pope listens. He smiles.

I continue.

The image of God Incarnate, become Man out of fascination with His own Creation, will triumph in the Third Millennium as the supreme emblem of Divine Sacrifice and Unfathomable Love.

It takes thousands of years to understand the Crucified Christ, I say. Why, for example, did He come down to live thirty-three years? Why not twenty? Why not twenty-five? You could ponder this stuff forever. Why did Christ have to start as a baby? Who wants to be a baby? Was being a baby part of our salvation? And why choose that particular time in history? And such a place!

Dirt, grit, sand, rocks everywhere—I've never seen so many rocks as in the Holy Land—bare feet, sandals, camels; imagine those times. No wonder they used to stone people! Did it have anything to do with the sheer simplicity of the clothes and hair, Christ coming in that era? I think it did. Page through a book on world costume—you know, a really good encyclopedia taking you from ancient Sumer to Ralph

Lauren, and you can't find any simpler clothes and hair than in Galilee First Century.

I am serious, I tell the Holy Father. Christ considered this, He had to. How could He not? Surely He knew that images of Him would proliferate exponentially.

Furthermore, I think Christ chose Crucifixion because henceforth in every depiction He would be seen extending His arms in a loving embrace. Once you see the Crucifix in that manner, everything changes. You see Him reaching out to all the World. He knew the image had to be durable. He knew it had to be abstractable. He knew it had to be reproducible. It is no accident that we can take the image of this ghastly death and wear it around our necks on a chain. God thinks of all these things, doesn't He?

The Pope is still smiling. "If you weren't a saint, I'd laugh at you," he says. "Exactly when are you expecting these Techno-saints, by the way?"

I'm happy. He looks like the old Wojtyla—the Pope who still went skiing until he was seventy-three. My visit has been worth it.

And after all, we can't all be Padre Pio or Mother Teresa. I'm Saint Lestat.

"I'll say hello for you to Padre Pio," I whisper.

But the Pope is dozing. He has chuckled and drifted off. So much for my mystical import. I've put him to sleep. But what did I expect, especially of the Pope? He works so hard. He suffers. He thinks. He has already traveled to Asia and Eastern Europe this year, and he will soon be going to Toronto and Guatemala and Mexico. I don't know how he can do these things.

I place my hand on his forehead.

Then I leave.

I go down the stairs to the Sistine Chapel. It is empty and dark, of course. It is chilly too. But never fear, my saintly eyes are as good as my vampire eyes, and I can see the swarming magnificence.

Alone—cut off from all the world and all things—I stand there. I want to lie on the floor face down in the manner of a priest at his ordination. I want to be a priest. I want to consecrate the host! I want this so badly that I ache for it. I DON'T WANT TO DO EVIL.

But the fact is, my fantasy of Saint Lestat is dissolving. I know it for what it is and I can't sustain it.

I know that I am no saint and never was or will be. No banner of me ever unfurled in St. Peter's Square in the sunlight. No crowd of hundreds of thousands ever cheered for my canonization. No string of cardinals ever attended the ceremony because it never took place. And I have no odorless, tasteless, harmless formula that exactly mimics crack, cocaine and heroin combined, so I can't save the world.

I'm not even standing in the Sistine Chapel. I am far away from it, in a place of warmth, though just as lonely.

I am a vampire. For over two hundred years I've loved it. I am filled with the blood of others to my very eyeballs. I am polluted with it. I am as cursed as the Hemorrhissa before she touched the hem of Christ's garment in Capharnaum! I live by blood. I am ritually impure.

And there's only one kind of miracle I can work. We call it the Dark Trick and I'm about to do it.

And do you think all this guilt is about to stop me? *Nada*, never, *mais non*, forget about it, get out of here, not in a pig's eye, pa-lease, gimme a break, no way.

I told you I'd come back, didn't I?

I'm irrepressible, unforgivable, unstoppable, shameless, thoughtless, hopeless, heartless, running rampant, the wild child, undaunted, unrepentant, unsaved.

And baby, there is a story to tell.

I hear Hell's Bells calling me. It's time to boogie!

SO SLAM CUT TO:

2

BLACKWOOD FARM: EXTERIOR; EVENING.

ALITTLE COUNTRY CEMETERY on the edge of a cypress swamp, with a dozen or more old cement graves, most names long ago effaced, and one of these raised rectangular tombs black with soot from a recent fire, and the whole surrounded by a small iron fence and four immense oak trees, the kind weighted down by their dipping branches, and the sky the perfect color of lilacs, and the heat of the summer sweet and caressing and—

—you bet I've got on my black velvet frock coat (close-up: tapered at the waist, brass buttons) and my motorcycle boots, and a brand-new linen shirt loaded with lace at cuffs and throat (pity the poor slob who snickers at me on account of that!), and I haven't cut my shoulder-length blond mane tonight, which I sometimes do for variety, and I've chucked my violet glasses because who cares that my eyes attract attention, and my skin's still dramatically tanned from my years-ago suicide attempt in the raw sun of the Gobi Desert, and I'm thinking—

—Dark Trick, yes, work the miracle, they need you, up there in the Big House, you Brat Prince, you Sheik among vampires, stop brooding and mourning down here, go to it, there's a delicate situation up there in the Big House—and it is

TIME TO TELL YOU WHAT HAPPENED AND SO I DO:

I PACED, having just risen from my secret hiding place, and I mourned bitterly for another Blood Drinker who had perished in this very cemetery, on the aforementioned blackened grave, in an immense fire, and of her own will, leaving us only last night, without the slightest warning.

This was Merrick Mayfair, only three years among the Undead or less, and I'd invited her here to Blackwood Farm to help me exorcise an evil spirit that had been haunting Quinn Blackwood since childhood. Quinn was very new to the Blood, and had come to me for help with this ghost, which, far from leaving him at his transformation from mortal to vampire, had only grown stronger and meaner, and had actually caused the death of the mortal dearest to Quinn—his great Aunt Queen, age of eighty-five, by causing the beautiful lady to fall. I had needed Merrick Mayfair to exorcise this evil spirit forever.

Goblin was the name of this ghost, and as Merrick Mayfair had been both scholar and sorceress before she sought out the Dark Blood, I figured she would have the strength required to get rid of him.

Well, she came, and she solved the riddle of Goblin, and, building a high altar of coal and wood which she set ablaze, she not only burnt the corpse of the evil one but went into the flames with it. The spirit was gone, and so was Merrick Mayfair.

Of course I tried to snatch her back from the fire, but her soul had taken flight, and no amount of my blood poured on her burnt remains could conceivably revive her.

It did seem to me as I walked back and forth, kicking at the graveyard dust, that immortals who think they want the Dark Blood perish infinitely more easily than those of us who never asked for it. Perhaps the anger of the rape carries us through for centuries.

But as I said: something was going on in the Big House.

I was thinking Dark Trick as I paced, yes, Dark Trick, the making of another vampire.

But why was I even considering such a thing? I, who secretly wants to be a saint? Surely the blood of Merrick Mayfair was not crying out from the Earth for another newborn, you can scrap that idea. And this was one of those nights when every breath I took felt like a minor metaphysical disaster.

I looked up at the Manor House as they call it, the mansion up on the rise, with its two-story white columns and many lighted windows, the place which had been the locus of my pain and fortune for the last few nights, and I tried to figure how to play this one—for the benefit of all involved.

First consideration: Blackwood Manor was buzzing with unsuspecting mortals, most dear to me on short acquaintance, and by unsuspecting I mean they've never guessed that their beloved Quinn Blackwood, master of the house, or his mysterious new friend, Lestat, were vampires, and that was the way Quinn willed it with all his heart and soul—that no untoward evil thing would happen, because this was his home, and vampire though he was, he wasn't ready to break the ties.

Among these mortals were Jasmine, the versatile black housekeeper, a stunner when it comes to looks (more on that as we go along, I hope, because I can't resist), and Quinn's one-time lover; and their little son Jerome, begat by Quinn before he'd been made a vampire, of course, four years old and running up and down the circular steps just for fun, his feet in white tennis shoes a little too big for his body; and Big Ramona, Jasmine's grandmother, a regal black lady with white hair in a bun, shaking her head, talking to nobody, in the kitchen cooking up supper for God knows who; and her grandson Clem, a sinewy black man seemingly poured into his feline skin, attired in a black suit and tie, standing just inside the big front door looking up the steps, the chauffeur of the lady of the house just lately lost, Aunt Queen, for whom they were all still painfully mourning, highly suspicious of what was going on in Quinn's bedroom, and with reason.

Back the hall upstairs was Quinn's old tutor Nash Penfield, in his bedroom, seated with thirteen-year-old Tommy Blackwood, who was actually Quinn's uncle by natural blood but more purely an adopted son, and the two were talking in front of the cold summer fireplace, and Tommy, an impressive young man by anyone's standards, was crying softly over the death of the great lady, to whom I just referred, with whom Tommy had traveled all over Europe for three years, "the making of him," as Dickens might have said.

Hovering about the back of the property were the Shed Men, Allen and Joel, sitting in an open lighted portion of the shed, reading the *Weekly World News* and howling with laughter at it, while the television was blaring Football. There was a giant limousine in front of the house and one in the back.

As for the Big House, let me go into detail. I loved it. I found it perfectly proportioned, which wasn't always the case with American Greek Revival houses, but this one, preening on its terrace of land, was more than agreeable and inviting, with its long pecan-tree drive, and its regal windows all around.

Interior? What Americans call giant rooms. Dustless, manicured. Full of mantel clocks, mirrors, portraits and Persian rugs, and the inevitable mélange of nineteenth-century mahogany furniture that people mix with new reproductions of classic Hepplewhite and Louis XIV styles to achieve the look they call Traditional or antique. Eh? And all pervaded by the inevitable drone of massive air-conditioning, which not only cooled the air magically but provided the Privacy of Sound, which has so transformed the South in this day and age.

I know, I know. I should have described the scene before I described the people. So what? I wasn't thinking logically. I was pondering fiercely. I couldn't quite leave behind the fate of Merrick Mayfair.

Of course Quinn had claimed that he saw the Light of Heaven receiving both his unwanted ghost and Merrick, and for him the scene in this cemetery had been a theophany—something very different from what it was for me. All I saw was Merrick immolating herself. I had sobbed, screamed, cursed.

Okay, enough about Merrick. But keep her in mind, because she will definitely be referred to later. Who knows? Maybe I'll just bring her up anytime I feel like it. Who's in charge of this book anyway? No, don't take that seriously. I promised you a story, you'll get one.

The point is, or was, that on account of what was going on in the Big House right now, I didn't have time for all this moping. Merrick was lost to us. The vibrant and unforgettable Aunt Queen was lost. It was grief behind me and grief before me. But a huge surprise had just occurred, and my precious Quinn needed me without delay.

Of course nobody was *making* me take an interest in things here at Blackwood Farm.

I could have just cut out.

Quinn, the fledgling, had called on Lestat the Magnificent (yeah, I like that title) to help him get rid of Goblin, and technically, since Merrick had taken the ghost with her, I was finished here and could go riding off into the summer dusk with all the staff hereabouts saying, "Who was that dashing dude, anyway?" but I couldn't leave Quinn.

Quinn was in a real snare with these mortals. And I was greatly in love with Quinn. Quinn, aged twenty-two when Baptized in the Blood, was a seer of visions and a dreamer of dreams, unconsciously charming and unfailingly kind, a suffering hunter of the night who thrived only on the blood of the damned, and the company of the loving and the uplifting.

(The loving and the uplifting??? Like me, for instance??? So the kid makes mistakes. Besides, I was so in love with him that I put on a damned good show for him. And can I be damned for loving people who bring out the love in me? Is that so awful for a full-time monster? You will shortly come to understand that I am always talking about my moral evolution! But for now: the plot.)

I can "fall in love" with anybody—man, woman, child, vampire, the Pope. It doesn't matter. I'm the ultimate Christian. I see God's gifts in everyone. But almost anybody would love Quinn. Loving people like Quinn is easy.

Now, back to the question at hand: Which brings me back to Quinn's bedroom, where Quinn was at this delicate moment.

Before either of us had risen tonight—and I had taken the six-foot-four inches tall, blue-eyed black-haired boy to one of my secret hiding places with me—a mortal girl had arrived at the Manor House and affrighted everybody.

This was the matter that had Clem looking up the steps, and Big Ramona muttering, and Jasmine worried sick as she went about in her high-heel pumps, wringing her hands. And even little Jerome was excited about it, still dashing up and down the circular stairs. Even Tommy and Nash had broken off their mourning laments earlier to have a glance at this mortal girl and offer to help her in her distress.

It was easy enough for me to scan their minds and get a picture of it, this grand and bizarre event, and to scan Quinn's mind, for that matter, as to the result.

And I was making something of an assault on the mind of the mortal girl herself as she sat on Quinn's bed, in a huge random display of flowers, a truly marvelous heap of helter-skelter flowers, talking to Quinn.

It was a cacophony of minds filling me in on everything from the beginning. And the whole thing sent a little panic through my enormous brave soul. Work the Dark Trick? Make another one of us? Woe and Grief! Sorrow and Misery! Help, Murder, Police!

Do I *really* want to steal another soul out of the currents of human destiny? I who want to be a saint? And once personally hobnobbed with angels? I who claimed to have seen God Incarnate? Bring another into the—get ready!—Realm of the Undead?

Comment: One of the great things about loving Quinn was that I hadn't made him. The boy had come to me free of charge. I'd felt a little like Socrates must have felt with all those gorgeous Greek boys coming to him for advice, that is, until somebody showed up with the Burning Hemlock.

Back to now: If I had any rival in this world for Quinn's heart it was this mortal girl, and he was up there offering her in frantic whispers the promise of our Blood, the fractured gift of our immortality. Yes, this explicit offer was coming from the lips of Quinn. Good God, kid, show some backbone, I thought! You saw the Light of Heaven last night!

Mona Mayfair was this girl's name. But she'd never known or even heard of Merrick Mayfair. So cut that connection right now. Merrick was a quadroon, born among the "colored" Mayfairs who lived downtown, and Mona was a member of the white Mayfairs of the Garden District and Mona had probably never heard a word spoken of Merrick or her colored kin. As for Merrick, she'd shown no interest ever in the famous white family. She'd had a path all her own.

But Mona was a bona fide witch, however—sure as Merrick had been—and what is a witch? Well, it is a mind reader, magnet for spirits and ghosts and a possessor of other occult talents. And I'd heard enough of the illustrious Mayfair clan in the last few days from Quinn to know that Mona's cousins, witches all, if I'm not mistaken, were undoubtedly in hot pursuit of Mona now, no doubt desperate with worry for the child.

In fact, I'd had a glimpse of three of this remarkable tribe (and one of them a witch priest, no less, a witch priest! I don't even want to think about it!), at the funeral Mass for Aunt Queen, and why they were taking so long to come after Mona was mystifying me, unless they were deliberately playing this one out slowly for reasons that will soon become clear.

We vampires don't like witches. Can you guess why? Any self-respecting vampire, even if he or she is three thousand years old, can fool mortals, at least for a while. And young ones like Quinn pass, no question. Jasmine, Nash, Big Ramona—they all accepted Quinn for human. Eccentric? Clinically insane? Yes, they believed all that about him. But they thought he was human. And Quinn could live among them for quite a while. And as I've already explained, they thought I was human too, though I probably couldn't count on that for too long.

Now, with witches it's another story. Witches detect all kinds of small things about other creatures. It has to do with the lazy and constant exercise of their power. I'd sensed that at the funeral Mass, just breathing the same air as Dr. Rowan Mayfair and her husband, Michael Curry, and Fr. Kevin Mayfair. But fortunately, they were distracted by a multitude of other stimuli, so I hadn't had to bolt.

So okay, where was I? Yeah, cool. Mona Mayfair was a witch, and one of supreme talent. And once the Dark Blood had come into Quinn about a year ago, he had forsworn ever seeing her again, dying though she was, for fear she might at once realize that evil had robbed him of life, and contaminate her he would not.

However, of her own free will and much to everyone's amazement:

She'd come about an hour ago, driving the family stretch limousine, which she'd hijacked from the driver outside the Mayfair Medical Center where she'd been dying for over two years. (He'd been walking the block, poor unlucky guy, smoking a cigarette, when she'd sped off, and the last image in her mind of him was of his running after her.)

She'd then gone to florist after florist where the Mayfair name was good as gold collecting giant sprays of flowers, or loose bouquets, whatever she could get immediately, and then she'd driven across the twin span as they call the long lake bridge and up to the Blackwood Manor House, stepping out of the car barefoot and wrapped in a gaping hospital gown, a perfect horror—a wobbling skeleton with bruised skin hanging on her bones and a mop of long red hair—and had commandeered Jasmine, Clem, Allen and Nash to take the flowers to Quinn's room, asserting that she had Quinn's permission to heap them all over the four-poster bed. It was a pact. Don't worry.

Scared as they all were, they did as they were told.

After all, everybody knew that Mona Mayfair had been the love of Quinn's life before Quinn's beloved Aunt Queen, world traveler and raconteur, had insisted Quinn go to Europe with her on her "very last trip," which had somehow stretched into three whole years, and Quinn had come home to discover Mona in isolation at Mayfair Medical quite beyond his reach.

Then the Dark Blood had come to Quinn in venality and violence, and another year passed with Mona behind hospital glass, too weak even for a scribbled note or a glance at Quinn's daily gift of flowers and—.

Now back to the anxious passel of attendants who rustled the flowers up to the room.

The emaciated girl herself, and we're talking about twenty years old, that's what I'm calling a girl, could not possibly make it up the circular staircase, so the gallant Nash Penfield, Quinn's old tutor, cast by God to be the perfect gentleman (and responsible for a great deal of Quinn's finishing polish), had carried her up and laid her in her "bower of flowers" as she'd called it, the child assuring him that the roses were thornless, and she had lain back on the four-poster twining broken phrases from Shakespeare with her own, to wit:

"Pray, let me to my bride bed, so bedecked, retire, and let them strew my grave hereafter."

At which point, thirteen-year-old Tommy had appeared in the doorway of the bedroom, and had been so upset by the sight of Mona, in his raw grief for lost Aunt Queen, that he'd begun to shake, and so the amazed Nash had taken him out while Big Ramona had stayed to declare in a stage whisper worthy of the Bard:

"That girl's dying!"

At which the little red-headed Ophelia laughed. What else? And asked for a can of cold diet soda.

Jasmine had thought the child was going to give up the ghost on the spot, which could easily have happened, but the child said No, she was waiting for Quinn, and asked everybody to leave, and when Jasmine had come running back with the cold soda in a bubbly glass with a bent straw, the girl would hardly drink it.

You can live all your life in America without ever seeing a mortal in this condition.

But in the eighteenth century when I was born it was rather common. People starved in the streets of Paris in those days. They died all around you. Same situation prevailed in nineteenth-century New Orleans when the starving Irish began to arrive. You could see many beggars of skin and bone. Now you have to go to "the foreign missions" or to certain hospital wards to see people suffering like Mona Mayfair.

Big Ramona had made a further declaration, that that was the very bed in which her own daughter died (Little Ida), and that it was no bed for a sick child. But Jasmine, her granddaughter, had told her to shush, and Mona had taken to laughing so hard she was in agony and began to choke. She had survived.

As I stood in the cemetery, monitoring all these marvelous mirrors of near immediate events, I reckoned Mona was five-foot-one or thereabouts, destined to be delicate, and once a famous beauty, but the sickness—set into motion by a traumatic birth which was despite all my power still unclear to me—had so thoroughly done its work on her that she was under seventy pounds in weight and her profuse red hair only heightening the macabre spectacle of her total deterioration. She was so dangerously close to death that only will was keeping her going.

It had been will and witchcraft—the high persuasion of witches—that had helped her get the flowers and to force so much assistance when she arrived.

But now that Quinn had come, now that Quinn was there with her, and the one bold idea of her dying hours was consummate, the pain in her internal organs and her joints was defeating her. There was also a terrible pain in the entire surface of her skin. Merely sitting amid all the precious flowers hurt her.

As for my brave Quinn renouncing every execration he had laid on his fate and offering her the Dark Blood, no big surprise, I had to admit, but I wished to Hell he hadn't.

It's hard to watch anyone die when you know you possess this evil paradoxical power. And he was still in love with her, naturally and unnaturally, and couldn't abide her suffering. Who could?

However, as I have already explained, Quinn had received a theophany only last night, seeing Merrick and his doppelganger spirit both passing into the Light.

So why in the name of God had he not consented to merely holding Mona's hand and seeing her through it? She certainly wasn't going to live until midnight.

Fact of the matter, he didn't have the strength to let her go. Of course Quinn never would have gone to her, I should add, he'd protected her from his secret valiantly, as noted, but she'd come here to Quinn, to his very room, begging to die in his bed. And he was a male vampire, and this was his territory, his lair, so to speak, and some male juices were flowing here, vampire or no, and now she was in his arms, and a monstrous possessiveness and high imaginative perception of saving her had taken hold of him.

And as surely as I knew all that, I knew he couldn't work the Dark Trick on her. He'd never done it before, and she was too frail. He'd kill her. And that was no way to go. Shoot, the child, having opted for the Dark Blood, could go to Hell! I had to get up there. Vampire Lestat to the rescue!

I know what you're thinking. You're thinking, "Lestat, is this a comedy? We don't want a comedy." No, it's not!

It's just that all the debasing subterfuge is falling away from me, don't you see? Not the glamour you understand, keep your mind on the image, baby! We're only losing those elements which tended to cheapen my discourse, and throw up a barrier of—artificial quaintness, more or less.

Okay. Onward. I went the human route, through the front door, clickity click, startling Clem, throwing him an ingratiating smile, "Quinn's friend, Lestat, yeah, gotcha, hey, and Clem, have that car ready, we're going into New Orleans afterwards, okay, dude?" and headed up the circular stairs, beaming down at little Jerome as I passed him, and giving Jasmine a quick hug as she stood stranded in the hallway, then telepathically turned the lock on Quinn's bedroom door and entered.

Entered? Why not went in? That's the artificial quaintness that has to go. You see my point? Matter of fact, I barreled into the room, if you must know.

Now, I'll let you in on a little secret. Nothing seen telepathically is ever one tenth as vivid as what a vampire sees with his own eyes. Telepathy is cool, no doubt about it, but our vision is almost intolerably vivid. That's why telepathy doesn't play much of a role in this book. I'm a sensualist anyway.

And the sight of Mona sitting on the foot of the big glowering four-poster was heartbreaking. The girl was in more pain than Quinn could conceivably realize. Even his arm around her was hurting her. I calculated without wanting to do it that she should have died about two hours ago. Her kidneys had shut down, her heart was sputtering and she couldn't fill her lungs with enough air to take deep breaths.

But her flawless green eyes were wide as she looked at me, and her fierce intellect understood on some complete mystical level, quite truly beyond words, what Quinn was trying to tell her: that the progress of her death could be utterly reversed, that she could join with us, that she could be ours forever. The vampiric state; the Undead. Immortal killer. Outside life for all time.

I know you, Little Witch. We live forever. She almost smiled.

Would the Dark Trick undo the damage which had been done to her miserable body? You betcha.

Two hundred years ago in a bedroom on the Ile St.-Louis, I had seen old age and consumption drop away from the emaciated form of my own mother as the Dark Blood realized its full magic within her. And in those nights, I'd been a mere postulant, compelled by love and fear to do the transformation. It had been my first time. I hadn't even known its name.

"Let me work the Dark Trick, Quinn," I said immediately.

I saw the relief flood through him. He was so innocent, so confused. Of course, I didn't much like it that he was four inches taller than me, but it really didn't matter. I meant it when I called him my Little Brother. I would have done just about anything for him. And then there was Mona herself. Witch child, beauty, ferocious spirit, almost nothing but spirit with the body desperately trying to hold on.

They drew closer to each other. I could see her hand clasping his. Could she feel the preternatural flesh? Her eyes were on me.

I paced the room. I took over. I put it to her in grand style. We were vampires, yes, but she had a choice, precious darling that she was. Why hadn't Quinn told her about the Light? Quinn had seen the Light with his own eyes. He knew the measure of Celestial Forgiveness more truly than I did.

"But you can choose the Light some other night, *chérie*," I said. I laughed. I couldn't stop myself. It was too miraculous.

She'd been sick for so long, suffered for so long. And that birth, that child she'd borne, it had been monstrous, taken from her, and I couldn't see to the core of it. But forget that. Her conception of eternity was to feel whole for one blessed hour, to breathe for one blessed hour without pain. How could she make this choice? No, there was no choice here for this girl. I saw the long corridor down which she'd traveled inexorably for so many years—the needles that had bruised her arms, and the bruises were all over her, the medicines that had sickened her, the half sleep in agony, the fevers, the shallow ruminating dreams, the loss of all blessed concentration when the books and films and letters had been put aside and even the deep darkness was gone in the seasonless glare of hospital lights and inescapable clatter and noise.

She reached for me. She nodded. Dried cracked lips. Strands of red hair. "Yes, I want it," she said.

And from Quinn's lips came the inevitable words: "Save her."

Save her? Didn't Heaven want her?

"They're coming for you," I said. "It's your family." I hadn't meant to blurt it. Was I under some sort of spell myself, looking into her eyes? But I could hear them clearly, the fast-approaching Mayfairs. Ambulance *sans* siren pulling into the pecan-tree drive, stretch limousine right behind it.

"No, don't let them take me," she cried. "I want to be with you."

"Honey bunch, this is for always," I said.

"Yes!"

Darkness eternal, yes, curse, grief, isolation, yes.

Oh, and it's the same old beat with you, Lestat, you Devil, you want to do it, you want to, you want to see it, you greedy little beast, you can't give her over to the angels and you know they're waiting! You know the God who can sanctify her suffering has purified her and will forgive her last cries.

I drew close to her, pushing gently against Quinn.

"Let her go, Little Brother," I said. I lifted my wrist, broke the inside skin with my teeth and put the blood to her lips. "It has to be done this way. I've got to give her some of my blood first." She kissed the blood. Her eyes squeezed shut. Shiver. Shock. "Otherwise, I can't bring her through. Drink, pretty girl. Good-bye, pretty girl, good-bye, Mona."

3

S HE DREW THE BLOOD from me as if she'd broken the circuit
that kept me alive, as if she meant to kill me. A witch had me by
the blood. I gasped and reached with my left hand for the post
of the bed and missed it, falling gently back with her on the nest of
flowers. Her hair was catching in the roses. So was mine.

In a blatant rush, I felt myself emptying my life into her—dank
country castle, Paris, the boulevard theater, stolen, stone tower, made
by Magnus, fire, alone, orphan weeping, treasure; did she laugh? I saw
her teeth in my heart, my very heart. I pulled back, dizzy, and clung to
the post, each one is unique, staring down at her.

Witchlet!

With glazed eyes she looked up at me. The blood was on her lips,
just a touch, and all her pain was gone, and the moment had come, the
moment of peace from pain, peace from struggle, peace from fear.

She simply couldn't believe it.

In the twilight between human and vampire, she breathed deeply
and slowly, hungry hybrid, doomed hybrid, her skin plumping exquisitely and the sweetness unfolding in her face as the cheeks formed and
her lips filled out, and the flesh around her eyes grew firm, and then
the breasts were rising beneath her cotton gown, and a roundness
came to her arms, such a delectable roundness, I am such a fiend, and
she sighed again, sighed as if ecstatic, looking at me, yeah, right, I'm
gorgeous, I know, and now she could endure the Dark Trick. Quinn
was stunned. So in love. Get away. I pushed him back. *This is mine.*

I snatched her up from the flowers. Vessel of my blood. Petals
falling. Whispered poetry was tumbling from her lips, "Or like a crea-

ture native and indued unto that element." I hugged her to me. I wanted my blood from her. I wanted her.

"Little Witch," I hissed into her ear. "You think you know all I can do!" I crushed her to me. I heard her sweet soft laugh. "Come on, show me!" she said. *I'm not dying.* Quinn was afraid. He put his arms around her and touched my arms. He was trying to hold us both. It was so warm. I loved him. So what? I had her.

I grazed her neck with my teeth. "I'm coming to get you, Little Girl!" I whispered. "You're playing in the big time, Little Girl!" Her heart was racing. Still on the brink. I sank my teeth and felt her body stiffen. Lovely paralysis. Slowly I drew on the blood, her salt mixed with my own. I *knew* her: child beauty, nymphet, schoolgirl scamp, the one on whom nothing was lost, pronouncements of genius, nursing drunken parents, freckles and smile, her life a romp, and always dreaming, restless at the computer keys, designée to the Mayfair billions, burying father and mother, no more worry there, lover of more men than she could count, pregnancy—now I saw it!—horror birth, monster child, *Look at it: woman baby! Morrigan. "Walking Baby," said Dolly Jean. Who are these people! What is this you are showing to me!* "You think you're the only monsters I know?" Morrigan gone forever, monster child, *What is this mutant that grows to be a full woman at its birth, wants your milk? Taltos! Gone, taken, ruined her health forever, made her start dying,* have to find Morrigan, emerald around Mona's neck, look at that emerald! Mona fastened to Quinn, so in love with Quinn, tell Quinn, no, poetry of Ophelia sustaining her soul, heart beat, catching breath, dying for too long, *Don't you realize what this is! I do, I do! Don't stop! Don't let me go! Who is that trying to take you from me? I knew that ghost! Oncle Julien!*

He came at me. Angry phantom! In the midst of my vision! Was he in the room? This tall, white-haired man assaulting me, trying to wrench her from me! Who the Hell are you? I sent him flying back, receding so fast he became a tiny speck. Damn you, let her go!

We lay on the bower of flowers, she and I in each other's arms, no time, look at him, he's coming again, Oncle Julien! I was blind. I drew back, tore my wrist again, pushed my wrist to her mouth, clumsy, spilling blood, couldn't see, felt her clamp hard, body lurch, *Oncle Julien, you're out!* She drank and drank. Oncle Julien's face furious. Faint. Vanish. "He's gone," I whispered. "Oncle Julien gone!" Did Quinn hear? "Make him go, Quinn."

I swooned, giving her my life, see it, see it all, see the devastated core, move beyond regret, go on, her body growing stronger, the iron of her limbs, her fingers digging into my arm as she drank from my wrist, go on, take it, sink those teeth into my soul, do it, now I'm the paralyzed one, can't escape, brutal little girl, go on, where was I, let her drink on and on, I can't, I snuggled my face against her neck, opened my mouth, no power to—.

Our souls closing to each other, the inevitable blindness between Maker and Fledgling meaning she was made. Couldn't read each other's thoughts anymore. Drink me dry, beautiful, you're on your own.

My eyes were shut. I dreamt. Oncle Julien wept. Ah, so sad, was it? In the realm of shadows, he stood with his face in his hands and he wept. What is this? An emblem of conscience? Don't make me laugh.

And so the literal dissolves. She drinks and she drinks. And alone I dream, a suicide in a bathtub with streaming wrists, I dream:

I saw a perfect vampire, a soul unlike any other, tutored in courage, never looking back, lifted from misery, and seeking to marvel at all things without malice or lamenting. I saw a graduate of the school of suffering. I saw her.

The ghost came back.

Tall, angry, Oncle Julien, will you be my Hound of Heaven? Arms folded. What do you want here? Do you realize what you are up against? My perfect vampire does not see you. Go away, dream. Go away, ghost. I have no time for you. Sorry, Oncle Julien, she's made. You lose.

She let me go. She must have. I drifted.

When I opened my eyes, Mona stood beside Quinn and they were both looking down on me.

I lay amongst the flowers, and there were no thorns on the roses. Time had stopped. And the distant commotions of the house didn't matter.

She was fulfilled. She was the vampire in my dream. She was the perfect one. Ophelia's old poetry dropped away. She was the Perfect Pearl, caught speechless in the miracle and staring down at me, wondering only what had become of me, as another fledgling of mine had done long ago—when I'd worked the Dark Trick just as fiercely and just as thoroughly and just as dangerously to myself. But understand that for Lestat there are only temporary dangers. No big deal, boys and girls. Look at her.

So this was the splendid creature with whom Quinn had fallen so fatally in love. Princess Mona of the Mayfairs. To the very roots of her long red hair the Blood had penetrated, and it was full and shining, and her face was oval with plumped and smiling cheeks and lips, and her eyes clear of all fever, those fathomless green eyes.

Oh, she was dazed by the Blood vision, of course, and above all by the vampiric power that pervaded the cells of her entire frame.

But she stood resolute and quick, staring at me, as robust no doubt as she'd ever been, the hospital gown now skimpy and straining to contain her. All that juicy and enticing flesh restored.

I brushed off the petals that clung to me. I got up on my feet. I was dizzy still, but healing fast. My mind was clouded and it was almost a nice feeling, a delicious blurring of the light and warmth in the room, and I had a swift, profound sense of love for Mona and Quinn and a profound sense that we'd be together for a long time, just the three of us. Three of us.

Quinn appeared shining and steadfast in this feverish vision of mine. That had been his charm for me from the beginning of knowing him, a secular crown prince of sorts, full of openness and self-confidence. Love would always save Quinn. Losing Aunt Queen, he had been sustained on the love he'd felt for her. The only one he had hated, he had killed.

"May I give her my blood?" he asked. He reached out for me, squeezed my shoulder and bent forward hesitantly and then kissed me.

How he could take his eyes off her I didn't know.

I smiled. I was gaining my bearings. Oncle Julien was nowhere about that I could see.

"Nowhere," echoed Quinn.

"What are you saying?" asked the shining newborn.

"Oncle Julien, I saw him," but I shouldn't have said it.

Sudden shadow in her face. "Oncle Julien?"

"But he was bound to—." Quinn said. "At Aunt Queen's funeral I saw him, and it was as if he was warning me. It was his duty, but what does it matter now?"

"Don't give her your blood," I said to Quinn. "Keep your minds open to each other. Of course you'll depend on words, no matter how much you read of each other's thoughts, but don't exchange blood. Too much, and you'll lose the mutual telepathy."

She reached out her arms to me. I embraced her, squeezed her tight, marveling at the power she'd already achieved. I felt humbled by the Blood rather than proud of any excess to which I'd taken the whole process. I gave a little accepting laugh as I kissed her, which she returned in her enchantment.

If any one trait in her made me a slave it was her green eyes. I hadn't realized how clouded they'd been by her illness. And now as I held her back, I saw a sprinkling of freckles across her face, and a flash of her beautiful white teeth as she smiled.

She was a small thing for all her magical health and restoration. She brought out the tenderness in me, which few people do.

But it was time to move out of the rhapsody. Much as I hated it. The practical matters came to intrude.

"Okay, my love," I said. "You're going to know one last bout of pain. Quinn will see you through it. Take her into the shower, Quinn. But first, arrange some clothes for her. On second thought, you leave that to me. I'll tell Jasmine she needs a pair of jeans and a shirt."

Mona laughed almost hysterically.

"We're always subject to this mixture of the magic and the mundane," I replied. "Get used to it."

Quinn was all seriousness and apprehension. He went over to his desk, punched in the intercom number for the kitchen and gave the order for the clothes to Big Ramona, telling her to leave them right outside the door. Okay, good. All the roles of Blackwood Farm are played smoothly.

Then, Mona, stunned and dreaming, asked if she might have a white dress, or if there might be a white dress downstairs in Aunt Queen's room.

"A white dress," said Mona, as if she were caught in some poetic net as strong as her mental pictures of drowning Ophelia. "And is there lace, Quinn, lace that nobody would mind if I wore . . ."

Quinn turned to the phone again, gave the orders, yes, Aunt Queen's silks, make it all up. "Everything white," he said to Big Ramona. His voice was gentle and patient. "You know, Jasmine won't wear the white dresses. Yes, for Mona. If we don't use them, they will all end up packed away. In the attic. Aunt Queen loved Mona. Stop crying. I know. I know. But Mona can't go around in this disgusting hospital gown. And someday, fifty years from now, Tommy and Jerome will be unpacking all those clothes and figuring what to do with it all and . . . just bring something up here now."

As he turned back to us his eye fastened on Mona and he stopped in his tracks as if he couldn't believe what he saw, and a dreadful expression came over him, as though he only just realized what had happened, what we'd done. He murmured something about white lace. I didn't want to read his mind. Then he came forward and took Mona in his arms.

"This mortal death, Ophelia, it won't be much," he said. "I'll get into the stream with you. I'll hold you. We'll say the poetry together. And after that, there's no pain. There's thirst. But never any pain." He couldn't hold her close enough.

"And will I always see as I see now?" she asked. The words about the death meant nothing to her.

"Yes," he said.

"I'm not afraid," she said. She meant it.

But she still had no real grasp of what had been done. And I knew in my heart, the heart I closed off from Quinn and the heart she couldn't read, that she really hadn't consented to this. She hadn't been able.

What did this mean to me? Why am I making such a big deal of it?

Because I'd murdered her soul, that's why.

I'd bound her to the Earth the way we were bound, and now I had to see to it that she became that vampire which I'd seen in my moment of intense dream. And when she finally woke to what she'd become she might go out of her mind. What had I said of Merrick? The ones who reached for it went mad sooner than those who were stolen, as I had been.

But there wasn't time for this sort of thinking.

"They're here," she said. "They're downstairs. Can you hear them?" She was alarmed. And as is always the case with the new ones, every emotion in her was exaggerated.

"Don't fear, pretty girl," I said. "I'm on to them."

We were talking about the rumblings from the front parlor below. Mayfairs on the property. Jasmine fretful, walking to and fro. Little Jerome trying to slide down the coiling banister. Quinn could hear all this too.

It was Rowan Mayfair and Fr. Kevin Mayfair, the priest for the love of Heaven, come with an ambulance and a nurse to find her and take her back to the hospital, or at least to discover whether she was alive or dead.

That was it. I got it. That's why they'd taken their time. They thought that she was already dead.

And they were right. She was.

4

I UNLOCKED the bedroom door.

Big Ramona stood there with an armful of white clothes.

Quinn and Mona had disappeared into the nearby bathroom.

"You're wanting this for that poor child?" Big Ramona said. Small-boned woman, white hair, sweet-faced, starched white apron. (Grandmother of Jasmine.) Deeply troubled. "Now, don't you just grab for all this, I've got it folded!"

I stood back to let her march into the room and lay the pile on the flower-strewn bed. "Now, there's underwear and slips here, too," she declared. She shook her head. The shower was running in the bath. She passed me as she went out, making her share of little grumbling noises.

"I can't believe that girl is still breathing," she said. "It's some kind of miracle. And her family down there brought Fr. Kevin with the Holy Oils. Now, I know Quinn loves that girl, but where does it say in the Gospel that you have to let a person die in your house, and what with Quinn's mother sick, you knew that didn't you, and Quinn's mother run off somewhere, did you know that, Patsy's up and gone—"

(Flash on memory of Patsy, Quinn's mother: country-western singer with poofed hair and painted fingernails, dying of AIDS in the bedroom opposite, no longer up to putting on her fringed leather outfits with the high boots and war paint makeup and going out, just pretty on the couch in white nightgowns when I had last seen her, lady full of irrational and overriding hate for Quinn, a twisted kind of sibling rivalry from a woman who'd been sixteen when Quinn was born to her. Now vanished.)

"—and leaving all her medicine behind, sick as she is. Oh Patsy,

Patsy, and Aunt Queen just laid in the grave, and then this redheaded child coming here, I'm telling you!"

"Well, maybe Mona's dead," I said, "and Quinn's washing her corpse in the bathtub."

She broke into laughter, muffling it with her hand.

"Oh, you're a devil," she said. "You're worse than Quinn," she went on flashing her pale eyes at me, "but don't you think I don't know what they're doing in that shower together. And what if she does die in there, what about that, are we going to be patting her dry with towels and laying her out like it didn't happen and—"

"Well, she'll be really clean," I said with a shrug.

She shook her head, trying not to laugh out loud, and then shifted emotional gears as she headed back to the hall, laughing and talking to nobody as she went on, ". . . and what with his mother running off, and she sick as a dog, and nobody knows where she is, and those Mayfairs downstairs, it's a wonder they didn't bring the sheriff." And into the back bedroom she went, The Angel of Hot Coffee, where Nash and Tommy talked in hushed voices, and Tommy cried over the loss of Aunt Queen.

It occurred to me with uncommon strength that I had grown too fond of all these people, that I understood why Quinn insisted on remaining here, playing the mortal as long as he could, why the entirety of Blackwood Farm had a hold on him.

But it was time to be a wizard. Time to buy some time for Mona, time to make her absence somehow acceptable to the witches below.

Besides, I was curious about the creatures in the double parlor, these intrepid psychics who fooled the mortals around them as surely as we vampires did, pretending to be wholesome and regular human beings while they contained a host of secrets.

I hurried down the circular stairs, grabbed up tiny Jerome with his big tennis shoes off the banister just in time to save his life as he nearly fell some ten feet to the marble tile floor below, and put him in the waiting arms of a very anxious Jasmine; and then, gesturing to her that everything would be all right, I went into the cooler air of the front room.

Dr. Rowan Mayfair, founder and head of Mayfair Medical, was seated in one of the mahogany chairs (picture nineteenth-century Rococo, black lacquer and velvet), and her head turned sharply as if jerked by a cord when I entered.

Now, we had seen each other before, as I noted, at Aunt Queen's funeral Mass in St. Mary's Assumption Church. In fact, I'd sat dangerously close to her, being in the pew right in front of her. But I'd been better camouflaged at the time by ordinary clothes and sunglasses. What she saw now was the Brat Prince in his frock coat and handmade lace, and I'd forgotten to put on my sunglasses, which was just a stupid mistake.

I hadn't had a really good look at her at all. Now I found myself instantly fascinated, which wasn't too comfortable since it was my role to fascinate as our conversation went on.

Her lean oval face was delicately sculpted and as clean as a little girl's and needed nothing in the way of paint to make it remarkable, with its huge gray eyes and cold flawless mouth. She wore a severe, gray wool pants suit, with a red scarf wrapped around her neck and tucked down into her lapels, and her short ash blond hair appeared to curl under naturally just below the soft line of her jaw.

Her expression was intensely dramatic, and I sensed an immediate and sweeping probe of my mind, which I locked up tight. I felt chills down my backbone. She was creating this.

She had fully expected to read my thoughts and she couldn't. And she was blocked from knowing what was going on upstairs. She didn't like it. But to put it more Biblically, she was deeply grieved.

And being shut out, she tried to make sense of my appearance, not at all concerned with the superficial eccentricity of the frock coat and my messy hair, but of elements which were more purely vampiric—the subtle sheen of my skin and the electric blue of my eyes.

I had to start talking quickly, but let me fill you in first on my instantaneous take on the other Mayfair—Fr. Kevin—who was standing at the far mantel, the only other occupant of the room.

Nature had dealt him the same cards as Mona—deep green eyes and red hair. In fact, he could have been her big brother, the genes were so close, and he was my height, six feet, and well built. He wore clerical black with the white Roman collar. And he was not the witch Rowan was, but he was more than slightly psychic, and I could read him easily: he thought I was weird and he was hoping Mona was already dead.

I sparked off the memory of him at Mass in his Gothic robes holding the chalice in his hands. *This is my blood.* And for reasons I couldn't possibly explain, I was taken slap back to my village childhood in France, to the ancient church and the village priest saying those very same words, chalice in hand, and for a moment I lost my perspective on everything. Other mortal memories threatened, perfected in color and lucidity. I saw the monastery where I'd studied, so happy, where I'd so wanted to be a monk. Oh, this was sickening.

And with another decided chill, I realized that Dr. Mayfair had caught these images out of my mind before I closed it up again.

I shook it off, annoyed for a moment that the double parlor was so crowded with shadow. Then my eyes latched on to the stark, don't belong, figure of Oncle Julien, three-dimensional and exquisitely solid in a slim gray suit, standing in the far corner, arms folded, eying me with calculating opposition. He was fiercely actual, and fiercely bright.

"What's wrong with you?" Dr. Rowan Mayfair asked. Her voice was deep, husky and sensual. Her eyes were still picking me apart.

"You don't see any ghost in here, do you?" I blurted out without thinking, the ghost just standing there all the while as it came clear to me that of course they didn't, neither of them. This shining and self-contained menace had it in for me.

"No, I don't see anything," Rowan answered promptly. "There's a ghost in this room that I ought to see?"

Women with these husky voices have a miraculous advantage.

"You do have your ghosts here," Fr. Kevin said acceptingly. Yankee accent. Boston. "As Quinn's friend, I thought you'd know."

"Oh, I do, yes," I said. "But I never get used to them. Ghosts scare me. So do angels."

"And didn't you hold an exorcism to get rid of Goblin?" asked the priest, throwing me off guard.

"Yes, and it worked," I said, glad of the distraction. "Goblin's gone from this house, and Quinn's free of him for the first time in his life. I wonder what it will mean to him."

Oncle Julien didn't budge.

"Where is she?" asked Rowan, meaning Mona, who else?

"She wants to stay here," I said. "You know, it's simple." I crossed in front of her and sat down in a chair with its back to the floor lamp, putting myself in a bit of shadow, and so I could see everyone, even my nemesis. "She doesn't want to die at Mayfair Medical. She managed to drive the limousine all the way over here. You know Mona. And she's with Quinn upstairs. I want you to trust us. Leave her with us. We'll take care of her. We can call Aunt Queen's old nurse to help us."

Rowan was staring at me as if I'd lost my mind.

"Do you realize how difficult it's going to be?" she asked. She sighed and a great weariness showed itself in her, but only for an instant. "Do you realize how difficult it can get?"

"You've brought the oxygen and morphine, haven't you?" I glanced over my shoulder in the direction of the ambulance out front. "Leave them. Cindy, the nurse, will know how to use them."

Rowan raised her eyebrows. Same weariness again, but her strength was greater. She was trying to figure me out. Absolutely nothing about me frightened her or repelled her. I found her beautiful. There was a limitless intelligence behind her eyes.

"Quinn can't possibly understand what he's taking on," she said gently. "I don't want him to be hurt. I don't want her to die in pain. Do you follow me?"

"Of course I do," I said. "Trust me that we'll call you when it's time."

She bowed her head, but only for a second.

"No, no, you don't understand," she said, the husky voice so expressive of concern. "There's no reasonable explanation for her being still alive right now."

"It's her will," I countered. *I'm telling you the truth, there is no reason to be concerned for her.* "She's resting, free of pain," I said.

"That's impossible," Rowan whispered.

Something flickered in her expression.

"Who are you?" she asked, that deep voice underscoring her seriousness.

I was the one being spellbound. I couldn't break loose of her. I felt the chills again. The room was too dim. I wanted to tell Jasmine to turn up the chandelier.

"My name doesn't matter," I said, but it was hard for me to speak.

What *was* it about this woman? Why was her stripdown beauty so provocative and threatening? I wanted to see into her soul but she was far too clever to let it happen. Yet I sensed secrets in her, a trove of them, and I felt an electric connection to the monster child that Mona had revealed to me when I made her, and other things.

I knew suddenly this woman was hiding something dreadful to her own conscience, that the dominant note of her character was this concealment and this conscience, and a great striving rooted in her brilliance and her guilt. I wanted it, whatever she was hiding, just to know it for a moment, just to know it in warmth with her. I would have given anything—.

She looked away from me. I had unwittingly stared her down and lost her, and she was fumbling silently, and I almost saw it: *a power over life and death*.

Fr. Kevin spoke up:

"I have to see Mona before we go," he said. "I must talk to Quinn, about the exorcism. I used to see Goblin, you understand. I'm concerned for both of them. You have to tell Mona we're here—."

He had taken a chair opposite me and I hadn't even noticed. "Perhaps we should both see her," he said to Rowan. "Then we can decide what to do." His was a gentle voice, perfect for a priest, humble yet totally unaffected.

I locked eyes with him, and it seemed for an instant I caught hold of shared secrets, things that they all knew, these Mayfairs, things they couldn't tell, things so profoundly connected to their wealth and their roots that they could never be outgrown or expurgated or overcome. With Fr. Kevin it was doubly hard because he was the confessor of this family, bound by that sacred oath, and also he'd been told things he could scarce believe and it had profoundly changed him.

But he too knew how to lock his mind. And again, all I got when I probed him was that aching memory of my own childhood schooling, of my wanting so badly to be good. An echo of my own mental voice coming back on me. I hated it. Away with it! It struck me, sharp and hard, that I had been given so many chances to save my soul that my entire life had been constructed around these chances! That was my nature—going from temptation after temptation, not to sin, but to be redeemed.

I'd never seen my life that way before.

Had that long-ago boy, Lestat, fought hard enough, he could have become a monk.

"Accursed!" whispered the ghost.

"That's not possible," I said.

"Not possible to see her!" Rowan said. "You can't be serious."

I heard a soft laughter. I turned around in the chair.

To my far right the ghost was laughing. "Now what are you going to do, Lestat?" he asked.

"What is it?" asked Rowan. "What are you seeing?"

"Nothing," I insisted. "You can't see her. I promised her. No one would come up. For God's sakes, let her alone." I threw all my conviction behind it. I suddenly felt desperate. "Let her die the way she wants, for the love of Heaven. Let her go!"

She glared at me, glared at this display of emotion. An immense inner suffering was suddenly visible in her face, as if she could no longer conceal it, or as if my own outburst, muted as it had been, had ignited the dim fire inside of her.

"He's right," said Fr. Kevin. "But you understand, we have to stay here."

"And it's not going to be very long," said Rowan. "We'll wait quietly. If you don't want us in the house . . ."

"No, no, of course you're welcome," I said. *Mon Dieu!*

Again came the ghostly laughter.

"Your hospitality is wretched!" said Oncle Julien. "Jasmine has not even offered them a cracker and glass of water. I am appalled."

I was bitterly amused by that, and I doubted the truth of it. I found myself worrying about it and became incensed! And at the same time I heard something, something nobody in the room could hear, except perhaps the laughing ghost. It was the sound of Mona crying, nay, sobbing. I had to go back to Mona.

All right, Lestat, be a monster. Throw the most interesting woman you've ever met out of the house.

"Listen to me, both of you," I said, fixing Rowan in my gaze, and then flashing on Fr. Kevin. "I want you to go home. Mona's as psychic as you are. It distresses her dreadfully that you're down here. She senses it. She feels it. It adds to her pain." (All this was true, wasn't it?) "I gotta go back up there now and comfort her. Please leave. That's what she wants. That's what gave her the strength to drive here. Now I promise you I will contact you when it's all over. Please go."

I rose, and I took Rowan's arm and all but lifted her out of the chair.

"You are a perfect lout," said the ghost, disgustedly.

Fr. Kevin was on his feet.

Rowan stared at me, transfixed. I guided her into the hallway and to the front door, and the priest followed. *Trust in me. Trust that it's what Mona wants.*

Could they hear Mona's sobs now?

Without taking my eyes off Rowan's eyes, I opened the front door. Blast of summer heat, scent of flowers. "You go now," I said.

"But the oxygen, the morphine," said Rowan. Whiskey voice, they called it. It was so seductive. And behind her delicate probing frown was this conflict, this unadmitted and sinful power. What was it?

We stood on the front porch, like dwarves underneath the columns. The purple light was suddenly soothing and the moment lost its proportions. It was like eternal dusk here in the country. I could hear the birds of the night, the distant unquiet waters of the swamp.

Fr. Kevin instructed the orderlies. They brought in the supplies.

I couldn't break away from this woman. What had I been saying to her? The ghost was laughing. I was getting confused.

What is your secret?

I felt a physical push, as though she had stretched out her two hands and laid them on my chest and tried to move me back from where I stood. I saw the ghost over her shoulder. It came from her, the push. It had to come from her.

Her face was engraved with a hostile beauty.

She tossed her hair just slightly, let it stroke her cheeks.

She narrowed her eyes. "Take care of Mona for me," she said. "I love her with all my heart. You cannot know what it means to me that I failed with her—that all my gifts, all my resources—."

"Of course. I know how you love her," I said. "I love her and I hardly know her." This was babble. This woman was suffering. Was I suffering? The ghost was accusing me. A tall man right behind her but she had no sense of him.

What was it that was slipping out of her conscious to me? Something so very dreadful that it had shaped her entire existence; and she felt it keenly at this moment. *I have taken life.*

I shuddered. Her eyes wouldn't let me move.

I have taken life again and again.

The orderlies swept by with more equipment. Cool air flooded out of the open front door. Jasmine was there. The ghost stood firm. It seemed to me that the curve of the limbs of the pecan trees marching down the gravel drive meant something, a secret communication from the Lord of the Universe, but what?

"Come to me," I said to Rowan. A life founded upon suffering, upon reparation. I couldn't bear it, I had to touch it, enclose it, save it.

I took her in my arms, Dear God Forgive Me, kissing her cheeks and then her mouth. *Don't fear for Mona.*

"You don't understand," she whispered. In a scalding moment I saw the hospital room, a torture cell of machines and pulsing numbers, glistening plastic bags feeding into dangling tubes, and Mona sobbing, sobbing the way she was now, and Rowan standing in the doorway. *Almost used the power, almost killed—.*

"I see, I do," I said. "And it was not the right time and she wanted to come to Quinn," I whispered the words in her ear.

"Yes," she said, her own tears rising, "and I frightened her. You see. She knew what I meant to do, she knew I had the power, it would have showed up as a stroke on the autopsy, just a stroke, but she knew! I almost. . . . I terrified her. And. . . ."

I held her so tight. I drew in my breath.

I kissed her tears. I wished I was a saint. I wished I was the priest who stood by the car waiting for her, pretending not to see our kissing. What was kissing? Mortal kissing? I kissed her mouth again. Mortal loving and all the while the thundering desire for the link of the blood, not her death, no, Dear God, no, just the link of the blood, the knowing. Who was this Rowan Mayfair! My head swam.

And the ghost beyond her glared as though he'd harrow Hell to bring its forces against me.

"How could you tell when was the right moment?" I answered. "And the thing to cling to is that you didn't do it. And now she has her time with Quinn." Oh, such deceitful euphemisms for one who detests all euphemisms, and with reason. I kissed her hard and eagerly and felt her body soften, felt her lock to me for one precious instant, and then the flash of icy coldness as she pulled away.

She hurried down the steps, her heels barely making a sound. Fr. Kevin was holding the door of the car open for her. The ambulance was already backing up. She turned and looked at me and then she waved at me.

Such a tender, unexpected gesture. I felt my heart grow huge, and its beating too much for me.

No, you poor darling. You didn't kill her. I did it. I killed her. I'm guilty. And she's sobbing again. And the ghost knows.

5

NONE OF THE MORTALS in the house could hear Mona sobbing. The walls were too thick.

Meantime, the middle of the dining room table was being draped and set for supper, and Jasmine wanted to know if Quinn and I would join Tommy and Nash; I told her No, we couldn't leave Mona, which she already knew.

I told her to please call Cindy, the Nurse, though she probably wasn't needed, and to put the oxygen tank and the medicine out of the way. (Actually, this lovely lady spells her name Cyndy, so we will start spelling it this way from here on.)

I went into the living room. I tried to clear my head. The simple perfume of Rowan on my hands paralyzed me. I had to get straight.

Snap to a tender affection for everybody in the house. Go to Mona.

What *was* all this succumbing to a human witch! The entire Mayfair family was full of troublemakers! Mayfair design and Mayfair will were quickening my pulse. I think I even cursed Merrick, that she had planned to immolate herself last night on that altar, that she'd somehow found a way to save her immortal soul, and left me to my own usual damnation.

And then there was the ghost. The Mayfair ghost had returned to his corner. He stood there giving me the most malevolent look I've ever seen on any creature, vampire or human.

I took his measure: a male, aged sixty perhaps, short curly hair, snow white; eyes gray or black; excellent facial features and regal bearing, though why the age of sixty I couldn't figure unless he'd felt most especially powerful at that earthly time of life, because I knew for a fact that he'd died long before Mona and could therefore haunt in any guise he chose.

These thoughts didn't bait him. There was something so intrinsically menacing in his stillness that I couldn't bear it.

"All right, then, be quiet," I said firmly. I detested the quaver in my voice. "Why the Hell are you haunting me? You think I can undo what I've done? I can't. Nobody can. You want her to die, haunt her, not me."

No change in him.

And no way could I trivialize and diminish the woman who'd just waved to me before stepping into the car, salt of her tears still on my lips to be licked. So why keep trying? What had befallen me?

Big Ramona, who happened to glance in from the hall, drying her hands on her apron, said, "And now we have another madman talking to himself, and right by the desk that Grandpa William used to go to all the time for no reason. Now that was a ghost that Quinn used to see, and me and Jasmine too."

"What desk, where?" I stammered. "Who is Grandpa William?" But I knew that story. And I saw the desk. And Quinn had seen the ghost over and over pointing to the desk, and they had searched it over and over, year in and year out, and found nothing.

Snap back, you idiot!

Upstairs Quinn tried tenderly and desperately to comfort Mona.

Tommy and the ever distinguished Nash came down for their dinner and passed, without noticing me, into the dining room across the way, their low conversation uninterrupted throughout, and seated themselves.

I went to the cameo case near the piano. That meant walking away from the ghost who was to my far right, but it made no difference. His eyes followed me.

This case was where Aunt Queen's cameos were displayed, and it was never locked. I opened the glass top—it was hinged like the cover of a book—and I picked up an oval cameo with a tiny display of Poseidon and his consort in a chariot pulled by sea horses, with a god to lead them over billowing waves, all of this spectacular progress intricately wrought. Cool.

I slipped the cameo into my pocket and went upstairs.

I found Mona lying on the bed, crying dreadfully among the flowers, with a desperate Quinn standing by the far side of the bed, leaning over her and trying to comfort her. Quinn was more frightened than I've ever seen him. I made a quick gesture to let him know everything was working well.

The ghost wasn't in the room. I could neither feel him nor see him. Cagey. So he doesn't want to be seen by Mona?

Mona was naked, Lady Godiva hair everywhere, her body shimmering and fine as she lay sobbing among the poetic blooms; and the neat stack of Aunt Queen's white garments had fallen and was scattered all over the floor.

For a moment I felt a deep stab of horror, a horror I deserved and couldn't escape, and which I didn't intend to confide to either Quinn or Mona as long as we all lived, no matter how many years or decades that might be; a horror of what whim and will can do and had done. But as usual with grand moral realizations, there was no time for it.

I looked at Quinn—my Little Brother, my pupil.

He'd been made by monsters he'd loathed and it had never occurred to him to weep in their presence. What Mona was doing was entirely predictable.

I lay down on the bed right beside her, and when I lifted her hair back and looked into her eyes, she went utterly silent.

"What the Hell's the matter with you?" I demanded.

A pause in which her loveliness struck me with all the subtilty of an avalanche.

"Well, nothing," she said, "if you're going to put it like that."

"For the love of God, Lestat," said Quinn, "don't be cruel to her. Surely you know what she's going through."

"I'm not being cruel," I said. (Who, me, cruel?) I kept my tight focus on her. "Are you afraid of me?" I asked.

"No," she said. Her eyebrows puckered. The blood tears stained her cheeks. "It's only that I know so well that I should have died," she said.

"Then sing a requiem," I said. "Let me supply some words: 'O heat, dry up my brains! Tears seven-times salt, burn out the sense and virtue of mine eye!' "

She laughed.

"Very well, honey bunch, let me hear it. I'm the Maker. Let it go."

"I knew that for so long, that I ought to die. God, when I think of it, it's the only thing I really know right now! I was supposed to die." Her words flowed calmly. "People around me got so used to it, they slipped up. They'd say, 'You used to be so beautiful, we'll never forget that.' Dying, that had become the central obligation of my life. I used to lie there and try to figure how to make it easier for people. I mean they were so miserable. This went on slowly for years—."

"Keep talking," I said. I loved her easy trust, her immediate openness.

"There was a period of time where I could still enjoy music and chocolate, you know, special things, like bed jackets with lace too. And I could dream of my child, my lost child. Then I couldn't really eat anything anymore. And the music only made me jittery. I kept seeing people who weren't really there. I thought Maybe I never had that child. Morrigan, gone so fast. But then I wouldn't have been dying if I hadn't had Morrigan. I saw ghosts. . . ."

"Oncle Julien?" I asked.

She hesitated, then: "No. Oncle Julien only came to me way, way back, when he wanted me to do something, and it was always in a dream. Oncle Julien is in the Light. He doesn't come to the Earth unless there's a really important reason."

(Deep carefully concealed shudder.)

She went on, the vampiric musicality sharpening her soft words: "These ghosts I saw were just really dead people like my father and my mother who were waiting for me—you know, the ones who come to take you across—but they wouldn't speak to me. It wasn't time yet, that's what Fr. Kevin said. Fr. Kevin's a powerful witch. He never knew until he came home South. He goes into St. Mary's Assumption Church in the night when it's completely dark except for the candles, you know, and he lies down on the marble, full-length, you know—."

(Secret heartache. *I know*.)

"—and with his arms outstretched, he contemplates Christ on the Cross. He imagines himself kissing the bloody wounds of Christ."

"And you in your pain? Did you pray?"

"Not very much," she said. "It was like prayer would have required a certain coherence. This last year, I was incapable of that coherence."

"Ah, yes, I see," I said. "Go on."

"And things happened," she said. "People wanted me to die. Something happened. Someone . . . People wanted me to get it over with. . . ."

"Did you want to get it over with?"

She didn't answer right away, then she said, "I wanted to escape. But when someone . . . someone. . . . My thoughts became—"

"—became what?"

"Became trivial."

"No, not so," I insisted.

"How to get out of the room, how to get all the way down the steps, how to scoot behind the wheel of the limo, how to get the flowers, how to get to Quinn—."

"I see. Poetic. Specific. Not trivial."

"A destination with the sanction of poetry, perhaps," she said. " 'There with fantastic garlands did she come.' And so I did."

"Most certainly," I said. "But before you could do it—you were going to say something, you were about to say something about someone. . . ."

Silence.

"Then Rowan came," she said. "You don't know my cousin Rowan." (I don't?)

Flash of pain in her clear brilliant eyes.

"Yeah, well, Rowan came," she said. "Rowan has this power. . . ."

"Was it for your sake or her sake that she was going to kill you?"

She smiled. "I don't know. I don't think she knew, either."

"But she realized you knew and she didn't use her power."

"I told her, I said, 'Rowan, you're scaring me! Stop it, you're scaring me!' And she burst into tears. Or was it me? I think I burst into tears! It was one of us. I was so scared."

"And so you escaped."

"Yes, I did, indeed I did."

" 'Which time she chanted snatches of old tunes.' "

She smiled again. Would she talk about the Woman Child? She lay very still.

I could feel Quinn's anxiety, and the outpouring of his love.

All the while, he hadn't moved the hand that lay on her shoulder.

"I'm not dying," she said with a shrug. "I'm here."

"No, you're not," I said, "that's finished."

"I've got to reach back and remember when I wanted things."

"No, you don't," I said. "That's mortal talk. You're Mona—Born to Darkness now." I tried to take it slowly, watching her smile come and go. Faint freckles on her face. The inevitable glister of her skin.

"That's it," I said. "Let your eyes drink me in. You're seeing colors you never saw before. You're realizing sensations you never even dreamt about. The Dark Blood's a magnificent teacher. You shiver because you think the pain's going to come back, but you couldn't go back to that pain if you wanted to. Stop shivering. I mean it. Stop."

"What are you asking of me?" she said, "that I surrender to you or to the Blood?"

I laughed under my breath. "I don't know why women always surprise me," I said. "Men don't. I think I underestimate women in general. They distract me. Their loveliness always strikes me as alien."

She laughed outright. "What do you mean, alien?"

"You're the Great Unknown, Sweetheart."

"Elaborate," she said.

"Well, think about Adam in the Bible, I mean this guy is the Wimp of All Time saying to Almighty God, the Creator, Yahweh Who made the stars, 'The woman gave me to eat!' I mean the poor slob is just a spineless hopeless jerk! And this is Original Sin, no less! The Primal Catastrophe. Oh, I mean—pa-lease. BUT! When you see a magnificent woman—like you—with your green eyes just the perfect distance apart, tinsel voice giving out intelligent words, lying naked and staring with an expression of keen unerring comprehension, you can sort of read into Adam an inevitable bafflement in the face of Eve, something that defies clarification, and that's how Adam could come up with such a ludicrous excuse! 'This completely weird, way out, strange, mysterious inscrutable seductive being which you made out of my rib, gave me to eat.' Get it?"

Quinn gave me a little laugh against his will. He was seething with possessiveness. Me and her on the bed. But this was nice, his laughter.

I locked in on her again. Enough about the Garden of Eden. (And enough about what had just happened downstairs on the front porch between me and someone infinitely better than any figment of my longing.)

Hell. It was the damned flowers all over the bed! She was patiently waiting, naked breasts against me, red hair snarled in the roses, just looking at me, green eyes and soft mouth actually sweet. A preternatural being, and I had known the most miraculous of them. What was getting to me? Kindly continue as if nothing was wrong. *As if you have not done Evil again, you fiend!*

"Surrender to both of us, me and the Blood," I said. "I want you and Quinn to be perfect the way I'm not. I want to take you through an apprenticeship that's flawless. You hear me? Quinn was twice maimed when twice born. Bad mothers. I want to erase that from his heart."

I felt Quinn's gentle squeeze on my arm. An assent even though I was lying practically on top of the succulent little love of his life, now transformed into his immortal companion.

"The Blood told me things," she said. She was in no hurry. Her tears were dried, like ashes flaking on her cheeks. "It was coherent, the Blood," she said. "I didn't realize it until it was over. It felt too good. Then came the thoughts. I know you've survived centuries. You've even survived yourself. You went into a desert place like Christ. You didn't die because your blood's too strong. You're afraid you can't die. Everything you've believed in has been shattered. You tell yourself you have no illusions, but that's not true."

She shivered again. It was advancing too fast for her. Maybe too fast for me. Where was that ghost? Tell her about the ghost? No. I was relieved she couldn't read my mind anymore.

"I have no theology of us," I said to her. I was really talking to Quinn too. "God tolerates us, but what does that mean?"

She smiled almost bitterly. "Who has a theology of now, anyway?" she asked.

"Lots of people. Your Fr. Kevin, it seems," I replied.

"He has a Christology," she replied. "It's different."

"Sounds awfully good to me," I said.

"Oh, come on, he couldn't convert you if he had the next hundred years."

I thought bitterly of Memnoch, the Devil. I thought of God Incarnate, with whom I'd spoken. I thought of all my doubts that any of it had been real, of all my suspicions that I was the mere pawn of spirits in some elaborate game, and of how I'd fled Perdition, with its myriad roaring holographs of confrontational guilt for the cold snow-filled streets of New York, avowing the material, the sensual, the solid above all illusions. Did I really not believe in those things which I saw? Or had I simply found that cosmos to be unendurable?

I didn't know. I wanted to be a saint! I was frightened. I felt emptiness. What was the nature of her monster child? I didn't want to know. Yes, I did.

And then I fixed my eyes on her. I thought of Quinn. And there flared for me in dim luminescence a scheme of meaning.

"We do have myths," I said. "We had a goddess. But now is not the time for all those things. You needn't believe all I've seen. What I do have to give you is a vision. I think a vision is stronger than an illusion.

And the vision is that we can exist as powerful beings without hurting anyone who's good and kind."

"Slay the Evil Doer," she said with inevitable innocence.

"Amen," I said. "Slay the Evil Doer. And then we do possess the world, the world you wanted when you were a crazed kid, daydreaming on your long restless walks all over New Orleans, your professed Wander Slut days, the little Sacred Heart Academy girl seducing all of her cousins, I know you, and thriving at home on junk food and the computer, yeah, I saw it, your drunken parents safely out of your hair, their names already inscribed in the Book of Death, all that before anything broke your heart."

"Whoa!" She gave me back a soft laugh. "So vampires can say all those words without taking a breath. You got it. And you just told me not to look back. You like to give orders."

"So we ransacked each other's souls during the Dark Trick, that's what's supposed to happen," I said. "I wish I could eat your little mind now. You've got me puzzled. Dreaming dreams. I'm forgetting things, like, for instance, that those I make in the Blood usually wind up despising me or leaving me for simpler reasons."

"I don't want to leave you," she said. Then came the pucker of her red eyebrows again, tiny distinct wrinkles in the smooth flesh that vanished instantly. "I'm thirsting," she said. "Am I supposed to thirst? I can see blood. I can smell it. I want it."

I sighed. I wanted to give her mine. But it wasn't the right way to go about things. She needed her appetite for the hunt. I was flustered suddenly.

Even Quinn, with all the adolescent mortal lust boiling in his brain, was handling her rebirth better than I was. Let's get a grip.

I withdrew from the flower-strewn bower. Woke up to the room. And Quinn standing there, patient, with so much confidence in me that he kept his jealousy in check. I sparked off his blue eyes.

She ruffled the flowers on the bed into ruin and mumbled poetry again.

I took her hand and brought her up off the bed and onto her feet. She shook all the petals out of her hair. I tried not to look at her. She was as ripe and glowing as any dream-world sacrificial virgin. She sighed and looked at all the scattered clothes.

Quinn gathered them up, swooping down, circling her carefully as if he didn't dare to touch her.

She looked at me. No flaw remained. All the bruises of those needles, they were gone as I knew they would be. But I must confess (to you) that I'd been a little unsure. She'd been so weak, so worked over, so torn. But the cells had been there, hiding, waiting for the renewal. And the Blood had found them out and re-created her.

Her lips were trembling a little and she said in a half whisper,

"How long do you think before I can go to Rowan? I don't want to fake my death, tell them lies, all that, disappear leaving a space where I was. I—. There are things I want to know from them. My child, you know, she went away. We lost her. But maybe now . . ." She was looking around at the most common objects, the bedpost, the edge of the velvet spread, the carpet under her naked toes. She flexed her toes. "Maybe now. . . ."

"You don't have to die," I said. "Isn't Quinn the clear proof of that? Quinn's been living here at Blackwood Farm for a year. Things are in limbo for you. Later on tonight you can call Rowan. Tell her you're all right, that the nurse is here . . ."

"Yes . . ."

"She's a sweet and loving nurse whom I can dazzle like that, I've done it, I know, and they'll feed her Creole chicken and rice in the kitchen. You're blinding me, Beautiful. Put on your clothes."

"Right-O, Boss," she whispered.

A smile flitted across her face, but I could tell her mind was giving her no peace. One minute she was looking at the flowers as though they were out to attack her and the next she was plunged into thought.

"But what about the people left in this house?" she asked. "They all saw me when I came in. I know what I looked like. We tell them it's a miracle?"

I burst out laughing.

"Is there a raincoat in your closet, Quinn?"

"I can think of something fancier than that," he replied.

"Cool. And you can carry her down the steps? I already told Clem we'd be going into New Orleans."

"Right-O, Boss," she said again, with a faint smile. "What are we going to do in New Orleans?"

"Hunt," I said. "Hunt and drink from the Evil Doer. You use your telepathic power to seek them out. But I'm going to assist you. I'm going to lead you to the kill. I'm going to be there with you."

She nodded. "I'm positively parched," she said. Then her eyes went wide. Her tongue had just touched her tiny fang teeth. "Good God," she whispered.

"He's in Heaven," I said softly. "Don't let Him hear you."

She took the panties from Quinn and slipped them on, pulling them up over her little nest of red pubic hair. That was ten times worse than pure nakedness. The lace slip with its delicate straps came over her head, a bit long for her because she wasn't as tall as Aunt Queen had been, but otherwise it was fine, snug over her breasts and hips, the broad lace hem just above her ankles.

Quinn took out his pocket handkerchief and wiped the caked blood off her cheeks. He kissed her, and she fell to kissing him, and for a moment they were just lost to each other, kissing and kissing, like two long graceful cats licking at each other.

He picked her up off her feet and wouldn't stop kissing her. They were both of them purring. He wanted so badly to drink just a taste of her blood.

I slumped down in the chair at Quinn's desk.

I listened to the house. Clatter of dishes in the sink, Jasmine talking. Cyndy, the Nurse, was there crying at the sight of Aunt Queen's room; and where was Quinn's mother, Patsy? Clem out front waiting for us with that big car, yes, right, don't frighten her by carrying her through the air; take the car.

In a daze of small considerations, I watched her slip on the silk dress. The silk dress appeared handmade with embroidered cuffs and a tight embroidered collar that Quinn clasped at the back of her neck. It hung to her ankles. It looked divine on her—like a gown rather than a dress. She was a barefoot princess. Oh yeah, that's a cliché, well then, so is a fulsome and comely young woman. Shove it.

She put on a pair of slightly scuffed little white slippers, the kind you can buy in any drugstore, the ones she'd obviously worn over here, and after she put her head back and tossed her hair, she was almost complete. It was vampire hair now, and it needed no real brushing, each strand fighting with the strand next to it, the whole voluminous and gleaming, her forehead high and well proportioned, with eyebrows divinely set, and then she flashed on me. I'm still here, guys.

"It's tricky," she said gently, as if she didn't want to be rude to me. "He knows you have a cameo in your pocket, and so I know because I can read his thoughts."

"Oh, so that's what I've done here," I said, laughing under my breath. "I forgot about the cameo." I gave it to Quinn. I could foresee this triangular telepathy being something of a nightmare.

Yes, I'd wanted them free to read each other's thoughts, so why the Hell was I jealous?

Towering over her, he pinned the cameo carefully in the center of the embroidered white collar. It looked old and fine.

Then in an anxious whisper he put a question to her.

"You wouldn't wear Aunt Queen's high-heel shoes, would you?"

She went into a riot of soft laughter. So did I.

Till her dying day, Aunt Queen had apparently gone about in breakneck high heels with ankle straps and open toes, some covered in rhinestones or, for all I knew, real diamonds. She'd had on such wondrous shoes when I made her acquaintance.

One of the enduring ironies of her death was that she had been in her bare stocking feet when she suffered the fall that killed her. But that was the evildoing of Goblin, who had deliberately startled her and even pushed her.

So the shoes were innocent and there were probably piles of them in her closets downstairs.

But slap together the image of Mona, the tramp kid, in saddle oxfords, and any vision of Aunt Queen's heels, and it was uproariously funny. Why would Mona do such a thing as that to herself? And if you knew how much Quinn noticed women's high heels—namely Jasmine's and Aunt Queen's, it was twice as uproariously funny.

Mona was stuck someplace between vampire trance and total love, gazing into Quinn's earnest face trying to figure this.

"All right, Quinn, I'll try her shoes," she said, "if you want me to." Now that was pure transnatural female.

He was on the phone to Jasmine in an instant. Bring upstairs Aunt Queen's finest big white satin wrapper—one of the full-length articles with the ostrich feather trim, and a pair of her new heels, very glittery, and hurry.

It didn't require a vampire's hearing to pick up Jasmine's answer:

"Lawd! You're going to make that sick girl put on those things? Have you lost your mind, Little Boss! I'm coming up there! And Cyndy, the Nurse, is here and she is as shocked as I am, and she's coming with me, and you better leave that child alone. Lawd! I mean Lawd! You can't go undressing her like a doll, Taw-quin Blackwood, you lunatic! Is that child dead already? Is that what you're trying to tell me? Answer me, Taw-quin Blackwood, this is Jasmine talking to you! Do you even know that Patsy's run off and left all her medicines, and nobody knows where the Hell she's gone? Now, I don't blame you for not caring about Patsy but somebody's got to think of Patsy, and Cyndy's crying her eyes out down here over Patsy—."

"Jasmine, calm down," Quinn said. He went on in the most courteous and calm manner. "Patsy's dead. I killed her night before last. I broke her neck and dumped her in the swamp and the alligators ate her. You don't have to worry about Patsy anymore. Throw her medicines in the trash. Tell Cyndy, the Nurse, to have some supper. I'm coming down for Aunt Queen's shoes and negligee myself. Mona is completely better." He put down the phone and went straight out the door. "Latch this after me."

I obliged.

Mona looked at me searchingly.

"He was telling the truth about Patsy, wasn't he?" she asked. "And Patsy's his *mother*???"

I nodded. I shrugged.

"They'll never believe him," I said, "and it was the smartest thing for him to do. He can repeat that confession until doomsday. But when you know more about Patsy, you'll understand."

She looked horrified, and the Blood was intensifying it.

"Which was the smartest thing?" she asked. "Killing Patsy or telling them that?"

"Telling them is what I meant," I pursued. "Killing her only Quinn can explain. Patsy hated Quinn, I can attest to that, and she was a hard merciless woman. She was dying of AIDS. She didn't have much time on the mortal clock. The rest he can answer."

Mona was aghast, a virgin vampire about to faint from moral shock.

"In all the years I've known him, he has never mentioned Patsy to me or even answered by E-mail one single solitary question about his mother."

I shrugged again. "He has his secrets as you have. I know the name of your child. Morrigan. But he doesn't."

She flinched.

There was the pounding sound of argument rising through the floor below. Even Nash and Tommy, fresh from the supper table, had been pressed into the cause on Jasmine's side, and Big Ramona declared Quinn a necromaniac. Cyndy the Nurse was sobbing.

"But still," said Mona, "to kill your own mother."

For one brief technicolor second, I let myself think of my own mother, Gabrielle, whom I had brought into the Blood. Where in the wide world was she—that cold silent unmovable creature whose solitude was unimaginable to me? It hadn't been so very long ago that I'd seen her. I'd see her again, some time or other. There was no warmth, no solace, no understanding there. But what did it matter?

Quinn rapped on the door. I let him in. I could hear the engine of the limousine started outside. Clem was getting ready for us. The night was hot. He was running the cooling. It would be sweet driving into New Orleans.

Quinn leaned back against the door when it was shut and bolted, and took a deep breath. "It would have been easier," he said, "to rob the Bank of England."

He thrust the glittering high-heel slippers into Mona's waiting hands.

She looked them over.

She slipped them on her feet, gaining a good four inches in height and a tension in her legs that even through the dress appeared ruthlessly seductive. The shoes were just a tiny bit too short, but it was hardly noticeable, the rhinestone-studded strap cutting across her toes exquisitely. He buckled one ankle strap as she did the other.

She took the long white negligee from Quinn and put it on, wrapping it about her and laughing as the shivering feathers tickled her. It was loose and shimmering and gaudy and glorious.

She ran all about the room in little and big circles. One of those things guys can't do????? Her balance was perfect. Just the beginning of her strength, and so some sense of frivolity inside of her wanted these impossible torturous slippers. Round and around, and then she froze against the far window:

"Why on earth did you kill your mother?" she asked.

Quinn stared at her. He seemed at a total loss. He went towards her in a great fluid gesture. He took her in his arms and pressed her to him as he'd done before and said nothing. Momentary fear. The mention of Patsy had enveloped him in darkness. Or maybe it was Aunt Queen's finery.

There came a loud rapping at the door. Jasmine's voice followed:

"You open up, Little Boss, and let me see that child, or I swear to God I'll get the sheriff."

Cyndy's sweet voice followed, so reasonable and kind. "Quinn? Quinn, please let me have a look at Mona?"

"Pick her up," I said to Quinn. "Carry her through them, past them, down the stairs and out the front door and into the car. I'm right with you."

6

W E WERE OUT OF THE HOUSE and on the road within three minutes, maybe less, moving on mortal time so as not to alarm any further the full chorus of those shouting at us. Mona had sense enough to pull up the shivering feathers of the wrapper over her face so that nothing could be seen of her but heaps of red hair and dangling bejeweled feet, and we made our exit with polished polite assurances to the clamoring herd, directing the profoundly indifferent Clem to head for New Orleans "immediately."

It was I who gave the command with a quick smile that elicited the driver's sarcastic expression and shrug, but the mammoth limousine was soon rocking down the gravel drive, and Mona was between me and Quinn in the back seat, and then and only then did I begin to scan the city of New Orleans for possible victims.

"I can hear the voices like the din from Hell," I said. "Toughen up, baby. I'm looking for the eternal scum. Call them grim soulless mortals feeding off the downtrodden or the downtrodden feeding off each other. I always wonder—and never learn—whether or not the genuine Power Thugs ever stop to look at the violet evening sky or the overhead branches of an oak. Crack peddlers, child killers, teenaged gangsters for a fatal fifteen minutes, the morgue's never empty in our town, it's an eternal brew of calculated malice mixed with moral ignorance."

Mona dreamed, staring out the windows, caught up in every shift of the landscape. Quinn could hear the distant voices. Quinn could tune in from afar. Quinn was anxious, so in love with her, but far from happy.

The car gained speed as it took to the highway.

Mona gasped. She slipped her fingers around my left arm. You can never tell just what a fledgling will do. It's all so intoxicating.

"Listen," I said. "Quinn and I are listening."

"I hear them," she said. "I can't take one thread from the knots, I can't. But look at the trees. There's no tint on these windows. Mayfairs always tint their limousine windows."

"That was not Aunt Queen's way," said Quinn, staring forward, washed in the voices. "She wanted the clear glass so she could see out. She didn't care if people looked in."

"I keep waiting for it all to settle," Mona whispered.

"It never will," said Quinn. "It only gets better and better."

"Then trust me," she said to him, her fingers tightening on my arm. "Don't be so afraid for me. I have requests."

"Hit me with them, go on," I said.

"I want to go past my house—I mean the Mayfair house on First and Chestnut. I've been in te hospital for two years. I haven't seen it."

"No," I said. "Rowan will sense your presence. She won't know what you are any more than she knew at Blackwood Manor. But she'll know you're close. We're not going there. There'll come a time, but this isn't it. Go back to the thirst."

She nodded. She didn't fight me. I realized she hadn't fought me on anything.

But I knew she had heavy thoughts, more than usual links in the chain that bound fledglings to their living past. Something was catching hold of her, something to do with the warped images she'd shown me in the Blood—the Monstrous Offspring, the Woman Child. What had that been, that creature?

I didn't let Quinn pick this up from me. It was too soon to reveal all that. But he might well have caught it all in the room when I'd brought her over. I'd belonged to her during those moments, exclusively and dangerously. He might know all I'd seen. And he might be reading it from her now, though I knew she wasn't ready to reveal it.

The car was speeding across the lake. The lake looked like a huge dead thing rather than a body of living water. But the clouds rose in a triumphant mass beneath the emerging moon. When you're a vampire you can see the clouds that others can't see. You can live off things like that when faith is destroyed—the random shifting shapes of clouds, the seeming sentience of the moon.

"No, I need to go there," she said suddenly. "I have to see the house. I have to."

"What is this, a damned mutiny?" I answered. I was just congratulating you in my mind that you didn't fight me."

"What? Do I get a merit badge for that?" she fired back. "We don't have to go close to the house," she went on, sob in her throat. "I just need to see those Garden District streets."

"Oh yeah, right," I said under my breath. "You care that you'll draw them right out of the house, right out of their peace of mind? You ready to follow up on that in some way? Of course I'm not saying you have to follow up. You understand, I'm just trying to respond to you and Mr. Quinn Blackwood as exemplary decent little people. I myself? I'm a scoundrel."

"Beloved Boss," she said with a straight face, "let me just go as close as we can, as close as you can figure. No, I don't want to rile them up. I hate the idea. But I was in solitary confinement for two years."

"Where *are* we headed, Lestat?" Quinn asked. "Will we hunt downtown?"

"Back of town is what I like to call it," I said. "No Creole like me is going to call it downtown. You know where the scum grows on the bricks. Listen for the city, Mona."

"I hear it," she answered. "It's like opening a floodgate. And then the discrete voices. Plenty of discrete voices. Bickering, threats, even the muffled snap of guns . . ."

"The town's full tonight in spite of the heat," I said. "People are out on the streets, thoughts flooding me in sickening waves. If I was a saint, this is what I would have to listen to all the time."

"Yeah, like prayers," she said. "All those petitions."

"Saints have to work," I said, as if I really knew.

And then with one fine blow it struck me. *Their presence.*

It hit Quinn at the same instant, and he said, "My God" under his breath. He was astonished.

"Close in on them," I said.

"What is it?" Mona asked. "I can't hear it." Then she locked her eyes on Quinn.

Oh, this was nothing short of providential! I was absolutely furious and deliriously happy at the same time. I closed my focus.

Oh, yeah, right, killing at random as they fed, a pair of male and female vampires, constitutionally cruel, high-toned, style versus character, brilliant gold and brand-name leather, drunk on their powers, lapping up New Orleans as if it weren't real, baiting the "great vampire Lestat," in whom they didn't really believe (who does?), prancing through my French Quarter streets to a lavish lair in a pricey hotel, key in the lock, blood full, laughter echoing to the ceiling, turn on the TV, done in for the night, innocent victims strewn in the back alleys, but not all of them, ready to groove on music or the color images of the mortal world, feeling totally superior, vague plan to sleep in the day in the filthy old whitewashed tombs of St. Louis No. 1 Cemetery, like, very bold! Unwittingly waiting to die.

I sat back laughing under my breath.

"This is too rich! Too deliciously wicked! She's up for it. Don't give it another thought. It's the lightning narcotic of enemy blood. It's perfect for her. And the sooner she learns to fight her own kind the better. Same for you, Quinn. You've never had to battle the cosmic trash that's out there."

"But this *has* to be perfect for her, Lestat," Quinn said. "You know what happened on my first night. I blundered. I can't let something ugly and bad happen to her—."

"You're breaking my tender little heart," I said. "Are you and she going in alone? I am going with you. You honestly think I can't handle this pair of mavericks? I've made myself too domestic for you, Quinn. You forget who I am and maybe I do too."

"But how will it end?" he persisted.

"Your innocence is so genuine," I responded.

"You should know that by now!" he said. And then at once, "I'm sorry. Forgive me. It's only—."

"Listen to me, both of you," I said. "We're talking the misbegotten of Hell. They've been swaggering through eternity for a decade at most, just long enough to make them very cocky. I'll get the lowdown on their souls before I dispatch them, of course. But as of now I know they're outlaws. And I don't like them. And vampire blood is always hot. And the fighting will be good. They're greedy filth. They break the peace on my streets. That's a death sentence, at least when I have the time for it. And right now I have the time, and you have the thirst, and that's what interests me. No more questions."

A little laugh came from Mona. "And I wonder how their blood tastes," she said, "but I wouldn't dare ask you. Let's just say I'm up for it if you say so."

"You're a mocking little thing," I replied. "Do you like to fight? Fighting with mortals is no fun because it's no fair. No honor-bound immortal would do it any more than necessary. But fighting with these revenants is going to be great. And you can never tell how strong they're going to be, absolutely never. Then there are the images that come through their blood—sizzling, more electric than those from the human prey."

Squeeze of her hand.

Quinn was distressed. He thought of the night he first hunted: a wedding in Naples, and the bride had pulled him into a bedroom, intent on a caper to cut her new spouse, and he'd drunk her dry, spilling the first draught all over her dress. Over and over he relived that fall from grace, that awful moment of the full curse.

"Little Brother," I said. "Those were human beings. Look at me."

He turned towards me, and in the flashing lights of the freeway I peered into his eyes.

"I know I've played it elegant with you up till now," I said. "I've played the sage European and now you're seeing the rough side of me. And I have to remember you've been through Hell just telling me your story, and what with the death of Aunt Queen, it's been pure torture for you, and you richly deserve any good thing that I can conjure or give. But I have to rid the world of these two Blood Hunters. And you and Mona mustn't miss this opportunity."

"What if they're strong, what if they were made like me by someone very old?" he asked.

I sighed. "I've given you my blood, Quinn. And Mona's been made with it. My blood, Quinn. They're no match for you now. They're no match for her, I told you."

"I wanna do it!" Mona interjected immediately. "If you say they're fair game, then they're fair game, and that's good enough for me, Beloved Boss. I can't tell my own heart and soul what I'm feeling now, how much I crave this little battle. I can't find the words, it's so raw, so rooted inside me! It goes way back into the human part of me that's not going to die, doesn't it?"

"Yes," I said. "Precisely."

"Bravo," she said. "I'm picking them up. But, something's, something's confusing me . . ."

"Save it, we're almost there," I said.

A soft subdued expression came over Quinn, unmistakable in the light of the cars that flew by.

"What if they beg for mercy?" he asked.

"You can count on that happening," I said with a little shrug.

"What if they know poetry?" he asked.

"It would have to be very fine," I said. "Don't you think? To make up for all those innocent victims?"

He wouldn't let up. He couldn't.

"What if they love you?"

7

Time out for one quick meditation on the matter of saints, as
you know how much I want to be one and can't.

Now, when we left the Pope he was safely in his quarters,
but in the time which it has taken me to faithfully record these events—
don't worry, we'll snap back in less than five minutes!—the Pope has
been to Toronto, Guatemala and Mexico, and in Mexico has canonized
a saint.

Why do I make mention of this when Pope John Paul II has done
many other things on this little trip, including beatifying a couple of
guys and canonizing a saint in Guatemala as well?

Because when it comes to this saint in Mexico, I am particularly
moved by the circumstances—that it was one Juan Diego, a humble
Indian ("indigenous person," as some headlines claim) to whom Our
Lady of Guadalupe appeared in 1531. This humble Indian, when first
he told the local Spanish bishop about the Virgin's appearing to him,
was ignored, naturally, until Our Lady worked a double miracle. She
provided some gorgeous red roses for Juan Diego to gather for the
bishop, roses growing impossibly in the snow on top of Juan Diego's
home mountain, and when the little guy gladly opened his *tilma* (pon-
cho) before the bishop to reveal these lovely blooms, there on the *tilma*
itself was a full-color picture of Our Lady in unmistakable Virgin Mary
form but with Indian skin.

This *tilma*, a garment made from cactus fibers, with its glorious picture of the Virgin Mary, still hangs intact in the Cathedral in Mexico
City, and thousands flock to it every day. It is called Our Lady of

Guadalupe, and there is no one in Christendom who has not seen this depiction of Christ's mother at one time or another in his or her life.

Okay. Now, I love this story. I always have. I think it's neat what happened to Juan Diego. When he was first trudging over the mountain, the Blessed Mother called to him: "Juanito!" Isn't that touching? And touching that thousands of Indians converted to Christianity after these miracles. And certainly it is wonderful that Pope John Paul II, ailing and eighty-two years of age, made it to Mexico to canonize Juan Diego.

But the Pope's critics aren't so happy. There are rumblings, says the press. Malcontents say there is no proof that Juan Diego ever existed.

Now, that is really rude!

And it points to a real misunderstanding of what the great spiritual wealth of Roman Catholicism is all about.

If nobody can prove that Juan Diego existed, then obviously nobody can prove that he did not.

But let's suppose for a moment that Juan Diego doesn't exist, or didn't. The Pope is still infallible, right? "Whatever you shall bind on Earth shall be bound in Heaven," Christ said to Peter. Okay?

Even the worst critics of the Papacy admit that it's a modern marvel, no?

Therefore, without doubt, and without rumblings, at the instant that John Paul declared Juan Diego a saint, the little guy popped into existence in Heaven! Now think about what probably went through Juan Diego's mind. And don't forget that this is "an indigenous person" of the Americas no less, and here he finds himself in a Heaven which is, by anyone's description, totally beyond description.

In fact, if the latest crop of mystics are correct and the Heaven to which we go when we enter the Light is very much shaped by our own preconceived notions, Juan Diego, endowed by the full definition given him through the arguments and decisions of the Roman Curia is probably roaming around in his *tilma* made of cactus fiber, picking roses. I wonder if he has shoes.

Is he going to be lonely? Of course not. Only an atheist would entertain such a notion. Take it from me, the indescribable Heaven is an indescribable hurricane of magnificence.

But let's tone it down for our Foot of Sinai senses. Surrounded by his ever blooming garden, Juan Diego can if he wishes keep company with dozens of other saints who spent no time on Earth whatsoever, including the Blessed Virgin Mary's famed parents, Joachim and Anne, and St. Veronica whom I have personally met.

But it is much more likely that Juan Diego will find himself besieged by prayerful petitions. The voices from "indigenous persons" on Earth as well as the descendants of colonists will bring him in contact with the suffering and the misery of the planet he escaped.

What am I talking about?

Simply this. Whether he existed on Earth or not, Juan Diego is probably hard at work, dipping down through the astral layers in his human-shaped soul, listening earnestly to the faithful and relaying their petitions to the All Knowing One. He has to be. He is a saint of immense importance. And no doubt Our Lady of Guadalupe is looking down benevolently upon a whole new stream of tourists and venerators in Mexico City.

And the Pope has gone home to the Vatican, having canonized in his lifetime 463 saints.

I wish I was one of those saints. Maybe that's why I had to write this chapter. I'm envious of Juan Diego. Hmmm.

But I'm not a saint. And that didn't even take five minutes and you know it, so don't complain. It's just that I cannot forget my passion to be officially canonized.

Alas. Anon. *Alors. Mais oui. Eh bien.* Proceed to Chapter Eight directly.

8

So, NOBODY EVER ACCUSED ME of acquiring any real wisdom in my two hundred years on this Earth. I know only one way to proceed.

Clem let us out in front of the hotel, a new one, quite luxurious, and most expensive, and in the thick of things, so to speak, with an address on Canal Street, the great shabby divide of New Orleans, and an entrance out back to the French Quarter, the little world I preferred.

Mona was in such a trance that we had to propel her to the elevator, I on her left and Quinn on her right. Naturally everyone in the lobby took note of us—not because we were blood-sucking immortals bent on destroying two of our kind on the fifteenth floor, but because we were exceedingly and severely gorgeous, especially Mona, wrapped in feathers and shimmering fabric and poised atop a pair of breakneck heels.

Quinn was thirsting now as strongly as Mona was, and it would see him through what we had to do.

But I wasn't immune to the questions he'd raised in the car. Poetry, love. And me secretly aspiring to sanctity! What an everlasting life! And remember, honorary Children of the Night, what I said about telepathy. It ain't the real thing, no matter how good it is.

As soon as we reached the suite, I pushed the door in fairly quietly, without breaking its hinges, since I intended to close it again, and the spectacle into which I plunged on feline feet astonished me.

Ah, the Savage Garden of this Earth that hath such creatures in it!

The mavericks were dancing in dim light to the most intense

music—a Bartók concerto for violin and orchestra flooding the room at max volume. The music was sad, ripping, overpowering—a command to abandon all things cheap and tawdry, a full-blown engulfing majesty.

And though they themselves were infinitely more arresting than I had ever anticipated, these two, I spied beyond them on the long deep burgundy-colored couch a cluster of mortal children, bruised, unconscious and obviously being used at random as blood victims.

All three of us were in the room with the door closed, and the insurgents danced oblivious to us, their senses drenched in lustrous sound and rhythm.

They were absolutely spectacular in appearance, with tanned skin, rippling jet black hair to the waist—being both of Semitic or Arabic descent—very tall and with large facial features, including magnificent mouths, and they were inherently graceful. They danced with closed eyes, oval faces serene, in huge swaying and arching gestures, humming through closed lips to the music, and the male, who was on the surface almost indistinguishable from the female, every now and then shook out his immense veil of hair and swung it rapidly around him in a circle.

Their sleek black leather clothes were stunning and unisexual. Supple pants, sleeveless and collarless tops. They wore gold bracelets on their naked upper and lower arms. They embraced each other now and then and let each other go, and as we watched, the female dipped down into the cluster of mortal children and brought up to her lips a limp little boy, and drank from him.

Mona let out a scream at the sight of this, and at once the two vampires froze, staring at us. So similar were their movements, one would have thought they were grand automatons operated by a central system. The unconscious child was dropped to the couch.

My heart became a little knot inside me. I could scarcely breathe. The music flooded my brain, the ripping, sad, compelling voice of the violin.

"Quinn, shut it off," I said, and scarcely had I spoken when the music stopped. The parlor was plunged into a ringing vibrant silence.

The pair drew together. The figure they made was statuesque.

They had exquisite arched black eyebrows, heavily lidded eyes with thick eyelashes. Arabic, yes, from the streets of New York. Brother and sister, petty merchant class, real hard work, sixteen when made. It came flooding out of them, and also a torrent of worship for me, a torrent of exuberant happiness that I had "appeared." Oh, God help me. Juan Diego stand by me.

"We didn't dream we'd see you, actually see you!" said the female, with heavily accented words, voice rich and beguiling and reverent. "We hoped and prayed, and here you are and it is really you." Her lovely hands unfolded and reached out to me.

"Why did you kill innocent victims in my town," I whispered. "Where did you get these innocent children?"

"But you, you drank from children yourself, it's in the pages of the Chronicles," the male said. Same accented words, courteous, gentle tone. "We were imitating you! What have we done that you have not done!"

The knot in my heart grew tighter. Those accursed deeds, those accursed confessions. Oh God, forgive me.

"You know my warnings," I said. "Everyone knows. Stay out of New Orleans, New Orleans belongs to me. Who doesn't know those warnings?"

"But we came to worship you!" said the male. "We've been here before. You never cared. It was as if you were a legend."

Suddenly they realized their immense miscalculation. The male raced for the door, but Quinn caught his arm effortlessly and swung him around.

The female stood shocked in the center of the room, her jet black eyes staring at me, then silently moving over Mona.

"No," she said, "no, you can't simply destroy us, you won't do it. You won't take from us our immortal souls, you will not. You are our dream, you are our model in all things. You cannot do this to us. Oh, I beg you, make of us your servants, teach us all things. We'll never disobey! We'll learn everything from you."

"You knew the law," I said. "You chose to break it. You thought you'd slip in and out, leaving your sins behind you. And you murder children in my name? You do this in my city? You never learned from my pages. Don't throw them in my face." I began to tremble. "You think I confessed what I did for you to follow my example? My faults were no template for your abominations."

"But we adore you!" said the male. "We come in pilgrimage to you.

Bind us to yourself and we'll be filled with your grace, we'll be perfected in you."

"I have no absolution for you," I said. "You stand condemned. It's finished."

I heard Mona let out a little moan. I could see the struggle in Quinn's face.

The male tensed his entire body trying to get loose. Quinn held him with one hand wrapped around his upper arm.

"Let us go," said the male. "We'll leave your city. We'll warn others never to come. We'll testify. We'll be your holy witnesses. Everywhere we go, we will tell others that we've seen you, heard the warning from your own lips."

"Drink," I said to Quinn. "Drink till there's no more to drink. Drink as you've never done it before."

"I begrudge nothing!" whispered the male and he closed his eyes. All the struggling left him. "I am your fount in love."

Without hesitation, Quinn put his right hand on the huge mass of springy hair of the male and brought the head to the proper position, twisting it until the neck was bared, and then, closing his eyes, he sank his teeth.

Mona stared enthralled, then turned sharply to the female. The thirst transformed Mona's face. She appeared half asleep, eyes fastened to the female.

"Take her," I said.

The female gazed fearlessly on Mona. "And you, so beautiful," the vagrant said in her sharpened words, "you so beautiful, you come to take my blood, I give my blood, here, I give it to you. Only spare me for eternity." She opened her arms, these arms with gold bracelets, long fingers beckoning.

Mona moved as if in a trance. She embraced the sleek body of the female with her left arm, and pushed the hair away from the right side of the female's face, and bent her supple body down and took her.

I watched Mona. It was always a spectacle—the vampire feeding, a seeming human with her teeth locked to another, eyes closed as if in deep sleep, no sound, only the victim shuddering and twisting, even her fingers motionless as she drank deeply, savoring the drug of the blood.

And so she was launched on the Devil's Road with this wretched sacrament, without the need of prodding, letting the thirst carry her through it.

The male collapsed at Quinn's feet. Quinn was dazed. He staggered backwards. "So far away," Quinn whispered. "An ancient one, from Jericho, can you imagine it, and he made them, and taught them nothing? What am I to do with this treasure of images? What am I to do with this curious intimacy?"

"Keep it close," I said. "Store it where the finer things are stored until such time as you need it."

I moved towards him slowly, then took the limp, soft victim from the floor and brought him into the tiled bathroom of the suite, a palatial marvel with a spacious tub completely surrounded by steps of green marble, and I threw the unfortunate one into the tub where he tumbled like a marionette without strings, settling silently. His eyes had rolled up into his head. He was murmuring in his native tongue, a fine collection of bronzed limbs and glints of gold, and the massive hair nesting beneath him.

In the parlor, I found Mona with her victim on their knees, and then Mona drew back, and for a moment it seemed she would lose consciousness herself, and they would be together in this, these two, their hair intermingling, but Mona rose and lifted the female.

I beckoned.

She carried the female, as a man would carry a woman, arm under her knees, arm around her shoulder. Dark hair streaming down.

"There in the tub, with her companion," I said.

Mona heaved her over with a sure gesture, letting her tumble in beside him.

The female was silent, unconscious, dreaming.

"Their Maker was old," Mona whispered, as if not to wake either of them. "He was tramping through eternity. Sometimes he knew who and what he was. And other times he didn't. He made the pair of them to run his errands. They found out everything on their own. They were so cruel. They were cruel for pleasure. They would have killed the children in the other room. They would have left them here."

"You want to kiss them good-bye?" I asked.

"I loathe them," she responded. She sounded so sleepy. "But why are they so lovely? Their hair so fine? It wasn't their fault. Their souls might have been beautiful."

"You think so? You *really* think so? You didn't taste their free will when you drank from them? You didn't taste an immense sweep of modern knowledge when you drank from them? And what was the summit of their existence, may I ask, other than bashing innocent souls; was it dancing and listening to fine music?"

Quinn came up behind her, keen for my words, and wrapped his arms around her. She raised her eyebrows and nodded.

"Watch what I do," I said. "Remember it."

I let loose the Fire with all my consuming power. Let it be merciful, Saint Lestat. I saw the outline of their black bones in the flames for a second, the heat blasting my face, and it was in that second, and that second only, that the bones moved.

The fire flashed to the ceiling, scorched it, and then shrank to nothingness. A tracery of the bones vanished. All that remained was black grease in the spacious tub.

Mona gasped. Her cheeks were beating with the blood she'd drunk. She stepped forward and peered down at the black bubbling grease. Quinn was speechless and plainly horrified.

"And so you can do that to me when I want to go, can't you?" Mona said, her voice raw.

I was shocked.

"No, dolly dear," I said. "I couldn't. Not if my life depended on it."

I let loose the Fire again. I sent it into the oily residue until there was nothing left.

And so the tall graceful long-haired dancers would dance no more.

I felt slightly dizzy. I shrank back into myself. I felt sick. I moved away from my own power. I collected all my force into my human-shaped self.

In the parlor, in the gentle manner of a human, I examined the children. There were four of them, and they had been beaten as well as bled. They were lying in a heap. All were unconscious, but I detected no blows to the head, no rushing of blood within the skulls, no permanent damage. Boys in shorts and skivy shirts and tennis shoes. No familial resemblance. How their parents must have been weeping. All could survive. I was certain of it.

The sins of my past rose up to taunt me. All my own excesses mocked me.

I made the requisite call to see to their care. I told the astonished clerk what I had discovered.

In the hallway, Mona was crying. Quinn held her.

"Come on, we're headed for my flat now. So it wasn't perfect, Quinn, you were right. But it's over."

"Lestat," he said, his eyes glittering as we pulled the weeping Mona into the elevator. "I thought it was nothing short of magnificent."

9

W E HAD TO DRAG MONA through the French Quarter streets. She fell in love with the colors made by spilt gasoline in mud puddles, with exotic furniture in the store windows of Hurwitz Mintz, with antique shop displays of threadbare gilded chairs and lacquered square grand pianos and idling trucks belching white smoke from their upturned exhaust pipes and laughing mortals passing us on the narrow sidewalks carrying adorable babies, who twisted their little necks to peer at us—

—and an old black man playing a tenor saxophone for money, which we gave him in abundance, and a hat-wearing hot dog vender from which Mona could not buy a hot dog now save to stare at it and sniff it and heave it into a trash bin, which gave her staggering pause—

—and of course we attracted attention everywhere, in very unvampirelike fashion, Quinn being taller than anyone we passed and perhaps four times as handsome, with his porcelain face, and all the rest you know, and every now and then Mona with hair flying broke from us and ran ahead frantically, the lazy evening crowds opening and closing for her as though she were on a Heavenly errand, thank God, and then she'd circle back—

—dancing and clicking and stomping like a flamenco dancer, letting the feather wrapper fly out, trail, sag, and then gathering it in again, and crying to see her reflection in shop glass, and darting down side streets until we grabbed ahold of her and claimed custody of her and wouldn't let her go.

When we got to my town house I gave two hundred dollars to my two mortal guards who were happily astonished, and as Quinn and I started back the open carriageway, Mona gave us the slip.

We didn't realize it until we'd reached the courtyard garden, and just when I was about to exclaim about the ancient cherub fountain and all the tropical wonders blooming against my much cherished brick walls, I sensed that she was totally gone.

Now, that is no easy feat. I may not be able to read the child's mind, but I have the senses of a god, do I not?

"We have to find her!" Quinn said. He was instantly thrown into protective overdrive.

"Nonsense," I said. "She knows where we are. She wants to be alone. Let her. Come on. Let's go upstairs. I'm exhausted. I should have fed. And now I don't have the spirit for it, which is a Hell of a situation. I have to rest."

"You're serious?" he asked as he followed me up the iron stairway. "What if she gets into some sort of jam?"

"She won't. She knows what she's doing. I told you. I have to crash. This is no selfish secret, Little Brother. I worked the Dark Trick tonight, and forgot to feed. I'm tired."

"You really believe she's all right?" he demanded. "I didn't realize you were tired. I should have realized. I'll go and look for her."

"No, you won't. Come on with me."

The flat was empty. No otherworldly bodies hovering about. No ghosts, either.

The back parlor had been cleaned and dusted earlier this very day and I could smell the cleaning lady's distant perfume. I could smell her lingering blood scent too. Of course I had never laid eyes on the woman. She came by the light of the sun, but she did her job well enough for me to leave her big bills. I loved giving away money. I carried it for no other purpose. I slapped a hundred on the desk for her. We have desks everywhere in this flat, I thought. Too many desks. Didn't every bedroom have a little desk? Why so many?

Quinn had only been here once and only under the most lamentable circumstances, and he was suddenly enthralled by the Impressionist paintings, which were quite divine. But it was the new and slightly somber Gauguin which caught my eye for a moment. Now, that was my purchase and had only been delivered in the last few days. Quinn hooked into that one too.

I made my usual beeline for the front parlor over the street, peeking into each and every bedroom on the way, as though I really needed to, in order to know that no one was home. The place had too much furniture. Not enough paintings. Too many books. What the hallway needed was Emile Nolde. How could I get my hands on the German Expressionists?

"I think I should go after her," Quinn said. He followed me, taking in everything reverently, mind on Mona, no doubt monitoring her every move.

Front parlor. Piano. There was no piano now. I should tell them to get a piano. Hadn't we passed an antique piano in a window? I had a sudden urge to play the piano—to use my vampiric gift to rip at the keys. It was that Bartók concerto still assaulting my mind, and the picture of those two macabre dancers accentuating the music.

Oh, give me all things human.

"I think I should go get her," Quinn said.

"Listen, I'm not one to talk much about gender," I said, flopping down in my favorite of the velvet wing chairs and throwing one foot up on the chair before the desk, "but you have to realize that she's experiencing a freedom you and I don't appreciate as men. She's walking in the darkness and she's afraid of nothing, and she loves it. And just maybe, just maybe she wants to taste a little mortal blood and she's willing to take the risk."

"She's a magnet," he whispered. He stood at the window, his hand pulling gently at the lace. "She doesn't know I'm tracking her. She isn't that far away. She's taking her time. I hear her idle thoughts. She's walking too fast. Somebody's going to notice—."

"Why are you suffering, Little Brother?" I asked. "Do you hate me for bringing her over? Do you wish it hadn't been done?"

He turned and looked at me as though I'd grabbed him by the arm.

"No," he said. He walked away from the window and sort of tumbled into the chair in the far corner opposite me, diagonally, his long legs sprawling as though he wasn't sure what to do with them. "I would have tried it if you hadn't come," he admitted. "I couldn't have watched her die. At least I don't think so. But I am suffering, you're right. Lestat, you can't leave us. Lestat, why are those guards outside the house?"

"Did I say I would leave you?" I countered. "I hired those guards after Stirling came here," I said. "Oh, it's not that I think any of the Talamasca will come back here. It's just that if Stirling could walk right in here, then somebody else might."

(Flash on the Talamasca: Order of Psychic Detectives. Don't know their own Origins. At least a thousand years old, maybe much older. Keep records on all sorts of paranormal phenomena. Reach out to the telepathically gifted and isolated. Know about us.)

Quinn and I had visited with Stirling at the Oak Haven Retreat House of the Talamasca right after the exorcism of Goblin, and the immolation of Merrick Mayfair. Merrick Mayfair had grown up in the Talamasca. Stirling had a right to know she was no longer one of the (sigh) Undead. The Retreat House was an immense square plantation house on the River Road just outside of town.

Stirling Oliver had not only been a friend of Quinn's during his mortal years, but he was a friend of Mona's as well. The Talamasca knew much more about the entire Mayfair family than they knew about me.

It gave me no pleasure to think of Stirling now, much as I admired him and liked him. Stirling was about sixty-five years old and very dedicated to the highest principles of the Order, which for all its avowed secularity might have been Roman Catholic with its strictures against meddling in the affairs of the world or using supernatural persons or forces for one's own ends. If the Order hadn't been so fabulously and mysteriously and undeniably wealthy, I would probably have been a patron of it.

(I am also fabulously and mysteriously and undeniably wealthy, but who cares?)

I felt compelled to go see Stirling at the Retreat House and tell him what had happened with Mona. But why?

Stirling wasn't Pope Gregory the Great, for the love of Heaven, and I wasn't Saint Lestat. I didn't have to go to Confession for what I'd done to Mona, but a terrible Contrition settled over me, a profound awareness that all my powers were dark powers and all my talents evil talents, and nothing could come from me but evil no matter what I did.

Besides, hadn't Stirling told Quinn last night that Mona was dying? What had been the meaning of that information? Wasn't he in some way in collusion with what had happened? No. He wasn't. Quinn hadn't left him last night to seek out Mona. Mona had come to Blackwood Manor on her own.

"Sooner or later, I'll explain all this to Stirling," I said under my breath. "It's as though Stirling will absolve me but that just isn't true." I looked at Quinn. "Can you still hear her?"

He nodded. "She's just walking, looking at things," he said. He was distracted, the pupils in his eyes dancing slowly. "Why tell Stirling?" he asked. "Stirling can't tell the Mayfairs. Why burden him with the secret?" He sat forward. "She's wandering along Jackson Square. A man's following her. She's leading him. He senses something isn't right with her. And she's on to him. She knows what he wants. She's luring him. She's certainly having a great time in Aunt Queen's high-heel shoes."

"Stop watching her," I said. "I mean it. Let me tell you something about your little girl. She's going to make herself known to the Mayfairs very soon on her own. Nothing's going to stop her. There are things she wants to know from the Mayfairs. I had a sense of it when—."

The room was empty. No Quinn. I was talking to all the furniture.

I heard the back door open and close, it was that fast.

I stretched out and scrunched down and put my head back and drifted, eyes shut at once.

I was half dreaming. Why the Hell hadn't I fed? Of course I didn't need to feed every night or even every month, but when you work the Dark Trick, no matter who you are, you must feed afterwards, you're giving from the very sap stream of your life. All is vanity. All is vanity under the sun and under the moon.

I'd been in a weakened state when I'd gone down to deal with Rowan Mayfair, that was my problem, that was why the creature obsessed me. Never mind.

Someone pushed my foot off the desk chair. I heard a woman's piercing laugh; I heard dozens of people laughing. Heavy cigar smoke. Glass breaking. I opened my eyes. The flat was full of people! Both windows to the front balcony were open and it was jammed with people, women in long low-cut sparkling dresses, men in fine black dinner jackets with flashing black satin lapels, the roar of conversation and merriment almost deafening, but deafening to whom, and a tray went by, held high by a waiter in a white coat who all but tripped over my legs, and there sat a child on the desk, a rosy child, staring at me, a dainty girl with quick black eyes and beautifully waved black hair, seven or eight, enchanting, precious.

"Ducky, I'm sorry!" she said, "but you're in our world now, I do hate to say it. We have you!" She was mocking up a British accent. She had on a little sailor dress, white with blue trim, and high white socks and little black Mary Janes. She drew up her knees. "Lestat," she laughed. She pointed at me.

Then, down into the desk chair facing me, slipped Oncle Julien, dressed for the party, white tie, white cuffs, white hair. The crowd pressed in on him. Someone was shouting from the balcony.

"She's right, Lestat," Oncle Julien said in flawless French, "we have you in our world now, and I must say you have a divine apartment here, and I so admire the paintings which have only just come from Paris, you and your friends are so very clever, and the furniture, there is so much of it, yes, it seems you've crammed every nook and cranny, yet who could have asked for anything finer?"

"But I thought we were mad at him, Oncle Julien," said the little girl in English.

"We are, Stella," he said in French, "but this is Lestat's house, and whether we are angry or not we are Mayfairs first and foremost, and Mayfairs are always polite."

This sent little Stella into a regular riot of laughter, and she gathered up her little self—soft cheeks, sailor suit, socks, shiny shoes—and leapt from the desk right into my lap, plop.

"I'm so glad," she said, "because you are so absolutely dandy; don't you think, Oncle Julien, he's too beautiful to be a man, oh, I know, Lestat, you're not one to talk about gender—."

"Stop it!" I roared. A flashing, cleansing power went out of me, flushing against the walls.

Dead quiet.

Mona stood there, eyes wide, wrapper gone, sleek silk, Quinn right beside her, towering over her, face full of concern.

"Lestat, what is it?" asked Mona.

I got up, I staggered into the hallway. Why was I walking like this? I glanced back at the room. All the furniture had been moved—just a little. Things were askew! The doors were open to the balcony!

"Look at the smoke," I whispered.

"Cigar smoke," said Quinn questioningly.

"What is it, Boss?" asked Mona again. She came up to me and put her arms around me and kissed me on the cheek. I kissed her forehead, smoothed back her hair.

I didn't answer her.

I didn't tell them. Why didn't I tell them?

I showed them the bedroom with the sealed-up window that was painted to look like a window. I showed them the steel plating on the door and the lock. I told them about the human guards twenty-four hours. They were to pull the curtains around the bed, and sleep in each other's arms. No ray of the sun, no immortal, no mortal intruder, no one would bother them here. Of course they had a long time before sunrise. Talk, talk, yes. They could wander. But no spying on the May-fairs, no. No probing for secrets, no. No searching for a lost daughter yet, no. No going home to Blackwood Manor, no. I told them I would meet them tomorrow at dusk.

Now I had to leave, had to.

Had to get out of here. Had to get out of there. Had to get out of everywhere.

The open country.

Near the Talamasca Retreat House.

Distant rumble of trucks on the River Road. Smell of the River. Smell of the Grass. Walking. Grass wet.

Field of scattered oaks. White clapboard house tumbling to ruin, the way they do in Louisiana, swaying walls and caving roof embraced and held suspended by the vines.

Walking.

I spun around.

He was there. Technicolor ghost, black tailcoat, walking as I had been, through the grass, tossing aside the champagne glass, coming on. Stopped. I lunged at him, grabbed him before he could vanish, had him by the throat, fingers dug into what sought to be invisible, holding him, hurting what would be immaterial. Yeah, got you! You impudent phantom, look at me!

"You think you can haunt me!" I growled. "You think you can do that to me!"

"I know I can!" he said in caustic English. "You took her, my child, my Mona!" He struggled to dissolve. "You knew I was waiting for her. You could have let her come to me."

"And just what crazy half-illuminated Afterlife are you from!" I demanded. "What are your half-baked mystical promises! Yeah, come on, what Other Side are you hawking, yeah, spill it, let's hear about Julien's Summerland, yeah, testify, how many ectoplasmic angels are on your side, give me the splendiferous images of your famous fabu-lous friggin' self-created self-sustained astral plane! Where the Hell were you going to take her! You're going to tell me some Lord of the Universe sends spooks like you to take little girls to Heaven!"

I was clutching nothing.

I was all alone.

It was sweetly warm and there was a numbing quiet in the vibration of the distant trucks, a winking beauty in the passing headlights.

Who missed the deep silence of so many past centuries? Who missed the deep darkness of the long ago pre-electric nights? Not me.

When I reached the Talamasca Retreat House, Stirling was standing on the terrace. Loose gray hair mussed, cotton pajamas, sashed robe, bare feet. A mortal couldn't have discovered him, standing in the shadows, waiting. An empathetic face, patient celibate alertness.

"I brought her over," I said.

"I know," he answered.

"I kissed Rowan Mayfair."

"You did what?" he answered.

"They're after me, the Mayfair ghosts."

He didn't respond, except for a small scowl and an undisguised look of wonder.

I scanned the Retreat House. Empty. Maid out in the back cottages. One postulant out there writing in a notebook by a gooseneck lamp. Saw her in her self-conception. Hungered for her. Had no intention of feeding on her. Ridiculous idea. Absolutely verboten.

"Give me a bedroom, please," I asked. "Just a room in which heavy draperies can be drawn."

"Of course," he said.

"Ah, the Talamasca, ready again to count upon my honor."

"I can depend upon it, can I not?"

I followed him into the front hallway and then up the broad staircase. How curious it was, to be his guest, to be walking on this wool carpet as if I were a mortal. Sleeping under the roof that wasn't mine. Next I'd be doing it at Blackwood Farm. This could get out of hand. Please let it get out of hand.

And here the fragrant and cozy bedroom with all its inevitable details. Pineapples carved into the four posts of the bed, canopy of hand-worked lace through which you could peer at the faint water stains on the ceiling, loving, caring, patchwork quilt of loops and circles and careening colors, parchment lamp shades, dark clots breaking through the old mirrors, needlepoint tiptoe chairs.

"What Mayfair ghosts are after you?" he asked softly. It was respectful, his manner. "What have you seen?" And when I didn't answer, "What have they done?"

"Mona gave birth long ago to a daughter," I whispered. Yes, he knew all about it, didn't he? "But you can't tell me, can you, what you know?"

"No, I can't," he replied.

"She wants to find that child," I said.

"Does she," he said politely. He was afraid.

"Sleep well," I said and turned to the bed.

He left me. But he knew the child's name. That much I'd filched from him. He knew its name and its *nature* but he couldn't tell.

10

I KNEW that Rowan Mayfair was in the Retreat House when I
opened my eyes. Heavy. Somebody who loved her was with her,
somebody who knew all about her too. Way heavy. And Stirling
in a state of angst.

I went to the right front window and drew back the velvet drape.
The sky was scarlet over the distant levee. Oak tree branches filled the
top of my view. It would have been a cinch to open this window and
slip out onto the porch and disappear from this place quietly.

But I wasn't going to do it. Why give up an opportunity to see her
again? There wasn't any harm in just seeing her. Maybe I could figure
out the source of her power over me. Maybe I could nullify it. And if
nothing else, I could give them some platitudes about Mona.

I stopped in front of the old mirror over the dresser to comb my
hair. My black frock coat looked all right. So did the lace at my collar
and cuffs. More than a bit of vanity there, and I knew it. So what? Have
I ever said I wasn't vain? I have lifted vanity to a poetical level, have I
not? I have transmuted vanity into the spiritual, have I not?

My body had fully restored itself from bestowing the Dark Gift, but
my thirst was strong, rather in the style of a craving than a physical
need. Was that because of her? Certainly not! I would repair to the first
floor to discover this woman was an ordinary woman and nothing
more and I would then come to my senses! How's that for a stiff upper
lip!

I paused to close in on New Orleans, scanning for the Romantic
Couple. They were just rising, crawling out from among the velvet pil-

lows, Long Tall Quinn still groggy, rambunctious Mona already on the prowl. Caught clear images of her through Quinn's overprotective mind. She wasn't sobbing. She was taking stock of the paintings, still wearing that dashing feather-trimmed wrapper with flair. This augured very well for the next hundred years.

Suddenly they were both talking at each other in rapid rips and slashes of life story and love professions. Hunt and feed now or later? Little Drink or something serious. Where was the Boss? I sent a swift silent message to Quinn.

Yo, Little Brother. You're the teacher for now. The Little Drink is the name of the lesson. I'll be with you soon enough.

I went out into the hallway of the Retreat House, where the sconces were already lighted, and sweet yellow and red flowers adorned the demi-lune tables, and made my way slowly down the main stairs. Saint Juan Diego, please preserve the Mayfairs from me.

Hum of heavy anxious mortal conversation below. Deep scent of mortal blood. Worry about the mortal Mona. Stirling intensely miserable, struggling to veil his conflicted heart. It takes the skills of a priest and a lawyer to be an effective member of the Talamasca.

All this coming from a garden room on the back of the house, just off the dining room, on the right side proper.

I made my way there. Real Rembrandts on these walls. A Vermeer. I took my time. Temples throbbing. Mayfairs, yes, witches again, yes. Why walk right into it? Nothing could have stopped me.

The furnishings of the dining room were regal and faintly charming. I saw the fine leavings of a recent meal on the long black granite table, with a mess of linen and heavy old silver. I stopped to examine the silver carefully.

Flash of Julien opposite in his everyday gray suit, eyes black. Hadn't they been gray before? "Enjoyed your rest?" he asked. He vanished. I caught my breath. *I think you're a cowardly ghost. You can't handle a sustained discourse. I personally despise you.*

Stirling called my name.

I moved towards the rear double doors.

The little conservatory was octagonal Victorian style, everything trimmed in white, and the wicker was white, and the floor was pink flagstone, and the whole was three steps down.

They were closely gathered at a round glass-top wicker table, far more cheerful than the dining room could ever have been, with lighted candles nestled among the countless flower pots, the sky already going dark beyond the glass walls and glass roof.

A lovely place to be. Scent of blood and flowers. Scent of burning wax.

All three mortals, who sat in comfortable wicker chairs virtually surrounded by magnificent tropical plants, had known I was coming. Conversation had stopped. All three mortals were watching me with a wary politeness now.

Then the two men shot to their feet as if I were the Crown Prince of England, and Stirling, being one of them, presented me to Rowan Mayfair as if I'd never met her, and then to Michael Curry, "Rowan's husband," and gestured for me to take the empty wicker chair. I did.

Rowan struck me immediately as uncalculatedly lovely, colorless and svelte in a short skirted gray silk suit and leather pumps. There came the chills again as I looked at her, in fact, an utter weakness. I wondered if she knew her dress matched her eyes and even the gray streaks in her dark hair. She was positively ablaze with an inner concentration of power.

Stirling wore a white vintage linen jacket with faded blue jeans and his pale yellow shirt open at the neck. I sparked off the linen jacket suddenly. It had belonged to someone who died of old age. It had been worn in the South Seas. Packed away for years. Rediscovered, loved by Stirling.

My eyes settled on Michael Curry. This was simply one of the most alluring mortal males whom I have ever struggled to describe.

First off, he was reacting powerfully to my own apparent physical gifts without even being aware of that dimension of himself, which always confuses and excites me, and secondly he had the exact attributes of Quinn—black curly hair and vivid blue eyes—in a heavier, stronger, more physically comfortable frame. Of course he was much older than Quinn. He was in fact much older than Rowan. But age doesn't really mean anything to me. I found him irresistible. Whereas Quinn's features were elegant, this man's were large and almost Graeco-Roman. The gray hair at his temples drove me crazy. The sunburnt tan of his skin was wonderful. And then there was the easy smile on his lips.

He was wearing something, I suppose. What was it? Oh, yeah, the de rigueur New Orleans white linen three-piece suit.

Suspicion. I caught it from both Michael and Rowan. And I knew that Michael was as strong a witch as she was, though in wholly different ways. I knew too that he had taken life. She'd done it with the force of her mind. He'd done it with the strength of his fist. It seemed that other invaluable secrets were going to slip right through his gaze when suddenly he closed himself off from me artfully yet completely naturally. And he began to speak.

"I saw you at the funeral for Miss McQueen," he said. New Orleans Irish voice. "You were with Quinn and Merrick Mayfair. You're Quinn's friend. You have a beautiful name. It was a lovely service, wasn't it?"

"Yes," I said. "And I met Rowan yesterday at Blackwood Manor. I have news for you both. Mona's doing well, but she doesn't want to come home."

"That's not possible," said Rowan before she could stop herself. "That simply can't be."

She was beyond exhaustion. She'd been crying and crying for Mona. I didn't dare try to draw her in as I'd done yesterday, not in front of this man. The chills came again. A wild vision possessed me of snatching her up and away from this place, my teeth pressed to her tender neck, her blood mine, all the chambers of her soul yielding to me. I banished it. Michael Curry was watching me, but the man's mind was on Mona.

"I'm happy for Mona," he volunteered now, putting his hand over Rowan's hand on the arm of the wicker chair. "Mona's where she wants to be. Quinn's strong. He always was. When that kid was eighteen, he had the poise of a full-grown man." He laughed softly. "He wanted to marry Mona the first time he saw her."

"She is doing better," I insisted. "I swore I'd tell you if she needed you." I gave Rowan my level gaze. "I will tell you. It makes her happy to be with Quinn."

"I knew it would," said Rowan, "but she can't survive off dialysis."

I didn't answer. I didn't know what dialysis was. Oh, I'd heard the word, but I really didn't know enough about it to bluff.

Standing behind her, indeed behind the cluster of flowers just over her shoulder, was the figure of Julien, with a grim smile on his lips, taking visible pleasure in my confusion.

A little shock went through me when my eyes met his, and suddenly Michael Curry turned and looked in that direction, but the figure had vanished. Hmmm. So this mortal sees ghosts. Rowan was unchanged. Rowan was examining me all too closely.

"Who is Stella?" I asked, looking again into Rowan's eyes. My only hope was to keep her talking. She was staring at my hand. I didn't like it.

"Stella? You mean Stella Mayfair?" she asked. Her low voice was sultry in spite of herself. She was feverish. She needed sleep in a cold room. Involuntary flash of the sorrow inside her, the knot of secrets. "What do you want to know about Stella Mayfair?"

Stirling was very uneasy. He felt deceitful but there was nothing I could do about it. So he was the confidant of the family, of course.

"A little girl," I said, "who calls people Ducky, and has black wavy hair. Picture her in a little white sailor dress trimmed in blue, with high socks and Mary Janes. Does it ring a bell?"

Michael Curry let out a genial laugh. I looked at him.

"You're describing Stella Mayfair all right. One time Julien Mayfair told me this story—Julien was one of the mentors of the Mayfair family—the story was all about Julien taking little Stella downtown with him, Stella and her brother Lionel Mayfair—he's the one who shot and killed Stella—but in the story Stella was wearing a sailor dress and Mary Janes. Oncle Julien described it. At least I think he did. No. He didn't describe it. But I saw her that way. Yeah, I saw her that way. Why in the world would you ask such a question? Of course I'm not referring to the living breathing Julien. But that's another tale."

"Oh, I know you're not. You're referring to his ghost," I answered. "But tell me, I'm just curious, I don't mean any disrespect, but what sort of ghost was Julien? Can you interpret? Was he good or was he bad?"

"My God, that's a strange question," said Michael. "Everybody idolizes Oncle Julien. Everybody takes him so for granted."

"I know Quinn saw Oncle Julien's ghost," I went on. "Quinn told me all about it. He'd come to see you and Rowan and Mona, and Oncle Julien let him in to the First Street property, or whatever you call it, and Quinn talked with Oncle Julien for a long time. They drank hot chocolate together. They sat in a rear garden. He thought Oncle Julien was alive, naturally, and then you guys discovered him back there all alone and there was no hot chocolate. Not that the absence of hot chocolate means anything metaphysically, of course."

Michael laughed. "Yeah, Oncle Julien's big on long conversations. And he really outdid himself with the hot chocolate. But a ghost can't do something like that unless you give him the strength to do it.

Quinn's a natural medium. Oncle Julien was playing off Quinn." He went sad. "Now, when the time comes, for Mona I mean, well, Oncle Julien will come and take her to the other side."

"You believe in that?" I asked. "You believe in the other side?"

"You mean you don't?" asked Michael. "Where do you think Oncle Julien comes from? Look, I've seen too many ghosts not to believe in it. They have to come from somewhere, don't they?"

"I don't know," I said. "There's something wrong with the way ghosts act. And the same holds true for angels. I'm not saying there isn't an afterlife. I'm only maintaining that those entities who come down here so beneficently to meddle with us are more than a little cracked." I was really getting heated. "You're not really sure, yourself, are you?"

"You've seen angels?" asked Michael.

"Well, let's just say, they claimed to be angels," I responded.

Rowan's eyes were moving sluggishly and rudely over me. She didn't care what I asked about Julien or what Michael said. She was back in that terrible moment when she'd come into the hospital room, the death room, to bring death, and Mona had been frightened. Back there and here studying me. Why couldn't I just hold her for a moment, comfort her, vanish with her into a bedroom upstairs, tear this house apart, fly with her to another part of the world, build her a palace deep in the Amazon jungles?

"Why don't you try!" said Oncle Julien. He stood behind her again, arms folded, sneering insofar as it didn't mar his charm. "You'd like nothing better than to get your hands on her. She'd be such a prize!"

"Kindly go to Hell!" I said. And to myself, Snap out of it.

"Who are you talking to?" asked Michael, turning in his chair as before. "What are you seeing?"

Julien was gone.

"Why are you asking about Stella?" Rowan murmured, but she was hardly thinking of it. She was thinking only of Mona and of me, and of that ghastly moment. She was noticing my hair and the way that it curled, and the way that the candlelight played on it. And then the grief over Mona again, *almost killed her.*

Michael fell into deep absorption, as if nobody was there. There was something defenseless about the guy. Stirling was studying me with a sharp angry expression on his face. So what?

Michael was plainly much more forthright than Rowan, more conventionally innocent. A woman like Rowan had to have a husband like Michael. If he'd known how I'd kissed her yesterday in that greedy fashion he'd be wounded. She hadn't told him. Not even he could roll with a punch like that. When a woman of that age lets you kiss her it means something entirely different from what it means with a young girl. Even I knew that and I'm not human.

"You can't figure it with Julien," Michael said, suddenly emerging from his thought. "He makes mistakes—sometimes absolutely awful mistakes."

"How do you mean?" I asked.

"Julien appeared once, trying to help me, I think, yes, it had to be," said Michael. "But it didn't work out. It led to a disaster. A total disaster. But he had no way of knowing. Absolutely no way at all. I suppose that's what I'm trying to say, that ghosts don't know everything. Of course, Mona has that old saying that a ghost just knows his own business, you know—and I guess that covers it, but there's more to it than that. Don't speak of it to Mona. Whatever you do, don't ask Mona these questions. I wouldn't . . . I mean, Julien made a dreadful mistake."

Well, now that's fascinating! So this dapper dude doesn't always know what he's doing. My thesis is correct! Why don't you appear now so that I can laugh at you, you impotent jerk?

I tried desperately to read the thoughts behind Michael's words, but I couldn't. These Mayfairs were so casually and maddeningly gifted. Maybe the man wasn't defenseless. He was just so strong he didn't bother to put up any defenses.

I glanced at Rowan. She was staring at my hand again. How could she not notice the sheen of my fingernails? All vampires have lustrous fingernails. Mine are like glass. She reached out, then drew back.

I had only moments here.

"Can you tell me what kind of mistake Julien made?" I asked.

"I think there's a photograph of little Stella in a sailor dress," Michael said, drifting off into his thoughts again. He didn't notice anything about me. He just alternated between intense thought and looking directly into my eyes. "Yeah, I'm sure there is."

"Did you say that Stella's brother shot her?" I asked.

"Oh, she was a woman by that time," Michael said, half dreaming. "She'd given birth to Antha. Antha was six years old. Stella nearly ran off with a man from the Talamasca. She wanted to escape the family and the ghost that went with it. Stirling knows all about it, of course." He looked at me as if startled. "But don't ask Mona. Don't say anything about all this to Mona."

"I won't say a word about it to Mona," I answered.

Rowan was sensing things about me, sensing that my heart rate was far too slow for a functioning mortal. Sensing things about the way that candlelight reflected off my face.

"I'll tell you what I think happens," said Michael. "When they come on an errand, they leave behind the totality of salvation."

"Ghosts, you mean," I said.

"What was that?" Stirling asked.

"Of course, the Totality of Salvation," I whispered. I smiled. I loved it. "Of course, they have to, don't they? Or every haunting would be a theophany, wouldn't it?" I flashed on Julien last night in my clutches, my questions to him coming angrily as accusations. He knew nothing about any Totality of Salvation, did he? Why, I'd already figured that out, hadn't I? That when I'd drifted to Earth in my fantasy as Saint Lestat I had to leave behind a certain Heavenly knowledge.

"I wouldn't trust any ghost, really," Michael said. "I think you're right about all that. But Julien tries to do good. He has the family's welfare in mind when he appears. If only—."

"If only what?" I pressed.

"Why did you ask that question about Stella?" Rowan asked. Her voice was rich yet sharp. "Where did you see Stella?" Her voice rose. "What do you know about Stella?"

"You don't mean the ghosts have already come for Mona, do you?" asked Michael. "You realize what that means, of course. Shouldn't we be there? Shouldn't we be near at hand?"

"No, they haven't come for her," I replied. "She'll tell us when that happens, I know she will." But I felt the lie catch in me. They were trying to come for her, weren't they, in some sort of grim game, or was it my soul they wanted?

I stood up.

"I'll let you know when she needs you," I said. "I promise you."

"Don't go," said Rowan crossly but under her breath.

"Why, so you can keep studying me?" I said. I was suddenly trembling again. I didn't know what I meant to say. "Would you like it if I gave you a sample of my blood? Is that why you're staring at me?"

"Lestat, do be careful," said Stirling.

"What would I do with a sample of your blood?" Rowan asked, eyes moving up and down my figure. "Do you want me to study you?" she asked coldly. "Do you want me to ask questions about you? Who you are, where you come from? I have the feeling you do. I have the feeling you'd like nothing better than to let me take a sample of your skin, your hair, your blood, everything you have to give. I see that," she said, tapping the side of her forehead.

"Do you really?" I asked. "And you'd analyze all this in May- fair Medical in some secret laboratory." My heart was pumping. My brain was on overdrive. "You're some genius doctor, aren't you? That's what's behind those gray eyes, those enormous gray eyes. Not the ordinary surgeon or oncologist, not you—." I broke off. What was I doing?

Julien's laughter. "Yes, isn't she a wonder? Play into her hands." Julien near the back door of the conservatory, deep in shadow, laugh- ing: "You're no match for her, you impudent fiend. Maybe she'll con- struct a glass enclosure for you. They have such marvelous materials in this new century. Even such exotica as you—."

"Shut up, you miserable bastard," I whispered in French. "It sounds to me like you're far more fallible than you let on. What was your disastrous mistake, would you like to tell me?"

"Are you talking to Julien?" asked Michael. He glanced to the very spot. But there was nothing there.

"Detestable coward," I said in French. "He's gone. He won't let anyone else see him."

"Come, Lestat," said Stirling, tugging at me. "It's really time for you to go. You have Mona waiting for you."

Rowan never once turned to look at the ghost. She was angry. She rose to her feet. I felt that push again, just as if she'd laid her two hands on my chest. Yet her face was radiant with a complex of anguish behind it that not even anger could mask.

"Where is Mona!" she demanded. Her husky voice had never been more effective. "You think I don't know you took her away from Black- wood Manor? I was there first thing this morning, as soon as I could get away from the Medical Center. Clem drove the three of you to the Ritz Hotel last night. I went to the Ritz Hotel. No Mona. No Quinn either. And no Lestat de Lioncourt. That's the name you signed in Aunt Queen's funeral book, isn't it? I checked the spelling and your flamboyant handwriting. You like signing your name, don't you?—

"—And you have such a lovely French accent, oh, yes. Where is Mona right now, Monsieur de Lioncourt? What in the name of Heaven is going on? Why are you asking questions about Stella? You think I don't know that you're behind everything that's happening? Jasmine and Big Ramona think you're some sort of foreign prince, with your melodious French accent and your mind reading gifts and your exorcism to rid the house of ghosts and spirits. And oh, yes, Aunt Queen absolutely adored you! But you sound more like Rasputin to me! You can't just steal Mona from me! You can't!"

A stinging hurt spread through me, over my face, my skin. I'd never felt anything quite like it.

Julien was back there, in the shadows, laughing cruelly, collecting just a seam of the light along the edge of his face and form.

Michael was on his feet and so was Stirling.

"Rowan, please, honey," Michael said, trying to calm her. He seemed hesitant to touch her, hesitant to enclose her with his arms, though this might have been welcomed by her.

"I've told you all I know," I said. I stammered.

"Let me see you out," said Stirling. I felt his hand on my arm.

"You tell Mona we love her," said Michael.

"Is Mona afraid of us?" Rowan whispered. The anguish inside her defeated her anger. She drew close to me. "She's afraid of us now, isn't she?" She and Mona, a shared history of horrors. Yes, an unbreakable link. *Child. Woman Child.* Morrigan. No admissions and explanations. Just an image. The same image I'd seen in the Blood. *Woman Child.* "I demand that you tell me! Is she afraid!"

"No," I said. I reached forward right through the aura of palpable power that surrounded her. I put my hands on her arms. Vague binding shock. To Hell with Michael. But Michael didn't stop me. "Not anymore," I said, peering into Rowan's eyes. "Mona's not afraid of anything. Oh, if only I could give you some peace of mind. I wish I could. Please, please wait for her to call you, and don't think about her anymore."

I felt her strength recede, and her eyes misted. A great glowing fire was quelled, and I had done it, and an ever present grief enfolded it. A protective surge rose in me and the wild fantasies reigned again inside of me as if no one else was present.

I let her go.

I turned and I left the company.

Behind me the ghost whispered contemptuously, "You're not a gentleman, you never were!"

I muttered all the obscenities I knew in French and English in a tight whisper.

I walked a little too fast for Stirling. But we came together at the front doors of the house.

Rush of sweet warm air. The night was purring and grinding with the tree frogs and the cicadas. I defy a ghost to distract me from this! The sky was rosey and it would be all night. I closed my eyes and let the warm air hold me close and lovingly and totally.

The warm air didn't care whether or not I was a gentleman, which I was not.

"What are you doing with Rowan?" Stirling demanded.

"What are you, her older brother?" I shot back.

We walked across the paved porch and onto the drive. Fragrance of grass. Roar of the River Road traffic as sweet as the roar of water.

"Perhaps I am her brother," he said shortly, "but I mean it. What are you doing?"

"Good God, man," I replied. "Night before last you told Quinn that Mona was dying. What was your motive? Weren't you tempting him to go to her? He didn't, as it turned out, but you were tempting him, goading him to use his power, to bring her over. Don't deny it. You provoked him. You with all your records. Your volumes. Your studies. Quinn had fed on you, almost taken you. I saved your life, man. You who knew. And now you question me for a little word game with a mortal who detests me?"

"All right," he said, "so in the back of my mind I abhorred the fact that Mona was dying, that Mona was desperate, and that Mona was so young, and I believed in sinister fairy tales and magic blood! But that woman is not dying. She is the magnate of her family. And she knows something's profoundly wrong with you. And you're playing with her."

"Not so! Leave me alone!"

"I will not. You can't entice her—."

"I'm not enticing her!"

"Did you see Stella?" he asked. "Is that who's haunting you?"

"Don't go back to a civil tone with me," I scolded. "Yes, I saw Stella. Did you think that was all part of a game? I saw her in the little sailor dress and she jumped into my lap. They were in my town house in the Rue Royale, both of them, Julien and Stella, with a whole crowd of

people. Julien was out there in your fine little conservatory, taunt-
ing me. But in my flat last night, they said threatening things to me.
Threatening things! Oh, I don't know why I'm telling you."

"Yes, you do," he answered.

"I've got to get back to the intrepid wanderers," I said. I took a deep
breath.

"Threatening things?" he asked. "What threatening things did
they say to you?"

"Oh, God in Heaven!" I said. "If only I were Juan Diego."

"Who is Juan Diego?" he asked.

"Maybe nobody," I said sadly. "But then again, maybe somebody,
maybe somebody very very important!" and I went away.

I WENT UP HIGH in the air. I traveled fast—faster than a ghost, or so I figured. I drifted above the city of New Orleans, lulled by its lights and its voices. I wondered how Mona would handle this power, if she'd be weeping again. I let myself believe there were no ghosts who could touch me up here or anywhere if I used all my considerable powers, no ghosts who could make me afraid.

I said No to hunger. I said to thirst Be still.

I slipped down silently into the realm of my fellow creatures.

I caught sight of Quinn in the Rue Royale, pulling behind him a pile of suitcases, all dependent upon one huge rectangular bag equipped with excellent little wheels. He was whistling a melody by Chopin and walking very briskly, and I fell into stride beside him.

"You're the most dashing man on the street, Little Brother," I said. "What's with all the suitcases?"

"Are you going to let us stay at the flat, Beloved Boss?" he asked. His eyes were fired with love. In our short acquaintance, I'd never seen him so happy. In fact, I'd never seen him happy before at all. "What do you think?" he asked. "Do we crowd you? Do you want us out?"

"Not at all, I want you there," I replied. "I should have told you." We walked along together, me trying to keep up with his long legs. "I'm the worst of hosts and Coven Masters, to use the old lingo. Not a gentleman. A thoroughgoing Rasputin. Settle in. You had Clem bring clothes to the Ritz? (Yes.) Clever. Where's Princess Mona right now?"

"In the bedroom, working on the computer we bought at sunset, first thing she had to have," he said with an airy gesture. "She's recording every experience, every sensation, every subtle distinction, every revelation—."

"I get it," I said. "Hmmm. You've both fed."

He nodded. "Greedily, among despicable wretches, though I had to oversee the operation somewhat. She falls into states of utter paralysis. Perhaps if I wasn't there she wouldn't. Physically she's stronger than I am. I think it confuses her. It was a couple bums back of town, both drunk, nothing to it."

"But it was her first human victim," I said. "Particulars."

"The men were unconscious, it was a cinch for her. She's yet to confront the living breathing struggling type."

"All right, that can wait. As regards her being stronger than you, you know I can level the playing ground," I said quietly. "I don't share the gift of my blood with many. But I'll share it again with you." Was there anything in the world I wouldn't have done for Quinn?

"I know that," he answered. "God, I love her. I love her so much it's overtaken everything else in my mind. I don't even think about Goblin being gone. I thought when Goblin was actually gone I'd suffer some crippling emptiness. I was sure of it. It seemed bound to happen. But Mona's the partner of my soul, Lestat, just the way I used to dream it would be when we first met, when we were both kids, before the Blood ever came between us."

"That's the way it's supposed to work, Quinn," I said. "And Blackwood Farm? Have you any news?"

It was fun walking along the street again. Feet on the summer pavements with the heat of the sun still rising from them.

"Perfect," said Quinn. "Tommy's staying the week. I'll be able to see him before he goes back to England. I wish he didn't have to go to school in England. Of course, they're making calls to anyone or everyone connected to Patsy. It's the damned medicine. I should have gathered up her medicine and thrown it in the swamp with her. Then they would have assumed that she'd run away. I told them again that I murdered her. Jasmine just laughed. She said she wished she could murder Patsy right now. I think the only one who loves her, really loves her, is Cyndy, the Nurse."

I pondered the matter, perhaps for the first time since Quinn had done it only a few nights before. A body couldn't survive being dumped in Sugar Devil Swamp. Too many gators. It made me smile bitterly to remember that once others had tried to dispose of me in just the same way. But poor dead Patsy had lacked my resources when she tumbled down into the darkness. Her soul had fled to the Totality of Salvation, of course.

We walked on together through a crush of valiant tourists. The town was drippingly hot.

Last week at this very time I'd been a wanderer, hopelessly without companions, and then Quinn had come into my life, with a letter in his pocket, needing my help, and Stirling had tiptoed into my flat, daring me to discover him, and soon all of Blackwood Manor had materialized around me, Stirling became a player in my life, Aunt Queen had been cruelly lost on the very night I'd made her acquaintance, and then our beloved Merrick, gone from us, and now I was being drawn into the knowledge of the Mayfairs, and I was what? Scared?

Come on, Lestat. You can tell me the truth. I'm your own self, remember? I was darkly and passionately thrilled by all this, and I felt those chills again, merely thinking of Rowan berating me with all that heat only an hour ago.

And then there was Julien, who just wasn't going to appear right now and run the risk of Quinn seeing him too. I searched the early evening crowds. *Where are you, you wretched coward, cheap second-rate phantom, accused blunderer?*

Quinn turned his head just a little, never breaking his stride. "What was that? You were thinking about Julien."

"I'll tell you all of it later," I said, and I meant it. "But let me ask you, you know, about the time you saw the ghost of Oncle Julien?"

"Yeah?"

"What vibe did you get in your secret soul? Good ghost? Bad ghost?"

"Hmmm, well, good, obviously. Trying to tell me I had Mayfair genes. Trying to save Mona from me, trying to keep us from breeding some *awful mutation*, which occurs now and then in the Mayfair family. A benign ghost. I've told you the whole story."

"Yes, of course," I replied. "A benign ghost and an awful mutation. Has Mona mentioned the mutation? The lost child?"

"Beloved Boss, what's bothering you?"

"*Nada*," I said.

Now just wasn't the time to tell him. . . .

We reached the town house. The guards gave us a friendly nod. I gave them a generous tip. It was, for mortal men in long-sleeved shirts, quite unbearably hot.

We could hear the clacking of the computer keys as we went up the iron stairs. Then the low chatter of the printer.

Mona came charging out of the bedroom clothed in last night's white duds, page in hand.

"Listen to this," she said. " 'Though this experience is undeniably evil, in that it involves predation upon other human beings, it is without question a mystical experience.' So, what do you think?"

"That's all you've written?" I asked. "That's one paragraph. Write some more."

"Okay." She ran back into the bedroom. Clack went the keys. Quinn followed her with the luggage. He winked at me, smiling.

I went into my bedroom, which was opposite theirs, shut the door, hit the button for the overhead light, and peeled off all my clothes with a shudder of utter disgust, threw them into the bottom of the armoire, put on a brown cotton turtleneck, black pants, and a lightweight black silk and linen jacket with a highly visible weave, a pair of completely smooth black shoes which had never been worn and looked like a modern sculpture, combed my hair until there was no dust in it and then stood there, awash in a moment of total stillness.

Then I stretched out on my bed. Satin tufted tester above me. Satin counterpane below. Fairly shadowy. I turned my face into the down pillows, of which I always had a sizable heap, and with all my muscles sort of scrunched up against the modern world.

Not a masculine thing to do, not a macho posture, not a show of strength to otherworldly entities, not a take-charge attitude at all.

I was comforted by the sound of Mona's clicking away, the low note of Quinn's voice. Footsteps on the boards.

But nothing could take the edge off Rowan's angry words, those eyes like hematite, her entire frame trembling with her passion as she accused me. How could Michael Curry stay so close to that blaze and not get scorched?

Suddenly, there was an agitation in me so great that only lying alone, scrunched up on the bed, could comfort me. Sleep. Sleep, but I could not. They weren't wicked enough for me, Quinn and Mona. No one was. *I* wasn't wicked enough for me!

And I had to see if the ghosts would come.

A clock ticked somewhere. A clock with a painted face and curlicue hands. Not a huge clock. A clock that with its whole soul knew only how to tick and might tick for centuries, maybe had ticked for centuries, a clock to which people would look, and which people would dust, and which people wound with a key, and which people might come to love; a clock somewhere in this flat, perhaps in the back parlor, the only piece of all this furniture that could talk. I heard it. I knew what it was saying. Its code was lovely to me.

There was a knock at the door. Funny. It sounded as if it was right by my ear.

"Come in," I said. Damn fool that I am. But I wasn't fooled by the sounds I heard. That wasn't the door opening. That wasn't the door being clicked shut.

Julien stood at the foot of the bed. He came walking up along the side. Julien in his downtown black tailcoat and white tie, hair very white under the chandelier. His eyes were black. I'd thought they were gray.

"Why did you knock?" I asked. "Why don't you just tear my world to pieces instead?"

"I didn't want you to forget your manners again," he said in perfect French. "You're atrocious when you're ill-mannered."

"What do you want? To make me suffer? Join the crowd. I've been tormented by much stronger creatures than you."

"You haven't begun to understand what I can do," he said.

"You made a 'disastrous mistake.' What was it?" I asked. "I wonder: do you even know?"

He paled. His placid face became visibly enraged.

"Who sends you here to play with the living?"

"You're not the living!" he said.

"Temper, temper," I said mockingly.

He was too angry to speak. It made him all the more vivid, blanched though he was with anger. Or was it sorrow? I couldn't bear the thought of sorrow. I had enough sorrow.

"You want her?" I asked. "Then tell her yourself."

He didn't reply.

I shrugged as best I could, being all snuggled up on the counterpane.

"I can't tell her," I said. "Who am I to say, 'Julien says you should expose yourself to the sun and thereby enter into the Totality of Salvation.' Or is it possible that my questions of last night were more than pertinent and you don't know where you come from? Maybe there is no Totality of Salvation. No Saint Juan Diego. Maybe you just want her with you in a spirit world where you wander, waiting for somebody who can see you, somebody like Quinn or even Mona herself or me. Is that it? She's supposed to want to be a ghost? I am showing you my best manners. This is my most polite voice. My mother and father would be pleased."

There was a real knock on the door.

He vanished. I thought I saw something out of the corner of my eye. Had Stella been sitting to my left all this time? *Mon Dieu!* I was going mad all right.

"Coward," I whispered.

I sat up and crossed my legs, Indian style. "Come in," I said.

Mona burst into the room, dressed in a fresh long-sleeved rose-colored silk dress and rose satin stacked heels, a quivering page of paper once more held aloft.

"Hit me with it," I declared.

" 'It is my ultimate goal to transmute this experience into a level of life participation which is worthy of the immense powers that have been bequeathed to me by Lestat, a level of life experience which knows no moral shrinking from the most obvious yet painful theological questions which my transfigured state has made utterly inescapable, the first of which is, obviously, How does God view my essential being? Am I human and vampire? Or vampire only? That is, is damnation, and I speak now not of a literal Hell with flames, but of a state which is defined by the absence of God—is damnation implicit and inherent in what I am, or do I still exist in a relativistic universe in which I may attain grace on the same terms as humans can attain it, by participating in the Incarnation of Christ, an historical event in which I totally believe, in spite of the fact that it is not philosophically fashionable, though what questions of fashion have to do with me now in this transcendent and often luminous condition is moot.' " She looked at me. "What do you think?"

"Well, I think you ducked out of the paragraph on that 'fashionable question.' I think you should scrap the thing about fashionable and try to make a more solid finish, perhaps with some very concise statement about the level on which you believe in the Incarnation of Christ. And you can always use 'transcendent' and 'luminous' in another sentence. Also you misused the word 'bequeath.' "

"Cool!" She dashed out of the room.

Naturally, she left the door open.

I went after her.

She was already pounding the keyboard, the computer humming on one of my many Louis XV desks; her red eyebrows puckered, her green eyes locked to the monitor when I took up my position, arms folded, looking down on her.

"Yeah, what, Beloved Boss?" she asked without stopping her writing.

Quinn was stretched out comfortably on the bed, staring at the tester. The whole flat was full of beds with testers. Well, six bedrooms, anyway, three on each side.

"Call Rowan Mayfair and tell her you're all right. What do you think? Can you pull it off? The woman's suffering."

"Bummer!" Clackity-clack.

"Mona, if you possibly could do it—for their sakes, of course. Michael is suffering."

She looked sharply up at me and froze. Then, without taking her eyes off me, she lifted the phone to the right of her on the desk and she punched in the number so rapidly with her thumb I couldn't follow it. Her generation, with Touch-Tone phones. Big deal! I can write with a quill pen in a flurry of curlicues you wouldn't believe; let's see her do that. And I don't spill a drop of ink on the parchment, either.

"Yo, Rowan, Mona here." Hysterical crying on the other end. Mona overriding: "I'm just fine, I'm hanging with Quinn, look, don't worry about me, I'm all better, totally." A storm of literal questions. Mona overriding: "Rowan, listen, I'm feeling great. Yeah, a kind of miracle. Like I'll call you later. No, no, no (overriding again), I'm wearing Aunt Queen's clothes, they fit me perfectly, yeah, and her shoes, really cool, like she has tons of these high-heel shoes, yeah, and I never wore shoes like this; yeah, fine, no, no, no, stop it, Rowan, and Quinn wants me to wear them, they're brand new, they're really great. Love you, love to Michael and everybody. Bye." Down with the phone over Rowan shouting.

"So it's done," I said. "I really appreciate it." I shrugged.

She sat there white faced, the blood having fled her cheeks, staring into space.

I felt like a bully. I was a bully. I've always been a bully. Everybody who knows me thinks I am a bully. Except perhaps Quinn.

Quinn sat up on the bed.

"What's the matter, Ophelia?" he asked.

"You know I have to go to them," she said, her eyebrows knitted. "I have no choice."

"What do you mean?" I said. "They just want off the hook. Now, admittedly, it's a very complex hook."

"No, no, no," she said, "for my sake." Her voice and her face were suddenly pitiless. "For what I have to find out," she continued coldly, shuddering all over as though a wind had blown through the room. "I know she's lied to me. She's lied to me for years. I'm afraid of how much she might have lied to me. I'm going to make her tell me."

"That was wrong of me, making you talk to her?" I asked.

"Ophelia," said Quinn, "take your time. It's yours to take."

"No, had to happen, you were right," she said to me. But she was shaking. Tears standing in her eyes. Preternatural emotions.

"It's about the Woman Child," I said under my breath. Was I free to reveal it to Quinn? What I'd seen: her monstrous woman offspring? "Doll face," I said, "why should we have secrets now?"

"You can tell him anything," she said, trying not to cry. "Dear God, I . . . I . . . I'm going to find them! If she knows where they are, if she's kept that from me. . . ."

Quinn was watching all this, keeping his counsel. But years ago she'd told him she had had a child, that she had had to give up that child. She had spoken of it to him as a mutation. But she had never explained the nature of that mutation.

And, to recap, in the Blood I'd seen a grown woman, something decidedly not human. Something surely as monstrous as us.

"You don't want to lay it all out for us?" I asked gently.

"Not now, not ready, not yet." She sniffled. "I hate it, all of it."

"I just saw Rowan Mayfair," I said. "I saw her at the Talamasca Retreat House. Something's deeply wrong with her."

"Of course something's wrong with her," she said with an air of exasperation. "I don't care what happens to her when she sees me. So she sees something that will never make human sense to her. I should care? I don't need to live with them the way Quinn lives with his family. I realize that now. It's impossible. I can't do what Quinn did. I need a legal name. I need some money. . . ."

"Think about it a little longer," I said. "There's no need to make such a decision right now. I got clear of Rowan and Michael tonight rather than disturb them, rather than create doubts that could harm them. It was hard. I wanted to ask them questions. But I had to give it up."

"Why do you care so much?" she asked.

"Because I care about you and Quinn," I said. "You offend me. Don't you know that I love you? I wouldn't have made you if I couldn't love you. Quinn told me so much about you before I ever saw you and then I fell in love with you, of course."

"I have to know things from them," she said. "Things they're holding back, and then I have to find *my daughter* on my own. But I can't talk about it just yet."

"Your daughter?" Quinn asked.

"You mean the Woman Child, it's living—"

"Stop! Not now," said Mona. "Leave me to my philosophy, both of you!"

Huge shift of gears. Her eyes shot to the computer.

She went back to banging on the keys. "What's a better word than 'bequeathed'?"

"Bestowed," I responded.

Quinn came up behind her and fastened a cameo at her neck without interfering with her ferocious writing.

"You're not trying to make her into Aunt Queen, are you?" I asked. She went on hammering.

"She's Ophelia Immortal," he said. He didn't take offense.

We left her. We went down the passage and out onto the rear balcony and down into the courtyard and found a couple of iron chairs. I realized I'd never used these chairs.

They were pretty after a fashion, Victorian, ornate. I didn't own anything that wasn't pretty after a fashion, or downright beautiful, if I could help it.

The garden enclosed us with its high banana trees and its night-blooming flowers. The music of the water in the fountain mingled with the distant sound of Mona writing, and Mona whispering as she wrote. I could hear the whine of the nightclub bands on the Rue Bourbon. I could hear the whole damned city if I tried. The sky was a faint lilac color now, overcast and reflecting the city glow.

"Don't think that," said Quinn.

"What, Little Brother?" I woke from listening to distant sounds.

"I see her as Aunt Queen's heiress," he said, "don't you see? Everything that Aunt Queen wanted to give of her clothes, her jewelry, all those things, whatever she wanted to give to Jasmine she'd already given, and there's plenty enough in bank boxes for Tommy's wife of the future or whoever little Jerome marries (Jerome was Quinn's son by Jasmine, let me remind you). And so I make Mona an heiress to maybe a tenth of the most extreme silk dresses. Jasmine never wore the extreme silk dresses anyway. And the glitter shoes which nobody really wants. And the shell cameos, which are common.

"If Aunt Queen somehow knew what had really happened to me, what I'd become, as we always say so delicately; if she knew that Mona was with me, finally, that Heaven and Earth had been moved, and Mona was with me, she'd want me to give those things to Mona. She'd be pleased that Mona was tripping around in those shoes."

I listened to all this and I understood it. I should have understood it before. But Mona's daughter, who and what was Mona's daughter?

"The clothes and shoes make her very happy," I said. "Most likely she's been sick so long that all her own clothes are gone. Who knows?"

"What did you see in the Blood when you made her? What was this Woman Child?"

"That's what I saw," I responded. "A daughter of hers who was a full-grown woman, a monster in her own eyes. It had come from her. And it was torn from her. She loved it. She nursed it. I saw that. And then she lost it, just like she told you. It went away."

He was aghast. He'd caught nothing like this from her thoughts.

But in the Blood you go where nobody wants to go. That's the horror of it. That's the beauty of it.

"Could it really have been so freakish, so abnormal?" he asked. His eyes veered away. "You know, years ago, I told you . . . I went to dinner at the Mayfair house. Rowan showed me the place. There was some secret, some dark hidden story present there the whole time. I could see it in Rowan's silence and in Rowan's drifting. But I couldn't see it in Michael. And even now Mona won't tell us."

"Quinn, you won't tell her why you killed Patsy, either," I said. "As we move on year by year in this life, we learn that telling doesn't necessarily purge; telling sometimes merely is a reliving, and it's a torment."

The back door opened with a splat.

Mona came clattering down the steps, two pages in her hand.

"Dear God, I just love these shoes!" she said, making a circuit of the courtyard. Then:

She stood before us, looking like a waxen doll in the light from the upstairs windows, with one finger pointing, like that of a nun in school:

" 'I must confess that it has already become undeniably clear to me, though I have existed in this exalted state for only two nights, that the very nature of my powers and means of existence attest to the onto-logical supremacy of a sensualist philosophy having taken up residence within me, as I proceed from moment to moment and from hour to hour both to apprehend the universe around me and the microcosm of my own self. This requires of me an immediate redefining of the con-cept of mystical, which I have heretofore mentioned to include a state both elevated and totally carnal, both transcendent and orgasmic, which delivers me when drinking blood or gazing at a lighted candle beyond all human epistemological constraints.

" 'Whereas the hermeneutics of pain had once completely con-vinced me of my own personal salvation, indeed, whereas I had once worked out a comprehensive Prayer of Quiet in which I had embraced Christ and his Five Wounds in order to endure the Finality which seemed inescapable for me, I now find myself approaching God on a totally undefined path.

" 'Can it be that being a vampire, and having a vampire soul as well as a human soul, I am therefore removed from human obligations and all human ontological conditions? I think not.

" 'I think on the contrary that I am now responsible for the supreme human obligation: to investigate the highest use of my pow-ers, for surely though I am vampire by my own free will and by a Bap-tism of Blood, I am still by birth, by maturity, by underlying physicality human, and must therefore share in the human condition despite the fact that I shall not in the ordinary scheme of things grow old or die.

" 'To return to the inescapable question of Salvation, yes, I do remain rooted in a relativistic universe, no matter how spectacularly defined I have become as to form and function, and I find myself within the same dimension in which I existed before my transforma-tion, and therefore I must ask: am I perforce outside the economy of grace established by Our Divine Savior in the very fact of his Incarna-tion, even before His Crucifixion, both events which I firmly believe to have occurred within human history and chronology, and to be know-able through both, and commanding a response in both?

" 'Or can the Sacraments of Holy Mother the Church redeem me in my present state? I must conclude on the face of it, from my short experience, from the ecstasy and abandon which have so rampantly replaced all pain and suffering within the organism which I am, that I assume that I stand excommunicated from the Body of Christ by my very nature.

" 'But it could be that I am never to know the answer to this question, no matter how thoroughly I investigate the world and myself, and does not this very unknowing only bring me all the closer to full existential participation in humankind?

" 'It seems wise to accept, in deepest humility and with an aim towards a validating spiritual perfection at the onset, that I may never hope at any juncture of my wanderings, be they for untold centuries or for a few short years of near unendurable ecstasy, to know whether I share in the Savior's Redemption, and that that very unknowing may be the price I pay for my extra-human sensibility and inherently bloodthirsty triumph over the pain I once suffered, over the imminent death that once tyrannized me, over the ubiquitous threat of human time.'

"What do you think?"

"Very good," I said.

Quinn piped up: "I like the word 'perforce.' "

She ran up to him and started beating him about the head and shoulders with the pages, and kicking him with her high-heel shoes. He laughed under his breath and carelessly defended himself with one arm. "Look, it's better than crying!" he said.

"You hopeless Boy," she declared, erupting in streaks of laughter. "You hopeless, egregious Boy! You are patently unworthy of all the philosophical considerations I have positively lavished upon you! And what, I ask, have you written since your Blood Baptism, why, the very ink has dried up in the circuits of your cruel little preternatural brain."

"Wait a minute, quiet," I said. "Someone's arguing with the guards at the gate." I was on my feet.

"My God, it's Rowan," said Mona. "Damn, I should never have called her on her cell."

"Cell?" I asked. But it was very much too late.

"Caller ID," Quinn murmured as he rose and took Mona in his arms.

It was Rowan, most assuredly—breathless and frantic, and, followed by both guards, who were protesting heavily, she came racing back the carriageway and stopped dead, facing Mona across the courtyard.

1 2

THE SHOCK OF SEEING MONA, of apprehending her in the light that fell from the upstairs windows and the inevitable light from the glowing sky, was such that Rowan was stopped as if she'd struck an invisible wall.

Michael at once caught up with her, and he too experienced a similar immense surprise.

As they stood baffled, not knowing what to make of the evidence of their senses, I told the guards to back off and leave the matter to me.

"Come on up into the flat," I said. I gestured towards the iron stairs.

It was useless to say anything at this juncture. It wasn't a vampire that they'd just seen. They knew and suspected nothing of supernatural origin here. It was Mona's spectacular "recovery" which had them in total disbelief.

It was in essence a scary moment. Because though a big frank smile of undisguised jubilation had broken out over Michael Curry's face, Rowan's scowling countenance was full of something akin to wrath. All her personal history was coiled behind that wrath, and I was fascinated by it as I'd been by all her emotions before.

Only reluctantly, and somewhat in the manner of a sleepwalker, Rowan let me take her arm. Her entire body was tense. Nevertheless, I led her to the iron steps, and then I went before her, in order to lead the whole party. And Mona gestured for Rowan to follow me, and Mona, tossing her hair back over her shoulders, looking miserable, followed her.

The back parlor was best for such gatherings, having no bookshelves and a deep velvet sofa and lots of tolerable Queen Anne chairs. Of course there was ormolu and inlaid wood everywhere, and a blazing new wallpaper of wine and beige stripes, and the garlands of flowers in the carpet seemed to be having convulsions, and the Impressionist paintings on the wall in their thick encrusted frames were like windows into a far far better, sun-filled universe, but it was a good room.

I shut off the overhead chandelier immediately and switched on two of the smaller corner lamps. It was softly dim now, but not uncomfortably so, and I directed everyone to sit down.

Michael beamed at Mona and said at once, "Darling, you look absolutely beautiful," as if he was uttering a prayer. "My lovely, lovely girl."

"Thank you, Uncle Michael, I love you," Mona answered tragically, and wiped at her eyes fiercely as though these people were somehow going to return her to her wretched mortal state.

Quinn was petrified. And his worst suspicion was rightly directed at Rowan.

She too appeared paralyzed except for her eyes, breaking away from Mona suddenly and fastening on me.

This had to be quick.

"All right, you see for yourself," I said, my eyes moving from Rowan to Michael and back again. "Mona's cured of whatever was wrong with her, and the entire wasting sickness has been reversed. She's utterly self-sufficient and whole. If you think that I am going to explain to you how this was done, or anything about it, you're wrong. You can call me Rasputin or worse names. I don't care."

Rowan's eyes quivered but her face did not change. The turbulence inside her was unreadable, indeed, unknowable, and if I caught anything definitive it was a high pitch of terror that hearkened back to things which had befallen her in the past. I couldn't fathom it, there wasn't time for such mental mining, and her confusion was putting up too much of a fight.

I had to go on.

"You're not going to walk away from here with any answers," I proceeded. "Get angry at me. Go ahead. Some night, many years from now, maybe Mona will choose to explain what happened, but for now you have to accept what you've seen. You no longer need to worry about Mona. Mona is on her own."

"It's not that I'm ungrateful," Mona said, her voice thick and her eyes filming red. She blotted them at once with her handkerchief. "You know I'm grateful. It just feels so good to be free."

Rowan fixed again on her. If Rowan found the slightest virtue in this miracle, it wasn't rising to the forefront of her mind.

"Your voice isn't the same," said Rowan. "Your hair, your skin—." She looked back to me. "Something's wrong." She stared at Quinn.

"This meeting's over," I said. "I don't mean to be harsh, truly I don't. But you know what you need to know. Obviously you know the phone number here, that's how you found us. You know where we are."

I rose to my feet.

Quinn and Mona followed but Rowan and Michael didn't move. Michael was taking his lead from Rowan, but then he reluctantly stood up, because Rowan or no Rowan, it was the courteous thing to do. This man was so lovable that even under these circumstances he didn't want to offend anyone, least of all Mona, and cause anyone any discomfort at all.

He simply did not see us the way Rowan did. He didn't look at people. He looked into their eyes. He studied Quinn's expression but not the physicality of Quinn. He didn't even care that Quinn was so tall. He scouted for the kindness in people and invariably found it, and his own kindness invested his entire being, infusing his considerable physical gifts. It was a rugged beauty he possessed, and he put behind him a calm self-assurance that can only arise from immense strength.

"Honey, do you need anything?" he asked Mona.

"I'm going to need some money," said Mona. She ignored Rowan's fixed stare. "Of course I'm not the Heiress anymore. Nobody wanted to talk about that when I was dying, but I've known that for years. And I'd retire now anyway, if it wasn't the case. The Heiress to the Mayfair fortune has to bear a child. We all know that I can't do that anymore. But I want to ask for a settlement. Nothing like the billions of the Legacy. Nothing like that at all. I mean, just a settlement so that I won't be poor. That's no problem, is it?"

"No problem at all," said Michael with a very loving smile to her and a shrug. The man was totally appealing. He wanted to hug her. But he took his lead from Rowan, and Rowan had not moved from the chair. "It's no problem, is it, Rowan?" he asked. His eyes swept the room a bit uneasily. He fixed for a few seconds on the brilliant Impressionist painting above the sofa in front of which I stood. He looked genially at me.

He couldn't begin to guess what had transformed Mona. But he never dreamt of anything sinister or evil. It was amazing the degree with which he accepted it, and only as I searched his mind now, in this moment when he was confused by Rowan and without his habitual defenses, only in this moment did I understand. He accepted Mona as she was because he wanted so very much for her recovery to be true. He'd thought Mona was doomed. Now a miracle had happened to Mona. He didn't need to know who'd worked the miracle. Saint Juan Diego? Saint Lestat? Whatever! It was fine with him.

I could have told him a harebrained story about us pumping her full of lipids and spring water and he would have bought it wholesale. He had flunked "Science" in school.

But Rowan Mayfair couldn't escape being a scientific genius. She couldn't ignore the fact that Mona's recovery was a physical impossibility. And in her mind were memories so painful they had no pictures or people to them; they had only dark inchoate feelings and awesome guilt.

She sat silent and motionless in the chair. Her eyes moved accusingly and wrathfully from Mona to me and back again and round once more.

I had a sense, perhaps flawed, that she was moving towards a brave curiosity, but . . .

Mona approached her. Not a great idea.

I signaled Quinn, and Quinn tried to stop Mona but Mona shook him off. Mona was determined.

Yet Mona appeared wary, as if Rowan was an animal that could scratch. I didn't like this at all. Mona stood between Rowan and everybody else in the room. I could no longer see Rowan, but I knew that Mona was only inches from Rowan and this was not good at all.

Mona bent down with her arms out. She apparently meant to kiss or embrace Rowan.

Rowan moved back so fast to get away from Mona that she knocked over the chair in which she'd been sitting and the table and lamp beside it, crash, thump, bang, shuffle, and plastered herself against the wall.

Michael went on full alert, shooting to her side. But what was there to see?

Mona stepped back to the center of the room, whispering "Oh, my God," under her breath, and Quinn took hold of her from behind and held her and kissed her cheek.

Rowan couldn't move. Her heart was pounding and her mouth was open and she shut her eyes as if she were about to scream. She had passed right through terror. It was utter revulsion, as if she'd seen a giant insect. It was the most explosive reaction on the part of a mortal to a vampire that I'd ever seen. It was panic.

I knew I could charm her because I'd done it before, crossed the barrier between the species without ever evoking that panic, and I determined to cross the barrier now with all my nerve. And this did take tremendous nerve.

"Very well, darling, very well, sweetheart," I said, advancing on Rowan as fast as I dared. "My precious, my darling," I said, as I slipped my arms behind her and under her, and caught her up and carried her past an astonished Michael, towards the door. Her body grew soft. (Thank Heaven.) "I have you, my sweetheart," I said to her, crooning in her ear, kissing her ear, "I'm holding you, precious darling," as I carried her out and down the steps, her body now completely limp, "I have you, my sweetheart, nothing can hurt you, yes, yes," her head falling against my chest and her hand clawing weakly at my shirt. She was gasping. "I understand, my precious," I said. "But you're safe, you're really safe, I would never let anything bad happen to you, I promise you, that's my promise, and Michael's here, he's with you, it's all right, darling, you know I'm telling you the truth, that these things are truly all right."

I could see these words sinking down, down into her mind, through the levels of guilt and remembrance and flight from the present, and what she'd sensed and couldn't deny and could only retreat from, and all the truths she had feared.

Michael was right behind me, and as soon as we reached the flagstones he took her from me effortlessly, and she fell into his arms in the same way.

Boldly I kissed her cheek, my lips lingering, and her hand found mine and her fingers coiled around mine. *Behold, thou art fair my love, thou art fair.* Her panic was still so great that she couldn't speak.

" 'A garden enclosed is my sister, my spouse; a spring shut up, a fountain sealed.' " I whispered in her ear. I kissed her again and again on her soft cheek. I stroked her hair. Her fingers gripped me, but the grip had softened, as she was softened.

"I've got you, darling," Michael said in exactly the same tone. "Rowan, my sweetheart, I have you, honey, I'll take you home."

As I backed off his eyes looked at me searchingly, and without enmity. I sensed something about his love for her, that it was immense and beyond pettiness, and that he claimed no dominion over her, that he adored her. It was difficult for me to really accept.

Rowan lost consciousness. Her head fell forward and against Michael. He realized it with total alarm.

"It's all right," I said. "Just take her home and lie down beside her and don't leave her alone."

"But what the Hell happened?" he whispered to me as he cuddled her.

"Doesn't matter," I said. "Remember that. It doesn't matter. What matters is that Mona has been saved."

I went back upstairs.

Of course Mona was sobbing.

She lay across the bed in their room where the computer purred, and she was sobbing, and Quinn sat by her, as was becoming the custom.

"What did I do wrong?" Mona asked. She looked up at me. "Tell me, what did I do wrong?"

I sat at the computer desk.

She sat up, cheeks streaked with blood.

"I can't live with them the way Quinn lives at Blackwood Manor; you see it, don't you? I didn't do anything wrong."

"Oh, stop lying to yourself," I said. "You know very well you're angry with her, deeply angry. Your intentions weren't pure when you approached her. She's done something to you, deceived you, something, something you can't forgive. You practically told us right here in this room. You had to show her your power, you had to push it—."

"You really think so?" she asked.

"I know so," I said.

"You think she's kept secrets from you. Magic secrets, secrets you haven't explained to Quinn and to me. You've resented her all these years as the doctor, the mad scientist, yes, right, the mad scientist, the keeper of the keys to the magic, coming in and out of your death chamber, ordering this medication and that medication and never really telling you what was happening, but other secrets, darker secrets, secrets that you and she and Michael know, not so?"

"I love her."

"And now here you knew you had the powerful magic. You had the keys to a powerful secret. You condescended to her. And so she saw through this duplicity, this display of patronizing affection, and she was panic-stricken when she realized *you weren't alive anymore*, just as you wanted her to be. You wanted her to acknowledge your power, that next to you, the way you are, she was nothing."

"You really think so?" Tears. Sniffles.

"I know so. And you're not finished with her. Not at all."

"Hold on, Lestat," said Quinn, "you're being unfair. Mona confessed that they had a score to settle. But surely she wasn't thinking of all those things, not when she went towards Rowan."

"Yes, she was," I insisted.

"You've fallen in love with her," said Quinn.

"In love with who? Mona? I told you I love both of you."

"No," said Quinn. "You know I don't mean Mona. You've fallen completely in love with Rowan in a way that's not like your infatuation with us. You've connected with something deep inside of Rowan and we can't compete with it. It started last night. But you can't have Rowan. You just can't."

"*Mon Dieu!*" I whispered.

I crossed the hall, went into my bedroom and shut and locked the door.

There stood Julien in his natty white-tie regalia, arms folded smugly as he gazed at me, leaning against the tall mahogany headboard of the bed.

"That's right, you can't have her," he said, laughing under his breath. "I watched you slip into it like the fly into the honey. I loved it. Her taking you so unawares, oh yes, your tasting that kernel of evil with your oh-so-refined senses, kisses in the shadows, yes, and falling so blithely in love with her, so tenderly for you with all your loathsome powers. And you cannot have her. No, never. Not Rowan Mayfair. Never ever. Not the Magnate, not the Creator of the greatest family enterprise, not the champion of the family's public dreams, the family's philanthropic wonder, the family's guiding star! You can't ever have her. And you shall have all the fun of watching her from afar and never knowing what might happen to her. Old age, sickness, accident, tragedy. Won't it be something to behold! And you can't ever interfere. You don't dare!"

There stood beside him little Stella, aged eight or nine, in a lovely white dress, drop waist style, a white bow in her black hair.

"Don't be so mean to him, Oncle Julien!" she said. "Poor darling."

"Oh, but he is a mean creature, Stella dearest," said Julien. "He took our beloved Mona. He deserves nothing but the worst."

"Listen to me, you cheap backstairs ghost," I said. "I'm no sentimental rake out of a bad Byronic poem. I'm not in love with your precious Rowan Mayfair. The love I feel for her is something you can't know in your shallow wanderings. And Rowan's in more trouble than you can ever imagine. Now why don't you tell me what disastrous mistake you made with all your clever machinations and visitations? Or shall I get it out of Mona or Rowan or Michael? You haven't been an angelic success, have you? Take your little girl in your arms and get out of my sight. Is God giving you the power to writhe and spit with anger?"

Pounding on the door. Mona calling my name over and over again.

They were gone, the ghosts.

She came into my arms. "But I can't bear it if you're angry with me, tell me you're not, I love you with my whole soul."

"No, no, never angry," I said. "Let me hold you tight, my fledgling, my darling, my newborn one. I adore you. We'll fix everything. We'll make everything perfect for everyone. Somehow."

13

HOTEL CORRIDORS. Muffled voices. On and on. Dark blue carpet. Candle flame electric lights. Door after door. That's a pretty table. Oh, you rank materialist, be done with tables, and be gone on your filthy errand. What if some ruthless enterprising individual did a catalog of all the furniture you have personally described in your Vampire Chronicles, then what, I'll tell you what, that would put you to shame, you avaricious, shameless, hoarding, ever-hungry Seven Deadly Sin Committing fiend, what did Louis once say to you, that you made a junk shop of eternity? Move it!

Bedroom interior. Mirrors and mahogany. Wreckage of room service. (Look Ma, no tables!) Olive-skinned woman, dark of hair, half conscious on the pillows. Smell of gin. Drapes open on the crowded sparkling high-rise night. Tumbler full of ice cubes and gin and tonic, catching light in frozen bubbles.

She turned on her back, rose up on her elbows. Beige satin nightgown, lank, nipples brown.

"So they sent you, did they?" she asked, lids half closed, eyes scornful, painted mouth hard. "So how will you do it? Hmmm. Get a load of that blond hair."

I lay down on the bed beside her, on my left elbow. Bed thick with her sweet human perfume. Luxurious hotel sheets and pillows.

"You're some hit man," she said, sneering. She picked up the beautiful tumbler. "You don't mind if I have a drink before I die, do you?" She drained the gin and tonic out of it. It smelled like poison to me.

Ahhhhh, gambling debts, millions, how does one do that, but it was only the tip of it, she'd been in much deeper, flying back and forth to

Europe, stashing the wealth for the wrong man. When she fired a gun she emptied it. Making a living. Her partner had vanished. She knew she was next. Didn't care anymore. All that money gone to waste. Drunk all the time now. Sick of waiting. Black hair oily and fine. One of those faces completely transformed by maturity. Lots of there there but who cares?

She fell back on the pillow.

"So kill me, you bastard," she purred. I mean slurred.

"You got it, sweetheart," I said. I covered her, and kissed her throat. Hmmm. Fragrance of nobody.

"What is this, Rape?" Snickering laughter. "Can't you find a two hundred dollar ho in this hellhole city? You know how old I am? You have to put a spin on the job, a guy with your looks?"

I covered her mouth. She gave just a little to the press of my lips.

"And kissy face on top of it," she drawled. "Stick to the pelvic moves, fancy man."

"I have something better, honey, you underestimate me."

I nuzzled against her neck, kissed the artery, heard the blood surging, opened my mouth slowly, tasting skin again, sank my teeth and drew fast so that she swooned before the pinprick pain could catch up. Oh, Lord God, this is from Somebody's Heaven.

Easy.

Weightless, timeless, apocalyptic. Oh, baby, you're no liar, don't expect me to give a hoot about the things I've done, never, how could I, I'm not God, honey bunch, well, then, who, the Devil, oh, sweet, I told you, didn't I, I don't believe in you, I hate you, keep it going, I am, I am, as much as I can bother to despise anyone, I love this! hmmm, yeah, tell me about it, and then what was it? I almost, if you want to give it up, do it, but if you don't, I don't need it, it's what you need, sidewalk hopscotch, colored chalk, I hate them, lemme go, jump rope, screen door bang shut, never could, kids crying, I just need the blood, oh, but wait, I see it, I never knew it could be so—back down that hallway, no, well, guess what? it isn't. Laughter, light and laughter, I should have—.

Her heart couldn't pump it any longer. I lifted her, drew harder, the heart stopped, arteries burst, blood blind, body slowly filling with weight, slipslide of satin, shock of downtown lights, the sparkle in the ice cubes, the Miracle of the Ice Cubes.

Blood to the brain, My Lord and My God, I'm out of here. Thou shalt not lie beside the corpse of thy victim, for the Deadly Sin of Pride I shattered the huge window, arms out, glass flying in all directions, Take me, Oh Twinkling Downtown Lights, Take me!—glass falling on the airwell gravel roof and the mighty modern unromantic ever-churning air machines. .

Won't the hit man be surprised?

14

THE NEXT NIGHT I AWOKE to discover the *National Catholic Reporter* had arrived in the mail, and I tore it open for news of Saint Juan Diego.

There was great coverage, including a wonderful black and white photograph of the Pope in his white mitre, listing badly to the right proper but doing fine otherwise, watching "indigenous dancers" at the canonization Mass in the Basilica of Our Lady of Guadalupe in Mexico City. Huge crowd. Of course the article HAD to mention the fact that some people doubted that Juan Diego had ever existed!

But what did that matter to the faithful like me?

Only after I had devoured all the articles on the Pope's travels did I realize there was a note lying on the desk from one of the guards, saying that Michael Curry had come by in the afternoon and asked if I might call him. No one was answering the phone.

I'd come back so late last night that I had not seen Mona and Quinn, and they had not yet risen.

The flat was ominously quiet. Apparently it was too early for Julien and Stella as well. Or maybe my last speech had routed Julien for a while. But I didn't think so. He was, if anything, probably more energized and waiting for a moment in which to strike.

I was about to pick up the phone and call the number which Michael had given to the guard when I realized that Michael had just come to the carriageway below.

I went down to meet him. The evening was all aglow and full of the scent of the kitchens of the Quarter.

I motioned for the guards to let Michael come on back.

He was in a frantic state. He was wearing the same three-piece white suit as yesterday, shirt now open and tie gone, and he was all rumpled and smudged with dirt and his hair was mussed.

"What's the matter, man?" I asked, as I reached to take his arm.

He shook his head. He was choking on the words he wanted to say. His thoughts were scrambled. On some unconscious level he blocked me from reading him, while appealing to me at the same time.

I led him into the courtyard. He was sweating badly. The garden was just too hot. I had to take him in where the artificial winds blow.

"Come on," I said. "Let's go upstairs."

Mona appeared in the doorway just as we reached the back parlor, pretty blue silk dress, heels strapped at the ankles, just her hair tousled from bed.

"Uncle Michael, what's wrong!" She was instantly distraught.

"Hey, baby," Michael said weakly. "You're sure looking fine." He collapsed on the velvet sofa and he put his elbows on his knees and his head in his hands.

"What is it, Uncle Michael?" she said, obviously shy of touching him, settling uncertainly on the edge of a nearby chair.

"It's Rowan," he said. "She's gone out of her mind, and I don't know if we can bring her back this time. It's worse than it ever was before."

He looked at me. "I came here to ask you point blank if you'd help. You have a power over her. You calmed her last night. You might be able to do it again."

"But what's happening to her?" Mona asked. "Is she catatonic like before?"

I caught only jumbled images from Michael's mind. He didn't appear to register Mona's question. I had to settle for his words.

"Stirling's with her now," Michael said, "but he's not getting through. This morning she insisted she wanted to go to Confession. I called Fr. Kevin. They were alone for about an hour. Of course he can't tell anybody what she said. You ask me, I think Fr. Kevin's on the brink too. You can't take a regular priest like Fr. Kevin and plunge him into a family like ours, and expect him to survive, expect him to represent something, expect him to exercise his priestly functions. It's not fair."

"Michael," I said. "What is Rowan doing?"

He didn't seem to hear me. He went on.

"Mayfair Medical, all her work on it has been frenetic, you know that, or at least you did know that—" he looked at Mona—"but nobody else really realizes it, that she works to the point of exhaustion so that there will be no inner life, no quiet life, no life of the mind other than that which is locked to Mayfair Medical, it's a complete vocation, yeah, marvelous, but it's also a complete escape."

"A mania," said Mona quietly. She was badly shaken.

"Right," said Michael. "Her public persona is the only persona she really has. The interior Rowan has utterly disintegrated. Or it has to do with the secrets of Mayfair Medical. And now this breakdown, this complete disconnection, this madness. Do you realize how many people are riding on her energy? Her example? She's created a world that's dependent upon her—members of the family from all over come here to study medicine, the new wing is under way at the hospital, there's the Brain Study Program, she's monitoring four research projects, I don't even know the half of it. You chuck my own selfish needs, and then there's all that—."

"What actually happened?" I pushed.

"Last night she lay on the bed for hours. She was whispering things. I couldn't hear her. She wouldn't talk to me. She wouldn't come out of it. She wouldn't dress for bed, or take anything to eat or drink. I lay beside her—what you told me to do. I held her. I even sang to her. Irish people do that, you know. We sing when we're melancholy. It's the strangest thing. I thought I was the only one. Then I realized all Mayfairs do it. That's the Tyrone McNamara blood down through Oncle Julien. I sang these melancholy songs to her. I fell asleep. When I woke up, she was gone.

"I found her in the back garden on the lawn under the oak. She was barefoot out there, in her pretty silk suit, digging, digging where the remains were." He looked at Mona. "She was in her bare feet and she was digging with one of the gardener's big shovels. She was talking to herself about Emaleth and Lasher and she was cursing herself. When I tried to stop her, she hit me. I tried to remind her she'd had the remains removed. As soon as Mayfair Medical was complete, she had had a team out to scour for the remains."

"Emaleth and Lasher?" I asked.

"I remember," said Mona. "I was there when it happened."

"She was crazy that day," Michael said. "She kept repeating herself. She said that she belonged in the Talamasca. They sifted through that dirt like a pack of archaeologists. Yeah, you saw them, and that fragrance, it was so strong."

Mona was fighting back her usual tears. My heart went out to both of them. They were prisoners of these secrets.

"Go on," said Mona.

"I tried to tell her. They'd excavated the entire area. They'd brought everything to Mayfair Medical. She didn't seem to understand. I told her what she'd told me at the time. It was cartilage, cartilage of an infinitely more elastic species . . . that it wasn't even the scene of a crime! But she wasn't listening. She keeps pacing and talking to herself. She says I don't know who she is. She's always told me that. She started talking again about joining the Talamasca, retiring into the Order. As if it was a convent. She said she belonged there. In the Talamasca. In the old days, when women had done evil things they could be sent to monasteries. She said she would make a bequest to the Talamasca, and they would take her, they would take the Mad Scientist, because that's who she really was. Mona, she doesn't believe in my understanding. She doesn't believe in my power to forgive."

"I know, Uncle Michael."

"I'm a moral child in her mind," Michael said, his voice shaky. "And then she said the worst thing."

"What?" asked Mona.

"She said that you were . . . you were dead."

Mona didn't reply.

"I kept telling her you were fine. We'd just seen you. You were all right, you were cured. She kept shaking her head. 'Mona's not alive anymore.' That's what she said."

Michael looked at me. "Lestat, will you come?" he asked.

I was vaguely amazed. This man was highly intuitive, but he was seeing in me only what he wanted to see.

"Will you talk to her?" he asked. "You had such a soothing effect on her. I saw it with my own eyes. If you and Mona could come. Bring Quinn. Rowan loves Quinn. Rowan doesn't notice many people. But she's always loved Quinn. Maybe because Quinn can see spirits, I don't know. Maybe because Quinn and Mona love each other, I don't know. She loved Quinn from the first time he came to call on Mona years ago. She's always trusted in Quinn. But Lestat, if you could talk to her . . . and Mona, if you could come and show her that you're alive, show her that you're fine, just hold her. . . ."

"Michael, listen to me," I said. "I want you to go home. Quinn and Mona and I have to talk this over. We'll come to you or call you as soon as we can. Be assured, we're very concerned about Rowan. There's no other concern on our minds right now except Rowan."

He sat back on the couch, closed his eyes and took a long breath. He looked defeated. "I was hoping you'd come back with me," he said.

"Believe me," I said, "our little consultation won't take long. We have strong obligations. We'll call or come just as quickly as we can." I hesitated. "We love Rowan," I said.

He stood up, heaved a sigh and headed for the door. I asked if he needed a ride back home and he murmured that his car had brought him downtown.

He looked back at Mona. She'd stood up but she was afraid to embrace him, that was plain.

"Uncle Michael, I love you," she whispered.

"Oh, sweetheart," he said, "if I had my life to live over again and could just erase that one night."

"Don't think about it, Uncle Michael," she said. "How many times do I have to tell you? I climbed in the back window, for God's sakes. It was all my fault, from start to finish."

He was unconvinced. "I took advantage of you, baby," he whispered.

I was stunned.

"Michael, it was Oncle Julien too," Mona said. "It was Oncle Julien's spell. He made a big mistake. Besides, it doesn't matter now, don't you see?"

I was stunned again.

He stared at her, narrowing his eyes. I couldn't figure whether he wanted a blurred focus or a fine one. It was as though he saw her loveliness afresh.

"Oh, you do look so good," he sighed. "My sweetheart." He closed the gap between them and embraced her totally, a bear of a man enfolding her. "My darling girl," he said.

I was afraid.

They rocked together, his arms completely enclosing her. He suspected nothing. He drifted in a dream. And she, newborn thing that she was, felt like a peach.

At last he broke away and said wearily that he had to return to Rowan, and I told him again that we would call him very soon.

He looked at me for a long moment, as though he was seeing me with new eyes, but it was only his weariness. He was seeing what he wanted to see in me, and he thanked me again.

"She called you Rasputin when she was angry," he said. "Well, I tell you, Lestat, you do have that sort of power and it's a good thing. I can sense the good in you."

"How in the world can you do that?" I asked. To ask that honest question felt extraordinarily sweet. This was truly one of the most baffling mortals I'd ever met. And to think, he was *her* husband, and I'd thought him the perfect husband for her when we'd first met.

He reached out and took my hand before I could stop him. Couldn't he feel how hard it was? Only the thinnest layer of flesh was permeable. I was a monster. Yet he peered into my eyes as though plumbing for something separate from the Deadly Sins that prevailed within me.

"You're good," he said, confirming it for himself. "You think I'd let you hold my wife in your arms if I didn't sense it? You think I'd let you kiss her cheek? You think I'd come to plead with you to calm my wife when I couldn't if I didn't know you were good? I don't make mistakes of that order. I've been with the dead. The dead have come to me and surrounded me. They've talked to me. They've taught me things. I know."

I held fast. I nodded. "I've been with the dead too," I said. "They left me in confusion."

"Maybe you asked too much of them," he said gently. "I think when the dead come to us they are crippled creatures. They look to us for their completion."

"Yes," I said. "I think that's true. And without a doubt I failed them. But I was with angels too and they asked too much of me and I refused them."

A look of quiet shock passed over his face. "Yes, you said it before. Angels. I can't imagine being with angels."

"Never mind my words," I said. "I talk too much of my own wounds and failures. With Rowan, something can be done, and I promise you, we will see to it."

He nodded. "Just come to the house, please, all of you."

"Are you and Rowan alone there?" I asked.

"Stirling Oliver is there, but—," he said.

"That's fine. He can stay," I replied. "We'll be there very soon. Wait there for us."

He nodded with a half smile that was trusting and grateful and kind. He went on out the door.

I stood trembling, listening to him make the stairs, and then the carriageway. I shut my eyes.

A solemn silence fell over the room. I knew Quinn had come to the door. I struggled to gain control of my heart. I struggled. Mona cried softly into her handkerchief.

"Mona of a Thousand Tears," I said. I fought them myself. I won. "How could he have so totally misunderstood me?"

"But he didn't," said Quinn.

"Oh, yes, he did," I insisted. "Sometimes I think the theologians have got it backwards. The big problem is not How to explain the existence of evil in this world. It's How to explain the existence of good."

"You don't believe that," said Quinn.

"Yes, I do," I said.

I fell into a sudden trance, thinking of the Pope in the Basilica of Our Lady of Guadalupe in Mexico City with the "Indigenous people" dancing in their feathered headdresses. I wondered if the Spaniards would have murdered those Indians in their feathered headdresses for doing that on consecrated ground two centuries ago or three or four. Well, Hell, it didn't matter. Saint Juan Diego would protect everyone now.

I shuddered in order to clear my mind.

I sat on the couch. I had to ponder what I'd learnt.

"So it was Michael who fathered your child," I said to Mona as gently as I could.

"Yes," she answered. She sat beside me. She put her hand over mine. "There are so many things I'm not free to tell. But at the time, Rowan wasn't there. Rowan . . . Rowan did a terrible thing. I can't tell what Rowan did. Rowan left Michael. Rowan was the thirteenth witch. I can't tell it. But Rowan left Michael on Christmas Day."

"Go on, you were talking about Michael," I said.

"It was weeks later. The house was all dark. I climbed in the window. Michael was supposed to be sick. He was grieving for Rowan. I crept up there to his room. I knew he wasn't sick as soon as I touched him."

Quinn sat down close to us. I realized he'd heard our conversation with Michael. He didn't care for what Mona was telling me. It came as a huge shock to him that Michael had fathered the child of which he knew so little. But he remained quiet.

"Then Oncle Julien cast a spell on both of us," said Mona. "He brought us together. He was trying to help Michael stop grieving over Rowan. He wanted to prove to Michael that Michael wasn't really sick. But I wanted it. I really wanted it. I was being the Wander Slut in those days. I kept a list on my computer of all the cousins I seduced. I seduced my cousin Randall, and I think he was eighty then. He nearly shot himself on account of it. Me being thirteen and all that. It was perfectly disgusting. I had to confess to my Aunt Bea that I'd seduced Randall and ask her to come bring the medics—Oh, never mind. But he's just fine now. Imagine. I like to think he's lived to be ninety, thanks to me."

"Yes, of course," said Quinn dryly. "But with Michael you conceived the child."

"Yes," said Mona. "The child that they took away from me."

"It was giving birth to the Woman Child," I said, "that brought on the wasting sickness, and the sickness wouldn't stop."

"Yes," Mona answered. "At first we didn't know what was happening. It came on very gradually. I had a little time. What good is it now to talk about these things? Rowan dug up the remains beneath the tree because she was trying to find something that might help me. At least in part that was the reason. But it doesn't matter now. What do we do?"

"But who were the creatures buried beneath the tree?" I asked. "Michael called them Emaleth and Lasher."

"Those are their secrets," Mona insisted. "Look, I escaped it all, on account of you, both of you. But there's no escape for Rowan, is there? Except Mayfair Medical. Except project after project. No. But I have to demand the truth from her. Did she try to find my child or not? Did she lie?"

"Why would she lie?" Quinn asked. "What would have been her motive? Don't you see, Mona, Lestat and I can't comprehend these things unless you tell us what they mean."

Mona's face grew dark. She was so pretty that it couldn't look sour, no matter how dreadful her thoughts. "I don't know," she said, tossing her hair. "I just had the feeling sometimes that if Rowan could get one of them . . . the mutation, the other species . . . she'd lock them up in

Mayfair Medical until she'd run every test she could to see what their flesh or their breast milk or their blood could do for human beings."

"The other species?" I asked.

She sighed.

"Their breast milk in particular, it had curative properties. I used to lie there in the dark and imagine that my daughter was somewhere locked in the building. It was a fantasy. Rowan would force drinks on me. I'd imagine the breast milk of my daughter was mixed in it. It's all wrapped up in what the mutation is. But it doesn't matter now. What does matter is now we have to help Rowan, and I still have to get the truth from her—how I go about finding my daughter myself."

"You still want to find her?" Quinn repeated, as if he hadn't really understood. "Even now, after what's happened to you?"

"Yes," said Mona. "Especially now. I'm no longer human, am I? We're equals now, me and Morrigan, don't you see? Morrigan will live for centuries and so will I! That is—if Rowan's been telling the truth all these years, if she doesn't know where my daughter is, if my daughter's really still alive. . . ."

"Another species," I said, "not really a mutation. Babies that grow to maturity soon after birth."

"The curse of the family . . . I can't explain it—," Mona protested. "Don't you understand? Only a tiny number of the Mayfairs know what happened. All the rest live in blissful innocence! That's the irony. The family is so large and so good, so very good. They really have no idea what happened, they never saw, they never experienced, they never knew—."

"I understand your loyalty to them," I said. "But don't you see that Quinn and you and I are a family now?"

She nodded. "I'm a Mayfair," she said. "What can I do to change it? Nothing. Even the Dark Blood doesn't change it. I'm a Mayfair, and that's why we have to go there. I have no choice."

"When Oncle Julien appeared to Quinn," I said, "to tell Quinn that he had Mayfair blood in his veins, Oncle Julien knew about the species? He feared Quinn would have the genes for the species?"

"Please," said Mona. "Don't ask me any more questions. So many bad things happened! By that time Oncle Julien knew because we knew. He wanted to keep Quinn and me apart. But so much damage was done to me by Morrigan's birth it didn't matter. I couldn't have another child of any kind."

"Morrigan," I said. "Did you love this creature? Did she have intellect? Could she speak?"

"You can't imagine what it's like to give birth to one of these creatures," said Mona. "They speak to you even from the womb, they know you, and you know them, and they're hardwired with the knowledge of their kind—." She broke off as if she'd shattered a vow.

I put my arm around her and I kissed her, and brushed the veil of hair back which separated us and kissed her cheek again. She quieted. I loved the texture of her skin. I loved the feel of her lips when my fingers touched them.

Quinn watched these things but he didn't resent me any more than Michael had with Rowan. I withdrew.

"Do you want me to go there alone?" I asked.

"No, absolutely not," cried Mona. "I want to see Rowan. I want to make her tell me. Is it true my child has never, never, ever tried to reach me? I have to know."

"I think you've both told me what we'll do," I said soberly. "We'll exchange secrets. That becomes the framework of our dialogue. We tell Rowan and Michael exactly what we are. And they tell us about the Woman Child and if they know anything at all to aid Mona in her search. They reveal to us the things that Mona can't."

Mona looked up. Her eyes appeared to focus more clearly. I looked at her.

"Are you willing, my darling one?" I asked.

"Yes," Mona said. "It's really their story, not mine."

"Mona, you almost died in this story," I said. "How could it not be yours as well?"

"Oh, I forced my way into it," she said. "I wanted Michael. And she'd deserted him. All those nights in the hospital—I wondered, had she really forgiven me? And my child had lived and—." She shook her head and raised her hand as though to banish a specter.

I stroked her hair back from her forehead. She inclined to me, and I kissed her forehead.

"We have to go there, Beloved Boss!" she whispered. "We promised Michael. She's got to tell me the truth."

"This is all wrong," said Quinn. He shook his head. He clearly didn't like the idea at all. No one at Blackwood Farm knew Quinn's secrets. Even his clever Aunt Queen had died believing him her innocent boy.

"It's the only way to save the sanity of Rowan Mayfair," I said. "She knows but she doesn't know for sure, and it will eat at her and it will obsess her, and on account of her bond with Mona, she and Michael will never let it go. The damage has been done. Only some form of truth will repair it."

"You're right," said Mona. "But if they tell you and Quinn about the Taltos, if they take you into their trust, tell you things that even most all of the Mayfairs don't know, there will be a bond, and maybe that bond can somehow save us all."

Taltos.

So that was the name of this species. That was the name of the creature of the curious fragrance and the back-garden graves and the dying womb.

"Michael and Rowan have obviously kept one terrible set of secrets," I said. "They're fit to keep another. And the innocent Mayfairs will come to receive Mona. And her life won't have to be of the shadows. She'll come and go as you do, Quinn. That's the way it will work."

Quinn studied me silently, respectfully. Then he spoke up.

"Are you in love with Rowan?"

"Doesn't matter one way or the other," I said.

Mona flashed on me, the blood rising in her cheeks very hot, and her eyes quivering.

Intense, painful moment. Why was my soul not crusted over with barnacles for every life I'd taken? I spoke with the tongue of a mortal.

"We're going there to save Rowan, are we not?" I said. "Quinn, call for a car, will you?"

I left them and opened the door and went out onto the rear balcony. The breeze had picked up. The banana trees were dancing against the brick walls. I could see the white roses in the dark. An illicit fire burnt inside me. " 'The rose of Sharon, and the lily of the valleys,' " I whispered. " 'Thou art all fair, my love, there is no spot in thee.' " How reverently the wind received these strange words.

I would have liked the long way—a walk uptown through streets narrow and wide, the open-mouthed roar of the streetcar or its heavy metal clatter through Chrondelet Street, the vision of the pilgrim oaks struggling on lower St. Charles Avenue, the festering flowers of the Garden District, and the glistening moss on the bricks.

But there was no time for that except in my memory. My heart was thudding. And in Quinn's heart my heart was on trial.

"You know," Mona said as we waited at the curb for the limousine. "I haven't seen the house on First and Chestnut for two years. The day the ambulance came I thought I'd be back in a week or two, like always. Hmmm. I wonder if Oncle Julien's on the prowl in the old rooms."

No, darling, I thought, though I didn't voice it. He's right across the street, in the shadows of a shop bolted for the night, the discredited spirit, glowering at me. *Goddamn you!* But who knows, maybe he'll come along.

15

Love. Who knows about another's love? The more you love, the more you know the burnt out loss of love, the more you heed the silence of unknowing in the face of another's spiritual bondage.

Behold the house, which Quinn described in years-ago summer days when he went to call on beloved Mona, the house with crape myrtles pressed against its black fence, and the two famous sentinel oaks with their erupting roots beneath the broken flagstones.

White columns upstairs and down, side hall door, long windows, rocking chairs on the porch, cast-iron railings beneath their spilling festoons of flowering vines. And the great secretive side yard stretching back into a private and concealed darkness. It was into that sunny gulf that Oncle Julien had lured the young Quinn and told him of his Mayfair blood and that he must never marry Mona. Some ghosts just never give up! I spied the sparkle of the waters of the swimming pool far back there, and who knows what beyond, the graveyard of the mysterious *Taltos*?

Led into the double parlor by a trusting Michael with a relieved smile, I sensed at once a telltale fragrance. *Alien species.* Faint but true. Mona caught it, nose uplifted in that quick, slight vampiric gesture.

Quite a room.

Soaring mirrors over twin fireplaces of white marble. Mirrors at each end multiplying the long shadowy chamber and its chandeliers into infinity. Aubusson carpets, are they not, and the scattered furniture both common and fine violating the built-in division of the rooms with a great gathering area of couch and chairs beneath the central arch, and beyond, the long black Bösendorfer piano beneath a genteel veil of dust. Paintings of ancestors on the wall, for who else could they be, a stalwart woman with black hair in handsome riding attire, and on this other side, guess who, with his gleaming eyes and a smile I'd never see, Monsieur Julien Mayfair, of course, and the great German tall-case clock ticking and swinging faithfully.

Rustlings, as if the house was full of ghosts. Glance of the real true hateful Julien out of the corner of my eye. It was Michael who turned. Then Julien on the other side, and the sound of taffeta as though from an old-fashioned floor-length dress. Michael turned again. Murmur: "Where are they?"

"They don't like us," I said.

"They don't make decisions for us!" Michael said angrily.

First time I'd seen that emotion in him. It came and went swiftly. There's a big word for that: "evanescent."

"Who?" said Mona. "What do you mean?" She shook off her private spell. Glaze of emotion in her eyes. Lived here, loved it, ripped out of it, lost, breath of death on her neck, gone, home, touch.

Do I have to read her mind to know that? I do not. I read it in Quinn's eyes, and he, child of a great house, feels a wondrous comfort here, frightened as he is of the loss of love of the whole Mayfair clan, as if they had come at us, winding up the mountain road with B movie torches in hand.

Michael's blue eyes fastened on me. He was worn down yet immeasurably strong, proud of the house and mildly happy with the way I looked at it.

"I've plastered it, painted it, run its new wires, sanded its floors, and laid the gloss." Rolling murmur. "I learned those skills out west, and all that time I lived out there I never forgot this house, used to pass it as a little boy, never forgot it, and never dreamed of course that one day I'd be the master of it (chuckle), that is, if any man can be the master of this house, what this house has is a mistress, or even two, and for a time, for a long time. . . ." He lost the thread. "Come, let me show you the library."

Only slowly I followed him.

The night outside beat hard on the windows, the song of the winged things, throb of the frogs, with the full authority of the big garden.

Narrow hallway, soaring walls. Evil stairs. Too straight, too long.

The alien fragrance again. But more than that the smell of mortal death. How did I come by this? Hand touching the newel post, sparked off it. Mortal tumbling down and down. Stairs made for the word "headlong." These doors like temple doors rise up in protest to this domestic constriction.

". . . added in 1868," said Michael, "everything just a little smaller in this room, but the best plasterwork in all the house." A wall of books, old leather.

"Oh, yes," I said, "a magnificent ceiling. Tiny faces up there in the plaster medallion."

Mona made a circuit of the room, heels silenced by the red carpet, went to the long window that opened on the small side porch and peered out as though measuring the world specifically by these particular lace curtains. Peacocks in the lace curtains. Then she pivoted and stared at Michael.

He nodded. Flash of menace to her in his remembrance. Something dreadful, something deadly come to the window. Hymns of death and dying. The family ghost made flesh and blood. Denial. *Hurry. Rowan waits. Rowan scared. Rowan very near.*

"Come on, sweetheart," he said to Mona.

Did I sound so intimate when I called her that?

For one moment I wanted to put my arm around her just to stake my claim. My fledgling now, my baby. Shameful.

Dining room a perfect square with a perfectly round table. Chippendale chairs. Surrounded by murals of the heyday of a plantation. A different sort of chandelier. But I don't know the name for it. It was set low, like so many candles.

Rowan sat alone at the table, perfectly reflected in the gloss.

She wore a dark purple robe, sashed, with satin lapels, mannish, except that with her piquant naked face and tiny shoulders she was so perfectly a female creature. Bit of white nightgown revealed. Indifferent hair second fiddle to her large gray eyes and virginal mouth. She stared at me as if she didn't know me. The pressure of knowledge behind her eyes was so immense, she might have been blind.

Then she looked at Mona. She rose out of her chair, right arm flung out, finger stabbing:

"Get her!" she whispered as though her throat were closing up. She ran round the table. "We'll bury her under the tree! Do you hear me, Michael!" She gasped for breath. "Get her, she's dead, can't you see it, get her!" She ran towards Mona, and Michael, brokenhearted, caught her in his arms. "I'll bury her myself," she said. "Get the shovel, Michael." A hoarse hysterical yet muted screaming.

Mona bit deep into her lip and cringed in the corner, eyes ablaze, Quinn struggling to hold her.

"We'll dig deep, deep," Rowan said, soft eyebrows knotted. "We'll bury her so she never comes back! Can't you see that she's dead! Don't listen to her! She's dead. She knows she's dead."

"You wish I were dead!" Mona sobbed. "You hateful, hateful thing!" The anger arched out of her like a great fiery tongue. "You hateful lying thing. You know the man who took my daughter! You always knew. You let it happen. You hated me because of Michael. You hated me that it was Michael's child! You let that man take her."

"Mona, stop," I said.

"Honey, please, my darling, please," Michael pleaded with Rowan for everyone and for his exhausted, bewildered self, holding Rowan effortlessly as she scratched at his arms.

I went to her, disentangled her from her lawfully wedded husband, and caught her up and peered into her intense manic eyes. I said:

"I did it because she was dying. Lay the sin on me."

She saw me. Truly saw me. Her body rigid as driftwood. Michael, behind her, stared. "Both of you attend," I said. "I speak now without sound."

Stuff of legend, vulgar names, hunters of the night, locked out of the day forever, live off human blood, hunt the evil ones only, feed on the trash lives if there are such things, always thriving among humankind, from the dawn of time, pass for human, body transformed by the Blood, perfected within its potential by the Blood, Quinn, Mona, me. You are right, you see, she is dead, but only dead to human life. I worked the magic. Filled her with the enlivening Blood. Accept. It's done. It's irreversible. I did it. A dying girl defined by pain and fear could not consent. Two centuries ago, I didn't consent. A year ago, Quinn didn't say yes to it. Maybe no one really consents. It was my conviction and my power. Lay the sin on me. And so she thrives. And so she hunts the filthy blood. But she is Mona again. The night belongs to her, and by day the sun can't find her. I am guilty. Lay all blame on me.

I went silent.

She closed her eyes. She gasped as though exorcising a deep invisible clotted horror from her lungs. "Blood Child," she whispered. She lay against me. Her left hand went up to clasp my shoulder. I held her close, my fingers reaching into her hair.

Michael looked down as though, the window having closed, he wanted to think in solitude. Leaving her to me, he seemed adrift in the room. But he had caught all of my revelation and it had sunk deep into him and he was wearied, and sad.

Mona went to him and opened up his arms, and he received her with the utmost tenderness. He kissed her cheeks as though the truth had broken open in him a powerful chaste communion. He kissed her on the mouth, the hair.

"My baby darling," he said, "my pretty girl, my baby genius." It was almost like the embrace he had given her only a half hour before, only this time I really understood it. And the knowledge of her nature worked on him, slowly transforming the way in which he touched her.

There was lust in him, yes, bred into him, and fed over many years, a practical, vital lust, and it was part of his constitution, his vision, but for her he didn't feel it. Six years of caring for her had punished it enough, and now this aberrant truth made it so he could caress her once again and kiss her freely, and croon to her, and smooth her hair with his hands, yes, and she was with him again, father of her child, father of her death.

"Like the Taltos," she murmured. She flashed her wholesome, sweet smile. Intrepid youth. And surely he saw in the dusky room her gleaming skin more truly now, and the unnatural glisten of her eyes, and the volume of her red hair as it surrounded her beaming face.

She didn't catch the drifting sadness in him, the enormous ache. He let her go with such tact, and took one of the chairs and sat at the table. He bent over and ran his hands through his hair.

Quinn took the chair opposite him. He looked at Michael. And then Mona went quietly to Quinn's side. And so they were settled.

I stood holding Rowan. Where was my lust? The blood tempest that sweeps into its vortex all desire to know, to absorb, to abide, to possess, to kill, to love? It was a drenching storm inside of me. But I am so very strong. That is a given, is it not? And when you love another as I loved Rowan, you don't strive to hurt. Never. The trivial operations of the heart are burnt away in quietude. Burnt away in humility that I could feel this, know this, and contain it within my prudent soul.

I lifted her face, my thumb pressed into her cheek, a gesture which if done to me I couldn't have borne, but I was tentative and ready to draw away had she showed the slightest unwillingness. She only looked at me with muted understanding. And all her flesh yielded to me, and the hand that held my shoulder closed warmly over my neck.

"And so," she said with that remarkable rich voice, that deep lustrous voice, "we Mayfairs of the inner circle, we have another sacrosanct secret, yet another breed of immortal come to us."

Slight and tenuous, she slipped from my embrace, and secretly kissing my hand, she went to Michael and laid her hands on his shoulders and looked across the table at Mona.

"And I will somehow wake from this gnosis," she went on, "and in the course of things, yes . . . the vital course of things, protect it utterly, this truth, and return to penetrate the world I've made to need me so much."

"Baby, you've come back," Michael whispered.

This was the creature I adored.

And when our eyes met I saw her full recognition, and a respect and comprehension of my devotion so profound that I could find no words in the swimming silence.

So poetry rises, surpassing the literal, *You are beautiful, my love, terrible as an army with banners, turn away your eyes for they have overcome me, a garden enclosed is my sister, my spouse: a spring shut up, a fountain sealed.*

16

WHY DID I LOVE HER so much? Surely someone will read these pages and ask: What was so lovable about her? What was it that caused you, of all beings, so to love? You, a lover of men and women, a vampire, a destroyer of innocent souls, so to love? You, the focus of so much easy affection, and forever flaunting your hopeful stinging charm—why did you love her?

What should I say? I didn't know her age. I can't write it here. I can't describe her hair other than to say it was clipped and turned-in on the ends, and her face was still smooth without the slightest trace of the furrows of age, and her figure boyish.

But one embraces such details in the boiling wake of the acknowledgement of such love. In and of themselves they are nothing. Or, if one believes that a woman so strong has shaped the lineaments of her face, the set of her brows, the straightness of her posture, the frankness of her gestures, the very way that her hair falls about her face, the length of her stride, the sound of her footfall—then perhaps they mean everything.

Beside the flaming red-haired Mona, she was the color of ashes, a woman drawn in charcoal, with a sexless and piercing gaze, and a soul so immense it seemed to fill every fiber of her frame and to emanate outwards into infinity, her knowledge of the world around her dwarfing that of everyone she'd ever known or would know.

Imagine it, such isolation.

She didn't talk down to people. She simply didn't talk to them. Only God knew the number of lives she'd saved. And only she knew the number of people she had murdered.

In the Mayfair Medical Center she had only just begun to fulfill her immense dreams. It was an engine of great and continuous healing. But what drew her through the world were projects yet unrevealed for which she had the wealth, the knowledge, the laserlike vision, the nerve and the personal energy.

What threatened this mammoth individual who had found for herself through tragedy and heritage the perfect goal? Her sanity. From time to time she gave in to madness as if it were strong drink, and when in her cups she fled from her sublime designs, drowning in memories and guilt, all judgment and sense of proportion lost, murmuring confessions of unworthiness and half-explored plots of escape that would seal her off forever from all expectations.

At this precious moment she regarded sanity as her State of Grace, and she saw me as the Demon who had brought her back to it.

For her I connected the two worlds. That meant that she could.

Blood Child.

She lusted for me. For the entirety of what I was—that is, for all she'd sensed in our three encounters, and what she knew to be true now, both from my profession and her apprehension.

She wanted me completely. It was a desire rooted in all her faculties, that overrode and obliterated her love of Michael. I knew it. How could I not? But she had no intention of yielding to it. And her will? It was iron. You can draw iron with charcoal too, can't you?

1 7

"THIS SECRET HAS TO BE KEPT by you from anyone else," Mona said. Her voice was quaking. She had a firm hold on Quinn's hand. "If you keep it from everybody else, then in time I can come to be with them. I mean the rest of the family. I can know them for a little while. The way Quinn knows everybody at Blackwood Farm. I can have some time for my leave-taking. What did you mean when you called me Blood Child?"

Rowan looked at her across the round table. Then with sudden impersonal impatience, Rowan tore off the thick purple robe and stepped out of it, as if from a broken shell, a tense figure in a sleeveless white cotton nightgown.

"Let's go out there," she said, her soft deep voice more sure of itself, her head slightly bowed. "Let's go where the other ones were buried. Stirling's out there. I've always loved that place. Let's talk in the garden." She started walking, and only then did I notice she was barefoot. Her hem just skirted the floor.

Michael rose from the table and followed her. It seemed his eyes avoided ours. He caught up with Rowan and put his arm around her.

Immediately Mona led the way after them.

We passed through a classic butler's pantry of high glass cabinets crammed full of vivid china, and then on through a modern kitchen, out French doors and down painted wooden steps onto a sprawling flagstone patio.

There ahead lay the huge octagonal swimming pool, shimmering with a wealth of submerged light and beyond that, a tall dignified cabana.

Long limestone balustrades enclosed the garden patches, which were bursting with tropical plants, and very suddenly the air was filled with the strong scent of the night jasmine.

Great arching branches of the rain tree poured over us from the left. And the cicadas sang loudly from the many crowding trees. There were no traffic sounds from the world beyond. The very air itself was blessed.

Mona gasped, and smiled and shook out her hair and turned for Quinn's reassuring embrace, murmuring fast like a hummingbird beating its wings. "It's all the same, so lovely, more lovely even than I remembered it. Nothing's changed."

Rowan stopped and looked up at the moving clouds as though allowing time for Mona to absorb it all. For one second she glared at me. *Blood Child. File folder of facts.* Then at Mona. Then at the clouds again. "Who would change such a place?" she asked gently in her low melodic voice, responding to Mona.

"We're only the custodians," said Michael. "Someday other Mayfairs will live here, long after we're gone."

We waited, clustered together. Quinn very anxious. Mona in bliss.

I scanned for the ghost of Julien. Nowhere around. Too risky with Michael able to see him.

From a black iron gateway to the left, Stirling came to meet us, ever the gentleman in crisp tailored linen, and strangely silent, and Rowan walked on, fearless in her bare feet, and pointed toward the garden from which Stirling had just come.

Stirling's eyes locked on Mona for one quick intake of information, and then he went after Rowan and Michael back the way he had come.

We all followed into a different world, beyond the measurements of Italian balustrade and perfectly square flagstone.

It was all rampant elephant ear and banana trees back here, and a broad lawn beneath a huge old oak, and an iron table there and modern iron chairs, more comfortable I suspected than the relics of my courtyard. A high brick wall bounded the place opposite the gateway and a row of yews concealed it from the carport to the left, and an old two-story wooden servants' quarters shut it off from the world to the right, the building itself mostly hidden from us by high thick ligustrum.

There was someone out there in the servants' quarters. Sleeping. Dreaming. An elderly soul. Forget about it.

Wet earth, random flowers, mingling, rattling leaves in the wet summer air, all the night songs, scent of the river only eight blocks from here over the the Irish Channel, where a train whistle cut the night, leading the distant soft roar of box cars.

The cicadas died down suddenly, but the song of the tree frogs was strong, and there were the night birds, which only a vampire could hear.

Low lights along the cement path provided a very feeble illumination. And there were other such beacons scattered in the farthest reaches of the garden. Two floodlights fixed high in the oak spilled a soft luminescence over the scene. As for the moon, it was full but veiled behind the pink panoply of clouds, and so we were in a thin rosy and penetrable darkness, and all around us the garden was alive and balmy and seeking to feed upon us with countless tiny mouths.

As I stepped on the lawn I caught the faint scent of the alien species, the scent that Quinn had caught when he came here as a boy led by the ghost of Oncle Julien. I saw the scent hit Mona with her heightened gifts. She drew herself up as though revolted, and then took a deep breath. Quinn dipped down to kiss her.

Stirling played host with the gathering of the chairs about the table. He tried to disguise his amazement at the vision of Mona. The miracle of Quinn as vampire he'd seen in frightening circumstances, and then again, later, the night we went to tell him that Merrick Mayfair was no more. But Mona . . . he couldn't quite keep it to himself.

Rowan's snow white gown dragged in the mud. She didn't care. She was murmuring or singing, I couldn't tell which or catch any words or meaning to it. Michael stared at the oak as though talking to it. Then he took off his wrinkled white jacket. He put it over the back of a chair. But he stood staring at the tree as though finishing a soliloquy. He was a big chunk of a man, gorgeously made.

Stirling helped Mona to her chair, and bid Quinn to sit beside her. I waited for Rowan and Michael.

Suddenly Rowan turned and threw her arms around me. She fastened to me about as tight as a mortal woman could do it, so much divine silk and softness to me, whispering feverish words I couldn't catch, eyes racing over me, while I stood stark still, my heart beating frantically. And then she began to touch me all over, open hands on my face, on my hair, then grabbing up my hands and slipping her fingers through my fingers. At last she thrust my hand between her legs and then drew back shuddering, letting me go and staring into my eyes.

I came quite close to losing my mind. Did anyone have a clue as to the crash and thunder inside me? I locked the casket of my heart. I punished it. I endured.

All this while, Michael never looked at us. He had sat down at some point, his back to the oak, facing Mona and Quinn, and he was talking to Mona, singing the fatherly chant again in a soothing voice as to how sweet and pretty she was, and that she was his darling daughter. I could see all that out of the corner of my eye, and then in sheer weakness, the lock inside me broke, and all was released. I gathered up Rowan's supple limbs and I kissed her forehead, the hard sweet skin of her forehead, and then her soft unresisting lips, and let her loose arms go, watching her slip into the chair beside Michael. Silent. Done.

I went to the other side of the table and sat beside Mona. I was bitterly full of desire. It was unspeakable to need someone in this way. I closed my eyes and listened to the night. Ravenous, repulsive creatures singing magnificently. And working the soft fertile earth, creatures of such loathsomeness I couldn't dwell on it. And the clatter of the riverfront train unendingly. And then the absurd song of the calliope on the riverboat that took the tourists up and down the waterway as they feasted and laughed and danced and sang.

"The Savage Garden," I whispered. I turned away as if I hated them all.

"What did you say?" Rowan said. Her eyes broke from their feverish movement just for one moment.

Everyone went quiet, except the singing monsters. Monsters with wings and six or eight legs, or no legs at all.

"It's just a phrase I used to use for the Earth," I said, "in the old times when I didn't believe in anything, when I believed the only laws were aesthetic laws. But I was young then and new to the Blood and stupid, expecting further miracles. Before I knew we knew more of nothing, and nothing more. Sometimes I think of the phrase again when the night is like this, so accidentally beautiful."

"And now you do believe in something?" Michael asked.

"You surprise me," I said. "I thought you'd expect me to know everything. Mortals usually do."

He shook his head. "I suppose I have a sense," he said, "that you're figuring it all out step by step, like the rest of us." He let his eyes wander over the banana trees behind me. He seemed preoccupied by the night, and deeply hurt by things I couldn't hope to learn from him. He didn't mean to show it off, this hurt. It simply became too great for him to conceal, and so his mind drifted, almost out of courtesy.

Mona was struggling not to cry. This place, this secret backyard, so well hidden from the world of the Garden District streets with its crowded houses, was obviously sacred to her. She slipped her right hand into my left. Her left hand was in Quinn's hand, and I knew she held him as tight as she held me, pressing for reassurance over and over again.

As for my beloved Quinn, he was severely discomforted and unsure of everything. He studied Rowan and Michael uneasily. Never had he been with this many mortals who knew what he was. In fact, he had never been with more than one, and that was Stirling. He, too, sensed the presence of the old one in the back house. He didn't like it.

And Stirling, who had correctly surmised that the disclosure had been made, that Rowan was now subdued and deep in thought, seemed frightened in a dignified way also. He was to my far left, and his eyes were on Rowan.

"What do you believe in now?" Mona asked me, her voice unsteady but insistent. "I mean, if the old resignation of the Savage Garden was wrong, what has replaced it?"

"Belief in The Maker," I replied, "who put it all together with love and purpose. What else?"

"Amen," said Michael with a sigh, "someone better than us, has to be—somebody better than every creature who walks the Earth, somebody who shows compassion. . . ."

"Will you show compassion to us?" Quinn asked. It was sharp. He looked directly at Michael. "I want my secret kept as well as Mona's."

"Trouble with you is you think you're still human," Michael replied. "Your secret's utterly safe. It will be exactly the way you want it. Wait a safe period of time. Then Mona can return to the family. It's not a difficult thing at all."

"This seems amazingly easy for you," Quinn replied suspiciously. "Why is that so?"

Michael gave a short bitter laugh. "You have to understand what the Taltos was, and what they did to us."

Rowan said in a low voice, "And what I did to one of them too quickly, too foolishly." Her eyes moved away into memory.

"I don't know or understand," said Quinn. "I think what Lestat had in mind was an exchange of secrets. There are things Mona simply can't explain. They hurt her too much. They involve you. She becomes caught up in a web of loyalty, and she can't be free. But one thing is clear. She wants to find her daughter, Morrigan."

"I don't know if we can help," said Michael.

"I can look for Morrigan now myself," Mona protested. "I'm strong again." Her hand tightened on mine. "But you have to tell me all you know. For two years I lay in that bed confused and crazy. I'm still mixed-up. I don't know why you haven't found my daughter."

"We'll take you all through it again," said Michael soothingly.

Rowan murmured under her breath, then came to the surface, eyes remote, uncertain, moving rapidly again over the table as over nothing.

"I knew about you," she said. Her words were hushed and ran on smoothly, "I mean, what you are—Blood Children, Blood Hunters, Vampires. I knew. It wasn't a simple matter. Michael knew. The knowledge came in stages." She looked directly at me for the first time as she continued:

"I had seen one of your kind one time, walking, in the Quarter. It was a male with black hair, very handsome, and set apart from everything around him. He appeared to be searching for someone. I'd felt a paralytic conflict, an attraction to him, and a fear of him also. You know my powers. They're not developed as they ought to be. I'm a witch who won't be a witch, a Mad Scientist who won't be Mad. I wanted to know *about* him. I wanted to follow him. It was a long time ago. I never forgot about it—knowing he wasn't human, and that he wasn't a ghost. I don't think I told anyone about him.

"But then this woman disappeared from the Talamasca. Her name was Merrick Mayfair. I hadn't known her, but I'd known of her—that she was a colored Mayfair, descended from a downtown branch of the family. I can't remember. I think it was Lily Mayfair, yes, or was it Lauren—I despise Lauren, Lauren has an evil mind—Lauren who told me there were lots of colored Mayfairs, but this Merrick wasn't very close to any of them. This Merrick, she had tremendous psychic powers. She knew about us, the First Street gang, but she really didn't want contact. She'd spent most of her life in the Talamasca and we'd never even known of her. Mayfairs hate it when they don't know about Mayfairs.

"Lauren said that she'd come once, this Merrick Mayfair, when the house was opened for a Holiday Tour, you know, a benefit for the Preservationists, after Michael had restored everything, after all the bad times were over, and before Mona was really sick. This person, Merrick, she'd gone through First Street with the tourists, imagine, just to see the nucleus. And we hadn't been here. We hadn't known."

A sword went through me at these words. I glanced at Stirling. He too was suffering. I flashed back on Merrick climbing on the flaming altar, taking with her into the Light the spirit that had plagued Quinn all of his life. Don't reveal. Don't revive. Can't help.

But Rowan was talking about a time long before the other night when Merrick disappeared forever. Rowan was talking about Merrick's turning to us.

"Then she disappeared," Rowan said, "and the Talamasca was thrown into confusion. Merrick gone. Whispers of evil. That's when Stirling Oliver came South." She looked at Stirling. He was watching her fearfully but calmly.

She lowered her eyes again, her voice continuing soft and low, just above a threatening hysteria.

"Oh yes," she said to me, "I know. I thought I was losing my mind at times. I built Mayfair Medical not to be the Mad Scientist. The Mad Scientist is capable of the unspeakable. Dr. Rowan Mayfair has to be good. I created this immense Medical Center to commit Dr. Rowan Mayfair to good. Once this plan was under way, I couldn't afford to go down into madness—dreaming of the Taltos and where they'd gone, dreaming of strange creatures I'd seen and lost without a trace. Mona's daughter. We tried everything we could to find her. But I couldn't live in a shadow world. I had to be there for all the ordinary people, signing contracts, rolling out blueprints, calling doctors all over the country, flying to Switzerland and Vienna to interview physicians who wanted to work in the ideal medical center, the medical center that surpassed every other in its equipment, its laboratories, its staff, its comforts, its protocols and projects.

"It was to rivet me to the sane world, it was to push my own medical visions to the very limits—."

"Rowan, it's a magnificent thing that you did," Quinn said. "You speak as though you don't believe in it when you're not there. Everyone else believes in it."

She went on in the same soft rush of words as though she hadn't heard him. "All kinds of people come to it," she said, her words flowing as if she couldn't stop them, "people who have never given birth to Taltos, people who have never seen ghosts, people who have never buried bodies in a Savage Garden, people who have never seen Blood Children, people who have never even hoped for the extraordinary in any form, it helps all manner of human beings, it embraces them, it's real to them, real, that's what was important. I couldn't let it go, I couldn't ever retreat into nightmares or scribblings in my room, I couldn't ever fail my interns and residents, my laboratory assistants, my research teams, and you know, with my background, the neurosurgeon, the scientist at heart, I brought to every aspect of this giant organism a personal approach; I couldn't run away, I couldn't fail, I can't fail now, I can't be absent, I can't. . . ."

She broke down, her eyes closed, her right hand forming a fist on the table.

Michael looked at her with quiet sadness.

"Go on, Rowan," I said. "I'm listening to you."

"You're making me angry," said Mona in a low sharp voice. "I think I hate you."

I was appalled.

"Oh, yes, you always did," Rowan said, raising her voice but not her wandering eyes. "Because I couldn't make you well. And I couldn't find Morrigan."

"I don't believe you!" Mona said.

"She's not lying to you," said Quinn in a chastising voice. "Remember what you just said. For years you've been sick, confused."

"Mona, honey, we don't know where Morrigan is," said Michael.

Mona leaned against Quinn and he put his arm around her shoulder.

"Tell us, Rowan, tell us what you have to say," I said. "I want to hear it."

"Oh, yeah, yeah," said Mona, "go on with the Saga of Rowan."

"Mona," I whispered, leaning to clasp her head and draw her to me, my lips at her ear: "these are mortals and with mortals we have a certain eternal patience. Nothing is as it was. Curb your strength. Curb your old mortal envy and spite. They have no place here. Don't you realize the power you have now to search for Morrigan? What's at stake here is the rest of your family."

Reluctantly she nodded. She didn't understand. Her mortal sickness had divided her from these people. I was only now realizing the extent of it. Though they'd come into her hospital room probably every day and all day, she'd been drugged, full of pain, alone.

A soft rustling sound broke my concentration. The person in the servants' quarters had awakened, and was rushing down the wooden steps. The screen door banged shut, and there came the skittering feet through the rattling foliage.

It might have been a tiny gnome, this creature that emerged from the elephant ears and the ferns, but it was simply a very old woman—a tiny bit of a thing with a small completely wrinkled face, black eyes and white hair in two long neat braids tied at the ends with pink ribbon. She was dressed in a stiff flowered robe, and clumsy padded fuzzy pink slippers.

Mona rushed to greet her, crying out: "Dolly Jean!" and picked up the bit of a creature in her arms and spun around with her.

"Lord, God in Heaven," cried out Dolly Jean, "but it's true, it's Mona Mayfair. Child of Grace, you set me down right now and tell me what's gotten into you. Look at those shoes. Rowan Mayfair, why didn't you tell me this child was here, and you, Michael Curry, giving me that rum, you think your mother in Heaven doesn't know the things you do, you thought you had me down for the count, I know, don't think I don't, and look at Mona Mayfair, what did you pump into her?"

Mona had no awareness that with her vampiric strength she was holding the woman in the air, and how perfectly abnormal it looked.

The spectators were speechless.

"Oh, Dolly Jean, it's been so long, so terribly long," Mona sobbed. "I can't even remember the last time I saw you. I was all locked up and taped up and dreaming. And when they told me Mary Jane Mayfair had run away again I think I just went into a stupor."

"I know, my baby," said Dolly Jean, "but they wouldn't let me in the room, they had their rules, but don't you think for a moment I wasn't saying the rosary every day for you. And one of these bright days Mary Jane'll run out of money and come home, or turn up dead in the morgue with a tag on her toe, we'll find her."

By this time we had all risen, except for Rowan, who remained sunk in her thoughts as if none of this was taking place, and Michael quickly took the apparently weightless Dolly Jean from Mona and set her in a chair between himself and Rowan.

"Dolly Jean, Dolly Jean!" Mona sobbed as Quinn led her back to her place at the table.

Rowan had never once even looked at either Mona or Dolly Jean. She was murmuring, her narrative moving along in her head, unbroken, and her eyes probing the dark for nothing.

"All right, settle down Dolly Jean, and you too Mona, and let Rowan talk," said Michael.

"Who in the world are you!" Dolly Jean demanded of me. "Holy Mother of God, where did you come from?"

Rowan turned suddenly and stared at Dolly Jean with apparent wonder. Then she turned back into her solitude and crowded reminiscence.

The old woman went quiet and still. Then muttered: "Oh me, poor Rowan, she's off again." Then, staring at me again, she let out a huge gasp and cried: "I know who you are!"

I smiled at her. I couldn't help it.

"Please, Dolly Jean," said Michael, "there are issues we have to settle here."

"Jesus, Mary and Joseph!" cried Dolly Jean, staring this time at Mona, who was hastily wiping away her latest tears. "My baby, Mona Mayfair, is a Blood Child!" Then her eyes discovered Quinn, and there came another huge gasp, and she cried out, "It's the black-haired one!"

"No, it's not!" Rowan declared in a furious rasping whisper, turning to the old woman again. "It's Quinn Blackwood. You know he's always loved Mona." She said it as if it was the answer to every question in the universe.

Dolly Jean made a jerky little turn in her chair, and with two dips or bobs of her head made a thorough examination of Rowan, who was looking at her with gleaming eyes as if she hadn't even seen her before.

"Oh, my girl, my poor girl," Dolly Jean said to Rowan. She put her tiny hands on Rowan and smoothed her hair. "My darling girl, don't you be so sad, always so sad on account of everybody. That's my girl."

Rowan stared at her for a long moment as though she didn't understand a word Dolly Jean spoke, and then she looked away again at nobody, half dreaming, half thinking.

"At four o'clock this very afternoon," Dolly Jean said, still stroking Rowan's hair, "this poor little soul was digging her own grave in this very yard. I noticed how well you covered it up, Michael Curry, you think you can cover everything up, and when I came down here to ask her what she was doing standing in a hole of wet mud she asked me to pick up the shovel and bury her while she was still breathing."

"Be quiet, be still," whispered Rowan, looking far off as if at the night sounds. "It's time now for a larger vision. The Initiates have multiplied, and this is the inner circle. Be worthy of it, Dolly Jean. Be quiet."

"All right, my girl," said Dolly Jean, "then you just talk on as you were, and you, my sparkling Mona, I'll say my rosary all day long for you, and you too Quinn Blackwood. And you, the blond one, you gorgeous creature! You think I don't know you, but I do!"

"Thank you, Madam," I said quietly.

Quinn spoke up: "So all of you will keep our secret? This grows more dangerous for us by the moment. What can come of this?"

"The secret can be kept," said Stirling. "Let us talk this out. There's no going back now, anyway."

"Why, you think we're going to try to make the whole Mayfair clan believe in Blood Children!" Dolly Jean laughed and slapped the table with both her hands. "That's just hilarious! We can't even get them to believe in the Taltos! This brilliant doctor, here, she can't make them believe in the giant helix, she can't get them to behave themselves on account of the risk of having another Walking Baby! And you think they'd listen to us if we told them all about the Blood Children? Honey, they just take the phone off the hook when we call."

For a moment, I thought that Rowan was going to start raving. She glared at Dolly Jean. She was trembling violently. Her face had gone white, and her lips were moving but she was not forming words.

Then the strangest laugh came out of Rowan. A soft free laugh. Her face became girlish and full of delight.

Dolly Jean went into ecstasy.

"Don't you know it," she cried to Rowan. "You can't get them to believe in pneumonia! You can't get them to believe in the flu!"

Rowan nodded and the laugh slowly but sweetly died in a smile. I had never seen such expressions in Rowan, obviously, and they were glorious to behold.

Mona was crying and trying to talk at the same time.

"Dolly Jean, please simmer down," said Mona. "We've got to get some things settled here."

"Then get me a drink of rum," said Dolly Jean, "for Heaven's sakes, go on your young legs, you know where it is, no, tell you what, bring me the Amaretto, go get it with a shot glass. That'll make me real happy."

Mona went off at once, darting across the lawn and towards the pool, high heels clicking when they hit the flagstones, and off around the bend on her errand.

Michael sat there musing and shaking his head. "You drink that on top of all that rum and you're going be sick," he murmured.

"I was born sick," said the old woman.

Stirling stared at Dolly Jean as though she was something perfectly horrible. I almost burst out laughing.

Rowan continued to smile at Dolly Jean. It was sweet and secretive and honest.

"I'm going to pour that bottle of Amaretto down your throat," Rowan said gently in her husky confidential voice. "I'm going to drown you with it."

Dolly Jean bobbed up and down in the chair with squeals of laughter. She grabbed Rowan's face and held her tight.

"Now, I made you laugh, I did, you're all right, my genius girl, my doctor, my boss lady, my mistress of the house, I love you, girl, I'm the only one in the entire Mayfair clan that's not afraid of you." She kissed Rowan on the mouth and then let her go. "You just keep on taking care of everybody, that's what God put you here to do, you understand, you take care of everybody."

"And I fail and fail again," said Rowan.

"No, you don't, darlin'," said Dolly Jean. "Put another wing on that hospital. And don't you fret anything, you sweet girl."

Rowan sank back in her chair. She looked dazed. Her eyes closed.

Across the lawn, Mona came flying, silver tray in hand, with several bottles of liqueurs and bright shiny glasses. She set this down on the iron table.

"Now, let me see," she said. "We have three human beings." She put the glasses in front of Stirling, Michael, Dolly Jean, and Rowan. "Oh, no, four human beings. Okay, now here you are, all human beings have glasses."

I thought Quinn would perish from mortification on the spot. I merely cringed.

Michael picked up the bottle of Irish Mist and poured himself a small amount. Dolly Jean took the bottle of Amaretto for herself and swallowed a good mouthful. Stirling poured a shiny nugget of cognac and sipped it. Rowan ignored the proceedings.

A silence ensued in which Mona took her old place.

"Rowan," I said, "you were trying to explain how you knew about us. You were talking about Merrick Mayfair, about when she disappeared from the Talamasca."

"Oh, that's a good one," said Dolly Jean. She drank more of the Amaretto. "I can't wait for this. Go on, Rowan, if you've a mind to talk for once, I want to hear it. Carry on as if I wasn't here to cheer you along."

"You have to understand what the Talamasca meant to us," Rowan said. She paused. Then went on in a low voice, filling the quiet completely. "The Talamasca has known the Mayfair family through all its thirteen generations. Mona understands. Quinn, I don't know that you ever understood, but we could tell them anything. They knew all about the Taltos. They knew. It was like going to Confession to go to them. They have the solidity and the eternal self-confidence of the Roman Church. And Stirling was so patient. Mona loved him."

"Don't talk about us as if we're not here," said Mona.

"Patience, Mona," I said.

Rowan continued as if she hadn't even heard:

"Then it was Dolly Jean, our precious Dolly Jean Mayfair from Fontevrault Plantation, who said that Merrick Mayfair had become a Blood Child: 'Sure enough! That's what happened to that one!' Dolly Jean knew it. She'd called Tante Oscar. Tante Oscar had told her."

Rowan smiled at Dolly Jean, who nodded and took another huge mouthful of Amaretto. Rowan leaned over and so did Dolly Jean and their foreheads touched, and then they kissed tenderly on the mouth. It was as if these two women were lovers.

"You do right by me, now," Dolly Jean retorted. "Or I'll shout you down. Truth is I can't recollect what happened."

"Hush up," said Rowan softly, with another tender smile.

Dolly Jean nodded and took another drink.

Rowan sat back and went on:

"Dolly Jean had Henri take her and me downtown in the big car to visit Tante Oscar. It was the French Quarter, off the beaten path. Tante Oscar's an elderly colored Mayfair who lives up three flights of stairs in a flat with a balcony from which you could see the River. Tante Oscar was over one hundred years old. Still is."

Rowan's words were gaining speed.

"Tante Oscar was wearing at least three sets of clothes, dresses over dresses, and at least four fancy worked scarves around her neck, and topped by a long maroon coat with golden fur along the collar, I think it was foxes, little foxes with heads and tails, I don't know, and she had a ring on every bony finger, and a long oval face, and jet black hair, and huge egg-shaped yellow eyes. And there was wall-to-wall furniture in the flat, three buffets in a row, and three desks in a row, and dining room tables in three rooms, and couches and chairs all over, and carpets laid on carpets, and little tables with doilies and bisque figurines and photographs in frames, and sterling silver tea services everywhere you looked. Armoires were bulging with clothes and all askew."

Dolly Jean began to cackle as she took another drink, and Mona laughed under her breath. Rowan continued as if she didn't hear them.

"Gorgeous little twelve-year-old mulatto children were running everywhere, getting us coffee and cake, and getting the mail, and running downstairs for the newspapers. There was a TV on in every room and an overhead fan blowing. I've never seen such beautiful children as I've seen in New Orleans. The colors of these children were simply indescribable.

"Tante Oscar went to the refrigerator, which she called the ice box though it was brand-new, and opened it to show us that the telephone was in there because she never talked on it, and there was the telephone all right, right there in the middle of the milk and the yogurts and the jars of jam, but when Dolly Jean had called, Tante Oscar had heard the ring through the refrigerator door because it was Dolly Jean, and she had answered.

"Tante Oscar told us that Blood Children had been living in the Quarter for two hundred years, feeding off the blood of the riffraff, and Merrick Mayfair was now one of them. It was meant to be. Merrick Mayfair's old Oncle Vervain had foreseen it, that his beloved little Merrick Mayfair would one day walk with the Blood Children, and he had told Tante Oscar and no one else. Oncle Vervain had been a great Voodoo doctor, and everyone respected him, but when he saw that in the future, it broke his heart. Tante Oscar said that now Merrick Mayfair would live forever."

I winced. If only I had seen that Light. . . . But how many chances would God give me?

"Of course Oncle Julien had tried to prevent this catastrophe—

I think Oncle Julien is paying for his sins by wasting his time on earth—."

"I like that very much," I uttered before I could stop myself.

Her words flowed right on.

"—Tante Oscar explained to us. Oncle Julien had come in a dream to Merrick Mayfair's Great Nananne when she was dying and told Great Nananne to give Merrick Mayfair to the Talamasca. But Tante Oscar said it was the curse of Oncle Julien that his interference in the world of the living always failed."

"Did she really say such a thing?" I asked.

Michael smiled and shook his head. He looked at Mona and Mona was looking at him.

Rowan continued her tale:

"When I described the black-haired one, the one I'd seen walking, Tante Oscar knew him. She called him Louis. She said the Sign of the Cross would drive him off, though it had no power over him. He merely respected it. She said the one to fear was the blond-haired one who had a strange name and who, 'talked like a gangster and looked like an angel.' I never forgot those words, I thought they were so strange."

She fixed me in her gaze. I was lost to her.

"And then years later and only days ago, you came into the double parlor at Blackwood Farm and Jasmine called you 'Lestat' and you talked like a gangster and looked like an angel. I knew what you were deep, deep down in my mind where I didn't want to know. I knew. I could remember the camphor-ball smell of Tante Oscar's apartment and the way she said, 'the black-haired one will never drink if it means a struggle, but the blond-haired one, he'll do terrible things to you. He's the one to fear.'"

"It's not true," I said softly. "Even the damned can learn. It isn't like it says in our prayer books. Even vampires and angels can learn. God has to be an all-merciful God. Nobody is beyond redemption."

"Redemption!" she whispered. "How can I ever be redeemed?"

"Darling, don't say that," said Michael.

"You can never love this girl enough," said Dolly Jean. "Every morning she gets up, eats breakfast and goes to Hell, I swear it."

Rowan smiled at me. In the pale light she looked girl-like, the lineaments of her face so refined and smooth, her gray eyes resting for the moment before they began their feverish searching again.

Oh to know the kiss of your lips, for your love is better than blood.

A pause. Her lawfully wedded husband distracted, unaware, and Rowan's eyes fixed on mine.

Forgive me.

"But I'm skipping all around in time," she said. "This is not an orderly story, is it?" She looked around herself, as if surprised to discover the garden and the dark, and the bottles glimmering in the light and the pretty shine of the glasses.

"Go on, Rowan, please," I said.

"Yes. Let me go back," she said, "to when Merrick Mayfair disappeared, yes." She nodded. "But overall, you see, I had heard and I had seen, and I told Michael these things, and Michael just listened as he always does to terrible things, with that ominous yet charming Celtic gloom growing ever greater in him year by year, but when I talked to Stirling I could see in his face that he understood everything. He wanted to meet Tante Oscar. And he did. He would only say, however, that they missed Merrick Mayfair, and nothing more than that.

"Then Lauren Mayfair, you know, the great lawyer of the firm of Mayfair and Mayfair, who knows all things legal and therefore knows nothing, she took it into her arid little mind to find out about this strange disappearance of a Mayfair who might just need her white family. Crap."

"Right on," said Dolly Jean. She took another slug from the bottle. "Lauren was just up in arms to find out a Mayfair of any kind was in the Talamasca, that's what she didn't like."

"She knew the house where Merrick Mayfair had been born," Rowan said, "and she checked it out and found that Merrick Mayfair still owned it. She went downtown. And whatever she saw frightened her. She called me. She said, 'It's renovated like a palace down there in a dangerous neighborhood, and all the neighbors are terrified to go near it. I want you to come with me.' And so I said I would. I was still laughing from that strange encounter with Tante Oscar. I thought, why not go downtown? I only have a hospital and research center to finish. Who am I to say that I'm too busy to do it?

"Dolly Jean said that we were fools to do such a thing—you just don't go near a Blood Child, specially if you know what it is, but if we were determined to go then do it after nightfall. A Blood Child only walked in the dark, and Dolly Jean said furthermore that we were to go by the front gate, very strictly, and knock on the front door, and not to do an untoward thing that would give a Blood Child legitimate cause to hurt us. (Dolly Jean was nodding and cackling all through this speech.) Then we rang up Tante Oscar, who heard our ring through the refrigerator door, and said all the same things all over again. Lauren Mayfair was fit to be tied, as they say here. She said she had had a bellyful of congenital insanity in the Mayfair family before her twenty-first birthday. She said if one more person used the words 'Blood Child' to her she would sue. So I said, naturally, 'Well, why don't we call them vampires?' "

Mona burst out laughing and so Dolly Jean laughed so hard she had to pound the table with her left fist. She almost choked. Mona finally dissolved into giggles. Michael gestured to them to be quiet. Rowan was obviously waiting.

Rowan went on, her eyes fixing on me, then moving away.

"We went down there. It was the most godforsaken slum I'd ever seen. The very slabs of the sidewalks had floated away in the mud, buildings had collapsed into heaps of lumber, and the weeds were like fields of wheat. And there stood this classic raised cottage with its fresh white paint and planted garden. It had a high picket fence and gate, and a bell at the gate and we rang, and up on the porch, a tall woman opened the door and stood there in her bare feet with the light of the hall behind her. It was Merrick Mayfair.

"She knew who we were. It was astonishing. She complimented me on the Medical Center, and she thanked Lauren for coming to Great Nananne's wake years and years ago. She was very pleasant to us, but she didn't ask us in. She was quite fine, she said. She hadn't really disappeared at all, just become a hermit. I remember using every grain of second sight that I might possess when I looked at her, and a deep spell overtook me. It was the timbre of her voice, and the way that she walked, which set her apart. The center of gravity was not in her hips as it should have been in a human female. And her voice, it had a rich musical dimension to it. As for the rest of her, she was a shadow up there.

"Of course, Lauren had satisfied her abysmal legal mind that all was well. The superficial idiot. And her next attack was upon the Talamasca, which she proposed 'to run out of Louisiana,' but when she came up against their endless list of London and New York law firms, and the fact that an entire contingent of the family went up in arms against her, myself and Michael included, she settled very quickly for a schism in the firm, and for telling me how 'insane' I was, and that she was going to 'put Tante Oscar in a home.' I grabbed her and shook her. I didn't mean to do it. I've never done that to any person before. It was a terrible thing to do. But when she said that about Tante Oscar, I lost my temper. I just did it. I told her if she dared to attempt such a thing with any Mayfair, colored or white, anywhere, at any time, I would kill her. I went sort of out of my mind. How could she think she had the power to do such a thing? I backed away from her. I was afraid that—. I was afraid I would do something even more dreadful to her. And the whole matter was dropped. And she doesn't come near me anymore.

"And I had so much to do with the Medical Center that I really didn't want to talk the night away with Dolly Jean about Blood Children and what they did or didn't do. Though I couldn't resist going up to Tante Oscar's apartment one more time with Dolly Jean, but when they started talking about the 'Walking Babies' born out in the swamps, and I knew they meant actual Taltos babies, and the way the terrified swamp Mayfairs hacked them to death, I thought I was going into trance mode, and I left.

"And now we come forward almost to the present, and suddenly Miss McQueen is dead, Quinn's beloved aunt, whom everyone adored, and it's her funeral we're gathered for, and Mona's much too sick to even be told, and the funeral's in grand New Orleans style, and there in the pew in St. Mary's Church before me I see you—Quinn, Lestat—and this tall woman, with the scarf around her head, and I see Stirling come up to her and he calls her Merrick, and I knew, I knew she was the same woman I'd seen before, and this time I was certain she wasn't human. Only I couldn't concentrate on it.

"At one point she turned and lifted her sunglasses and looked directly into my eyes, and I thought, What does it have to do with me? She smiled. And after that I felt sleepy and unable to concentrate on any thought in particular, except that Aunt Queen was dead and everyone was the lesser for it.

"I wouldn't look at Quinn. I wouldn't think about the change in Quinn's voice on the phone—how over a year ago, his voice and his entire audial demeanor had changed. That might be a mistaken notion after all. What did it matter to know such things? And what if the blond-haired tan-skinned guy next to Quinn in the pew looked like an angel? How was I to guess that when I met him in the double parlor at

Blackwood Manor only a day or two later he would have 'captured' Mona and he'd talk like a gangster?" She laughed softly, just a little sweet private laugh.

"I had Mayfair Medical as my life, my mission in the real world. And this was a funeral Mass, I closed my eyes and prayed, and then Quinn stood at the podium and said warm and lovely things about Aunt Queen, and he had young Tommy Blackwood with him. Now would somebody who is not alive do that?

"And I had to get back to the Medical Center and find Mona in her bed of needles and bandages and the tape tearing her skin, and somehow convince her that Quinn was hale and hearty and fine, and had grown four inches since he'd gone to Europe so long ago, her beloved. . . ."

She stopped again, as though all the words had run out. She was staring at nothing in front of her.

"These matters are of no use to us," said Mona in a hard voice.

I was shocked.

Mona went on: "Why do you tell us all this? You're not the prima donna of what's happened here! All right, so, you tried to help me not die for years! If it hadn't been you, it would have been some other doctor. And you dug up the corpses of the Taltos out here, so what—."

"Stop, no!" Rowan whispered. "You're talking of my sins, you're talking of my daughter!"

"That's the whole point! I can't!" Mona cried. "That's why you have to do it. But you ramble on—."

"So you gave birth to one of them too," I said gently to Rowan. I reached across the table and covered her hand with mine. Her hand was cold, but at once she clasped my fingers.

"Traitor!" Mona said to me.

"Poor darling girl," said Dolly Jean, who was now drunk and falling asleep, "having those Walking Babies, and getting her womb torn out."

Rowan gasped at those words. She drew back her hand and her shoulders slumped as though she was drawing into herself.

Michael was deeply alarmed and so was Stirling.

"Dolly Jean, put a lid on it," Michael said.

"Rowan, can you go on?" I pleaded. "I understand everything you've said. You've been telling us exactly how and why you can keep our secrets."

"That's right," Quinn said. "Rowan's telling us how she can abide what we are."

The deep hurt flashed in Michael's eyes, private and almost lonely. "That's very true," he said under his breath.

"I gave birth to two," Rowan said. "I let the evil in after twelve generations. That's what Mona wants to hear. That's the secret we have to divulge in exchange for yours—."

"Oh yes!" cried Mona sarcastically, "more of the saga of Rowan! I want to know about my own child! About the man who took her away."

"How many times must I tell you, I can't find them!" said Rowan. "I've searched and searched."

I became furious at Mona. I had to take a deep breath. I reached over and snatched her out of Quinn's protective hold and turned her to face me.

"Now you listen to me," I said in a small voice. "Stop abusing your power. Stop forgetting that you have it. Stop forgetting the inevitable limitations of your kindred here! If you want to search for your daughter now, you have resources that Rowan and Michael can't even dream of! Quinn and I are here to find out what the Taltos is because you won't tell us! (She stared at me wide-eyed and slightly in terror.) Every time we ask you about it you dissolve into tears. In fact, you've wept more in the last thirty-six hours than any fledgling I've ever encountered in all my years, and it's becoming an ontological, existential, epistemological, and hermeneutical nuisance!"

"How dare you ridicule me!" she hissed. She took a deep cool breath. "You let me go this instant. You think I'm going to obey you in thought, word and deed! You're dreaming. I'm not the Wander Slut you make me out to be. I was the Designée of the Legacy of the entire Mayfair family. I know what it means to have self-possession and power. You don't look like an angel to me, and you sure as Hell don't have the charm of a bona fide gangster!"

I was stunned. I let her go. "I give up!" I said disgustedly. "You're a brash little infidel! Go your own way."

Quinn whipped her around and looked down into her eyes.

"Be still, please," he said. "Let Rowan talk the way she wants to talk. If you're ever to be Mona Mayfair again, that must be allowed to happen."

"Mona, this is very true," said Stirling. "Remember, this is an exposition of souls, a bartering of extraordinary revelations."

"Oh, let me get it straight," said Mona. "I triumph over death, and we gather here to listen to the personal memories of Rowan Mayfair?"

Dolly Jean, who had been dozing with the bottle, suddenly jumped into life, bouncing up and down and leaning forward, crinkled little eyes staring hard at Mona.

"Mona Mayfair, you button your lip," she said. "You know perfectly well, no matter how sick you've been, that Rowan almost never talks at all, and when she does talk she's got something to say, you and your fancy friends are learning about the Mayfair family, now how's that supposed to hurt you, I'd like to know, don't you want your handsome escorts to understand you? Shut up."

"Oh, you're just joining in with the chorus!" Mona said sharply to Dolly Jean. "Drink your Amaretto and leave me alone!"

"Mona," said Quinn as amiably as he could. "There are things we do need to know for your sake. Does it hurt so much to listen to Rowan?"

"Very well," Mona replied miserably, and she sat back in the chair. She wiped at her face with one of her thousands of handkerchiefs. She glared at me.

I glanced at her, then back to Rowan.

Rowan was watching all this with a remote expression, her face more relaxed than it had been all evening. Dolly Jean took another drink of Amaretto and sat back and closed her eyes. Michael was studying the three of us. Stirling waited, but our cross words had fascinated him.

"Rowan," I said. "Can you tell us what the Taltos is? We lack that basic knowledge. Can you give it to us?"

"Yes," she answered in a resigned voice. "I can tell you as much as anyone can."

18

ER EXPRESSION REMAINED PLACID, though she looked away, her inner focus gathering.

"A mammal," she said, "evolved totally apart from Homo sapiens, on a volcanic island in the North Sea thousands of years before us. We share perhaps forty-five percent of our genes in common. The creatures look like us except that they tend to be taller and more long of limb. Their bone structure is almost entirely what we would call cartilage. When the pure creatures mate, the female ovulates on demand and the fetus develops within a matter of minutes or hours, it isn't clear to me—but whatever the case, it puts tremendous stress upon the mother. Birth is accompanied by severe pain, and the infant unfolds as a small adult and begins to grow to maturity immediately."

Mona's entire demeanor changed at these words. She moved closer to Quinn, and he put his arm around her once more, kissing her quietly.

"The Taltos craves its mother's milk in order to grow," said Rowan. "And without that milk it cannot develop properly. In the hour right after birth it runs the risk of being stunted forever. With that milk, and with its mother's full telepathic nurture, the baby reaches its full height within that hour. Six and a half feet is the usual. The males can be seven feet. It will go on drinking its mother's milk as long as it can. Weeks, months, years. But the toll on the mother is heavy."

Rowan stopped. She put her hand up to support her forehead. A deep sigh came out of her. "The milk . . ." she said. "The milk has curative properties. The milk can work a cure in humans." Her voice broke apart. "Nobody really knows what that milk could do. . . ."

Deliberate flash of images. *A bedroom with an elaborate half-tester bed and Rowan in the bed, sitting up, taking milk from the breast of a young female.* Shut out. *Gunfire. Several shots. Flash of Rowan digging in this very yard. Michael with her. Rowan wouldn't let go of the shovel. Body of the young female lying limp in the moist earth.* Heartbreak.

Rowan began again, voice strong, automatic:

"Nobody knows the lifespan of a pure Taltos. It could be thousands of years. Females clearly can become infertile in time. I've seen one who was past her prime. She was a simpleton. She was found in rural India. Males? I know of only one in existence—the one who took Morrigan. They may remain potent till they die. Taltos tend in their natural state to be extremely naive and childlike. In ancient times, many died through clumsiness and accidents." She paused for a moment and then went on:

"The Taltos is telepathic, curious by nature and hardwired with a tremendous amount of basic historical and intellectual knowledge. It is born 'knowing,' as they say, all about the species itself, the island continent from which they came, and the places in the British Isles to which they migrated after the island was destroyed by the same volcano that created it. The glen of Donnelaith in Scotland was one of those strongholds. Maybe one of the last.

"That's what the Taltos was . . . when it was pure, before it knew about humankind or had any mixture with it. The population was culled by accidents, occasional pestilence, the females by overbreeding."

"What does this mean, hardwired?" I said. "I want to be sure I understand you."

"We're not hardwired," she said. "We don't come into this world knowing how to build a house or speak a language. But a bird is hardwired to build its nest, to do a mating call, or a mating dance. A cat is hardwired to hunt for food, care for its kittens—even to eat them if they are weak or deformed."

"Yes, I see," I said.

"The Taltos is a highly intelligent primate that is hardwired with a tremendous fund of knowledge," she said. "That and its extraordinary reproductive advantage are what make it so dangerous. Its naivete, its simplicity and lack of aggression are its vulnerabilities. It's also extremely sensitive to rhythm and music. You can almost paralyze a Taltos when you utter a long rhyme or sing a rhythmic song."

"I understand," I replied. "How did they become mixed with humans?" I asked.

She seemed at a loss. "Medically," she said, "I don't know the answer. I only know that it happened."

"Humans inevitably came to the British Isles," said Michael. "And there is a long history of "the tall people" and their fight with their more aggressive invaders. Interbreeding occurred. For human females it's almost always fatal. The woman conceives and then miscarries and bleeds to death. You can imagine the hatred and fear this inspired. As for the other way around, a human male would bring about an insignificant hemorrhage in a female Taltos. Nothing important there, except that if it happens repeatedly over years and years, it will use up the female's eggs." He paused, caught his breath and went on:

"Some successful breeding occurred and the offspring gave rise both to malformed 'little people' and Taltos with human genes, and humans with the genes of the Taltos. And as the centuries passed, all this became a matter of superstition and legend."

"Not so very neatly," said Rowan. Her voice was firmer than before, though her eyes still moved feverishly. "There were terrible wars and massacres and unspeakable bloodshed. The Taltos, being far less aggressive than humans by nature, lost out to the new species. The Taltos were scattered. And they went into hiding. They pretended to be humans. They concealed their birthing rites. But as Michael said, couplings with humans did happen. And unbeknownst to the early inhabitants of the British Isles, there developed a kind of human who carried a giant helix of genes, twice the number of a normal human, and capable at any time of giving birth to the Taltos or a malformed elfin child struggling to be one. When two such humans happened to mate, a Taltos birth was even more likely."

Rowan paused. Michael hesitated, and then, as she put her face into her hands, he continued the story.

"The secret genes were passed on by the Earls of Donnelaith, Scotland, and their kith and kin, this we know for certain, and superstitious legends grew up about any occasional Taltos child born to their household.

"Meantime, a May Day orgy gave way to a misalliance between an Earl and a common woman of the glen, which led in three generations to the foundation of the Mayfair family. The Taltos genes were passed on in this way to what would later become a great colonial clan, first on the Caribbean island of Saint-Domingue, and then here in Louisiana.

"But even before the Mayfair family had a name, the Talamasca had become intimately involved with its origins—recording the story of a witch by the name of Suzanne, who had called up a spirit quite by accident, a spirit who appeared to be a brown-eyed man who answered to the name Lasher—a spirit who was to haunt the family right down to Rowan's generation. The ghost originated in the glen of Donnelaith, as did the Mayfairs."

Rowan broke in:

"You see, we thought it was the ghost of a human being," she said, "or some astral being without a human story. I believed this even as it courted me, and I tried to control it."

"And it was a Taltos ghost," I said.

"Yes," she said, "and it was biding its time, generation by generation, until a witch would come who would bear a Taltos child, a witch with psychic powers enough to aid it to possess that unborn Taltos fetus and be reborn within it."

Michael interrupted: "And I didn't know I had Mayfair genes in my blood. I never even dreamed. It was a dalliance between Oncle Julien and a riverfront Irish girl, and the child went to an Irish Catholic orphanage. And that was one of my ancestors."

"Oh, this Lasher was a clever ghost," said Rowan, shaking her head with a bitter smile. "Over the generations he brought this family great wealth in any number of ways. Strong witches appeared in various generations who really knew how to use him. And the men he despised and punished if they got in his way. Except for Julien. Julien was the only Mayfair male strong enough to use Lasher to perfection. And Julien regarded Lasher as an evil thing, but even Julien thought that Lasher had once been human."

"Lasher himself thought so," said Michael. "The ghost didn't fully understand who he was or what he wanted, except to be reborn. He guided everything to that purpose: to come through, to be flesh and blood again. I saw the ghost from the time I was a little kid, passing the fence outside. I'd see him standing in the garden. I never dreamed that one day I'd live in this house. I never dreamed that one day—." He stopped, clearly unable to continue.

"The Legacy was established very early on," said Mona. "You had to keep the name Mayfair, whether you married out or not, if you were to be part of the family, if you were to be connected to the Legacy."

"And that way, the clan was kept close," said Rowan, "and there was much interbreeding."

"And there is one Heiress in each generation," said Mona, wiping her nose, "and that Heiress lives in this house and must be able to bear children."

"It was a matriarchy in legal and moral fact," said Rowan softly. "And Michael and I . . . we fit the design of Lasher perfectly. Of course my child was not pure Taltos. It was Taltos mixed with human. It was perhaps five months in the womb. And on the night of its birth, there came Lasher with all his force down into the infant manniken making it grow and cry out to me to use all my power. Rowan the Mad Scientist knew the circuitry and the cells! Rowan the Mad Scientist knew how to guide the monstrous offspring." She closed her eyes. She turned away, as though the remembrance was pressing against her.

Brilliant flash of the Man Baby, tall, slippery, face evincing wonder, gawky, pinkish limbs. Rowan clothing it as the creature laughed delightedly. Flash of it clutching her breast, drinking. Rowan sinking to the floor in unconsciousness. The creature drinking hungrily from the other breast as well. My Darling, what secrets these are, indeed.

Silence.

A look of pure torment on the face of Michael. How well I understood his pain now, that he had fathered these creatures, and apparently no others.

Stirling appeared fearful as before, yet shamelessly fascinated. Mona, her eyes closed, leaned against Quinn as he watched Rowan. Sounds of the garden—soft, inevitable, indifferent, sweet.

"Walking Babies, horrible things," said Dolly Jean from her sleep. "If only I'd a known that ghost was a Walking Baby, but the thought never entered my head. . . ."

"Not my girl," whispered Mona. "My girl wasn't a horrible thing. Her father was the demon, but not her."

Michael fighting with the creature called Lasher. Snow and ice. The creature tremendously slippery and crafty and flexible and invulnerable to the blows. The creature laughing and mocking Michael. The creature knocking Michael into the ice-cold swimming pool, Michael sinking down to the bottom. Sirens, trucks, Rowan and the creature running towards the car . . .

"I left with it," Rowan whispered. "This Man Child thing with no name other than the name of a ghost. I left Michael. I took it away. The Mad Scientist thought first and foremost to save it from those who might have destroyed it, and it had possessed the body of Michael's child and sent that child's true soul Heavenward, and I knew that Michael wouldn't stop until he'd killed it, and so I fled with it. It was a dreadful error."

Silence.

Rowan remained turned to the side, as though away from all that she'd said, her eyes closed, her hands limp on the table. I wanted to enfold her in my arms. I did nothing.

Michael remained still. Father of this monster. No. *Sent that child's true soul Heavenward.* Father of the mysterious body only, the vehicle for the mystery.

"The Taltos," I said to Rowan, "it fathered a daughter in you? You bore two of these creatures?"

Rowan nodded. She opened her eyes and looked at me with a steady gaze. There might as well have been no one else there.

"The male was an atrocity," she said. "A spiritual monster. It had two goals—to remember what it had been, as Taltos memories inundated it—and to father a female with which to breed. I lost control of it almost immediately. I miscarried again and again as it drank my breasts dry. Only in the very beginning could I lure it into laboratories or hospitals, where, using my authority, I managed to accomplish some tests and secretly forward the material on to a laboratory in San Francisco.

"As the Heiress of the Legacy, I could draw all the money we needed from our foreign accounts, as long as I stayed one jump ahead of the family, which was searching for me. So the creature had the funds to drag me on a world odyssey. In the glen of Donnelaith, a torrent of memories came back to it. But it was soon desperate to get back to the States.

"I chose Houston as a city where we might settle and I could study it. Among hospitals and medical centers, I thought I could order the equipment for a laboratory and not be discovered. Unbeknownst to me this was perfect for the fiend. Having no luck with me, he was soon leaving me tied up, starved and near insane. Only much later did I learn that he was making the short journey to New Orleans to mate with random female Mayfairs. Of course his victims fatally miscarried, and were found dead in their own blood.

"The family was in a panic.

"Mayfair women began dying one after another. And they couldn't trace Rowan who had abandoned Michael for the fiend. And Rowan was now a prisoner. Soon Mayfair women everywhere were surrounded by armed guards. The creature came to First Street and almost gained access to Mona.

"But Mona, in the time of my desertion, had made love with Michael and was already carrying a Taltos child, though she didn't know it.

"At last, when I'd almost given up hope of life, I conceived another child of my own. And the child spoke to me. It said the very word 'Taltos.' It told me its name: Emaleth. It spoke of times its father couldn't remember. In the secret telepathic voice, I told it that when it was born it was to go to Michael in New Orleans. I told it about the house on First Street. If I should die, it must reach Michael with word of my death. We talked to each other in silence.

"Lasher was jubilant when he heard the child's voice! He would soon have his bride. It was then, as he softened to me, that I managed to escape. With the filthy clothes on my back I made for the highway.

"I never made it home. They found me comatose in a roadside park, bleeding from an apparent miscarriage. No one dreamed I'd given birth to Emaleth, and she, poor orphan, unable to rouse me or draw more milk from me, had started her long trek to New Orleans on foot.

"I was rushed home. In the hospital they had to remove my organs to stop the hemorrhaging. It probably saved me from the wasting sickness that later almost destroyed Mona. But my brain had been severely damaged. I remained in a deep coma.

"I was unconscious upstairs when Lasher, dressed as a priest, slipped past the guards and into this house, and appealed to the Talamasca and to Michael to let him live. After all, was he not a priceless specimen? He counted on the Talamasca to save him. He poured out a tale of his former life. It's a fascinating study of the innocence of the Taltos. But Lasher wasn't innocent. Lasher had brought death. Michael fought him and killed him. And so his long rule of the Mayfair family came to an end. I was still comatose when Emaleth came and bent to give me her healing milk.

"When I woke and saw the Taltos daughter I had birthed, and realized I was drinking from her breast, I was horrified. This gangly creature with a baby face terrified me. It was a moment of dislocated lucidity.

And here I was nursing from the creature as if I were a helpless baby. I grabbed the bedside gun. I killed her. I did that. I destroyed her. That quick and she was no more."

She shook her head. She looked away as we do when we sink into the past. Guilt, loss . . . her pain seemed beyond these words.

"It didn't have to happen," she murmured. "What had she done but make her way to the house as I had taught her? What had she done but brought me back to consciousness with her plentiful milk? One lone female Taltos. How could she hurt me? It was the loathing of Lasher that warped my mind. It was the revulsion at this alien species and my own atavistic behavior.

"And so she died, my girl. And there were two graves beneath this oak. And I, risen from the coma, a monster now myself, buried her." She sighed. "My lost girl," she said. "I had betrayed her."

Quiet. Even the garden was hushed. The low roar of a passing car seemed as natural as a breeze stirring the trees.

I was suspended in Rowan's sadness.

Stirling's eyes were moist and aglow in the shadows as he studied Rowan. Michael said not a word.

Then Mona spoke very gently.

"There was trouble in the Talamasca," she said. "It all had to do with the Taltos. Some members had tried to get control of Lasher. They'd even done murder. Michael and Rowan took off for Europe to try to investigate the corruption inside the Order. They felt a familial tie with the Talamasca. We all did. And during that time, I realized I was pregnant. My child began to grow out of control. It began to speak to me. It told me its name was Morrigan." Her voice broke. "I was enchanted, crazed."

"I went south to Fontevrault plantation house where Dolly Jean was living, and she and Mary Jane Mayfair, my cousin, my friend who later ran away, she and Dolly Jean, they helped me to give birth to Morrigan. It was really, really painful. And beyond scary. But Morrigan was tall and beautiful. No one could look at Morrigan and not say she was beautiful. She was shining and fresh and magical."

Dolly Jean gave a little cackle in her half sleep. "She knew a whole jumble of human things," she said. "Just a real beastie!"

"You loved her at the time," said Mona, "you know you did."

"I'm not saying I didn't," said Dolly Jean, squinting at Mona, "but what do you make of somebody who tells you she's going to take over the whole family and make it a clan of Walking Babies? Was I supposed to be tickled at that?"

"She was just born!" said Mona softly. "She didn't know what she meant. She had my ambition, my dreams."

"I don't know where she is," said Rowan in her deep heartfelt voice. "I don't know whether she's alive or dead."

Mona was deeply miserable, but I had so shamed her over her tears that she held them back painfully. I tried to take her hand. She drew away.

"But you knew the Taltos who came and took her!" Mona said to Rowan. "You had met him in Europe. He had heard the story of you and Lasher in your wanderings." She turned to me. "That's what happened. He had found them. Yes, another one, an ancient survivor. He was their friend. Of course, they didn't tell me and they didn't tell Morrigan. Oh no, we were children! They kept it to themselves! Imagine. An ancient one. Hadn't I suffered enough to be told about him? And when he came here, they let him take my daughter away."

"How could I have stopped them?" asked Rowan. "You were with us," she said to Mona. "Morrigan was maddened by the scent of the male on our clothes, on the gifts we'd received from him. And why he came, we'll never know. All we know is what you know. He was out in the garden. She went to the window. She ran out to him. There was no stopping either of them. We never saw them again."

"Mona, we searched for him by every conceivable means," said Michael. "Surely you must believe us."

"I want the files," said Mona, "the paperwork. His name, the names of his companies in New York. He was a rich man, a powerful man, this ancient wise one. You admitted that much."

"I'll be glad to give it to you," said Rowan, "but please understand, he liquidated everything. He vanished."

"If only you'd searched right away," Mona said bitterly.

"Mona, you agreed with us at the time," said Rowan. "We would wait until they contacted us. We respected their choice to be together. We didn't think they would simply disappear. We couldn't imagine it."

"We were afraid of hearing from them," said Michael. "We had no idea how they could multiply or survive in the modern world, how Ash could control them."

"Ash was the name of the man," I said.

"Yes," said Michael. His pain opened up as he spoke. "Ash Templeton. Ash *was* ancient. He had been alone for so long it was unimaginable. He'd seen his species become extinct. He was the one who told us the history of the Taltos. He believed that the Taltos couldn't survive in the world of humans. After all, he'd seen them wiped out. His was a tragic history. Of course, as we listened to his stories we had no idea that Morrigan even existed. We left Ash in New York. We loved him. We pledged eternal friendship. Then we got home and discovered Morrigan."

"Maybe it was some telepathic sense that guided him to Morrigan," I said.

"We don't know," said Rowan. "But he came here, he entered the side garden, he saw her through the windows, and she picked up his scent and she ran to him."

"For years we were afraid," said Michael. "We combed the news services for any story that might involve the Taltos. We were on the alert and so was the Talamasca. Mona, you must think back to the time before you were so sick. You must remember. We were afraid because we knew that the species might do great harm to human beings."

"Well put!" said Dolly Jean. "And Morrigan all fired up to rule the world, preaching that her vision came from her human father and mother. When she wasn't looking back she was looking ahead, or dancing in circles or sniffing at scents, she was a wild beastie."

"Oh hush up, Dolly Jean, please," whispered Mona, biting her lower lip, "you know you loved her. And all of you—I wanted to look for them long before you did. For years you wouldn't tell me that name. Oh, just leave it in your hands. Leave it in the hands of Mayfair and Mayfair. And now you say it as if it's nothing. Ash Templeton. Ash Templeton." She started to cry.

"That's not true," said Michael. "I acknowledged this creature as my daughter. You know I did. We began to search before we told you about it. We didn't know how sick you would get." His voice was raw, but he swallowed and moistened his dried lips with his tongue, and then he continued: "We didn't know yet how badly you would need the Taltos milk. We only learned that in time. But we tried to contact Ash, and we discovered that he had sold all his holdings. He'd vanished from the banks, the stock exchanges, the world markets."

"Whatever his feelings for us," Rowan said, "he chose to disappear. He chose to keep his future secret."

Mona was sobbing against Quinn. It broke Michael's heart to see it. Stirling spoke up, his voice assuming a reverent authority:

"Mona," he said, "the Talamasca began to search for Ash and Morrigan almost immediately. We tried to do it in an unobtrusive way. But we searched. We found some evidence that they had visited Donnelaith. But after that, the trail went cold. And please believe me now when I tell you again: we've never found the slightest trace of them anywhere."

"That's actually quite surprising," I said.

"I'm not speaking to you," cried Mona, glaring at me and then drawing close to Quinn as if she was afraid of me.

"Some evidence of them should have turned up," I said, "no matter what happened to them."

"That's what I've always thought," said Michael. "For two, three years we lived in dread of their surfacing in some catastrophic way. I can't tell you all my fears. I thought: what if the young ones bred out of control? What if they rose up against Ash? What if they committed murders? And then when we stopped living in fear and started to search, nothing."

Dolly Jean chuckled again, bringing up her shoulders and letting her head sink down and rocking back and forth. "Walking Babies can kill humans easy as humans can kill Walking Babies. They could be breeding somewhere, breeding like fire, spreading in all directions, hiding in the valleys and the hills, in the mountains and on the plains, traveling over land and sea, and then comes the ringing of a loud bell, and they all walk out all over the world at the same time and they shoot one human being apiece, bang, and they take over the entire planet!"

"Save that for Tante Oscar," said Rowan under her breath with a cool lift of her eyebrows.

(I winked at Dolly Jean. She nodded and wagged her finger.)

Michael looked directly at Mona and leaned in towards her as he addressed her.

"I hope we've given you what you need," he said. "As for the files, I'll see that they're all copied and delivered to you wherever you like. They'll prove our efforts to track down every lead. We'll give you every scrap of paper we have on Ash Templeton."

"Of course," said Dolly Jean, "they could both be stone-cold dead in the grave like Romeo and Juliet! Two Walking Babies all wrapped up in each other's arms, just rotting away somewhere to cartilage. Like maybe he couldn't stand her ranting and raving and all her plans, and he tied a silk stocking around her neck and—."

"Stop it, Dolly Jean!" cried Mona. "Don't you say another word or I'll scream!"

"You're screaming now, be still!" whispered Quinn.

In my heart of hearts I entered into a debate with myself, and then I spoke:

"I'll find them," I said quietly.

I startled everyone.

Mona turned to me resentfully. "Just what do you mean by that!" she demanded. Her handkerchief was full of blood tears.

I looked at her as disdainfully as I could, considering how tender and pretty she was, and how wicked and fiendish I was, and then I looked across the table at Rowan.

"I want to thank you all for sharing your secrets with us," I said. I looked at Michael. "You've trusted us, and treated us as if we were sinless and kind, and I don't know that we are. But I know that we try to be."

A slow broad smile lit up Rowan's face, extraordinary to behold. "Sinless and kind," she repeated. "How marvelous are those words. If only I could work them into a hymn and sing it under my breath day and night, day and night. . . ."

We looked at each other.

"Give me a little time. If they still exist, if they've parented a colony, if they're anywhere in the wide world, I know those who will know where they are—without question."

Rowan raised her eyebrows and looked off thoughtfully, and the smile came again—a lamp of loveliness. She nodded.

Michael seemed vaguely stimulated by my words, and Stirling was curious and respectful.

"Sure enough," said Dolly Jean, without opening her eyes, "you didn't think he was the oldest Blood Child in the world, did you? And you mark my words," she said to me, "you big old great thing, you sure are pretty as an angel, and you've got plenty charm enough to be a gangster. I've seen every gangster movie ever made three times and I know what I'm talking about. They put a little boot black on your hair, you could play Bugsy Siegel."

"Thank you," I replied soberly. "It was always my ambition to play

Sam Spade, actually. I was all alone and forlorn when the *Black Mask* magazine first published *The Maltese Falcon*. I read the novel by the light of the moon. Sam Spade captured my ambition."

"Well, no wonder you talk like a gangster," said Dolly Jean. "But Sam Spade's small time. Go for Bugsy Siegel or Lucky Luciano."

"Stop this!" screamed Mona. "Don't you realize what he's just said?" She was painfully confused, trying to crush her sobs, trying to crush her rage against me. "You can really do this?" she asked in a little bewildered voice. "You can find Ash and Morrigan?"

I didn't answer. Let her suffer for a night.

I rose from the table. I bent to kiss Rowan on the cheek. My hand found hers and held it tight for a small, heated moment. *A precious garden closed against me, is my sister, my beloved bride.* Her fingers caught mine and held them with all her strength.

The gentlemen had risen to see me off. I murmured my superficial farewells, and only then did the secret grip release me.

I walked slowly into the formal garden beyond the pool, and would have gone up into the roaring clouds, to be as far away from the Earth as I could be. But Mona's piteous cry rang behind me.

"Lestat, don't leave me!"

Across the lawn she came running, her silk dress billowing.

"Oh, you miserable girl!" I said, deliberately gnashing my teeth. I received her in my embrace, sweet bundle of panting limbs. "You intolerable witch. You wicked undisciplined Blood Child. You contemptible pupil. You worsling, you rebellious and obstinate fledgling."

"I adore you with my whole soul, you're my creator, my mentor, my guardian, I love you," she cried. "You have to forgive me!"

"No, I don't," I said. "But I will. Go take a proper leave of your family. I'll see you tomorrow night. I must be alone now."

Off to the deepest pocket of the garden I went—

—and thence to the clouds, and the merciless unknowing stars, and as far from mortaldom as I could get.

"Maharet," I called out to the very most ancient one, "Maharet, I've made promises to those I love. Help me to keep them. Lend your most powerful ear to those whom I love. Lend your most powerful ear to me."

Where was she, the tower of ivory? The great ancestor. The one who now and then came to our aid. I had no clue, because I had never bent my stiff neck to go in search of her. But I knew that in her centuries of endurance she had acquired powers that surpassed all dreams and fears of mine, and that she could hear me if she chose. Maharet, our guardian, our mother, listen to my plea.

I sang the song of the tall ones, the long-extinct ones, come again to form a colony, lost somewhere in the modern world. Gentle beings, out of time, out of place, and maybe out of luck. And of such tragic import to my fledgling and her human kindred. Don't make me say so much that other immortals might gather up my intent and use it to bad ends. Hear me, Sweet Maharet, wherever you are. Surely you know this world as no one else knows it. Have you spied these tall children? I don't dare to say their name.

And then I wrapped myself in comforting phantasms, roaming the winds for my own sake, dissolved now and then in the poetry of love, and envisioning bowers of love, places of Divine safety foreordained beyond Good and Evil, where I and the one I coveted could dwell. It was a doomed vision and I knew it, but it was mine to enjoy.

19

POST SUNSET. First taste of autumn in the warm air.

Mona and Quinn appeared at the garden doors five minutes after I'd called them. Every man on the dimly lit hotel terrace turned to check out the daring beauty with the flowing red hair. Whoa, short sequined job with straps, hem above her knees, and the audacious heels making her naked calf muscles flex, yes, hmmm, and Quinn in minutely tailored khaki and dress shirt and red tie, was her dazzling escort.

I'd been hanging back on the outskirts of the thick sinister little party, scanning one mind after another, letting the hubbub crash against me, smelling the perfume of the cigarette smoke, hot blood and male cologne, and grooving now and then on the pure avarice and cynicism of the group.

Speakers all around poured out a low thumping steel-band music that came on like a collective heartbeat.

The subject was women, Russian women, imported through the young arrogant pimp—slick brown hair, fashionably emaciated, Armani jacket, shiny enthusiastic face, who worked his guests, buyers all, in methamphetamine fits and starts, bragging about the "white flesh, the blond hair, the freshness, the class" he had coming in from his connections in Moscow and St. Petersburg. "You've never seen so much white gash."

The trade was so rich they could replace the girls every six months; we pass them on down the line, don't you worry, how was that for a guarantee? "I'm talking crème de la crème, I'm talking girls who'll score a thousand a half-hour, we package with clothes or without, I'm talking unbroken flow to point of purchase—." Slam. He'd seen Mona.

She and Quinn caught up with me. Buzz on her thickening. She was the only woman on the terrace. What gives? Was she the door prize?

I narrowed in on the pimp, and the big rawboned oversold body-guard who was hovering around him, a drone in a badly cut dinner jacket with traces of white powder on his lapels. Drug slobs. All of them drug slobs.

"We're going to do it right here," I said in a whisper. Mona let out a cool laugh. Look at those naked arms. Whiff of cedar to the dress. Aunt Queen's closets. Quinn only smiled, sharpened for the hunt.

The music thumped and went into Brazilian jazz samba.

Even the white-jacketed waiters passing everywhere with little bits of ridiculous food and splashing glasses of champagne were high. The bald-headed man from Dallas pushed his way to the pimp: how much for the redhead? He wanted a right to top anybody's price, "hear me?" They were all giving him the word in passing whispers, and he was now staring at me full-time. A guy from Detroit with beautiful white hands was murmuring on about how he'd put her up in a pad in Miami Beach and give her anything she wanted, girl like that, you couldn't let this business dumb you down to where—.

I smiled at the pimp. I had my elbows on the black iron fence behind me, heel hooked on the lower bar, violet sunglasses down. Purple turtleneck, formal cut, butter-soft black leather suit coat and pants, how I love my own clothes. Mona and Quinn were dancing just a little, back and forth, Mona humming to the music.

The pimp sidled over, throwing sharp highly personal smiles here and there like cheap necklaces at Mardi Gras. On my right side (she was on my left) he said, "Give you a hundred grand for her now, no questions asked, got the cash in my coat."

"What if she doesn't go for it?" I asked, eyes on the shifting clattering party. Sudden smell of caviar, cheeses, fresh fruits, hmmm.

"I'll take care of that," he said, with a scornful laugh. "You just take the other guy and leave her here."

"And later on?" I asked.

"There is no later on. Don't you know who I am?" He felt sorry for me. "You're fancy but you're stupid. Two hundred thousand for her. Take it or leave it. Five seconds. No more."

I burst into a soft laugh.

I looked into his heartless frenzied eyes. Pupils enormous. Harvard Law School, drug trade, female slavery. Up and up and down and down. He flashed his glossy perfectly bleached teeth. "You should have asked around about me," he said. "Want a job? I'll teach you so much people will think you're smart."

"Let's rock, baby," I said. I slipped my hand under his left armpit and gently swung him around so that he hit the fence between me and Mona. I bent over and covered his mouth with my left hand before he could make a sound. She pivoted and opened her lips on his throat, her hair a perfect veil of privacy.

I felt the life drawn out of his frail limbs, heard her gasping swallows, his whole frame giving one full spasm.

"Leave him alive," I whispered. Who was I kidding?

Hand on my shoulder. I looked up. The big stupid-eyed bodyguard, almost too stoned to know why he was suspicious or what to do about it, yeah right, but Quinn was already drawing him away and had him paralyzed, the guy with his broad hunched back to the press of the party and Quinn drawing quietly and slowly for the blood. What does that look like, that he's whispering in the dude's ear? Most likely.

The laughing, gulping, gurgling crowd rolled on, a waiter nearly stepping on me with his precarious tray. "No thanks, I don't need a drink," I said, which was true.

But I liked the pale yellow color of the champagne in those glasses. And I liked the spattering and burbling and dancing of the water in the fountain in the middle of the crowd, and I liked the pure rectangular lights of all the hotel windows climbing and climbing in beauteous parallel rows above us to the rosy sky, and I liked the low raw saxophone of the jazz samba dancing with itself, and I liked the fluttering of the leaves in the potted trees, which everyone on the terrace ignored but me. I liked—.

The dazed bodyguard staggered. An underling caught his arm, scheming and proud to have him at a disadvantage. The pimp was dead. Oops. Such a brilliant career slumped over the fence. Mona's eyes were electric. Drugs in the blood.

"Get the host a chair," I said to the first waiter I could snare. "I think he's overdosed and he's holding."

"Oh MaGod!" Half the drinks on his tray crashed into the other half. Customers turning, murmuring. After all, the host had slipped down to the tile floor. Not so good for the slave trade.

Out of there.

Luscious gloom of hotel mezzanine floor, marble and golden lights, mirrored elevator, swoosh of doors, glowing fields of carpet, gift shop full of pink stuffed monsters, heavy glass, outside pavements, filth, shrieks of tourist laughter, innocent and deodorized half-naked people of all ages in wrinkle-free scraps of brightly dyed clothing, paper trash in the gutters, glorious heat, screeching roar of the crowded St. Charles Street car rounding the bend onto Canal.

So many . . . many good people . . . so very happy.

20

W E WERE BACK at the flat. Rear parlor. My darlings on
the couch. The drugs in their blood had played out on
the walk back. Me at the desk but facing them.

I told her to change clothes. That short sequined dress was just
too damned distracting. And we had some heavy matters to address
immediately.

"Are you serious!" she demanded. "You're not honestly telling me
what I can and cannot wear, you don't for one minute think I'm going
to listen to this, this is not the eighteenth century, baby. I don't know
what castle *you* grew up in, but I assure you I don't change my mode of
dress for feudal lords, no matter—."

"Beloved Boss, could you not simply ask Mona to change her dress
instead of telling her!" said Quinn with restrained exasperation.

"Yeah, what about that!" she said, leaning forward, accentuating
her cleavage swelling under the sequined band across her breasts.

"Mona, my darling," I said with perfect candor, "*ma chérie*, my
beauty, please change into something less fetching. I find it hard to
think, for you are so lovely in that dress. Forgive me. I lay my shameful
omnisensual impulses at your feet. A tribute. I, having spent two centuries in the Blood, should possess a wisdom and restraint that makes
such a request unnecessary, but alas, within my heart I feed a human
flame that it may never completely go out, and it is the heat of this
flame which distracts me now and renders me so powerless in your
presence."

She narrowed her eyes and puckered her brows. Exploring me as best she could for mockery. Finding none. Then her lower lip began to tremble.

"Can you really help me find Morrigan?" she asked.

"I don't talk till you change the dress," I replied.

"You're a bully and a tyrant!" she said. "You treat me like a child or a slut. I won't change it. Will you help me find Morrigan or not? Now make up your mind."

"You're the one who has to make up her mind. You act like a child and a slut. You have no dignity, no gravitas! No mercy! We have things to discuss before we get to the finding of Morrigan. You didn't behave very well last night. Now change your clothes, before I change them for you."

"You dare touch me!" she said. "You liked it well enough when every human being at that party turned to look at me. What don't you like about this dress now?"

"Take it off!" I said. "It's needlessly distracting."

"And if you think you're going to preach to me about the way I behaved with my family. . . ."

"That's just it, they're not simply your family now. There's infinitely more to it, and you know it. You're forfeiting your intelligence for cheap emotional outbursts. You abused your powers last night, your singular advantages. Now change that dress."

"And what are you going to do if I don't change it!"

Her eyes were blazing.

I was flabbergasted.

"Have you forgotten that this is my flat?" I said. "That I am the one who has made you welcome here! That you exist because of me!"

"Go on, throw me out!" she declared. Her whole face went red. She shot to her feet and leaned over me, her eyes on fire.

"You know what I did last night after you left us and went away just because you were oh, so in love with Rowan! Oh, so very in love with *La Doctor Dolorosa*. Well, guess what! I read your books, your maudlin mawkish melancholy Vampire Chronicles, and I can see why your fledglings despise you! You treated Claudia like a doll just 'cause she had the body of a child! And what was that all about, making a child a vampire in the first place?—"

"Stop it, how dare you!"

"And your own mother, you give her the Dark Gift, and then you try to stop her from cutting her long hair or wearing men's clothes, and this in the eighteenth century, when women have to go around looking like wedding cakes, you're an autocratic monster!"

"You insult me, you abuse me! If you don't stop—."

"And I know why you're so fired up over Rowan, she's the first adult female other than your own mother who's ever caught your attention for more than five minutes, and Hello! Lestat Discovers The Opposite Sex! Yeah, females do come in grown-up sizes! And I happen to be one of them, and this is not the Garden of Eden, and I am not taking off this dress!"

Quinn got to his feet. "Lestat, wait, please!"

"Get out!" I roared. I stood up. My heart was cut so deep I could hardly talk. I felt that stinging hurt again all over my skin, the hurt I'd felt when Rowan had been railing at me at the Retreat House, an enervating, crippling pain.

"Out of my house, you wretched little ingrate," I shouted, "get out now before I throw you down the steps! You're a Power Slut, that's what you are, using every edge your sex or youth can give you, a moral lilliputian in grown-up shoes, a career adolescent, a professional child! You don't know the meaning of philosophical insight, or spiritual engagement, or true growth—. Out, out of here now, Heiress to the Mayfair Legacy, what a fiasco that must have been, go beat up on your mortal family at First Street, rave at them until you drive them out of their minds and they crack you over the head with their shovel and bury you alive in the backyard!"

"Lestat, I beg you—." Quinn put his hands out.

I was too angry. "Take her to Blackwood Farm!"

"Nobody's taking me anywhere!" she cried. She ran out the door, hair whirling, sequins sparkling, slamming the door shut. Clatter down the iron steps.

Quinn shook his head. He was in silent tears. "This just shouldn't have happened," he whispered. "It was entirely avoidable. You don't understand, she's not even accustomed to being out of a sickbed, to putting one foot in front of the other, to putting one word after another—."

"It was inevitable," I said. I was shaking. "It's why I gave her the Dark Gift instead of you, so the anger would come at me, don't you see? But how could she attack so violently the things that have happened to me! She has no moral modulation, no moral rhythm, no moral patience, no moral kindness. She's a pitiless little hellion! I don't know what I'm saying. Go after her. She's so blatantly and arrogantly careless! Just go."

"Please, please," he said, "don't let this be a split between us."

"Not between you and me," I said, "no, never. Just go."

I could hear her sobs from the courtyard.

I stormed out onto the balcony. "You get off my property!" I shouted down to her. She was glowing in the dark. "Don't you dare stand there weeping in my courtyard. I won't have it! Get out!" I came down the steps.

She fled from me down the carriageway. "Quinn!" she wailed. "Quinn!" as if I was murdering her. "Quinn, Quinn," she squealed.

He brushed against me as he passed me.

I turned around and went up the steps. I clung to the balcony railing for a long moment, forcing some calm upon myself, my hands trembling, but it did little good.

As soon as I'd closed the door I saw Julien out of the corner of my eye. I tried again to quell my pounding heart. I refused to tremble. I collected myself, eyes roving the ceiling, ready for the next cheap diatribe to be flung in my face.

"*Eh bien*," he said, going on in French, his arms folded, his dinner jacket very black against the damask striped wallpaper. "You've done a fine job, *Monsieur*, haven't you? You've fallen deep in love with a mortal who'll never yield to you, only succeeding in driving a true rivet into her heart which her innocent husband won't fail to detect sooner or later. And now my innocent niece, whom you've so cleverly brought over into your world, is running rampant through the streets with a boy lover who hasn't a clue as to how to comfort her or contain her mounting madness. You are a fine example of the Ancien Régime, *Monsieur*, oh, but I should be calling you Chevalier, should I not? Or, what precisely was your title, anyway? Was there something lower?"

I sighed, and then slowly I smiled. I wasn't shaking too badly.

"*Les bourgeois* have always disappointed me," I said gently. "My father's title means nothing to me. That it means so much to you is tiresome. Why don't we let the matter drop?"

I took my chair at the desk, caught the heel of my shoe on the rung and just looked at the ghost admiringly. Flawless white shirt. Patent leather shoes. Now, he knows how to dress, doesn't he? In my exhaustion and my grief for what had just taken place with Mona, I looked into his eyes and I prayed silently to Saint Juan Diego. What is there that can come of this that might be good?

"Oh?" he asked. "You've come to be fond of me?"

"Where's Stella?" I asked. "I want to see Stella."

"You do?" he asked, arching his eyebrows and tipping his forehead slightly.

"I don't like to be alone," I said, "as much as I give out. And I don't want to be alone at this moment."

He lost his look of resolute superiority. Grim gaze. He'd been a handsome man in his time, trim white curls, clever black eyes.

"Sorry to disappoint you," I said. "But since you do go and come as you will, it seems I must get used to you."

"You think I like what I do?" he asked with sudden bitterness.

"I don't think you know much about what you do," I replied. "Maybe we have that in common. I've been hearing about you. Rather ominous things, it seems."

Blank expression, then a slow yield to appraisal.

I heard a skipping step in the hall, definitely a child skipping. And there she came into the room, in a snow white dress, with her white sox and her black Mary Janes, a darling girl.

"Hello, Ducky, you have the most amazing digs," she said. "I simply love your paintings. This is the first time I've had a chance to look at them. I love the soft colors. I love the sailboats and all the agreeable people, people in lovely long dresses. There's a sweetness to these paintings. If I weren't a little girl, I'd suspect that they soothe people's nerves."

"I can't claim to have chosen them myself," I replied, "someone else did. But now and then I add one or more to the collection. I like the brighter, stronger colors. I like the greater, more savage force."

"What do you intend to do about all this?" asked Julien, plainly irritated by this exchange.

My heart had begun to assume its normal rhythm.

"About all what?" I asked. "And let me assure you that your mixing in it isn't a good omen, from what I've learnt. Seems some of your mortal descendants believe you're doomed to failure in all your Earthly visitations, did you know that? It's a special curse visited upon you, apparently, or so I'm told."

Stella had plopped into a Louis XV chair, her white dress going poof all around her. She looked up at Julien with alarm.

"You do me a bitter injustice," he said coldly. "You can't know my accomplishments. And only very few of my descendants know them either. Now let's get back to your present obligation. Certainly you don't intend to let my niece run rampant with the powers you've given her."

I laughed. "I told you before," I said, "that if you want her, you will have to tell her. Why are you so afraid of her? Or is it that she won't acknowledge you? That she's completely unreceptive? That she's off on a supernatural tear and you're small potatoes to her now, hmmm?"

His face became hard.

"You're not fooling me, not for a moment," he said. "You're cut to the quick by Mona's words, you're cut to the quick by Rowan, that you can't have her, no matter how much harm you try to do to her. You're paying for your sins. You're paying now as we speak. You're terrified you'll never see either of them again. And maybe you won't. And maybe if you do, they'll show you a defiance that will demoralize you even more truly than you're demoralized now. Come, Stella. Let's leave this mountebank to his nightmares. I tire of his company."

"Oncle Julien, I don't want to leave!" she said. "These are new shoes and I love them. Besides, I find Lestat charming. Ducky, you must forgive Oncle Julien. Death has had the most oppressive effect upon him. When he was alive, he would never have said such things!"

She bounced to the floor, ran to me and threw her soft little arms around me and kissed my cheek.

"Bye, Lestat," she said.

"*Au revoir,* Stella."

And then the room was empty.

Perfectly empty.

I turned, disconsolate and shuddering, and put my head down on my arm, as if I could go to sleep on my desk.

"Ah, Maharet," I said, naming again our great ancestor, our mother, one who was for all I knew on the opposite side of the globe. "Ah, Maharet, what have I done and what can I do? Help me! Let my voice reach you over the miles." I closed my eyes. Once again, I used the very strongest of my telepathic power. *I have such need of you. I come to you ashamed of my failures. I come to you as the Brat Prince of the Blood Drinkers. I don't claim to be anything better or worse. Listen to me. Help me. Help me for the sake of others. I beg you. Hear my prayer.*

I was in this dark frame of mind, alone with this message, which engaged my soul completely, when I heard a step on the iron stairs outside.

Knock at the door.

My guard from the gate: "It's Clem from Blackwood Farm out front."

"How in the world did he find this address?" I asked.

"Well, he's looking for Quinn, says they need Quinn back there right away. Seems he's been up to the Mayfair house looking for Quinn and they sent him over here."

I might as well hang out a tasteful neon sign.

Now I had an immediate and mundane use for my telepathy: scan the blocks around for the Dazzling Duo and relay this message to Quinn.

Zap: nothing to it.

Quinn and Mona were in a small café on Jackson Square, Mona sobbing into an immense heap of paper napkins, Quinn enfolding her and hiding her from the world.

Gotcha. Tell Clem to meet me at Chartres and St. Ann. And please, Lestat, I beg you, come with me.

Meet you at Blackwood Farm, sweet boy.

Eh bien, so after the proper messages were conveyed to Clem, who was presiding over the choking, wheezing, seething limousine outside in the Rue Royale, at least I had a moment of stillness in which to think, and then a destination.

And I was NOT riding over the lake in the car with that unforgivable Valkyrie in her sequined chemise! I would take to the clouds, thank you.

I went outside.

That twinge of autumn again in my beloved heat. I didn't so much like it. I fretted the winter coming on. But what was all this to me with my broken heart, and illegitimate soul, and what *had* I done to Rowan with my furtive, disgraceful whispers? And Michael, that powerful and soft-spoken Michael, who had trusted me with his wife's heart, what had I done to him?

And how could Mona say such hurtful things, how could she? And how could I have behaved so childishly in response?

I closed my eyes.

I cleared my mind of all distractions and random images.

Again I spoke only to Maharet. Wherever you are, I need you.

And now came some artifice—to describe once more my needs without casting to the winds unnecessary details for every other immortal who might pick up my message and ponder the precise nature of what I sought. *To find a tribe of tall beings, tender of bone, ancient, simple, tangled with my fledgling, unknown to the world of records, history and location essential to the sanity of those I love. Guidance. Mistakes I've made with my fledgling, spiraling out of control. Give to me your wisdom, your keen hearing, your vision. Where are the tall creatures? I am your loyal subject. More or less. I send my love.*

Would she answer? I didn't know. In all honesty (yeah, like all the rest of this is a pack of lies?), I had only once, years ago, called out to her for help, and she had not answered me. However, I'd been guilty of the most ridiculous blunder at the time. I'd switched bodies with a mortal, and been abandoned by him. Idiocy. I had to go after my own supernatural body and recover it. And on my own—well, almost on my own—I'd found a solution to my problem. And so it had ended well.

But I had seen her since, this mysterious ancestor, when she did come to my aid of her own volition, and she had taken great pains with me. She'd forgiven my ranting and raving and my temper. I'd described her in my writings, and she had borne it. From me, she'd borne many things.

Perhaps she had heard me last night. Perhaps she would hear me now.

If nothing came of the call, I would try again. And again. And if her silence continued, I would call to others. I would enlist Marius, my sometime mentor, and wise Child of the Millennia. And if that failed, I would scan the Earth on my own for the Taltos, be they one or many.

I knew I had to make good on my promise to find the Taltos—for Michael and for Rowan, my precious Rowan, even if Mona utterly deserted me, which was most likely the case.

Yes, I felt my heart shrinking. I had already somehow lost Mona. And soon Quinn would follow. And precisely how I'd done it, I really didn't grasp.

Somewhere in the back of my conscious was taking shape the horrid realization that a modern-minded fledgling was as complex as a nuclear reactor, a communications satellite, a Pentium 4 computer, a microwave oven, a cell phone and all the other intricate overarching newfangled creations I couldn't understand. Of course, it was all a matter of exploding sophistication.

Or mystification.

Vixen. I hated her. That's why I was crying my own blood tears, wasn't it? Well, there was nobody to see it.

Eh bien, it was on to Blackwood Farm, and as I ascended I prayed to Maharet. Maharet was my prayer of the winds all the way there.

BLACKWOOD MANOR WAS LIT UP like a lantern in the rural dark, doors thrown open on the front porch, floodlights on, Jasmine sitting on the steps crying with a white handkerchief, knees up, black heels, navy blue sheath, chocolate skin and bleached curls looking lovely as was routine, her crying brokenhearted and exhausting and terribly sad.

"Oh, Les-Dot, help me, help me!" she cried. "Where is Quinn? Where is Little Boss? I need him. I'm going out of my mind! And that boy's running rampant. Nash doesn't believe in ghosts, Tommy's scared to death of them, and Grandma's sending for the priest to drive the Devil out of me! As if it was my doing!"

I walked up to her, picked her up, with her utter soft silky willingness, and carried her inside. She lay her head against my chest.

The front room was full of people.

"The car's turning into the drive," I said, "what's wrong?"

We sat down on the living room couch, me with her in my lap. I patted her. She was really drained and miserable.

"I'm so glad you're here," she cried, "we've been so alone out here."

Little Tommy Blackwood, aged thirteen, Quinn's uncle by blood, sat in one of the chairs opposite and watched me in a really formal sort of way, his fingers on one arm of the chair. He was a truly marvelous young man, much as Quinn had described, and from his travels with Aunt Queen and the all too human Quinn in Europe, he had imbibed an entire attitude towards life which would stand him in good stead always.

Cool to see him again.

Nash Penfield, his tutor, was there also, attired in an impeccable herringbone suit, a man who seemed born to have a calming effect on others, though why he could not calm Jasmine I wasn't certain. He seemed puzzled as he stood near to Tommy's chair, eying Jasmine with profound concern, and nodding to me respectfully.

Big Ramona, Jasmine's grandmother, sat glowering near the couch, in a somber wine-colored gabardine dress with an ornate diamond pin just below her right shoulder. Big Ramona's hair was brushed back artfully to a twist on the back of her head, and she was wearing stockings and fancy black shoes.

"Oh hush up, girl," Big Ramona said at once to Jasmine, "you're just drawing attention to yourself. Sit up straight! Stop talking like a fool!"

Two of the Shed Men, still in their work clothes, were standing awkwardly behind her. One of them was cheerful Allen, with the round face and white hair. I didn't know the name of the other one. Correct. Yes I did. Joel.

And nobody said anything after Big Ramona bawled out Jasmine.

Before I could begin a mind search, Quinn came into the room, and Mona, the sequined harpy, went on back the hall like a streak of silver light, and into Aunt Queen's bedroom. Aunt Queen's bedroom was the only bedroom on the main floor.

A ripple of interest and wonder went through the assembly as to Mona's presence and Mona's appearance, but nobody had gotten a really good look at her. The insolent little monster.

It was Quinn who mattered here. He sat opposite me just inside the huge hallway door. His characteristic innocence slowly alchemized into a gentlemanly air of command as he scanned the gathering. Then he rose to his feet quickly as Cyndy, the Nurse, came in, looking quite lovely in her starched white uniform, also quite tearful and sad, and took a chair far away, by the piano.

Next there appeared the sheriff, a rotund and jocular human being whom I'd met the night of Aunt Queen's death, followed by a person whom I identified at once as Grady Breen, the family lawyer, aged, portly and stuffed into a three-piece pinstriped suit, whom Quinn had described to me when he'd been telling me his life story.

"Whoa, this is quite serious," I said under my breath.

Jasmine was shuddering against me, and clinging to me. "Don't you let me go, Lestat," she said. "Don't you let me go. You don't know what's after me."

"Honey bunch, nothing can get you when you're with me," I whispered. With loving hands I tried to distract her from the fact that my body feels like a chunk of marble.

"Jasmine, get off that man's lap," whispered Big Ramona, "and start behaving like the Head Housekeeper here, where you are supposed to be! I tell you, the only thing holding some people back is their own selves!"

Jasmine did not obey.

The two official gentlemen found chairs in the shadows rather close to Cyndy, the Nurse, as though they didn't want to invade the family circle. The sheriff's belly poured over his belt, which was laden with weapons and a crackling walkie-talkie, which he silenced with embarrassed suddenness.

Jasmine put her left arm around me and hung on as though I were trying to release her, which I wasn't. I stroked her back and kissed her head. She was a delicious little person. Her long silky legs were stretched out to my left.

The fact that Quinn had once made love to her, fathered little Jerome by her, was suddenly uppermost in my heated evil ever-churning half-human half-vampiric mind. Indeed people's charms should not go to waste, that is my motto, may it never have dire consequences for the mortal world.

"If only I hadn't been so mean to her," Jasmine said. "She's never going to leave me alone." She ground her forehead against my chest. She tightened her grip. I closed my arm completely around her.

"You're just fine, honey bunch," I said.

"What in the world do you mean?" asked Quinn. He was deeply distressed to see Jasmine suffering. "Jasmine, what's going on? Somebody please bring me up to speed."

"So there's news of Patsy?" I asked. For that was clearly everybody's concern, and I was getting it in sputters and waves, whether I searched for it or not.

"Well, seems so," said Grady Breen. "But it seems to me that Big Ramona, well, what with Jasmine unable to talk, maybe you should tell the story."

"Who says I'm unable to talk!" Jasmine cried, head still bowed, body shuddering. "You think I can't tell you what I saw with my own eyes, coming right to the window of my bedroom, all soaked and wet and streaming with duckweed and swamp water; you think I don't know what I saw, that it was Patsy, you think I don't know Patsy's voice, when she said, 'Jasmine, Jasmine,' over and over again? You think I don't know it was a dead person who said, 'Jasmine, Jasmine,' over and over again? And me in that bed with little Jerome, and me scared to death he would wake up, and her clawing at the window with her red fingernails, saying, 'Jasmine, Jasmine,' in that pitiful voice?"

Quinn went bloodless with shock.

Cyndy, the Nurse, burst into tears. "She has to be buried in consecrated ground, I don't care what anyone says."

"Buried in consecrated ground!" said Big Ramona. "All we have of her is some of her hair pulled out of her hairbrush, what are you talking about, Cyndy? Are we going to bury a hairbrush, for the love of Heaven?"

Nash Penfield was so frustrated, I could feel it. I didn't have to read it from his thoughts. He had wanted to take charge for some time, for the sake of everyone. But he felt he had no authority to speak here.

Mona came clicking down the marble-tiled hall and appeared in the door, soberly dressed in a high-neck black dress with long sleeves and tight cuffs and a high hem, and black heels, calves once again flexed magnificently. She took a place to the left of Quinn. Her face was very sweet and serious, the little dissembler.

Everyone looked at her at once, even Jasmine, with a covert turn of her head, but no one knew what to make of it. I refused to even give her a glance. I have excellent peripheral vision.

"When did this ghost appear to you?" I asked at once to distract everyone from Mona and the inevitable questions about her transformation.

"Now tell the story from the start," said earnest and forthright Grady Breen, "as we are dealing with what constitute legal documents."

"What legal documents?" said Quinn patiently.

"Well," said Big Ramona, moving just a little bit forward in her chair, her dark face very commanding, "I think that everybody present knows that for years the ghost of William Blackwood has appeared often in this very room, pointing at that French desk there between the windows, and no one has ever known what to make of it. Quinn, you saw that ghost plenty times, and Jasmine, you did too. And I have to confess, as God is my witness, so did I, though I always said a Hail

Mary and the ghost went away like that, just like pinching out a candle flame. And when we opened up that desk, well, we always found nothing. Just nothing. And we put the key back into the cup in the kitchen, though why we so carefully kept locking up nothing I'm not the one to explain.

"But what you don't know is that right after you took Mona Mayfair out of here, Quinn, that is, right after your mother went missing, leaving all her medicine behind, the ghost started to appear again night and day! I'm telling you, all I had to do was to walk in this room and there was Grandpa William standing there pointing at that desk! And same held true for my grandchild Jasmine. Jasmine, sit up straight!"

(The desk in question was fancy Louis XV, with one central drawer, cabriole legs and much ornate ormolu.)

"Well, finally, Jasmine says to me she just can't stand this any longer, and she couldn't reach Quinn and she couldn't do her work, and neither could I, and then my boy Clem comes in here and even he sees this ghost, and so we decided, well, we were going to search that desk one more time, whether Quinn was here or not to give his permission. But before we had made up our minds that we were going to do this, Jasmine is laying up in the bed asleep with her blessed little boy, Jerome, and up to her window out there comes Patsy, yes, I'm telling you, Patsy, all full of swamp water and crying, 'Jasmine, Jasmine,' and scratching at the glass with her long painted fingernails, and Jasmine grabs up little Jerome and runs out of the house screaming!"

Jasmine nodded furiously, making of herself a tiny ball in my lap.

"Fact was," said Big Ramona, "Jasmine was the only one on this property who was ever kind to Patsy! Except for you, Cyndy, honey, but you didn't live here! And how's Patsy's ghost gonna crawl out of the swamp and find you all the way over in Mapleville? And then we told Grady Breen we were opening that desk, he best come on over here, because it was locked and the key was not in the cup in the kitchen after all these years of that key being in that cup in the kitchen, and we had to use a knife to get the desk open."

"That makes perfect sense," said Quinn agreeably.

Big Ramona cast her eyes in the direction of Grady Breen, a most respectful man, who now drew from his brown leather briefcase what appeared to be a sheaf of handwritten papers in a clear plastic folder.

"And when we opened the drawer of the desk," Big Ramona proceeded, "what did we find but Patsy's handwritten letters, saying that 'by the time you find this I will be dead,' and then going on to describe how she meant to go out into Sugar Devil Swamp and lean over the edge of the pirogue and shoot herself in the right side of her head so she'd fall in the water, and that not one scrap of her remains would be left to put in the family tomb next to her father on account of her hating him, which we all knew that she did."

"She was so sick," cried Cyndy, the Nurse. "She was in pain. She didn't know what she was doing, God help her."

"Yes, indeed," said Grady, "and fortunately, well, no, not fortunately, but, conveniently, well, no, not conveniently, but coincidentally, Patsy had been arrested many times for drug possession and her fingerprints were on file, and so we were able to match up the prints on these pages with her prints, and also this is her handwriting—." Grady rose and hurried across the room and presented the plastic cache to a stunned and silent Quinn—"and she did write about ten drafts of her letter, as she apparently wasn't satisfied, even with the very last, when she apparently jumped the . . . I mean when she finally decided to go out there and execute her plan."

Quinn held the packet as though it was about to explode, merely staring at the letter that he could see through the plastic, and then he reached out and laid the packet on the famous haunted desk in which it had been discovered.

He said softly, "That's her handwriting."

Everybody nodded, mumbled, concurred, the Shed Men murmuring that Patsy was a great one for scribbling notes saying, "Have my van gassed-up right now!" and "Wash my car and do it right," and they knew that that was her writing too.

Then the hefty sheriff, a devoutly ignorant man, cleared his throat and announced: "And then of course we found the conclusive evidence in the pirogue."

"Which was what?" asked Quinn with a small frown.

"Her hair," said the sheriff, "which matched right up to the hair on her brushes upstairs, and everybody knew Patsy'd never gone out there for any other reason, so it had to be she shot herself out there, 'cause why else would she come to be in the pirogue?"

"You've made a DNA match this quickly?" asked Quinn coldly.

"We didn't have to. Everybody could see it was the same hair all stuck with her hairspray, you could smell it," said the sheriff, "but the DNA will be coming if you mean to bury the strands in that little cemetery of yours where you like to bury things and hold séances with big fires and such!"

"Sheriff, please be kind to this boy," said Cyndy, the Nurse, in a sweet voice, "we are talking about his mother."

"Yes, please, if we could stick to the facts at hand," said Nash Penfield, in his deep authoritative voice. His frustration had gotten the better of him. He felt protective of just about everyone, but especially Tommy.

"So the coroner is satisfied?" asked Quinn. "And has ruled it suicide?"

"Well, yes, he would be!" declared the sheriff, "if you'd stop going around the house saying you murdered your mother and threw her to the gators, Quinn Blackwood! And Jasmine here would stop telling everybody Patsy's come a-crawling up to her window, all full of swamp weed, crying for help, for the love of the Lord in Heaven."

"She did, she did," gasped Jasmine under her breath. "Lestat, don't you let me go!"

"I won't," I whispered. "No ghost is going to get you, Jasmine."

"But Jasmine," said Quinn, "when did you see this ghost? Was it after you all found this note?"

"No, Grandma just told you, I saw her before I even knew about the letters, she came to the window, crying and clawing. And she's done it again! And I'm scared even to go to sleep out there. I don't know what she wants, Little Boss, what can I do for her? Little Jerome is upstairs in Tommy's room playing video games right now, I'm scared to even let him stay in the back house, what can I do? Quinn, you've got to hold another séance for Patsy!"

Suddenly Mona spoke up, and it was as if a light had gone on in that corner of the room.

"The poor creature probably doesn't know she's dead," Mona said tenderly. "Someone has to tell her. She needs to be guided into the Light. This often happens to people, especially if they die suddenly. I can tell her."

"Oh, please, could you do that?" said Jasmine. "That's it, you got it, she doesn't know, and she's wandering around, all forsaken and lost, coming out of the swamps back of my house and doesn't know what's happened to her."

The sheriff was smirking and raising his eyebrows and squinting his eyes. Nash was becoming extremely uncomfortable as he watched the man.

"That's what happened with Goblin, wasn't it?" Big Ramona asked. "You all told him he was dead and he went on. Well, you all have to do it again, you just got to."

"Yes, it was," said Quinn. "I'll tell her to go on. I don't mind doing it. I don't think it will require an entire séance."

"Well, you people ought to do that right away," said the sheriff, now on his feet and primed to depart, tugging at his heavy belt, "but I must tell you, it is the darnedest thing that every time you have a death out here you have a ghost right smack dab in the middle of it. Sure enough! Do you see the ghost of Miss McQueen carrying on like this? No, you do not! She's not scratching at any windowpane. Now that was a great lady!"

"What are you talking about!" Quinn demanded in a low voice. He looked up angrily at the sheriff. I'd never seen Quinn take on such an expression. I'd never heard Quinn talk in such a voice. "You trying to give us a lecture on who's a good dead person and who's not? Seems like you should wait outside of Jasmine's window and give that lecture to Patsy. Or why don't you just go back to your office and dictate a book on manners for the lately dead?"

Big Ramona chuckled under her breath. I swallowed my laughter. Nash was greatly worried. Tommy was afraid.

"Don't you talk that way to me!" the sheriff said, leaning over Quinn. "You're nothing but a crackpot kid, Tarquin Blackwood. It's the scandal of the parish that you've inherited Blackwood Farm! It's the end for this place out here and everybody knows it. And there's other things you've done that are the scandal of the parish, and now you go around saying you murdered your mother. I ought to run you in."

A cold rage came over Quinn. I could see it happening.

"I did murder her, Sheriff," he said in an iron voice. "I snatched her up from her couch upstairs, broke her neck, carried her out into the pirogue and went deep, deep into the dark swamp until I saw the backs of the gators in the light of the moon, and then I threw her body into the muck. And I said, 'Eat up Mother.' That's what I did."

The entire room was thrown into consternation, with Big Ramona and Jasmine crying No no no, and Nash murmuring desperate confidential reassurance to Tommy, and Tommy glaring at Quinn, and one of the Shed Men laughing, and Cyndy the Nurse avowing that Quinn would never really do such a thing. Grady Breen was speechless, shaking his head and shuffling papers in his briefcase uselessly, and even Mona was shocked, staring at Quinn with her glassy green eyes in vague wonder.

"You going to run me in, Sheriff?" asked Quinn, looking icily up at the man.

The room fell silent.

The sheriff was squint-eyed and speechless.

Nash was fearful and poised to act.

Quinn uncoiled from the chair and rose to his full height and looked down on the sheriff. The combination of Quinn's youthful face and imposing height alone was frightening, but the menace flowing from him was palpable.

"Go on, Big Boy," Quinn said in a stage whisper. "Put those handcuffs on me."

Silence.

The sheriff froze, then turned his head away, backed up two feet, and sidled towards the door and went off into the hall and out the front, muttering that nobody at Blackwood Farm had a lick of sense, and, it was such a crying shame that the house would now go to rack and ruin, yes, indeed, RACK AND RUIN! Slam went the door. No more sheriff.

"Well, I think I'd better be going along," said Grady Breen in a cheery loud voice, "and I'll get you a copy of the coroner's report first thing." He made for the front door so quickly that he might have suffered a heart attack later in his car. (But he did not.)

Meantime, Tommy ran to Quinn and threw his arms around him. Nash looked on helplessly.

This caught Quinn very much off guard. But he at once reassured the boy.

"Don't you worry about anything," he said. "You go on back to Eton. And when you come home, Blackwood Farm will be here, always, safe and sound and beautiful as it is now, and making lots of people happy, with Jasmine and Big Ramona and everybody, the same as it is today."

The Shed Men murmured that that was certainly the case. And Cyndy the Nurse said it was true. Big Ramona said, "Yes, Lawd."

Now Jasmine saw that she was needed, and, giving her face a final wipe with her handkerchief, she released her grip on me, received a little torrent of my kisses and went to put her arms around Tommy.

"You come on in the kitchen with me, Tommy Blackwood," she said. "You too, Nash Penfield, I've got a pot of stewed chicken on the stove; you too, Cyndy . . ."

"*You* have a pot of chicken on the stove? Who is this 'You'?" asked Big Ramona, "that's *my* pot of stewed chicken. And just look at this Mona Mayfair, why the child's totally recovered."

"No, no, you all go on," said Mona, rising and gesturing for them to leave us. "Quinn and Lestat and I have to talk."

"Little Boss," said Jasmine, "I'm not sleeping downstairs in that house. I've moved upstairs with Jerome and Grandma, and I'm locking the shutters over the windows. Patsy's after me."

"I'll find her out there," said Quinn. "Don't worry."

"Does she come at any certain time?" Mona asked very kindly.

" 'Bout four in the morning," said Jasmine. "I know 'cause she stops the clock."

"That's about right," said Quinn.

"Now, don't you start again with that!" Jasmine rebuked him. "Now they found all those letters and they think she shot herself, you're off the hook, now cool it!" And she pulled Tommy away with her.

"But wait a minute," said Tommy, at once clabbering up and losing a little of his manly dignity in the pure sadness of a child. "I really want to know." He swallowed. "Quinn, you didn't kill her, did you?" It was heartbreaking.

For a long moment everyone was silent, and then Quinn said:

"No, Tommy, I didn't. It's important that you believe me, that I would never do a thing like that. It's just, I wasn't kind to her. And now she's gone. And I feel sad about it. And as for the sheriff, I don't much care for him, and so I said mean things to him."

It was the most perfect of lies, executed with such determination that it shone in the darkness of Quinn's thoughts as it was uttered. It was inflamed with the vibrant love that Quinn felt for Tommy. His hatred of Patsy was as intense as ever. That her ghost was on the prowl infuriated him.

"That's right," said Jasmine. "We just all wish we'd treated her better. She was an independent person, wouldn't you say now, Little Boss, and sometimes we didn't understand her."

"Very well put," said Quinn. "We didn't try hard enough to understand her ways."

"Of course Tommy understands," said Nash. "We all understand.

Perhaps I can explain this a little better, if Quinn will allow. Come, Tommy, let's have some supper in the kitchen. Now that Quinn's here, there's nothing to worry about any longer, and Miss Mayfair, if you'll allow me to say, you do look absolutely lovely. It's marvelous to see you again, and so fit."

"Thank you, Mr. Penfield," said Mona, as if she wasn't a wild beast.

But Quinn's face was very dark, and as soon as the room was empty except for the three undercover monsters, we drew together.

"Let's go upstairs," said Quinn, "I really need your advice just now, Lestat. I have to figure out some things. I have some ideas."

"You know I'll do anything I can," I responded.

I calculatedly ignored Mona in her penitential black, who led the way up the circular staircase.

22

QUINN'S IMPRESSIVE BEDROOM SUITE—bedroom and parlor divided by a huge arch—had been completely cleaned since the making of Mona Mayfair into an irresponsible little demon. And the bed on which the Dark Gift had been given was all made up with its fancy dark blue velvet comforter and draperies.

There was the center table where Quinn and I had sat for hours as he'd told me the story of his life, and Mona and I took our places there, but Quinn seemed stunned by the sight of the room, and for a long moment he simply appraised his surroundings as if they meant something wholly new to him.

"What gives, Little Brother?" I asked.

"Pondering, Beloved Boss," he said. "Just pondering."

I was not looking at the harpy. Was I glad she was sitting to my right rather than roaming the world all vulnerable and tearful in her sequined chemise? Yes, but I was under no obligation to say so to one who had so furiously rejected me. Was I?

"Come, talk to us," I said to Quinn. "Sit down."

Finally, he did, taking his old place with his back to the computer desk, and just opposite me.

"Lestat, I'm not sure what to do."

"I can go out to her at four a.m.," said Mona, "I'm not afraid of her. I can try to reach her."

"No, darling," Quinn said, "I'm not thinking of Patsy just yet. I couldn't give less of a damn about Patsy, except for Jasmine's sake, really. I'm thinking of Blackwood Manor. I'm thinking of what's going to happen to it. You see, all the time we were in Europe, Aunt Queen and I were in charge by phone, by fax, by some means, and then all this last year we were both here, figures of security and authority. Now all that's changed. Aunt Queen is gone, simply gone, and I don't know that I want to be here very often. I don't think that I can be."

"But can't Jasmine and Big Ramona run the place, as they did while you were in Europe?" Mona asked. "I thought Jasmine was a whiz at that. And Big Ramona was a genius chef."

"All that's true," said Quinn. "They can do everything, actually. They can do the cooking and the cleaning, and they can meet and greet the drop-in guests. They can host the Easter Feast and Christmas Supper and every other imaginable event. Jasmine is extremely talented as a manager and a guide. Fact is, they can all do far more than they believe they can. And they all have plenty of money, money enough to walk away from this place and be comfortable wherever they go. That gives them a feeling of security, and an air of independence. But they want to be right here. This is their home. But they want for there to be a presence, a Blackwood presence, and without that, they're insecure."

"I see," she said. "You can't make them think like owners of the place."

"Exactly," he said. "I've given them every opportunity," he went on. "Every type of advancement and profit sharing as well, but they want me in residence. They want my authority. And Tommy wants it. And then there's Tommy sister Brittany to think of, and Tommy's mother, Terry Sue. They'll be coming frequently to visit. They've become part of Blackwood Farm because of Tommy. Someone has to be at the very heart of this house to receive them. And Jasmine wants me to be that heart, not only for herself but for my son, Jerome, and I'm not sure that I can continue to be the Master of Blackwood Farm as I would have been if only—."

"The answer's simple," I said.

"What is it?" Quinn asked, startled.

"Nash Penfield," I said. "You make him resident curator, to run and maintain this property on your behalf and on behalf of Tommy and Jerome."

"Resident curator!" Quinn's face brightened. "Ah, that sounds brilliant. But would he take the job? He's finished his Ph.D. He's ready to start teaching."

"Of course he'll take the job," I said. "The man spent years in

Europe with you and Aunt Queen. You described it as a luxurious journey."

"Oh, yes, Aunt Queen broke the bank," replied Quinn. "And Nash did seem to make the most of it in the best ways."

"Exactly. I suspect Nash is thoroughly ruined for ordinary life. He would love nothing better than to be curator here, to maintain the Easter and Christmas traditions for the sake of the parish, and whatever else you want, while earning a high salary, having a gorgeous bedroom and ample time to write a couple of books in his academic field."

"Perfect," Quinn said. "And he has the style and the grace to pull it off. Oh, this could be the answer."

"Run the idea by him. Suggest that in his idle hours he could begin to build a proper library on shelves put up on the inside walls of the double parlor. And he could write a short history of Blackwood Farm, to be printed up for the tourists, you know, with architectural details and blueprints and legends and such. Throw in the limousine and driver twenty-four hours a day, and a new car of his own every two years, and a deep-pocket expense account and paid vacations to New York and California, and I think you'll have him."

"I know he'll go for it," said Mona. "Downstairs he was desperate to intervene when the sheriff was acting like an idiot. He just didn't feel he had the right to do it."

"Precisely," I said, without looking at Mona. "It's a dream position for a man of his gifts."

"Oh, if he only would," said Quinn, with mounting excitement, "that would be key. And I could come and go from this room, with you and Mona, anytime that I wanted."

"It's far more interesting than what awaits Nash elsewhere," I said. "And he can play proper host to Tommy's mother, Terry Sue, and exert a guiding influence on little Jerome, maybe tutor him, in fact, and you don't have to tell him how to treat Jasmine and Big Ramona; he knows. He adores them. He was born in Texas. That's the South. He isn't some ignorant Yankee who doesn't know how to speak two civil words to a black person. He respects them completely."

"I think you've hit on it," Quinn said. "If he were ensconced in Blackwood Farm, it would work. It would work for a long time. Jasmine would be ecstatic. She loves Nash."

I nodded and shrugged.

"That's a grand idea," said Quinn. "In time I'll tell them Mona and

I were married in Europe. They won't protest. It will be perfect. Mona, you really think he'll go for it?"

I refused to look at her.

"Quinn, he's already part of Blackwood Farm," she said.

Quinn went to the phone. "Jasmine," he said, "I need you up here."

Almost instantly we heard the vibration of the staircase as Jasmine came running up, and then breathlessly she opened the door.

"What's the matter, Little Boss?" She was panting. "What's going on?"

"Sit down, please," he said.

"You scared me to death, you miserable boy!" she declared. She took her chair. "Now what's on your mind to call me like that! Don't you know this whole place is in a state of crisis? And now Clem's saying he won't sleep in the bungalow, either, because he's scared of Patsy coming to him too."

"Never mind all that, you know perfectly well Patsy can't hurt you!"

He sat back down and he told her the whole plan, how Nash would be the curator, but before he was halfway through what he meant to say, she threw up her hands and declared it was a miracle. The whole parish would be happy. Nash Penfield had been put on this Earth for Blackwood Farm.

"Now, it's Aunt Queen who put that idea in your head, Little Boss, she's looking down from Heaven," Jasmine said. "I know she is. And so is Mamma, who died right there in that very bed. God bless us all. You know what people round here believe? They believe Blackwood Farm belongs to everybody!"

"Everybody?" asked Mona. "Everybody who?"

"All the parish around, girl," said Jasmine. "The phone's been ringing off the hook since Aunt Queen died. Are we still going to do the Christmas Dinner? Are we still going to have the Azalea Festival? I'm telling you, they think this place belongs to the whole parish."

"Well, they're right," said Quinn. "It really does. So do I have your consent to ask Nash Penfield to take the job?"

"Yes, indeed!" Jasmine said. "I'll tell Grandma, you'll get no argument from her. You just talk to Nash Penfield. He and Tommy are down in the parlor. I wanted them to play the piano. Nash knows how to play. Tommy knows one song. But Tommy says you don't play the piano for weeks after a person dies. Now, we never abided by that here because we were always a Bed-and-Breakfast. And I say that Tommy can play that song."

Quinn got up and went out with Jasmine.

I followed them down the stairs. I wanted to see this thing through. I ignored the fact that Mona came afterwards and was behaving with such obvious grace and reticence. A complete facade.

Wise ones must not be deceived by such ploys.

Tommy was sitting at the square grand in the double parlor, an antique that apparently still worked. And he was crying just a little and Nash was standing over him. I could feel the pure love of Nash for Tommy.

"Tommy," Quinn said. "There was this woman in Beethoven's time who lost her child. She was bereft. Beethoven would come into her house, unannounced, and he would play the piano for her. She would be lying upstairs, distraught, and she would hear him playing down there in the drawing room, and the piano music was his gift to her, to comfort her. You play the piano if you like. You offer the music up to Aunt Queen. You go on. Part the gates of Heaven with your music, Tommy."

"You tell Little Boss what you mean to play," said Jasmine.

"It's a song by Patsy," said Tommy. "Patsy sent the CD to us while we were in Europe. I wrote home for the sheet music. Aunt Queen saw to it we had suites with pianos so I could learn the song. It's very Irish and very sad. I wanted to play it for Patsy, to see if it would quiet her soul."

Quinn said nothing. His face went pale.

"You go on, son," I said. "That's a good idea. Aunt Queen will be pleased and so will Patsy. Patsy will hear you. You play the song."

Tommy laid his hands on the keys. He began a simple, very Celtic-sounding ballad. It had its Kentucky Bluegrass sound too. Then, startling us all, he began to sing the lyrics in a low competent boy soprano that was as mournful as the music:

> Go tell my friends for me
> That I'm not coming back.
> Go tell the gang for me
> That I can dance no more.
> Go tell the ones I love
> That I have gone on home.

I'm walking in the graveyard now
And I am all alone.
And I'll be gone before the leaves
Begin to fall again.

They're rushing up and down the stairs
The bed is wide and soft.
But I lie still and oh, so cold.
Because my mother's gone.

Will I soon see her simple face?
I have no dreams or faith.
I wish that I could make a song
That tells how good it's been.

I had the stage, I had the light.
The music was the tale.
But things are tinged with purple now
And these sad notes I play.

I wait until the autumn comes
And I will be no more.

We stood together, bound by the sorrow of it, as if we were in a deep enchantment.

Quinn leant down to kiss Tommy on the cheek. Tommy just stared at the printed music before him. Jasmine had her arm around his shoulder.

"Now that was beautiful," she said. "And Patsy wrote that, now, she knew what was coming, she knew."

Then Quinn drew Nash off with him into the dining room. Mona and I went with him, but there was no real need for us.

I saw this as they sat down to talk.

I saw that Nash understood from the first words, and was completely desirous of this position that Quinn was describing to him. I saw that it had been Nash's secret dream. Nash had only been waiting for the time to present such a proposal to Quinn.

Meanwhile, in the parlor Jasmine was asking Tommy to play the song again.

"But you didn't really see that awful ghost of Patsy, did you?" Tommy was asking.

"No, no," said Jasmine, trying to comfort Tommy, "I was just carrying on, I don't know what got into me, don't you be afraid of Patsy's ghost, don't you think about that, besides, you see a ghost, you make the Sign of the Cross, nothing to it, now you sing that song again, I'll sing it with you. . . ."

"You play the song again, Tommy," I said. "You keep playing it and you keep singing it. If her spirit's wandering, she'll hear it and it will comfort her."

I went out the unlocked front door into the warm humid air, down the steps and away from the light, and I walked back behind the house and over to the far right where the bungalow stood in which Jasmine and Big Ramona and Clem lived.

It was lighted cheerily. And only Clem was there, sitting on the front porch, rocking and smoking a very aromatic cigar. I gestured for him not to get up on my account, and I walked back behind the house and along the treacherous soft bank of the swamp.

I could hear Tommy singing. I sang the words along with him, soft, in no more than a whisper. I tried to picture Patsy as she had been in her heyday—country-western star, in her leather jackets with fringe and skirts and boots, with teased and bouffant hair, belting her original songs. It was the image that Quinn had given to me. Grudgingly he had said she could truly sing. Even Aunt Queen had mentioned to me with some reserve that Patsy could really sing. Ah, there hadn't been a single soul in the world of Blackwood Farm who had felt love for Patsy.

And all I'd glimpsed was the sick Patsy, bitter and full of hate, sitting on the couch in her white nightgown, knowing she'd never be well enough to perform anymore, hollering for Cyndy, the Nurse, to give her another shot, hating Quinn out loud and with her soul, her pinched and twisted soul, Patsy, who'd caught the plague from drug needles and didn't care how many times she'd passed it on.

And Quinn had done her in just exactly as he'd described it to the sheriff.

I walked on, with the swamp beside me. I let my vampiric hearing rove. Nash had begun to play Patsy's song, with more notes and a bolder expression. He and Tommy were singing it together. Sadness. Jasmine cried. Jasmine whispered, "Ah, the pure pitifulness of it."

The rural dark fell down around me. I let go of the music.

The swamp seemed the most savage and devouring place, with no pastoral symmetry or harmony to it. What thrived there was ravenous and battling to the death, and would never find a safe haven for itself—a landscape eating itself alive. Quinn had told me it was like that. But how could I not have known it?

Centuries ago, I'd been dumped for dead in the swamp by my fledglings, Claudia, the murderer, Louis, the coward; and I, a hideous and grasping thing, had survived in those stagnant, polluted waters, survived to come back and take my battered and shapeless revenge, sharpened to a fatal point by others.

I don't care about that.

I don't know how long I walked.

I took my time.

Patsy. Patsy.

The night sounds were at once particular and at the same time a deep hum on the warm breeze, and the moon was high, sometimes penetrating a break in the swamp that only revealed its jagged hateful chaos more harshly.

Now and then I stopped.

I looked at the scattered stars—so cunningly bright in the country night. And I hated them, as usual. What comfort was it to be lost in the endless universe, a simpleton on a tiny speck of revolving dust, whose forefathers had read patterns and meanings into these countless unknowable points of cold white fire, which only mocked us by their unchanging indifference?

So let them shine over the vast pastureland to my right, over the distant clusters of oaks, over the warmly lighted houses now far behind me.

My soul was with the swamp tonight. My soul was with Patsy.

I walked on.

I hadn't known so much of Blackwood Farm bordered on the swamp. But I wanted to know. And I kept as close as possible to the water without slipping right into it.

Soon I knew Mona was somewhere near me. She was doing her best to conceal herself, but I heard the little sounds that she made, and I could smell a faint perfume from her that had clung to Aunt Queen's dresses, a scent I hadn't noticed before.

After a little while, I knew Quinn was with us, too, staying behind me with Mona. Why they so faithfully followed I didn't know.

I used my strongest vision to penetrate the reeking darkness to my left.

A strong chill came over me, moving down my back, a chill such as I'd felt when Rowan Mayfair and I had first met, and she had used her power to study me, a chill that was from a source outside of me.

I stopped, and I faced the swamp, and at once I perceived that a female figure was right before me. It was so close that I could have touched it without extending my hand more than a few inches.

It was tangled in the moss and creeper vine, still and lifeless as the cypress tree which appeared to support it, and it was soaked through and through, its hair in dank rivulets on its filthy white gown, and gleaming faintly in a light mortal eyes could not have seen, and it was staring at me.

It was Patsy Blackwood.

Weak, silent, suffering.

"Where is she!" Quinn whispered. He was at my left shoulder. "Where? Patsy, where are you?"

"Be quiet," I said. I kept my gaze on her, on her large miserable eyes, and the streaks of hair that ran down her face, and her parted lips. Such yearning, such agony.

"Patsy," I said. "Darling girl, all your tribulation in this place is finished."

I saw her eyebrows close in a slow listless frown. It seemed I heard a deep long sigh from her.

"You best go on, beautiful girl," I said. "Go on to glory. Don't roam this dismal realm, Patsy. Don't make this darkness your home when you can turn to the Light. Don't you wander here searching and moaning. You go on. Turn your back on this time and place and beg for the gates to open."

Something quickened in her face. Her eyebrows went smooth, and it seemed that she shuddered.

"Go on, honey," I said. "The Light wants you. And here in this world, Quinn will gather all your songs, every song you ever recorded, Patsy, and put them all together, and they'll go out far and wide, Patsy, every single one, old and new, for always. Isn't that a splendid thing to leave behind, all those wonderful songs that people love, that's your gift, Patsy."

Her mouth opened, but she didn't speak. Her white cheeks were slick with the water of the swamp, her nightgown torn, her arms scratched and streaked with filth, her fingers struggling to close but unable to do it.

I heard Mona cry out. I felt a force move the damp air around me. Quinn was vowing in a low-running whisper that, having sinned in taking her life, he would give her songs life forever.

But nothing changed for me in the agonized and straining apparition, except that Patsy raised her right hand just a little, and her parted lips made just a small bit of a word. I couldn't hear it. It seemed she inclined towards me. And I inclined towards her—

—*love me, love the way love must be, unsparing love, love Patsy!*—

—across the perilous void I moved, as if stepping off the very world itself, and I kissed her lips, wet and reeking of the foul water, and I felt a great current come from inside me, a wind out of the deepest root in me that swept inexorably into her and carried her far, far away, up and out, her form growing faint and immense and brilliant—.

"Into the Light, Patsy!" Mona wailed, her words borne on the wind and swallowed by it—.

—teenaged cowgirl strumming her guitar, belting it: *Gloria!* stomping her foot, crowd screaming, searing flash of angels, numberless monsters of the unseen, those wings, no, I didn't see, yes, I did, get away! *Gloria!* I didn't see—*Gloria!* I'm clawing the grass trying to get into the Earth—Oncle Julien smiling, beckoning. *Gloria! This is the most dangerous game. You're no Saint Juan Diego, you know.* I will not, I will not, I will not go with you! Patsy in pink leather, arms raised, blinding light, belting *Gloria in Excelsis Deo!*

Blackness. It is done. I am separate. I am here. I feel the grass beneath me.

I whispered: "Laudamus te. Benedicimus te. Adoramus te. In Gloria Dei Patris!"

When I opened my eyes, I was lying on the ground, and except for Mona who cradled my head in her hands, and Quinn who knelt beside her, the night was quiet and empty.

23

E VERY NOW AND THEN, I demand to be treated like the supernatural hero that I am.

I strode back to the house, ignoring Quinn and Mona (especially Mona), and opened the kitchen door, and told Jasmine that
Patsy's spirit was definitely gone from the Earth, and that I was spent
and that I needed to sleep in Aunt Queen's bed, no matter what anybody thought about it.

Obstreperous little Jerome jumped up from his tiny table and cried:
"But I never got to see her! Mamma, I never got to see her."

"I'll draw you a picture, sit down!" said Jasmine and, with the incon-
testable authority of the lady with the keys, she led me across the hall
and admitted me to the sacrosanct chamber at once, mumbling that
Mona had made a mess of the closets only two hours before, but everything was now put right, and I flung myself theatrically upon the rose
satin bed, beneath the rose satin canopy, nuzzled into the rose satin
pillows and lay there, drenched in the scent of Chantilly, allowing Jasmine to pull off my dirty boots because it made her happy, and protected the bed, and I closed my eyes.

At once Quinn said in a soft, respectful voice, "Lestat, may Mona
and I keep watch with you? We're so grateful for what you did."

"Out of my sight," I said. "Jasmine, please light all the lamps and
then make them get out of here. Patsy is gone, and my soul is weak! I
have seen the feathered wings of angels. Don't I deserve to sleep for
this little while?"

"You get out of here, Tarquin Blackwood and Mona Mayfair!" Jasmine said, "Thank the Lawd that Patsy's gone! I can feel it. That child was just lost and now she's way up home and no more searching. I'm taking these boots to Allen. Allen's the boot expert on this property. Allen can clean these boots. Now, you two go on, you heard what the man said. His soul is weak. Now let him be. Lestat, I'm getting you a blanket."

Amen.

I drifted.

Julien was at my ear in heated French: "I'll follow you to the ends of the Earth through all your endeavors until you are ruined in madness! Vanity of vanities, all is vanity. All that you do is vanity, and for your own pride and glory! You think the angels don't know what you do and for whom you do it!"

"Aw, yeah!" I whispered, "you spiteful ghost, you thought you had me between the worlds, didn't you? Is that where you live forever, watching them pass you by? You didn't give a damn for Patsy's soul, did you? And did she not descend from you as surely as Quinn? And Mona? You did the beast with two backs in this very house with Patsy's ancestor too, did you not, you don't know your own descendants when they're not to your taste, you merciless astral panhandler. . . ."

I drifted deeper, brain descending into the sweetness of human exhaustion—far from the ring of the anvil between the worlds, far from the torrent of Heaven. Adieu, my poor doomed Patsy. Yes, and I had done it with a kiss, and yes, with a step, and yes, she had gone up, and wasn't it good? Had I not done good? Could anybody deny it was good? Yo, Juanito, wasn't it good? Wasn't the exorcism of Goblin good? I sank back into the safety of know-nothing sleep. And round about, the golden lighted room protected me.

What could I do that was good for Mona and Quinn?

Two hours later I was awakened by the chiming of a clock. I didn't know where in the house it was or what it looked like and I didn't care. The room was wholesome and reassuring, as if the purity and generosity of Aunt Queen had totally infused it.

I was refreshed. The evil little cells in my body had done their dirty and inevitable work. And if I'd had any terrible dreams I didn't remember them.

Lestat was Lestat again. As if anyone cared. Do you care?

I sat up.

Julien was sitting at Aunt Queen's little round table, the table at which she had taken her meals, the table between the bed and the closet doors. He wore his fancy dinner jacket. He smoked a little black cigarette. Stella sat on the couch in her pretty white dress. She was playing with one of Aunt Queen's floppy boudoir dolls.

"*Bonjour*, Lestat," said Stella. "At last you wake, you handsome Endymion."

"Everything you do," Julien said in French, "you do for your own selfish aims. You want these mortals to love you. You bask in their blind adoration. You devour it like blood. Are you tired of killing and destroying?"

"You're not making sense," I replied. "Being dead, you should know better. The dead should have an edge. You don't have one. You hang out in the alleyways of the other world. I saw you for what you are."

He smiled a wicked little smile.

"Exactly what is your paltry plan?" he asked in French, "to send me through the cloudy Heavens the way you did Patsy Blackwood?"

"Hmmm. Why should I bother with your salvation?" I asked. "As I told you before, I'm getting used to you. I feel privileged, having these little tête-à-têtes, no matter where you come from. And then there's Stella. Stella is a delight always."

"Oh, you're so sweet," said little Stella. She held the doll up by the arms. "You know, Ducky, you present the most bizarre problem."

"Do explain," I said. "Nothing delights me more than children who spout philosophy."

"Don't be sure that I'm capable of a philosophical observation," she replied, frowning and smiling at me at the same time. She let the doll flop in her lap. She lifted her shoulders, then slowly relaxed. "This is what I think about you, Ducky. You have a conscience without a soul to back it up. Quite unique, I should say."

A dark shiver passed through me. "Where is my soul, Stella?" I asked.

She seemed at a loss, but then she spoke: "Entangled!" she said. "Caught in a web! But your conscience flies free of your soul. It's simply marvelous."

Julien smiled. "We'll find a way to cut that web," he said.

"Oh, so you mean to save my soul?" I asked.

"I don't care where it goes once it leaves this Earth," Julien replied. "Haven't I told you that? It's the fleshly shell I detest, the evil blood that enlivens it, the appetite that drives it, and the consuming pride that motivated it to take my niece."

"You're overwrought," I said. "Remember the child. You must have had some purpose in bringing her with you as a witness. Behave decently in her presence."

The knob on the hall door turned.

They vanished. Such shy retiring individuals.

The doll fell over on the couch, and, having no elbows or knees, looked most bereft as it stared with its big painted eyes at the room around it.

Quinn and Mona entered. Quinn had changed into a big cable knit sweater and simple slacks, for the air-conditioning at Blackwood Farm was a force to be reckoned with, and Mona was still in her gorgeous black dress, her pale face and hands glowing. A cameo was now fixed at her neck, a very large and beautiful one of white and blue sardonyx.

"Can we talk now?" Quinn asked in a very polite tone. He looked at Mona with great concern, then his eyes returned to me.

I realized that Quinn had been quite right in his early description to me of his love for Mona. Mona's unhappiness—indeed Mona herself, whether happy or sad—continued to supplant all Quinn's own woes and griefs in his own heart. She continued to deliver him mercifully, at least for now, from the loss of Aunt Queen, and the loss of his doppelganger, Goblin. Whatever the little scorpion did to me, his love for her was a blessing.

How else explain the ease with which he accepted me usurping Aunt Queen's magnificent bed in my, how shall we put it, vanity?

I pushed back against the pillows until I was firmly planted in an upright position, with legs comfortably stretched out and ankles crossed, and I nodded.

Seldom did I see my feet in black socks. I knew almost nothing personally about my feet. They looked rather small for the twenty-first century. Bad luck. But six feet was still a good height.

"I want you to know that I adored Aunt Queen," I muttered. "I slept on top of the counterpane. I was shaken."

"Beloved Boss, you make a picture there," Quinn said kindly. "Make this your place here. You know my aunt. She slept all day. Every window's fitted with a black-out blind beneath the fancy velvet."

These words had an immensely soothing effect. I gave him to know that silently.

He sat on the bench before Aunt Queen's dressing table, with his back to the big round mirror and the soft lamplight. Mona sat on the couch, very near to the doll that the ghost of Stella had just left there.

"Are you rested now?" Mona asked, pretending to be a decently behaved creature.

"Do something useful," I said disdainfully to Mona. "Pick up that boudoir doll and set it down properly, so it doesn't look so lost."

"Oh, yes, certainly," she said, as if she wasn't a roaring revenant from Hell. She set the doll against the padded arm of the chair, crossed its legs and put its little hands in its lap. It stared at me gratefully.

"What happened to you out there, Lestat?" Quinn asked. His manner was very solicitous.

"Not certain," I replied. "Some force wanting to take me with her, maybe. We were connected as she started to rise. But I managed to get away. Not sure. I see angels sometimes. It's frightening. Can't talk about it. Don't want to relive it. But Patsy is gone on. That's what's important."

"I saw the Light," said Quinn. "I saw it without mistake, but I never saw the spirit of Patsy." He had such a sincere manner about him, nothing fanciful.

"I saw it too," said the banshee. "And you were fighting with someone, and you were cursing in French, and you cried out something about Oncle Julien."

"Doesn't matter now," I said, eyes on Quinn. "As I said, I'd rather not relive it."

"Why did you do it?" Quinn asked, respectfully.

"What on Earth do you mean?" I asked. "It had to be done, didn't it?"

"I realize that," said Quinn. "But why you? I'm the one who murdered Patsy. And you went out there alone and drew her spirit to you. You brought the Light down for her. There was a struggle. Why did you do it?"

"For you, I suppose," I said with a shrug. "Maybe I didn't think anybody else could do it. Or I did it for Jasmine, because I'd promised her the ghost wouldn't get her. Or for Patsy. Yes, for Patsy." I brooded. I said, "You're both so young in the Blood. You've seen so little. I've seen the howling wind of the Earthbound Dead. I've seen their souls in the void between the realms. When Mona said that Patsy didn't know she was dead, that settled it for me. So I went out there and I did it."

"And then there was the song," said the little harpy, looking at Quinn. "Tommy played the Irish song and it was so mournful."

"Speaking of her songs, I made good on the promise," said Quinn. "Or at least I've started. I called Patsy's agent, got him out of bed. We're going to reissue all her recordings, do a special publicity release—all that she could ever have wanted. Her agent's so thrilled that she's dead, he could hardly contain himself."

"What!" said Mona.

"Oh, you know, dead recording stars make plenty of money," Quinn replied with a little shrug. "He'll publicize her tragic demise. Bracket her career. Package it."

"I knew you would make good on the promise," I said. "And I would have seen to it, if you hadn't—that is, if you had given me leave. Now it's over, isn't it?"

"Her voice was marvelous," Quinn said. "If only I could have murdered her and not her voice."

"Quinn!" said Mona.

"Well, I think that's what you've done, Little Brother," I remarked.

He laughed softly. "I suppose you're right, Beloved Boss," he said. He smiled at Mona and her innocent shock. "Some night I'll tell you all about her. When I was little, I thought she was made of plastic and glue. She was always screaming. Enough about her."

Mona shook her head. She loved him much too much to press. Besides, she had other things on her mind.

"But Lestat, what did you see out there?" she asked me.

"You are not listening to me," I said with exasperation. "I told you, you maddening little miscreant, I won't relive it. It's closed for me. Besides, give me one good reason why I should even speak to you. Why are we in the same room?"

"Lestat," said Quinn, "please give Mona another chance."

I got furious—not at Mona, I wasn't going to fall into that trap again—but simply furious. They were such beautiful children, these two. And—.

"Very well," I said, thinking as I spoke. "I'm going to lay down the law to you. If I am to remain with you, I am the Master here. And I refuse to prove myself to you. I won't spend my tenure with you being constantly questioned as to the virtue of my authority!"

"I understand," said Mona. "I really, really do!" So seemingly heartfelt.

"Case in point," I said. "Whatever I saw out there, I choose to forget. And you have to forget it too."

"Yes, Beloved Boss," said Mona eagerly.

Pause.

I wasn't buying it.

Quinn was not looking at her. He was looking attentively at me.

"You know how much I love you," he said.

"I love you too, Little Brother," I said. "I'm sorry that my disagreements with Mona have put a distance between us."

He turned to Mona. "Say what you have to say," he told her.

Mona looked down. Her hands were folded one on top of the other in her lap and she looked abruptly forlorn and full of warmth, her coloring all the more intense on account of the black dress, her hair quite incidentally magnificent.

(Big deal! So what!)

"I showered you with abuse," she confessed. Her voice was smoother and richer than it had been before now: "I was so very wrong." She looked up at me. I had never seen her green eyes so placid. "I was wrong to speak of your other fledglings the way I did, to speak of your long-ago tragedies with such coarseness and attempted cruelty. I should have never spoken to anyone with such callousness, let alone to you. It was spiritually and morally crude. And it was not my nature. Please trust me when I say that. It was not my nature. It was downright hateful."

I shrugged, but I was secretly impressed. Good command of the English language. "So why did you do it?" I asked, feigning detachment.

She appeared to be thinking about it, during which time Quinn looked at her with obvious concern. Then she said:

"You're in love with Rowan. I saw it. It frightened me, really, really frightened me."

Silence.

Inexpressible pain. No image of Rowan in my heart. Simply an emptiness, an acknowledgement that she was far, far away. Maybe forever. *"Or ever the silver cord be loosed, or the golden bowl be broken."*

"Frightened?" I asked. "How so?"

"I wanted you to love me," Mona said. "I wanted you to remain interested in me. I wanted you to be on my side. I . . . I didn't want you to be swept away by her." She faltered. "I was jealous. I was like a prisoner let out of a solitary confinement cell after two years, and having found riches all around me, I feared losing everything."

Again I was secretly impressed.

"Nothing was at risk," I responded. "Absolutely nothing."

"But surely you understand," said Quinn, "what it means for Mona to be deluged with our gifts and unable to modulate her feelings. There we were in that very garden behind the First Street house, the very place where the Taltos bodies had been buried."

"Yes," Mona said. "We were talking of things which had tortured me for years and I . . . I. . . ."

"Mona, you must trust in me," I said. "You must trust in my principles. That's our paradox. We do not leave behind the Natural Law when we receive the Blood. We are principled creatures. I never stopped loving you, not for an instant. Whatever I felt for Rowan at the family gathering in no way affected my feelings for you. How could it? I warned you twice to be patient with your family because I knew it was right for you to do so. Then the third time, all right, I went too far with a little mockery. But I was trying to curb your insults, and your abuse of those you loved! But you wouldn't listen to me."

"I will now, I swear it," she said. Again, the assured voice, a voice I'd not heard last night or tonight earlier. "Quinn's been instructing me for hours. He's been cautioning me about the way I treat Rowan and Michael and Dolly Jean. He's told me I can't just blithely call them 'human beings' right in front of them. It's ill-mannered for a vampire to do that."

"Indeed," I said withcringly. (You gotta be kidding.)

"He's explained that we have to be patient with their ways, and I see that now, and I understand why Rowan had to talk as she did. Or that it wasn't my place to interrupt her. I see it. I won't make those blundering remarks anymore. I have to find my . . . my maturity in the Blood." She paused and then: "A place where serenity and courtesy connect. Yes, that's what it is. And I'm far from it."

"True," I said. I studied her, the picture she made. I wasn't quite convinced by this perfect Act of Contrition. And how lovely her little wrists looked in the tight black cuffs, and of course the shoes, with their wicked heels and winding snakelike straps. But I liked her words: "A place where serenity and courtesy connect." I liked them a lot, and I knew they'd come from her. All she had said had come from her, no matter what Quinn had taught her. I could tell by the way that Quinn responded to her.

"And about the sequined dress," she said, startling me out of that line of thought. "I understand now."

"You do?" I asked soberly.

"Of course," she said with a shrug. "All males are obviously much more stimulated by what they see than females. And why should we people of the night be an exception?" Flash of big green eyes. Rosy mouth. "You didn't want to be distracted anymore by all that skin and cleavage, and you were very honest about it."

"I should have made my wishes known with more tact and respect," I said in a dull monotone. "I will be gentlemanly in the future."

"No, no," she said with an honest shake of her red hair. "We all knew the dress was highfalutin trash, it was supposed to be. That's why I wore it to the hotel terrace. It was deliberately seductive. That's why when I walked into this house, I went right to change into something more presentable. Besides, you *are* the Maker. That's the word that Quinn used. The Maker, or the Master. The Teacher. And you have the authority to say to me, 'Take off that dress,' and I knew what you were talking about.

"But you see—I've been sick for a very crucial part of my life. I never knew as a mortal girl what it was like to wear a dress like that. I was never a mortal woman, you see."

A great sadness descended on me.

"I just went from being a kid to being an invalid," she said. "And then this, this range of powers which you've entrusted to me. And what have I done but strike out at you because I thought you . . . thought you loved Rowan." She stopped, puzzled, looking off. "I suppose I wanted to reveal to you . . . that I was a woman, too, in that dress. . . ." she said dreamily. "Maybe that was it. That I was a woman as much as she was."

It struck me in the soul, her words. The soul I wasn't supposed to have, the entangled soul.

"Ironic, isn't it?" she said, her voice roughened by emotion, "what womanhood means. The power to mother, the power to seduce, the power to leave behind both, the power to. . . ." She shut her eyes. She whispered: "And that dress, such an outrageous badge of it!"

"Don't battle with it anymore," I said. It was the first warmth I'd shown to her. "You said it the first time around, really. You said it."

She knew it. She looked up at me.

"Power Slut," she whispered. "That's what you called me, and right you were, I was drunk on the power, I was spinning, I was—."

"Oh, no, don't—."

"And we can transcend, we are so blessed, even if it is a dark blessing, we are miracles, we are free in so many marvelous respects—."

"It's my task," I said, "to guide you, instruct you, remain with you until you're able to exist well on your own, and not to lose my temper as I did. I was in the wrong. I played out the power hand same as you did, baby. I should have had much more patience."

Quiet. And this sorrow too will lift. It must.

"You do love Rowan, though, don't you?" she asked. "You really really love her."

"Accept what I'm saying to you," I said. "I am a very mean guy. And I am being nice."

"Oh, you're not mean at all," she said with a little laugh. She cleared her saddened face with the brightest smile. "I absolutely adore you."

"No, I am mean," I said. "And I expect to be adored. Remember your own words. I'm the teacher."

"But why do you love Rowan?"

"Mona, let's not delve into that too much," said Quinn. "I think we've accomplished a great reconciliation here, and Lestat won't leave us now."

"I was never going to leave," I said under my breath. "I would never abandon either of you. But now that we're gathered together, I think we can move on. There are other matters on my mind."

Quiet.

"Yes, we should move on," said Mona.

"What other matters?" Quinn asked a little fearfully.

"Last night we talked about a certain quest," I said. "I made a promise. And I mean to keep it. But I want to clarify certain things . . . about the quest and what we hope to gain from it."

"Yes," said Quinn. "I'm not sure I fully understand everything about the Taltos."

"There's too much for us to understand," I said. "I'm sure Mona would agree with that."

I saw the trouble come back into her bright face, the pucker of her eyebrows, the soft lengthening of her mouth. But even in this I saw a new maturity, a new self-confidence.

"I have some questions. . . ." I said.

"Yes," said Mona. "I'll try to answer them."

I reflected, then plunged: "Are you absolutely certain that you do want to find these creatures?"

"Oh, I have to find Morrigan, you know that! Lestat, how could you, you said you—?"

"Let me phrase it differently," I said, raising my hand. "Never mind whatever you've said in the past. Now that you've had time to think— to become more accustomed to what you are, now that you know that Rowan and Michael weren't lying to you, that you do know everything, and that there's nothing to know—do you want to search out Morrigan simply to know that she's safe and sound, or to reveal yourself to her in a true reunion?"

"Yes, that is the essential question," said Quinn. "Which is it?"

"Well, for a true reunion obviously," she answered without hesitation. "I never thought of any other possibility." She was bewildered. "I . . . I never considered just finding out if she was all right. I . . . always thought we'd be together. I want so much to put my arms around her, to hold her, to—." Her face went blank with hurt. She fell silent.

"You do see," I asked as tactfully as I could, "if she wanted that, she would have come back to you a long time ago."

Surely such thoughts had occurred to her before. They must have. But as I watched her now I wondered. Maybe she had dwelt on fantasies and lies—that Rowan knew the whereabouts of Morrigan and kept it secret. That Rowan had smuggled her the magic milk and it did no good.

Whatever the case, she was shaken now. Badly shaken.

"Maybe she couldn't come to me," she whispered. "Maybe Ash Templeton wouldn't let her." She shook her head and put her hands to her forehead. "I don't know what kind of creature he is! Of course Michael and Rowan thought Ash was a . . . hero, a great all-knowing, wise observer of the centuries. But what if—. I don't know. I want to see her. I want to talk to her. I want to hear it from her, what she wants, don't you see? Why she didn't come to me all those years, why she didn't even . . . Lasher, he was cruel, but he was an aberrant soul, a. . . ." She covered her mouth with her right hand, her fingers trembling.

Quinn was beside himself. He couldn't bear to see her so unhappy.

"Mona, you can't give her the Blood," I said softly, "no matter what her circumstances. The Blood cannot be passed to this species of creature. It is too unknown for us even to consider such a thing. The Blood very likely can't be passed on to them. But even if it could, we can't make a new species of Immortal. Believe me when I say there are ancient ones of our kind who would never tolerate such a thing happening."

"Oh, I know that, I haven't asked for that, I wouldn't—." She went quiet, obviously unable to speak.

"You want to know she's alive and well," said Quinn in the gentlest manner. "That's paramount, wouldn't you say?"

Mona nodded, looking away. "Yes—that there's a community of them somewhere, and they're happy." She frowned. She battled her pain. She drew in her breath, cheeks reddening. "It isn't likely, is it?" She looked at me.

"No, it's not," I said. "That's what Rowan and Michael were trying to tell us."

"Then I have to know what happened to them!" she whispered bitterly. "I have to!"

"I'll find out," I said.

"You really mean that?"

"Yes," I said. "I wouldn't make a promise to you like that unless I meant it. I'll find out, and if they have survived, if they do have a community somewhere, then you can decide whether or not you want to meet with them. But once a meeting occurs, they'll know about you, what you are, everything. That is, if they have the powers that Rowan ascribed to them."

"Oh, they have those powers," Mona said. "They do." She closed her eyes. She took a deep painful breath. "It's an awful thing to admit," she said, "but the things Dolly Jean said were all true. I can't deny them. I can't withhold the truth from you and Quinn. I can't. Morrigan was . . . almost unbearable."

"How so, unbearable?" asked Quinn.

I could see this was a radical admission. She had said things quite to the contrary.

Mona threw back her hair, her eyes searching the ceiling. She was facing something she had always denied.

"Obsessive, incessant, maddening!" she said. "She went on and on about her schemes and plans and dreams and memories, and she did say that Mayfairs would become a family of Taltos, and once she caught the scent of the Taltos male on Rowan and Michael, she was absolutely unendurable." Mona closed her eyes. "The thought of a community of such creatures is—almost beyond my imagination. This old one, Ash Templeton, the one that Rowan and Michael knew—he had learned to pretend to be a human being, he had learned that centuries ago. That's the thing. These creatures can live indefinitely! They are immortals! The species is utterly incompatible with humans. Morrigan was new and raw." She looked imploringly at me.

"Take it slowly," I said. I had never seen her suffering so. In all her bouts of tears there had been a generosity and selflessness that made them seem quite challengeable. As for her rage, she'd positively enjoyed it. But now she was truly in torment.

"It's like me, don't you see?" she said. "She was a newborn Taltos. And I'm a newborn Blood Child, or whatever you want to call me. And we share the same faults. She was unruly and crashing into everything around her! And that's the way I've behaved, raving to you as I did about your written confessions, I . . . she . . . presuming, assuming, even rushing to the computer just the way she did, recording my responses the way she did, and going on and on the way she did, but she, she never stopped, she . . . I . . . she . . . I don't know. . . ." Her tears came and she couldn't talk anymore. "Oh, dear God in Heaven, what is the squalid secret behind all this?" she whispered. "What is it? What is it?"

Quinn's face was torn.

"I know the secret," I said. "Mona, you hated her as much as you loved her. How could you not? Accept it. And now you have to know what happened to her."

She nodded, vigorously, but she couldn't speak. She couldn't look at me.

"And we have to go about this with great care," I said, "this search for the Taltos, but I vow to you again that we will do it. And I will find them or find out what became of them."

Quiet.

She finally looked at me.

A sorrowful motionlessness settled over her. She wasn't trying to stare me down. I don't think she even realized I was looking back at her. She looked at me for the longest time and her face grew soft and giving and tender.

"I'll never be mean to you again," she said.

"I believe you," I said. "I took you to my heart the first moment I saw you."

Quinn sat staring with patient eyes, the round mirror behind him like a great halo.

"You really do love me," she said.

"Yes," I said.

"What can I do to prove that I love you?" she asked.

I thought for a long moment, sealed off from her and from Quinn. "You don't have to do anything," I said. "But there is one small favor I might ask."

"Anything," she answered.

"Never mention my love for Rowan again," I said.

She locked on me, eyes so full of anguish that I could hardly bear it. "Only one more time, to say this," she said. "Rowan walks with God. And Mayfair Medical is her sacred mountain."

"Yes," I said with a sigh. "You are so very right. And don't ever think that I don't know it."

24

AN HOUR BEFORE the first light.

Mona and Quinn had already retired into Quinn's bedroom.

It was confirmed that I would take the bedroom of Aunt Queen whenever I visited Blackwood Farm. As for Jasmine, she was so grateful to me for getting rid of the ghost of Patsy that she held me to be infallible and was overjoyed with the arrangement.

It was a sin, my taking that room! But I did it. And Jasmine had already closed Aunt Queen's daytime curtains on the coming sun, and turned down the covers, and tucked under the pillow as always the copy of Dickens' *The Old Curiosity Shop*, as Quinn had said to do.

Enough on that.

I stood alone in the little Blackwood Farm cemetery. Did I like being alone? I hated it. But the cemetery drew me, as they always do.

I called to Maharet, as I had done earlier on this same evening. I didn't even know if it was night where she was. I knew only that she was very far away, and that I needed her. Once again I poured out with all my strength the tale of the tall children and the young ones I couldn't name, and how much I needed Maharet's wisdom and guidance.

As the dawn came near to the moist Louisiana sky, I felt a vague foreboding. Find the Taltos on my own? Yes, I could do that. But what would happen?

I was about to retire, so that I could enjoy the process of falling asleep instead of blanking out like a smashed light bulb, when I heard a car turn on the pecan-tree drive and head steadily and confidently for the front of the house.

As I mounted the rise of the lawn, I saw it was an antique roadster, a venerable English MG TD, one of those irresistible cars you don't see anymore except at car shows. Real low-slung, British Racing Green, bumpy canvas top, and the person who pulled it to a halt was Stirling Oliver.

Being only slightly less telepathic than a fledgling vampire, he saw me immediately, and we moved to greet each other.

The morning light was still well behind the horizon.

"I thought you once promised me to keep away from here," I said, "and to leave Quinn alone."

"I've kept that promise," he said. "I'm here to see you, and if I'd missed you, which I didn't think I would, I would have given this to Jasmine."

He took out of his linen coat a single folded page on which somebody had written my name.

"What is this?" I asked.

"An E-mail I received for you, care of me, an hour ago. Came in from London. I've been on the road since to bring it to you."

"Then this means you read it?" I took him by the arm. "Let's go into the house."

We went up the front steps. The door was never locked. And apparently the lights in the parlor were never turned off.

I sat on the couch.

"Did you read it or not?" I said, staring at the page.

"I did," he said. "That would have been very difficult to avoid. It was also read by our man in London who sent it to me. He doesn't know where it originated, and he doesn't really know what it means. I've bound him to confidentiality."

"Why am I afraid to open this?" I asked. I unfolded the sheet.

To: Lestat de Lioncourt
New Orleans, Louisiana
c/o Stirling Oliver
Talamasca
Hand deliver without delay

My dearest indefatigable one:
    If you absolutely must: Private isle, St. Ponticus, southeast of Haiti, once a resort, apparently taken over by those you seek

six years ago. Harbor, airstrip, heliport, hotel, beach houses closed to public. Population of those you seek once numerous, cautious, secretive. Heavy human presence from beginning. Present state extremely unclear. Sense conflict, danger, rapid and confusing activity. Approach with caution from undeveloped east coast. Guard your children. Weigh wisdom of intervention if such is even possible. Ponder question of inevitability. Situation apparently localized. And *s'il vous plaît, Monsieur,* take the time to learn how to use E-mail! Both your young ones possess this knowledge! For shame! Be assured of my love, and the love of those here. M.

I was speechless. I read the letter over again.

"And this, all this confusing information, this is how I reach her by E-mail?" I said, pointing to the other data contained on the page.

"Yes," said Stirling. "And you can reach her instantly. Show this to either Mona or Quinn. Dictate your message to either Mona or Quinn. They'll send it."

"But why would she betray her location like that?"

"She hasn't betrayed anything. All you know is her screen name. And the message was probably relayed through several points. Believe me, she's quite clever enough to be untraceable."

"You don't have to tell me how clever she is," I said. "But I guess I asked you, didn't I?"

I was still stunned. I was holding in my hand a response to my most serious telepathic communication.

He handed me a map. He had folded it to the appropriate section and circled the island. I instantly committed it to memory.

"Why do you think she sent this message through you?" I asked.

"For convenience, obviously. She gathered the intelligence. She wanted you to have a precise summary of it. And also, it shows a kind of trust in us. She's acknowledging that the Talamasca is not your enemy or her enemy."

"That's certainly true," I said. "But what can she mean with all this about intervention and inevitability?"

"Lestat, if you'll forgive me, it's plain. She's asking you not to become involved in something where Darwinian forces may be at work. And she's telling you a drama is being played out on an isolated island where the world might not take notice."

"That isn't what she said. She said she couldn't tell what was going on. This message is extremely tantalizing. Well, to me, anyway. I don't think it will be to Mona."

"Both interpretations are correct," he said with a sigh. "What are you going to do?"

"Go there, old boy, what do you think?" I said with relish. "I can't wait. I mean, I have to wait. But I'll head out with them at sunset."

I folded the letter and put it inside my coat. I did the same with the map.

"Tomorrow I teach Mona about our most frightening gift. I've been putting it off—not wanting to overwhelm her. Quinn and I can take her to that island in less than half an hour."

"You have to teach her more than the art of flight," Stirling said. "The Taltos are much stronger perhaps than you imagine."

"In what particular way?"

He thought for a long moment. "You've met humans with the telekinetic ability to kill," he said.

"Yes," I said. "You're talking about Rowan. You don't have to be so cagey with me, Stirling. I've sought your hospitality. At First Street we sat at a round table together. For me, that's rather like the human custom of breaking bread. And now this E-mail from Maharet. So what are you driving at?"

"That Rowan's power, formidable as it is, didn't work for her with Lasher. That's why he was able to abuse her and keep her prisoner. The Taltos are simply too strong, too resilient, too elastic."

"That's a good point, but surely you don't think these creatures are a match for me," I said. "You have no idea of the evil engine that lurks behind this fancy facade of mine. Worry not. But I'll take the time to find out Mona's full capabilities. There's no calculating Mona's strength. We've spent so much time on her state of mind, we haven't developed those talents. Thank you for coming with this. Now I have to bid you *au revoir*. Why don't you stick around? I can smell bacon cooking in the kitchen."

"Take care," he said. "I'm devoted to you, all of you. I'll be anxious on your account until I hear from you."

I headed back to Aunt Queen's room.

Big Ramona, black cotton uniform, white apron, came barreling down the hall.

"Didn't you offer that Englishman a cup of coffee? All you had to do was stick your head in this kitchen, Lestat. You're underfoot enough around here to do that. Don't you go, Mr. Oliver! Can't you smell that coffee perking on the stove? You sit right down. You're not driving off without some grits and biscuits and scrambled eggs. I got bacon and ham on the stove. And Lestat, don't you go tracking that mud all around in Aunt Queen's room. Do you go looking for mud when you go outside? You're worse than Quinn. You take off those boots now, and Allen'll polish them again. Got to hand it to you, four o'clock, Patsy's ghost did not come! And I had a dream not half an hour ago, Patsy's in Heaven."

"*Eh bien, Madame,*" I called out, reverting at once to stockinged feet and standing the boots neatly side by side outside the bedroom door. "Never have my boots received such loving attention. You know, this is really like living somewhere."

"Yes, indeed," she hollered over her shoulder, "should have seen that gal, all dressed in pink cowboy leather, singing, 'Gloria in Excelsis Deo!' "

I froze. *You saw that!*

I went into the bedroom, latched the door tight, surveyed the inviting bed, dove into it and pulled the covers up over my head. No more. No more! Down pillows, yes, Oblivion, will you please get on with it!

There came a nudge against my back, and I rolled over.

Julien on his elbow, white flannel nightshirt. Face-to-face.

"*Dormez bien, mon frère.*"

"You know what's going to happen to you if you keep this up?" I asked.

"What," he replied sardonically.

"You're going to fall in love with me."

25

QUINN'S BEDROOM. *Conférence extraordinaire.*

Mona was hysterical with joy over the message from Maharet. And by my leave at once E-mailed a letter of thanks on Quinn's computer, which somehow devolved into two pages, with me taking over the keyboard at one juncture to outline my intention of going at once to the island with my children to ascertain what had become of the Taltos. Mona signed off with her "screen name" of Ophelia Immortal, but not before including Quinn's name as well: Noble Abelard.

No sooner was that sent off by the magic of electronics than we were fast at work ascertaining that Mona had the power to light candles by the force of her mind, ignite also the kindling in the fireplace, and the logs, and that she could levitate to the ceiling with no effort whatsoever.

I wagered she could very likely make journeys of considerable length by air, but we had no time right now to test it. As for telekinetic power to push, she was very strong on this, able to push me back to the wall if I did not resist, and so could Quinn, but again we weren't able to test this to the max with resistance. No guinea pigs. My vocal suspicion was they could bring death to a mortal easily with this power, breaking down the heart and its feeding vessels inside his or her body with no difficulty.

"You visualize it, you send it, you stand behind it with the full force of your will, you feel it leave you."

Ultimately Mona and Quinn would only learn the full extent of their powers if the situation on the island involved real danger. If they couldn't fend for themselves with full effect against hostile forces, they could certainly escape with supernatural speed and dexterity, and I could easily take care of them.

Now, as to clothes, my instincts prevailed.

I had a little theory of what we might find on the island. I nixed the idea of Aunt Queen's safari clothes for Mona and Quinn's hunting clothes for him. Forget the jungles and the far east side of the island.

"What's the flashiest and fanciest suit you own?" I said to Quinn, all the while rooting through Aunt Queen's closets.

"Well, I guess the gold lamé suit I had made for the Halloween feast. It's a three-piece beauty, but—."

"Put it on," I said, "with the fanciest dress shirt you own and a sequined tie if you've got one."

At last I drew from Aunt Queen's neat lineup exactly the thing: a black satin pinched-waist, deep slashed neck, sleeveless, knee-length dress trimmed in black ostrich feathers down the front and along the hem. Only an absolute stunner could wear such a thing. I tore off the ancient price tag and presented it to my princess.

"Go girl," I said. "And here are the black sequined shoes to match. (Four-inch heels, rhinestones galore.) Let's hit the road."

"This is how we go sneaking up to people hunting on a Caribbean island?" she said. She loved the duds. She was changing immediately.

I went to the dressing table.

Quinn had just returned in the shiny gold suit. Like all Quinn's suits, exquisitely tailored. The boy just didn't wear anything that wasn't finely sewn. Fact was, he had found a pale lavender satin shirt and sequined tie, and he was luscious.

"How about the pearls, can I heap them on her?" I asked.

"Absolutely," he replied. He went to work, putting necklace after necklace over Mona's head. All you saw was the richness of it, between the shuddering black feathers, her rounded little arms very peachy and her legs breathtaking under the flared short skirt.

She shook out her tangled hair.

"I don't get this," she said. "Aren't we supposed to be stealthy and careful and proceeding through the jungles?"

"We will be," I said. "But we're not mortals, honey pie. We're vampires. You can push the jungle out of your way with your mind, sweetheart. And if we run into hostile dudes, this is the perfect armor."

(As for me, beloved reader, allow me to remind you I am in a three-piece butter-soft black leather suit, with purple turtleneck and the shiniest boots in Christendom.)

Off we went to find the island of St. Ponticus.

I carried Mona with me up into the air, comforting her as much as I could and urging her to use her own power as much as I could, and Quinn journeyed on his own, being very adept at this gift and having used it since his Blood Baptism.

Within ten minutes Mona had her legs wrapped around me as well as her arms, she was so scared, but it didn't matter, she was hanging on, and she was learning, and I had her in my firm grip, and I resisted the urge to tease her by swinging her loose and holding her by one hand (chuckle, men are beasts), and we were headed for the gleaming rolling waters of the Spanish Main, now known as the Caribbean.

When I spotted the island in question, I made a swift descent until I spied the topography Maharet had described. Any closer and the gravity would have taken hold of me.

The decisive element was the airstrip with the words "St. Ponticus" painted in enormous letters on it. Probably faded to the human eye, but we could read them. There was a small Cessna plane on one runway, and then another very long vacant runway fit for a jet landing.

When I verified this I went back up to judge the island as a whole before drawing close to the buildings.

The island was oval-shaped. The resort covered the crescent-shaped south and southwest shore, with a huge margin of beach, and the rest of the island was jungle with rocky cliffs, apparently totally undeveloped.

I went low again. It was clear the island had plentiful electricity.

One immense villa dominated the landscape, fronting on the deepest southwest beach, with sprawling left and right wings and five stories of windows and spacious balconies. Its broad terraces led right down to the sand itself, and rooms on the lower floors of the palace had French doors and their own small courtyards, including gemlike swimming pools with low walls, and open gates to the beach.

On the west side was a giant swimming pool, sparkling with underwater light, and to the west of that deserted tennis courts.

Quite an affair, and off to the east what seemed to be a huge utility building with a restaurant attached to it. I could identify it by the open bar and the stools and the scattered tables, though not a soul was using it.

Then came the harbor, or marina, I'm sure they preferred to say, with a huge fancy white cabin cruiser at dock and many small boats tethered to the pier, and beyond it a heliport with what seemed to me to be a giant copter.

Last of all, and furthest from the villa, was the airstrip with the faded letters.

There were busy little beings visible on the island, carrying what appeared to be white crates between the cabin cruiser and the small plane.

I whispered to Mona: "Look down and use your vampiric gifts. What sort of people are these?"

"Those aren't Taltos," she whispered in my ear.

"You bet they're not," I said.

"They're carrying automatic weapons," she said in my ear, "they've got gun belts."

"Right you are," I said. "And knives in their boots, most likely. They're fair game, you understand, they're drug pirates and they're dirty."

Some of the men wore colored bandannas around their foreheads. All wore jeans. Racial characteristics varied. The blood scent rose in my nostrils. I was hungry for it.

"It's a positive feast!" she said. "But how are we going to do this! And what have they done to the Taltos!"

I felt my heart tripping. I ought to have been ashamed. I was getting more heated by the second.

I took her up again, and went towards the jungle of the east coast as Maharet had cautioned me to do. The whole island wasn't very big. One could have walked straight across it, even given the mountainous heights, in about two hours. But that is a great deal of jungle, really.

We arrived at the foot of an awesome cliff, where there was a little strip of beach, just enough for us to come together. Beautiful and boring.

I scanned the jungle around us. I picked up nothing clear. But the sheer thickness of the jungle, the sounds of all the little beasts, all this bothered me. It was a perfect hiding place, this jungle.

I scanned afar for the voices of the drug pirates. Activity of phones. Some music. I let my scan grow in power. It was all drug maneuvers. Cabin cruiser had brought in a load. The load would go out in the plane and the copter. Transfer was almost complete. A chaos of voices.

Party going on in one of the rooms of the villa, maybe other rooms as well.

Mona was very shaken. "What if they've killed them all!" she cried. "What if they've taken over this island?"

"What if they're working for the Taltos," said Quinn. "What if this is how the Taltos support themselves?"

"I can't believe that," said Mona. "Besides, Ash Templeton had wealth. He didn't need anyone to help him to acquire more of it. He wouldn't have done this. He would have contacted Rowan and Michael had he needed help." She was fast becoming hysterical.

"Get a grip, Mona," I said. "The information's five minutes away. As for Maharet's advice, I'm overruling it. I'm going straight to the other end of the island. You can proceed through the jungle towards the back of the building if you like, but I want to enter by the front door. My blood's too hot for waiting. Are you with me?"

"You're not leaving us here," said Mona. She clung to Quinn all the same. "Can we follow your lead?"

"That's what I had in mind."

Quinn was plainly reticent. "I say we do what Maharet told us to do."

"Come on, Little Brother, get into the action," I said. "We're on the moral high ground."

We came down right above the airport-control building. Empty. Went around it, walking in a leisurely manner until we reached the enormous runway where the drug drones were just finishing their work with the little plane.

You couldn't have imagined more dangerous-looking creatures than this trio, in their cut off T-shirts and jeans with knives visible on their belts, guns stuck inside them, plus the big automatic weapons slung over their lean muscular shoulders.

When they happened to see us, they nodded and politely looked away. The clothes completely blinded them. Obvious presumption we were guests. Unwise to stare at us.

Then came strolling along the pilot, a cut above the little crowd, but just as mean, burnt brown from the sun, a human raisin, armed to the teeth but wearing a dirty bill cap instead of a bandanna.

They were all talking fast and a little hostile to each other in Spanish, a generally resentful and bristling bunch. Had the plane been overloaded? Was anything pilfered? What took them so long? I caught the greed and the impatience and the universal distrust. Nothing at all about any tall children who inhabited this place before.

The pilot glanced at us, checked us out from head to toe, nodded, then went back to his conversation with the trio.

"I get it," said Mona under her breath, meaning the clothes. I nodded.

I walked across the distance between us, ignoring Mona's desperate plea for me not to do it.

"So where's the boss?" I said.

"Man, if you don't know, how should I know?" countered the pilot. Snarl for a face. Empty black eyes. "I'm off schedule. Don't hold me up."

"Where you headed?" I asked.

"Get that info from Rodrigo," he said. "You shouldn't be down here anyway. Get back to the villa."

Rodrigo.

I whipped him away from the others, sank my teeth, sought the blood fast and drew it out: *Where are the tall ones, the ones who lived here first?* Know nothing. Whoa, delicious rush of blood to my brain and eyes. Floating for one second. Heart exploded. Flung him down on the tarmac, dead, staring up at me, last breath of air through his dead mouth.

The trio of bandits stood trapped, then bolted. I hooked one and held him.

Mona and Quinn caught the remaining pair, quickly seeking for the blood. For a second Mona had a struggle on her hands, the bandit going for his knife of all things, but she hung on, pitching it away, and finally subdued him, using more nerve than innate strength.

Quinn was lithe and silent and perfect.

"Tell me about Rodrigo," I said to the man I held helpless by the neck, my fingers getting tighter. I jerked him around and sank my teeth. *Who is on this island?* The boss, his mother, his women, this is his sanctuary, he'll cut you to pieces—. The heart and the blood went dead. I had had enough.

The fresh blood swam up in my eyes, ignited my brain. I savored it, savored the tingling in my arms and legs. Battle juice.

" 'They are corrupt. They have done abominable works,' " I quoted with a sigh as we came together. Quinn was dazed by the feeding. Mona was reeling.

"They've been here for over a year!" she whispered. "That's all I could get. But where in the name of God is Morrigan?"

We passed the heliport and its adjacent building. Two inside, breaking for coffee before takeoff. Same mold, heavily muscled arms, jeans low on their hips, looked up at me calmly from their steaming cups.

I sauntered to the table, Mona and Quinn inside the door. I sat down:

"You know what I'm talking about. The tall people who owned this place before Rodrigo took over. What's happened to them?"

The shortest of the two shrugged and smiled: "You asking me? I never been here before last week. That's the way Rodrigo works. Ask Rodrigo." He turned around and gave Mona the once-over with his eyes, then looked back to me with a sinister smile.

The taller of the two shrugged.

"Say your prayers," I said.

After that little fatal skirmish we headed for the big restaurant utility building, which stood seemingly vacant and all lighted up, the bar stools standing empty outside under the thatched roof and the tables scattered on its pink tiled terrace.

Stainless steel kitchen, glaring lights, groaning, rumbling, rattling machines. Scent of pine cleaners and soap. Countertops covered with trays of dirty dishes, stench of rotting food. Giant dishwasher churning.

"Come on," I said, "no life here."

We pushed on towards the immense palazzo.

We had to pass the ground floor suites with their private swimming pools, and here the internal lamps burnt and there was chattering and laughter.

I caught the sound of the Bossa Nova coming from somewhere deep in the main part of the building, a soft seductive music pulsing over the breeze-swept sands.

In the dark, beyond the low walls of the suites, we weren't visible as we moved along, scanning room after room. It was all drug goons who functioned as lackeys, bodyguards, unquestioning assassins, whatever the boss wanted, hooked to their giant televisions or chattering away on their cell phones, or even up to their waists in the pools. Blue walls. Bamboo furniture. Their rooms were pits of garbage, girlie magazines, bottles of tequila, beer cans, packaged chips spilling out of bags and bowls.

We scanned desperately for knowledge of the tall people. We got nothing for our pains.

My urge was to kill all of them. "They are all gone aside, they are all together become filthy, there is none that doeth good, no not one," saith the fourteenth psalm. But who am I, Saint Juan Diego, to mete out such a fate to these souls who might in some distant future repent and become saints of the Lord on High?

Nevertheless! I'm a ruthless dude. And they had to go if we were to extricate even one Taltos from this island.

Besides, there just wasn't any other way to do it.

Gathering Mona and Quinn to me, I blasted the lackeys one after another, feeling the strength leave me in the instant that it hit them. This was not exhilarating. This was not fun. This became repulsive, and the only thing that made it endurable was my abhorrence of their boot leather souls.

We came on a pair, fancier than the others, Miami-retro Hawaiian shirts. Mona took the comely one with the dazzling rings and the naked chest, and I clamped down on the older, frightened one, who gave up images of contrition in the blood.

"They can't give us anything!" Mona said, wiping her lip. Her eyes were glassy and large. "Why don't they know?"

"Because they come and they go, and they know nothing about what actually happened here," I said. "We're cleaning them up, that's the point. When the big man calls for help he won't get it. Move on."

Two more suites. Low-level, groveling servants. Snorting coke and listening to salsa. Mad that they couldn't turn up the volume. Orders of the guy in the main building. The strength was getting a little more difficult, and I let Quinn have a go at them and he took them down swiftly, eschewing the blood.

Then Pay Dirt!

The last suite fitted partially into the body of the main building. Considerably larger than the others. Forget the powder blue walls and the rattan furnishings. This was a palatial cell of pure whiteness. White leather couches, chairs, broad pillow-laden bed strewn with glossy magazines. Vases of fresh flowers bursting with color. A wall of books. Immense dressing table laden with cosmetics. Burgundy carpet. Shining in the night.

And maybe just the strangest creature I'd ever seen in my long wanderings on the planet.

Mona let out the expected gasp, and Quinn put his hand resolutely on her shoulder.

As for the occupation of the beast, he was clacking away on his computer, which had a large printer connected with it, and he did not sense our presence any more than the drug bums in the other chambers. He paused in his work to pick up a full glass of milk and drain it. He set the glass on the table to his left, beside a large opaque pitcher.

He was easily seven feet tall, apparently male, though it was difficult for me to tell until I really caught the scent, thick and sweet, and his lustrous black hair was cut maybe shoulder length and brushed back and held away from his bone-hard face by the common red bandanna.

Sweet fragrance. Remarkable fragrance.

He had huge black eyes, enormous and beautiful cheekbones and baby fresh skin all over. Clothes? Sleeveless gleaming satin T, chocolate brown leather mock jeans exquisitely stitched up, enormous feet in open sandals. Spiderlike hands, and fingernails and toenails polished in shimmering metallic blue. Mouth baby soft and large.

He played delicately with the keys, oblivious to us, oblivious to all things, humming and turning his head from side to side as he wrote or calculated or sought or talked, and then—

—he rose up to his height of seven feet and pivoted and pointed to us, eyes wide, hostile, mouth open.

"Blood Hunters!" he cried out in a weary exasperated and disgusted voice. "Pass over me, you fools of the night, I assure you my blood is bitter to you. What do you want me to do? Cut my wrist and paint the door post? Pass over. Go feast on the humans on this island! Kindly don't disturb me again."

Mona darted across the courtyard and around the pool and we went after her.

"Taltos!" she said. "I'm Mona Mayfair, the mother of Morrigan! You came down from me! You have my genes in you! Where is Morrigan!"

Rocking back on his heels, he gazed upon her as though he pitied her.

"You're a cute little pixie to be such a liar," he said with withering scorn. "You never birthed a human being in your life," he went on contemptuously and coldly. "You're a Blood Hunter. You can't birth. Why come into my room to lie to me about Mona Mayfair of all people, Morrigan's mother? Who are you? Don't you know where the party is, darling dear? Listen to the Bossa Nova, and go dance with the Drug Lord and his select minions. Drink their blood. It's hot with evil, you ought to love it."

The contrast between this large-boned baby fresh face and this dark free-flowing disdainful voice was shattering. But we were far from interesting to the creature, obviously, who was about to sit down again at the desk when Mona protested.

"I was human before this," said Mona, reaching out to take the creature's right arm. (He pulled back.) "I did birth Morrigan," Mona said. "I love Morrigan. My love has crossed into the Blood. I've come to find out if Morrigan is well and happy. Ash Templeton took Morrigan from me. You're descended from them. You have to be! Talk to me. Answer me! This is the goal of my life!"

The creature took the measure of each one of us. More easy scorn. A little amazed laugh. He slouched back with a gorgeous grace, the lids of his eyes coming just perfectly halfway over his big glistening eyes, and his baby mouth smiling brilliantly. He raised one eyebrow.

"Goal of your life?" he said mockingly. "Little redheaded Blood Hunter on stilts? Why should I care about the goal of your life? Ash Templeton, you said. Ash Templeton. Now that name is not known to me. Unless you refer to Ashlar, my father."

"I do, yes, I do!" said Mona.

I was cautious in studying him, out of courtesy and full awareness that this was a Taltos, this was the mysterious being, and we had found at least one, but then my eyes saw what I should have seen before—the creature was shackled to the wall by his right leg.

He wore a cuff of steel connected to a very long chain that was hooked to the wall behind the desk. It was a chain long enough to allow him access to the pool in the courtyard behind us, and conceivably to the bath, which lay to the right of the immense bedroom.

"You know where Morrigan is, don't you?" said Mona. She seemed suddenly so tragic as she spoke these words. She'd been asking them forever, and now even this being wouldn't answer her.

I focused my force on the chain and broke it with a loud snap. I knelt on one knee and severed the cuff.

The creature jumped back, staring at the remnants of the shackles.

"Well, aren't we the little band of wingless angels," he conceded, his voice still sneering, "but how on Earth am I to escape? These stunted apes control everything. Listen to them. You hear the Bossa Nova? That's the big boy's song. Rodrigo, Lord of All. And his Mother, Lucia. Can you imagine living with this music for a year now? Isn't it sweet?"

"Oh, you'll escape all right," I said. "We'll take you out of here without question. Every human between here and the airstrip is already dead. And the others will soon join them. But we want to rescue all the Taltos. Where are the others? Do you know?"

"Morrigan," said Mona. "When did you last see her?"

"Morrigan!" the creature said, his head falling back, his voice like a black ribbon as the words flowed: "Stop saying her name. You think I don't know who she is? She's the mother of the entire Secret People. Of course I know her name. Morrigan is probably dead. Anyone who didn't cooperate with these Drug Merchants is dead. Morrigan was dying before they ever came. She birthed five males before she birthed Miravelle. That's too many children in too short a time."

He gave a weary shake of his head, eyes still half-mast, weight shifting from one hip to the other.

"Her own sons rose up and raped her in the hope of a female birth. At last Miravelle! And da da da DA! The tribe goes on! Morrigan was sick unto death, and her milk dried up, and then came the poison. If the Drug Men shot her they wasted their bullets. She was my mother, by the way, I loved her. Past tense. Get on with it."

I expected Mona's tears to come and I thought them justified, and I held her tight with my right arm. But they only stood in her eyes, forming a glaze in the light as she followed this cold, hard speech. She looked suddenly like a costumed waif in her feathered finery, gazing up at the face of this bizarre and sardonic creature.

This was a blow of such weight falling upon her that she could only stand there and let me support her. I wondered if she would slip from consciousness, so grave was her stare, so still her figure in my grip.

"Take it easy, my little one," I whispered. I kissed her cheek. "We have yet to explore the main building."

"Oh, Beloved Boss," she said in a faltering voice. "Oh, Beloved Boss, I have sought and so I have found."

"Not yet," said Quinn, eying the creature grimly. "Not till we search the island end to end."

"Well, aren't we the gallant little gang of Blood Thieves," said the tall being, "and we all love each other, kissy, kissy! I'm impressed. Seems in my fathomless noisome memories of Paradise Lost and Come Again and Gone Underground and Lost and Species Wiped Out that you merciless little beings preyed upon humans rather ruthlessly. What is this, Valentine's Day for Vampires?"

"We're going to get you out of your little prison," said Quinn with equal coldness. "Will you kindly cooperate with us and tell us what Taltos are left here?"

"And I'd oh, so love it if you told us your name," I said sarcastically. "It's a bit hard to read your mind. I keep stumbling in the ice and snow when I try."

He gave a bitter laugh in a small show of sinister spontaneity.

"Oh, so the outside world has finally come," said the being, swaying with undeniable grace, his words flowing like glossy syrup. "Well, you're a year too late. I don't know who's left or where they are. I might be the sole specimen." He made a broad upward gesture with both hands, and a broad hateful smile.

"And you did say that Morrigan was your mother?" Mona asked tenderly.

"Out of Morrigan and Ashlar," he said. "Pure as they come. Oberon of the first rank, known by the younger ones as a cynic and eternal wet blanket. Though I've never called them by name. They are Mother and Father to me. If I'd killed my brother Silas when he first started talking sedition maybe none of this would have happened. But I don't think the Secret People could have gone on forever."

"The Secret People, that's a lovely name," I said. "Whose idea was that?"

"Yes, I've always thought it was sweet," he said. "And our life wasn't bad at all, let me tell you. But Father was naïve to think it could last. Even Morrigan told him that. You can't keep a community of twenty Taltos perfectly under your supervision, you know, that sort of thing, no matter how much diversion and education and stimulation you provide. Father was a dreamer. Morrigan was an oracle. Silas was the poisoner. So it came to a bloody end."

Suddenly I divined a human presence behind the far door, and so did the Taltos.

A tall dark-skinned woman came in, perhaps fifty years in age, but extremely well groomed and seductive—black-rimmed eyes, heavily made-up face, blood red lips, and a head of luxuriant dark hair and a pinched waist, breast-heavy figure.

She was holding in her hand an obviously religious statue. She was fastidiously dressed in a mauve silk dress with a golden chain for a belt, black net stockings and sharp heels, flashy gold earrings, and she spoke immediately in heavily accented Spanish.

"Well, I finally found it but I had to move Heaven and Earth, I tell you, you'd think it should be common enough, with the Pope going all the way to Mexico, but I had to go on the Internet and find it, and here it is."

And there it was!

She set it down on the low white table along the wall! A brilliantly painted statue of Saint Juan Diego!

I was thunderstruck.

There he stood, brave little fellow, with his arms out, and the unmistakable image of Our Lady of Guadalupe in full rich color emblazoned on his *tilma*, and the famous roses dropping to his feet, and all this in unmistakable detail! Of course, the image of Our Lady was glued on, and the flowers were paper, but so what, it was Juan, my Juan Diego.

"And you left the party just to give this to me?" said Oberon with dripping mock affection.

"Oh, shut your filthy mouth," she said. "And who are these people?" Flash of brilliant smile. "Ah, you are my son's guests, are you not? Welcome."

"I'll give you a thousand dollars for that statue," I said. "No, I'll make you a better deal. I'll let you live. After all, what good would a thousand dollars be to a dead woman? Go get in one of those small boats in the marina and take off. Everybody else on this island's doomed, except for the tall people."

She stared at me with immense curiosity and utter fearlessness, eyes opaque, mouth hard. In a flash she had a black pistol in her hand. And in a flash I'd taken it from her and thrown it on the bed.

"You think my son won't cut you and your fancy friends to pieces? How dare you!"

"Better take my offer," I said. "Woman, thy faith has saved thee! Head for the marina, now."

"Lucia, I think he's telling you the truth," said Oberon in the same languid disdainful voice with which he spoke to us. "I can smell death.

It's all around us. I think the rule of the Drug Merchants has come to an ignominious end. Alas, your Ariel is free, my precious and prosperous pussycat, why don't you go?"

Oberon moved slowly across the room, swaying a little from one hip to the other, dipping his head to this side and that, and dipping down to pick up the gun, and looking at it as if it was a curiosity, and as Lucia watched, perplexed, enraged, frustrated, furious, helpless, Oberon slipped the gun into the right position and shot Lucia three times in the face.

So much for Lucia. She went down with knees bent, arms out, face pulp.

"She was kind to me." he said. "The statue is for me. I visited the Cathedral of Our Lady of Guadalupe when the Secret People went to Mexico City. You can't have the statue. Even if you rescue me, I won't give it to you."

"Cool," I replied. "You're in such a good bargaining position. But who am I to steal Saint Juan Diego from anyone? I'm sure I can find another statue. But why did you kill her if she was so kind?"

Oberon shrugged. "To see if I could do it," he said. "Are you ready now to go after the others? Now that I'm packing, I am more than ready to play my part."

"Oh God in Heaven," Mona sighed. I could see the shudder pass through her. She took several shaky steps forward and then collapsed in the white leather chair, her heels together, her hand to her forehead.

"Oh, do tell me what's wrong, pretty little grandmother of the tribe," said Oberon. "What, you thought we were all little flutter-wing angels like Morrigan? Must I describe to you nature's purpose in designing the double helix, regardless of its number of chromosomes? It's to produce a variety of creatures within the species. Cheer up. We've a party to go to, don't we?"

Quinn's face was grim. "Maybe you should give one of us that gun," he said.

"Not on your life," Oberon replied. He slipped the gun into his low-slung waist. "Now where should we start? Let me fill you in on such facts as I possess. Now pay attention."

"Marvelous," I said. "Something besides performance art and gilded insults."

He chuckled. He went on undaunted, the voice black syrup again pouring thickly and slowly:

"I can tell you that Silas and the vast majority of the Secret People were gunned down on the day that the Drug Merchants came. Torwan and several other females were kept for a while. But they cried all the time. Torwan tried to get away in a boat, and they caught her on the pier and stabbed her to death. I saw that. Of the men, only Elath and Hiram and I were kept. Then Elath killed one of the Drug Merchants and they shot him, and Hiram disappeared. And I think I saw Isaac once, but I'm not sure. I think they're all dead. Except for Miravelle and Lorkyn."

"What about Mother and Father?" I asked.

Oberon shrugged.

"Handsome Blood Thief, I must confess I hold out no hope. They were dying from the poison when the Drug Merchants landed here. Father told us to hide. Miravelle took care of them. Miravelle slept with them. We'd long ago put a stop to the poisoning but the damage was done. And no one could stop Silas and his rebellion. Right before Silas made his fatal mistake, Miravelle and Mother apparently had an opportunity to blind Silas with a screwdriver, but Miravelle, precious little thing, just couldn't bring herself to do it, sob, and Silas got free of Mother and knocked her unconscious. Oh, so tragic. I know now that I should have killed Silas first time I ever laid eyes on him. Father should have killed Silas as soon as Silas started threatening the Secret People. Lorkyn could have done it. She was the coldest female ever birthed on this island. A beast, I tell you. Alas! Who would have ever dreamed that Silas would rise up and try to take on the outside world."

I shook my head. "Cut to the connection between the rebellion of Silas and the coming of these drug people?"

He shrugged. One of his great spidery hands smoothed his hair and firmed the red bandanna.

"Silas started the war against them," he said. "He spied upon their work on a small nearby island. Don't ask me where. I never went there. But Silas plotted against them. He took a gang of the most aggressive and warlike of the tribe to their island, and went in smiling and saying kind things, and slowly and systematically murdered the whole gang. He took their drugs and their weapons.

"Silas said the reign of Father had to end. Father was ancient, pure Taltos, unfit for the modern world. Silas said we had Mayfair genes, human cleverness, human dreaming."

I stood beside Mona as she cried silently.

"The tribe celebrated, snorted the cocaine and shot off the guns. They smoked marijuana and went absolutely crazy. They killed two of us—Evan and Ruth—by accident. Can you imagine how stupid? Nobody had ever seen a dead Taltos before. It was ghastly. Silas had them ceremoniously dumped in the sea. Flowers flung into the water! Ludicrous. Silas began to shoot those whom he suspected of disloyalty!" He gave a deep disgusted laugh.

"Lorkyn made a speech. She said that going to the drug island had been a typical Taltos blunder. The drug people belonged to a great cartel. Their cohorts would come to get us. We had to take Father and Mother and get onto the yacht and leave the island. We could do it. Silas tried to kill her, but the others stopped him. Now that was a revelation. But Lorkyn has a way with her. No one was prepared to see her go down."

He shrugged, rolled his eyes, pushed the gun more firmly into the belt of his beautiful brown leather jeans.

"The drug people came," he said, swaying languidly as he went on. "By nightfall they were here. Silas and his allies ran at them, shooting off the guns they'd stolen. Rat tat tat! Can you picture it? They didn't even shoot from under cover." He sneered. "The Drug Merchants shot every Taltos in sight. They kicked open doors all over the villa. Quite an unforgettable experience, waiting for them to kick open one's door.

"It was the complete end of the Secret People. Those of us who were kept for a while? We were the quiet ones. The ones who didn't rush into battle.

"They didn't find me till the third day. I was simply lying in my room, upstairs in the villa. In they walked. They made a servant of me. They taught me to mix Caipirinhas out of cachaça and lime juice for Carlos. I knew the computer very well. I did the bookkeeping, spread sheets, payroll, all of that too. Then Lucia fell passionately in love with me. How could she not? She's well past the age where a male Taltos can make her bleed to death—.

"—That's what we males do to human women, you know, unless they're past their menarche. Lucia showered me with attention. She did this room all in white for me. She went to Miami Beach to have her inviting little privy chamber surgically tightened till it felt like the sheath of a twelve-year-old. She did that for me. Very nice. Of course

I've never been with a human twelve-year-old. She was a delicious lover."

"Hmmm," I said. "You don't mind her lying there with a pool of blood for a face?"

"Not particularly. You said every human on the island was going to die. Didn't you mean it?"

He sat down in his desk chair. He turned, poured himself another glass of milk from the pitcher and drank it down.

He fell to studying the three of us again, Quinn and I standing and Mona on the edge of the white chair, knees up, her face beating with the blood, and her tearfilled eyes so unutterably sad they were indescribable.

"Is that computer connected to the outside world?" Mona asked. Her voice was feeble, but she was still holding back the tears.

"Of course not," he said sardonically. "What kind of idiot do you think I am? If it had been, I would have gotten help. I would have tried to reach Rowan Mayfair at Mayfair Medical in New Orleans."

We were all of us silently shocked.

"How did you know about Rowan?" asked Mona. She wiped at her eyes. The black feathers of her dress brushed her cheeks.

"Father told all of us—if ever we found ourselves in grave trouble, we were to contact Rowan Mayfair at Mayfair Medical in New Orleans. I think that was two years after I was born. Father was already being poisoned by Silas but he didn't know it. He only knew he was getting weaker. He thought he was dying of old age. He had been to see his lawyers in New York. Very secret. No names. No numbers. That was Father's way. Morrigan was seldom if ever awake. Father knew things were going on behind his back. Morrigan woke up one time and accused Father of being in love with Rowan Mayfair."

In love with Rowan Mayfair.

"Why did she say that?" asked Mona in a broken voice.

"I don't know," he said wearily, with mock innocence. "All I know is, she's my only lifeline to the human world. Then suddenly you show up, Grandmother Dear, and you want to rescue us. Aren't you a child? You look like one. Playing with your mother's clothes perhaps?"

"Were you always of this disposition?" I asked. "Or has this enslavement altered you?"

He laughed a mirthless knowing laugh. He stared at the dead woman on the floor.

"You're a tricky one," he said. "I was born knowing Father and Mother were doomed." He smiled. "Father didn't have the temperament to control the young males. There were secret births all the time. You might say I sang a tragic song from the beginning. After all . . ." He stopped, yawned and then continued: "How is one to rule a community of Taltos unless one is willing to kill the unwanted births and those who breed against one's rules?" He shook his head. "I don't see any other way. Unless of course one puts chastity belts on the females. That could be done. You know, modern nylon chastity belts or some such. But that was certainly not the way of Mother and Father."

"What did the Secret People do here?" Mona asked. She was trying to speak firmly. "Did you simply live pleasurably on this island?"

"Oh, certainly not," Oberon responded. "Father and Mother provided a marvelous life for us. Father had a wonderful plane. It's in New York somewhere, stranded, dead, orphaned. Like Little Boy Blue's toys, waiting for him to come back. In that plane we visited all the great cities of the world. I loved Rome and Bombay in particular. I would love to see them all again—London, Rio, Hong Kong, Paris. And Mexico City. We were shepherded everywhere. And we were taught to observe human beings and pretend to be human beings. As long as we did that, Father and Mother took complete care of us. Simply terrific life. Father was very strict and very cautious. No telephones, no Internet. That might have been a fatal error in the long run."

"Did you ever want to escape?" asked Quinn.

"Not me," he said with a shrug. "I loved the Secret People. Besides, human beings generally kill male Taltos. The women they let live. They use them. But the males they always kill. Everyone knew that. Our life here was good. We had superb teachers here on the island. Father had them flown in for two to three weeks at a time. Of course they didn't know what we really were, but that didn't matter. We had an excellent library in the main building—books, films, all that."

He took another glass of the milk, making a slight face.

"It's not cold enough," he whispered. Then: "Sometimes we had human guides on our trips. Like when we went to India. We had the yacht, you know, the cabin cruiser for going out on the water. And the

cleanup crew came in twice a week and went through the entire property. And then there was the jungle. Elath and Releth loved to go off
in the jungle. So did Seth. I'm not much for gnats and scratches
and snakes and that sort of thing." He made a weary gesture with his
long arm.

"No, it was quite a nice life. Until Silas started his rebellion with
the slow poisoning of Mother and Father. And of course, though Silas
never lived to find out, there were others breeding behind his back,
and plotting against him too at the end. It was out of control, totally
out of control." He shrugged again. "You might say it was a disaster."
He leaned back and looked down at Mona as she sat crouched on the
edge of the white chair.

"Don't be so sad," he said hatefully, "Little Grandmother of the
tribe. It's not your fault. It's the way it is. Taltos can't live with humans.
Taltos make fatal blunders. Father told me if it hadn't been Silas, it
would have been another. The Secret People was an absurd idea. Near
the end he talked a lot about Rowan Mayfair. Rowan Mayfair would
know what to do. But he was a virtual prisoner in the penthouse by
then. And Mother was only conscious occasionally."

Mona's heart was broken. The cautions in Maharet's electronic
letter made sense. Darwinian principles, Stirling had called them. I
wanted to wrap Mona in my arms.

But we had yet to enter the main body of the villa. And I could hear
shouting now. A handful of mortals had discovered the dead we had
left behind in the other suites.

The door burst open again, and this time the black greasy barrel of
a gun preceded the man who had kicked it in. I sent the discrete power
to hurl him backwards and destroy his heart. A spray of bullets struck
the white ceiling. Too close. They might have killed this vile talking
creature. What a loss!

I plunged through the door. I found myself in a long thatch-roofed
porch. Another mortal lifted his weapon. I sent the Fire. And in the
sudden brilliant illumination, I saw another man running. The Fire
caught him. *Be quick.*

When I turned around, a young woman, jeans, shirt, snarling curses
in my face, came at me with a big automatic weapon. I disarmed her,
and sent the power. She collapsed, blood gushing from her mouth. I
closed my eyes. I was sickened.

I hoped to God that we'd cleared away most of the underlings. Maybe all.

The Bossa Nova was very loud now here in this courtyard. I could hear the whispered words in Portuguese, the swooning dance. The music said Peace. It said Slumber. It was so sweet, so hypnotic.

Through huge open doors I could see the deserted lobby with its lavish plants, the pink tile running to the broad central stairs. I was eager to get up there, get to the heart of the evil.

I went back into the white-walled room, shut the door, stepped over the dead Lucia and got to the point:

"When was the last time you saw any Taltos, living or dead?"

Shrug. "Maybe nine months ago? Every so often I think I hear the voices of Miravelle and Lorkyn. I woke up once and saw Miravelle walking out there on the beach with Rodrigo. Perhaps they were taken prisoner too for these ungodly men. Miravelle was sugar and spice—the idiot kind of Taltos, if you pardon my candor. When Miravelle plays tennis with you, she wants you to win! Notoriously stupid. It would have been easy to keep her. Lorkyn is cunning enough to hide her true spirit, and exceedingly beautiful. Red hair like Granny here. I know I've seen Lorkyn. But is she still alive now? Who knows?"

"Don't call me that," whispered Mona. She gave him a glacial smile. She seemed at a breaking point. "Oh, I know you mean it out of heart-felt respect, you're such a thoughtful creature, so full of innate love for everyone, but I will settle for Gorgeous, or Beautiful, or Darling One, or Toots, or even Sweetheart. You call me Granny again and I may chain you up to that wall and leave you here."

Another spontaneous laugh. "Very well, Toots," he said. "I didn't realize you were the boss of this little operation. I thought that position resided with the blond beauty here."

"And where is the room of Mother and Father?" I went on.

"Penthouse suite," he said. "Believe me, they were probably thrown into the sea a long time ago."

"How many people do you think are left in the main building now? I've wiped out all the men in this wing of the building, and one woman."

"Aren't you the feisty one!" he sighed. "How should I know? I can make a guess. Rodrigo, his two bodyguards, maybe a goon or two to fetch, and maybe . . . maybe . . . Miravelle and Lorkyn. It's a party in the first-floor bridal suite, that's Rodrigo's home away from home, one

level above, dead center looking out to sea. Or so his mother told me."
He pointed to the dead mother. "I'd love to shoot one of the goons,
assuming you haven't taken care of all of them."

"What about women? Does Rodrigo bring other women here? Are
there likely to be some innocent guests up there?"

"Very unlikely," he said, head to one side. "If there are guests,
they're dirty. This is a hideaway, a depot. Which has always given
me the faint hope of seeing more of Miravelle or Lorkyn. You know,
female Taltos are always, shall we say, feverish for fun? There's inevitably a slight issue of blood, but it comes afterwards and can be dealt
with privately. And the milk! Well, let me tell you, the milk's delicious.
Human beings can use them ad nauseam."

"All right, wait here for us, don't shoot anybody unless you have to
and we'll take you out of here, Mona and Quinn, come."

"I have no intention of being left behind," said Oberon. He
checked the gun in his belt. "I'll follow you. I told you I want to shoot a
goon or two. Besides, if Lorkyn and Miravelle are here I want to see
them. They're my sisters, for the love of Heaven. You think I'm going
to sit in this room and listen for bullets flying?"

"Don't you know by their scent if they're here?" asked Mona.

He gave another amazingly soft laugh. "The males give off the
scent, Grandmother," he retorted. "You should have studied up on the
breed."

"That's what I'm trying to do," she said bitterly, the tears spilling.
"Rescue it and study up on it, Oberon, my darling dear! I've come a
long way to find you, you blessed little sweetheart of a thing. What a
joy it is that we've met. I warned you, you call me Granny or Grandmother one more time, and I may just knock you flat on your back."

Rolling sarcastic laughter. "Okay, Toots," he said. "No more slips
of the tongue. And you are gorgeous."

He stood up and stretched like a cat. Gave her a warped smile.

"Have any of you brilliant and crafty and conscientious Blood
Thieves lifted a cell phone off your human victims? I want to call
Rowan Mayfair."

"I have my own," said Quinn. "And I did lift a couple. But it's too
early to call. Let's move."

"Well, come on, you little sugar pot," Oberon said, offering Mona
his hand. "Let's go kill Rodrigo so he can be with his mother. And then
we'll come back for Saint Juan Diego."

"Why do you like him so much?" I asked.

"Who, Rodrigo?" he asked. Big raise of his eyebrows. "I detest the man, I assure you."

"No, Saint Juan Diego," I said.

"Oh." Laugh. "I told you. I went to the Cathedral. Besides, when Lucia told me he'd been made a saint, I prayed to him for a miracle." Suddenly his eyes got wide. "Good Lord!" he said.

"What is it?" I asked. "Something has come as a surprise to the Cynic for All Seasons?"

"Don't you see?" He was flabbergasted. "Saint Juan Diego answered my prayer! You're the miracle!"

26

R ODRIGO WASN'T A SLOB. The lobby was clean, not a scrap of paper on the desk or in it.

Nevertheless, the hotel had the air of a haunted place, having been robbed of its vitality and purpose.

Mammoth kitchen, machines grinding away, countertops clean except for fresh trays littered with fancy china, remnants of lobsters, glasses of milk, fish bones, etc.

No human presence.

"Don't you see what that means?" Oberon said, staring at the plates. "That's Taltos food, all white. They very well might be up there." He was sloughing off his languor, growing even slightly excited.

I checked out the storage room, cases of powdered milk, some split open, powder on the floor, footprints, cans of condensed milk, empties in a pile.

"And explain that to me?" I asked.

He stared at it, shook his head. "I can't," he said. "Unless one of them comes down here in the night and guzzles. It's a possibility. You starve a Taltos for milk, and it will go after it. But let's get upstairs, my sisters are here! I know it."

"Hold on," said Mona, her eyes rimmed in red, her voice still quavering. "This doesn't prove a thing."

The big central stairway led to the mezzanine floor and into the spacious rooms of what had once been the library. Litter of laptops, bigger computer stations, walls of books, maps, world globes, televisions, huge windows open to the sea. Dust everywhere, or was it sand? The music from above was extremely loud. The place looked uninhabited and untouched.

"This was Heaven here," said Oberon, "you can't imagine the hours of pleasure I spent in these rooms. Saints Preserve Us, I detest that music. Maybe we should hit the breaker box to shut that off."

"Bad idea," said Quinn.

Oberon held his gun with both hands, and he had dropped his disdainful demeanor altogether. He was almost what one would call enthusiastic. But the music was attacking him like a horde of mosquitoes. He shuddered over and over again.

"First thing I'm going to shoot is that speaker system," he said.

Again we took the carpeted stairs. Scanning for humans. I caught the scent of one.

The suite was dead center and wide open to the broad iron-railed porch that looked down on the lobby, the emperor himself seated in a huge gold satin–sheeted bed to the right, bleached wood headboard carved with mermaids, talking rapidly into a phone, costume sleek leather pants, purple satin shirt open to reveal a chest of oiled muscles, lustrous short black hair brushed back from a polished brown face with extraordinarily pretty eyes.

Thick beige carpet, scattered chairs, lamps. Doors open to other rooms.

He clicked off the phone as soon as we entered.

"Oberon, my son, I wasn't expecting you," he said, musical voice barely accented with Spanish, drawing up one knee, eyes moving over the rest of us as he smiled cordially, toenails manicured and buffed to a shine. Extremely amiable manner. "And who have we here? It must be party time. But let's introduce ourselves first, shall we?"

He lifted a small black gadget and the inundation of purring dance music came to an end. The sound of the breeze was born again, sweeping through the great empty wall that fronted on the Caribbean.

"Oh, Rodrigo, I am ever so grateful to you for that," sighed Oberon. "I was looking everywhere for the source of that infernally simpering music."

"So that's why we're waving that gun around," said Rodrigo agreeably. "And where's my Mamma, didn't you bring her up with you? I can't raise anybody on this island. I'm humiliated. Please, my guests! Be seated! The bar is there—everything you could wish. Miravelle!"

he shouted suddenly. "I have guests here! Where exactly did you come from? It's once in a blue moon a boat ties up at my dock. But you're most welcome. We are very private here, you understand, I can't invite you to stay—"

"Don't you worry at all about that," I said, "we'll soon be on our way. Just wanted to connect with Miravelle and Lorkyn."

"Is that so?" he asked skeptically. "Miravelle!" he called out again in a short Latin bark.

This time with results.

She entered from the left, the genuine article without doubt, maybe six and a half feet tall, yellow hair, oval face, baby flesh like Oberon, simple black linen sleeveless dress, sandals, round blue eyes, and when she saw Oberon she screamed and ran into his arms. He had only time to shove the gun in his belt before he enfolded her.

He lost all reserve embracing her and running his lips all over her. He pushed her hair back and broke into sobs suddenly as he kissed her.

"That's it, get back!" declared Rodrigo from the bed. He clapped his hands imperiously. "You hear me, both of you, I said get back! Oberon, did you hear what I said?"

But the two had fallen to kissing and speaking what seemed an alien language in high-pitched whistling words that none of us could understand, astonishing Quinn, though Mona seemed not one bit surprised by it. It was a spectacle.

Rodrigo was off the bed in an instant. He had the cell phone unfolded and was barking orders in Spanish. Then shaking the phone.

"They're all dead," I said. "I killed them all."

"What are you talking about?" he said, the graciousness gone, his face the picture of rage. He drew his gun out of his belt and leveled it at me. "You're being rude to me in my own room," he said, "which I won't tolerate."

I sent the power to push the gun out of his hand and far to the right wall. It hit the sheetrock and fell to the floor. His eyes grew large, but he wasn't humbled by this display of strength. He glared at me, trying to make sense of what he'd just seen, then scoping Mona and Quinn.

Meanwhile the two Taltos had settled down somewhat and were watching him. Mona came up beside them. Quinn was beside me.

I scanned the hotel. There was another being walking on the floor above, but I didn't know whether it was Taltos or human.

"All right, what do you want from me?" Rodrigo said. "You want money, what? You killed all my men, you did that? For what reason? You want this island, it doesn't belong to me, take it. I was leaving tonight anyway. I don't care what you do. Miravelle, get away from him!"

He was suddenly distracted by a roar and a particular sound which I knew and couldn't place until he named it:

"The copter! They're taking off without me!" He ran to the open balcony. "Stop them, damn them." He want into a Spanish aria of denunciations and execrations.

I sent the scan. Two human beings. Male. What good was it to us or the future of this place to have them escape? I held tight to the iron railing of the balcony and I sent the Fire.

I didn't know if the power was viable over such a distance, but no one would know if I failed. My body was rigid with the attempt, the knot inside me burning with all the energy I could feed it, and suddenly the Fire hit the copter with a force that knocked it to one side. I gave every particle of consciousness in me to the heat. *The Fire.* The copter went up in flames. Then it exploded.

It was plenty far away from us, but everyone in the room cringed from the blast. It lit up the island.

Rodrigo was speechless.

I hung on to the rail, dizzy, sweating all over, and then I backed away, glaring at the spectacle of the huge machine coming down lopsided to the runway. It was slowly incinerated. I was sickened again, to think that I could do that, to think that I had done it. And the feeling of emptiness, of meaninglessness took hold of me. I believed in nothing. I was good for nothing. I ought to die. All that seemed fixed in my mind. I couldn't move or speak.

Quinn took over; I could hear his crisp voice right beside me.

"Well, old man," he said to Rodrigo, "it's no longer leaving without you. Any more favors you want from us? And now tell me: What did you do with the pair in the penthouse suite, the ones that Miravelle and Oberon call Mother and Father?"

Rodrigo turned slowly and looked at me, eyes narrow and vicious, and his mouth twisted with anger. He picked up his little cell phone again, and let loose a barrage of Spanish into it with only one recognizable word: Lorkyn.

Steps overhead.

"Hmmm. So she's alive too," said Oberon, from behind him.

A light singing voice came from Miravelle:

"Oh, please, please, if you're here to save us, let us go up to Mother and Father's room. Let us see them. Rodrigo promised they are there, they are on ice, let us go! They are safe and sound on ice. Please, Oberon, please! Before Lorkyn comes."

"You imbecile," said Rodrigo, his eyes fixed on me, then darting to Mona and Quinn, trying vainly to comprehend what we were, how to play this. He had no gun, but there was a knife in his boot, and he was desperate for the appearance of Lorkyn.

And Lorkyn satisfied everyone on that score immediately.

We could hear her striding down the steps from the floor above. We could hear her tread on the balcony, and then she appeared in the open doors to the suite.

I heard Oberon's deep despairing sigh before I made sense of what I saw, and Mona let out a bitter laugh.

The creature was the predictable six and a half feet tall, with the predictable baby flesh face and naked arms and legs, but her face was round, not oval, and she had almond-shaped green eyes, extraordinarily pretty, with lashes so thick you'd think they were fake but they weren't, and a kitten nose, and a sweet mouth, very pink, and a small firm chin. She had Mona's red hair, brushed back from her shining forehead and apparently clipped on the top of her head, because it appeared to be spilling down behind her.

She wore a leather sleeveless shirt, low-slung belt, miniskirt and high-heel boots, laced up the back.

The shocker? She was armed, not just with a gun in a holster over her shoulder, but with an AK-47 slung over her shoulder as well.

She sized up the situation in an instant. But for insurance Rodrigo let loose with another aria of Spanish in which he told her to kill us all, including Oberon, but to spare Miravelle.

"You move for that gun, precious," I said, "and I'll burn you to a cinder where you stand."

Oberon was transformed with rage.

"You filthy trash!" Oberon declared. "You murderous little traitor to the Secret People!" He began to shake all over, the tears spilling from his eyes. "You're in with them and you let me rot in that room below! You treacherous beast!" He drew out his gun and aimed it right at her.

Mona snatched it out of his hand.

"Honey darling," she said, shivering all over, "she's a specimen now. Rowan Mayfair can decide what to do with her."

"Rowan Mayfair?" asked Lorkyn in a soft ironic voice. "Rowan Mayfair has found this island?"

"Shoot them!" Rodrigo cracked out in English.

Lorkyn didn't move. "And Rowan Mayfair sends Blood Hunters to take us away from here?" Her voice had a sweetness to it that was entirely physical and had little to do with her intentions. Her facial features were mobile, expressive of emotion. But she dropped her voice to a whisper. "No wonder Father fell in love with this woman. What amazing resources she commands."

"Oh, he never did, he loved Mother!" cried Miravelle. "Please don't say all those old hateful things! We have Oberon free again. We're together! Rodrigo, you have to let us stay together."

"Shoot them!" screamed Rodrigo. He cursed Lorkyn a thousand times over in Spanish.

"Why not kill this one now?" Quinn asked pointing to Rodrigo.

"Lorkyn, where are the Mother and the Father?" I asked. "Do you know?"

"Safe on ice," she said.

"And where precisely would that be?" Mona asked with exhausted exasperation.

"I won't speak to anyone but Rowan Mayfair," said Lorkyn.

"Let me see them, please!" cried Miravelle. "Oberon, make her unlock the penthouse."

"Rodrigo, I don't think there's any reason now to keep you alive," I said.

"Let me shoot him," said Oberon.

"No," I said, "you'd take the gun and shoot Lorkyn."

Rodrigo went mad after a fashion. He tried to jump from the front balcony. I turned his head around on his neck, killing him instantly. I dropped him down to the tiles below. He lay there in a splat of blood.

I turned around in time to see Lorkyn shoved back against the wall, her arms out in the form of a crucifix. She'd reached for the gun in her holster and Quinn had done this by pure force. Lorkyn was staring at him. Her calm was impressive.

Mona was studying her as if trying in vain to understand her.

Oberon was glaring at Lorkyn, and bitterly weeping. Miravelle clung to him.

"You were in with them all the time," Oberon said despairingly. "What were you, the brains behind Rodrigo's glory? You with all your intellect and cunning? You could have reached help! You could have gotten us off this island! Damn you for what you did! Why did you do it?"

Lorkyn of the kitten face didn't answer. Her face never lost its softness, its expression of receptivity.

I went to her and gently removed her automatic weapon and broke it into pieces. I took the gun and threw it way out over the patio into the sea. She had a knife in her boot. Beautiful knife. I took it and put it in my own boot.

She said nothing to me, her exquisite eyes watching me as patiently as if I was reading her a poem.

I scanned but it got me nowhere.

"Take us to the Mother and the Father," I said.

"I'll reveal them to Rowan Mayfair and no one else," said Lorkyn.

"They're in the penthouse on ice!" said Miravelle. "Rodrigo always said. On ice. Let's go. I can lead the way. Rodrigo said that when he came into the penthouse, Father said 'Don't kill us, we can't do you any harm, keep us on ice and you can sell us to Rowan Mayfair and Mayfair Medical for millions of dollars.' "

"Oh, please," said Oberon through his tears, "Miravelle, darling dear, for once don't be a perfect idiot! They can't be in the penthouse on ice. I know where they are. I know where they have to be. If you can keep Lorkyn in custody, I know precisely where to go."

We moved as quickly as we could. Quinn had Lorkyn firmly by the arm. Oberon led the way. Down the stairs and down the stairs.

Once again, the giant kitchen.

A pair of huge doors. Refrigerator? Freezer? One was laden with locks.

I broke them off immediately.

As soon as the white mist cleared I stepped inside and I saw in the light over my shoulder the bodies frozen on the floor.

The tall black-haired man with the white hair above his ears, and the red-haired woman, both with their eyes closed, serene, tender to behold in each other's arms, white cotton garments, bare feet, angels sleeping together. Covered with frost, as if in the deep claw of intentional winter.

Scattered end to end on them, but not on their faces, were frozen yet once beautiful flowers.

I stood to one side gazing down at them, as the others peered through the door. I gazed at the frozen fluids on the floor, at the discoloration of their skin here and there, at the perfection of their embrace and their utter stillness.

Miravelle let out a high-pitched scream: "Mother. Father."

Oberon sighed and turned away. "And so down the long centuries he comes to this," he murmured, "at the hands of his own sons and daughters, and she the mother of us all who might have lived a millennium. And who put the flowers here, may I ask? Was it you, Lorkyn, you traitor to everything they believed? It had to be, did it not? You petty deserter. May God forgive you that you made peace with our enemy. Did you lead them here by the hand yourself?"

Mona stepped into the lighted rectangle of the door. "That's my daughter," she whispered. No tears. No sobs.

I felt the immense falling off in her of hope, of dreams, of love itself. I saw the bitter acceptance in her face, the deep drifting.

Miravelle was crying. "So he made them hard as ice, that's what he did," she cried. She put her hands to her face and cried and cried.

I knelt down beside the pair, and I laid my hand on the man's head. Frozen solid. If there was a soul in there, I couldn't feel it. But what did I know? Same with the red-haired woman, so resembling Mona in her fresh Nordic beauty.

I walked carefully out of the freezer until I reached the warm air, and I took Mona in my arms. She was shaking all over but her eyes were dry and squinting in the white mist. Then she roused herself as best she could.

"Come on, Miravelle, my dear," she said. "Let's close the door. Let's wait for help to come."

"But who can help?" said Miravelle. "Lorkyn will make us do what she wants us to do. And all the others are gone."

"Don't worry about Lorkyn," said Quinn.

Oberon wiped away his tears disgustedly, and once again he took Miravelle in his arms and embraced her warmly. He reached out his right hand, with its long delicate fingers, and stroked Mona's bowed head, and drew her close to him.

We closed the freezer door.

"Quinn," I said, "punch in First Street for me, then give me the little phone."

He obliged with one-handed dexterity, still keeping Lorkyn prisoner with a left-handed grip.

Lorkyn's face was sweet and musing, revealing nothing. Oberon, though he held Miravelle and Mona both, was glaring at Lorkyn with undisguised malice.

"Watch," I whispered to Mona.

Then I was on the phone:

"Lestat to speak to Rowan about Morrigan."

Her low husky voice came on the line: "What have you got for me, Lestat?"

I told her everything. "How fast can you get here?"

Mona took the phone from me. "Rowan, they could be alive! They could be in suspended animation!"

"They're dead," said Lorkyn.

Mona surrendered the phone.

Rowan asked: "Will you stay until I get there?"

"We're creatures of the dark, my beloved," I said. "As mortals are wont to say: Make it snappy."

It was two a.m. when the jet landed. It barely made it on the long runway.

By that time, Mona and I—leaving Oberon and Lorkyn in the custody of Quinn—had spent two hours getting rid of every corpse on the island. To the devouring sea we fed the remains even to the grisly remnants of the charred and smoking copter—a grim task, save for the placid overpowering waves of the Caribbean, so quickly forgiving every unclean offering.

Just before the plane landed, Mona and I had also discovered Lorkyn's digs—quite gorgeous, with a computer that was indeed hooked up to the outside world, and loaded with information about the Drug Merchants, and bank accounts in a dozen places at least.

But what had astonished both of us was the medical information of all kinds—countless articles downloaded from seemingly respectable sources on every aspect of health care, from studies of diet to neurosurgery and the intricacies of heart bypass operations and the removal of tumors of the brain.

In fact, there was far more medical information than we could conceivably examine.

Then we hit the material on Mayfair Medical.

And it was there, in that strange place, in moments sandwiched between violence and mystery, that I realized how immense the Mayfair Medical project was, how multifaceted and daring and full of promise. I saw the layout of the hospital and laboratories. I saw lists of doctors, lists of units and programs and research teams.

In addition, Lorkyn had downloaded dozens of articles about the Center which had appeared in medical journals.

And finally we came upon an immense amount of material on Rowan herself—her career, her achievements in research, her personal plans for the Center, her pet projects, her attitudes, her goals.

We couldn't possibly cover it all.

We decided we had to take the microprocessor with us. No choice really. Had to take Oberon's as well. No traces of the tragedy would be left for strangers.

Rowan and Stirling were first off the plane, Rowan in jeans and plain white shirt and Stirling in a tweed suit. Immediately they reacted to the spectacle of the three Taltos, in fact, Rowan appeared to go into a silent shock.

I presented Rowan with the microprocessors from the two computers, which she entrusted to an assistant who put them safely on the plane. Lorkyn watched all this with eyes as unreadable as Rowan's, though they looked much softer, perhaps part of a very sweet mask. She had been absolutely silent all during the wait and she showed no change now.

Miravelle was weeping. Oberon, having relieved himself of the bandanna and brushed his hair, looked beyond handsome, and deigned to give Rowan a slight nod of his head.

Then Rowan said to Mona:

"Where are the bodies?"

Out of the plane as if on cue came a crew of men in white scrubs, on down the metal stair carrying what looked like a giant sleeping bag. They had other equipment I couldn't decipher or describe.

We went back to the freezer.

All this time Lorkyn made no protest, though Quinn held her tightly, but she kept her large exquisite eyes on Rowan, except for occasional glances at Oberon who never stopped staring at her with a look of pure venom.

Rowan stepped cautiously inside the freezer as I'd done before. She examined the bodies minutely. She touched the stains of frozen fluid on the floor. She studied patches of discoloration on their skin. Her hands returned to their heads. Then finally she withdrew and let the team do its work of taking the bodies to the plane.

She looked at Mona:

"They're dead," she said. "They died a long time ago. Most likely right after they first lay down together here."

"Perhaps not!" said Mona desperately. "Maybe they can survive temperatures that we can't." She looked frail and worn in her black feathered dress, her mouth shuddering.

"They're gone," Rowan said. Her voice was not cruel. It was solemn. She was fighting her own tears and I knew it.

Miravelle began to cry again. "Oh Mother, oh Father. . . ."

"There's evidence of widespread decay," Rowan said. "The temperature was not consistently maintained. They didn't suffocate. They fell asleep as people do in the snow. They were probably warm at the end, and they died peacefully."

"Oh, that is so lovely," said Miravelle with the purest sincerity. "Don't you think, Mona? It's so very pretty. Lorkyn, darling, don't you think it is very sweet?"

"Yes, Miravelle, dear," said Lorkyn softly. "Don't worry anymore about them. Their intent has been fulfilled."

She had not spoken in so long that this warmth took me by surprise.

"And what was their intent?" I asked.

"That Rowan Mayfair know of their fate," said Lorkyn calmly. "That the Secret People not vanish."

Rowan sighed. Her face was indescribably sad.

She opened wide her arms and shepherded us out of the kitchen, a doctor leading us away from a deathbed.

We went out into the warm air, and the landscape seemed peaceful and given over to the rhythm of the waves and the breeze—cleansed by violence and mercilessness.

I looked beyond the lighted buildings to the huge mass of hovering jungle. I scanned again for any presence, human or Taltos. The dense growth was too thick with living things for me to detect any one creature.

I felt soul sick and empty. At the same time the three Taltos were worrying me in the extreme. What precisely was going to happen to them?

The crew with the frozen bodies ran past us to board the plane, and we made our way slowly to the metal steps on the tarmac.

"Did Father really ask for this, this freezing?" Oberon wanted to know. He had lost all of his scornful manner. "Did he go willingly to this death?" he asked sincerely.

"That's what Rodrigo always said," replied Miravelle, who was now in Stirling's arms, weeping piteously. "Father had told me to hide from the bad men, so I wasn't with him. They didn't find me until the next day. Lorkyn and I were together, hiding in the little house by the tennis courts. We didn't see what happened. We never saw Father and Mother again."

"I don't want to board this plane as a prisoner," said Lorkyn very politely. "And I'd like to know where I'm going. It's unclear to me, the source of authority here. Dr. Mayfair, would you please explain?"

"You're the victim of concern right now, Lorkyn," said Rowan in the same mild tone that Lorkyn had used with her.

Rowan reached into her pants pocket, pulled out a syringe and, as Lorkyn stared in horror and desperately struggled, sank a needle into the arm by which Quinn held her. Lorkyn went down clawing at Quinn and then finally totally collapsed, all hips, knees and spidery hands, kitten face asleep.

Oberon watched with narrow eyes and a chilling smile.

"You should have slit her throat, Dr. Rowan Mayfair," he said, with the rise of one eyebrow. "As a matter of fact, I think I can break all the bones in her neck if you'll kindly allow me to try it."

Miravelle spun around out of Stirling's loving grip and glared at Oberon: "No, no, you can't do such a horrible thing to Lorkyn. It's not Lorkyn's fault she's wise and knowing! Oberon, you can't do mean things to her, not now."

Mona gave a short bitter laugh. "Maybe you've got your prize specimen, Rowan," she said in her frail voice. "Hook her up to every machine known to science, vivisect her, freeze her in fragments and on slides, make her lactate the marvelous Taltos milk!"

Rowan stared so icily at Mona it was difficult to tell if she heard the words. She called for help from inside the plane.

The sleeping Lorkyn was placed on a stretcher with restraints and taken on board as we waited in silence.

Stirling followed with Miravelle, who was still weeping for Mother and Father. "If only Father had called Rowan Mayfair when he wanted to. But Mother was so jealous. She knew Father loved Rowan Mayfair. Oh, if only Father had not listened. And now the Secret People are just us three."

Rowan caught those words, glanced at me and then at Mona. Mona registered them too with a dark flashing glance at Rowan. The darkness overcame Rowan.

Oberon stood quite free, the picture of relaxation, with his weight on one hip, thumbs in his back pockets, studying Rowan in detail, his huge eyes half-mast again and his cheeks still wet from weeping.

"Don't tell me," he drawled, his head thrown back, "you want me to get in that plane too and go back with you to your Center of Medical Marvels."

"Where else are you going to go?" asked Rowan with a coolness that matched his own. "You're going to leave Miravelle and Lorkyn?"

"Rowan's your kin," said Mona, her voice strained and impatient, "she's your family, she'll take care of you, Oberon. If you have an ounce of sense let it override your crushing sarcasm and caustic wit, and get on the plane, and behave yourself. You might just discover you belong to an extremely rich clan of remarkably generous people."

"Your optimism touches me," he tossed off to Mona. "Shall we assume that it was devotion to the remarkable generous clan that drove you to run away with a couple of Blood Hunters and allow them to transform you into what you are?"

"Oberon," I said. "I set you free, did I not?"

"Here it comes," he said, rolling his eyes, "for the sake of Saint Juan Diego, will I please behave for Rowan Mayfair, the only human being Father ever truly loved, and will I not blind Lorkyn with my thumbs first chance I get, or something even more deliciously cruel?"

"Precisely," I said. "Cooperate with Rowan in every respect. You have nothing to lose by it. And don't jump Miravelle and make a baby. Okay? And when you're tempted to do otherwise, remember Saint Juan Diego."

Oberon gave a short laugh, threw up his hands, then lowered them and turned them out, then went up the metal steps to the open door.

"This must be one hell of a saint," said Rowan under her breath.

"On board," I said, "Oberon can tell you all about him."

"Wait, I'm forgetting the statue!" Oberon cried out at the top of the stairs. "How could I do such a thing?"

"I promise to bring it to you," I said. "Besides, the Mayfairs will buy you whatever you want. Go on, board."

He did as I told him to do, then appeared again:

"But remember, that's the statue connected to the miracle! You have to get it!"

"I have no intention of forgetting it," I said. He disappeared.

Now only Rowan was left, standing there with Mona and Quinn and me.

"Where are you going now?" asked Rowan.

"Blackwood Farm," said Quinn. "We three, we stick together."

Rowan looked at me. No one has ever looked at me in quite the same way that Rowan does.

She nodded.

She turned to go, then turned back and put her arms around me, a warm bundle of life entrusted to me. Every barrier inside me collapsed.

We kissed as if no one was there to see it, over and over, until it was a little language of its own, her breasts very hot against my chest, my hands clutching her hips, my eyes closed, my mind mute for once as if my body had driven it back, or so inundated it with sensation that it could not tell me what to do. And at last, she pulled away, and I turned my back. The blood thirst was paralyzing me. The want was paralyzing me. And then there broke loose the love, the pure love.

I stood motionless, realizing it for what it was. Pure love. And connecting it suddenly and helplessly with the love I'd felt when I'd kissed Patsy's phantom at the edge of the swamp: pure love.

And my mind cast back over the centuries, like the mechanism of conscience determined to ferret out sin, only it searched for moments of *pure love*. And I knew them, secret, silent, few, splendid. Splendid in their own power, whether the loved one ever knew it or not, splendid to have loved—.

Flash on the couple in each other's arms, Ash and Morrigan, the white mist rising from them. Emblem of pure love.

The awareness dissolved. Quinn moved me away from the roar of the jet engines. We walked off the tarmac.

We were silent in the noise of the departing plane. At last it made its smooth ascent. And was gone into the clouds.

The age-old mystery of the Caribbean unfolded—another tiny island soaked in blood—that this most glorious part of the world should bear witness to so many tales of violence.

Mona stood looking out to sea. The breeze lifted her full red hair. Her eyes were beyond tears. She was the very picture of mourning.

Could she begin now? Really begin, my perfect one?

I drew close to her. I didn't want to intrude on this bereavement. But she reached out with her left arm and brought me in, and let her weight rest against me.

"This was my search," she said, eyes faraway, "this was my dream, my dream that overleapt the Dark Blood—the dream that carried me through all the pain that preceded it."

"I know," I said. "I understand you."

"That I would find my Morrigan," she said, "that I would find them living in happiness, that I would know her again with all her madness and we would talk the long nights away, exchanging kisses, our lives touching and then parting. And now . . . it's all ruin."

I waited, out of respect for what she'd said. Then I spoke:

"They did live in happiness for a very long time," I said. "Oberon described it to us. They lived for years as the Secret People." I reminded her as best I could of what Oberon had told us.

Slowly she yielded to a nod, her eyes on the placid and warm sea. It made no impression upon her. "They should have let us help!" she whispered. "Michael and Rowan would have helped! Oh, the folly of it! To think that Morrigan wouldn't let him call Rowan. Because she was jealous! Oh, Rowan, Rowan."

I held my thoughts to myself.

"Come home to Blackwood Farm," said Quinn. "There's time to mourn and time to know Miravelle and Oberon and even Lorkyn."

She shook her head.

"No," she said. "These Taltos are not for me, not now. Miravelle is some pure and lithesome thing without my fire, without her mother's fire. The link is broken. Morrigan went down in pain. They'll care for Miravelle. Poor tender creature, salvaged from the ancient one and a mutant birth. I have nothing to give to Miravelle. As for Oberon, he's too dark for me, and what can I give him? He'll kill Lorkyn sooner or later, don't you think? And how will Rowan justify the keeping of Lorkyn? It's not my concern. It's not my passion. I want to be with you, you are my people."

"Don't try to decide these things now," I said. I felt so sorry for her. And in my heart I felt a burning concern for the tasks that lay ahead of Rowan.

"Maharet's words are clear." She went on in the same torn voice, her eyes never turning to me or to Quinn. "It was nature taking its course. It was inevitable."

"Perhaps, perhaps not," said Quinn. "But it is finished."

I turned, and looked at the distant villa with all its lighted windows. I looked at the broad mass of rocky jungle rising behind the brashly illuminated beach. I scanned. I caught the small beasts of the wild place, the tamarinds, the birds, perhaps a wild boar deep in there. I couldn't tell.

Yet I was reluctant to leave. I wasn't sure why.

I wanted to move through the jungles. The jungles I had not searched, and they were thick. Only this was not the time.

We bid the island good-bye. Quinn took Mona in his arms, and they made for the clouds.

I went back for the statue of my beloved saint, and was soon on my way to the safe refuge of Blackwood Farm.

27

I STOPPED at the flat, stripped off the leather clothes, put on a lavender dress shirt, purple tie, black linen three-piece suit, new boots, cut out for Blackwood Farm, dived into Aunt Queen's bed and went sound asleep.

(Saint Juan Diego was on the bedside table right beside me.)

Vague memory of Mona coming in before sunrise and telling me she'd E-mailed to "the mysterious Maharet" an account of the entire event. I said: "Bravo. I love you. Get out of here."

At sunset, when I awoke, I went out into the house to discover Stirling Oliver had come. He'd had an early supper with Tommy and Nash, who had gone into New Orleans for the evening, and was now waiting for me on the "wicker terrace" on the east side of the house.

I was so comforted by every aspect of Blackwood Farm and its unsuspecting humans that I could have wept, but I didn't. I made a little circuit of the big rooms. No sign of Julien's ghost. Why was he letting me off the hook? I rejoiced, whatever his reasons. Here at Blackwood Farm, the island of St. Ponticus seemed remote, the horrors of last night imagined.

The Dazzling Duo had not risen yet.

I took the statue of Saint Juan Diego and I headed outdoors.

The wicker terrace had been created by Quinn out of all the antique wicker furniture he'd found in the attic of Blackwood Farm when he was still a teenager, and he'd had it all restored and put out here, and it was quite atmospheric and charming.

The floodlights weren't on. There were just a couple of hurricane lamps flickering away, and Stirling, in a light tweed Norfolk jacket, was smoking a cigarette. His neatly trimmed gray hair was ruffled a bit by the breeze. But otherwise he was the picture of dignity. And the picture of a mortal with whom I could be at ease and talk as if I wasn't a monster.

I sat down in the chair opposite him, with Saint Juan Diego out of sight at my side.

There was that Fall bite in the air. I resigned myself to it, and breathed in the pure freshness of the breeze, and let my eyes linger on the pearly clouds and the frightening and inevitable little stars that soon shone through them.

"So hit me with it, baby," I said.

"Well," he said, his youthful eyes at once alert. "A plane of our people descended on the island as swiftly as could be managed, and collected the laptops and every other computer they could find in the mezzanine library that Oberon described to us, remnants of the Secret People that Oberon wanted saved, and they were about to take their leave when a boatload of the unsavory characters arrived. We had an escort of five or six soldiers of fortune, you might call them, not members of the Talamasca you understand, but quite loyal in their work for us, so there was a parley of sorts. The unsavory individuals deemed it prudent to depart. Very quickly in fact. I would say that they surmised that their time on the island had ended. Our plane took off without mishap. Chalk it up to poise and persuasion on the part of our soldiers.

"Meanwhile, the firm of Mayfair and Mayfair traced the entire history of the island, finding a clear chain of title revealing the transfer from Lost Paradise Resorts to The Secret Isle Corp., only officer and stock holder Ash Templeton. Attorneys for the Corporation in New York notified other attorneys, who then notified other attorneys who were the true managers of Ash's affairs.

"They flew down this afternoon. Saw his body at Mayfair Medical. Revealed Last Will and Testament executed four years ago, leaving everything to Michael Curry and Rowan Mayfair, with some sort of trust arrangement for Ash's children. That was years after Ash left New Orleans with Morrigan. There was a bundle of accompanying letters. 'To be given to Michael Curry and Rowan Mayfair should I die or become incapacitated.' They've been given to Michael and Rowan."

"I don't quite get it," I said.

"Ash was taking steps," said Stirling. "He knew the Secret People were in trouble. He simply didn't take the steps fast enough. Communication was always sporadic. The estate lawyers didn't know the location of the Secret People or their name. Communication broke off two years ago. Ash should have given one of the firms a timetable and a course of action: 'If you don't hear from me every six months, etc.' "

"I see," I answered. "Any clue as to what was in the letters?"

"From what Michael told me, the letters are full of polite warnings, observations and requests that Rowan and Michael and the Mayfair family care for his children. Ash was immensely wealthy. The money in essence passes to Rowan and Michael in trust for Oberon, Lorkyn and Miravelle.

"No problem there. I don't know whether anyone's ever made you aware of it, but Rowan and Mona both made immense profits for the Mayfair Legacy. Rowan sits on the boards who invest the funds of the Medical Center Endowments and she's considered an incredibly shrewd moneymaker. I suppose what I'm struggling to say is that the Mayfair fortune continues to grow, in spite of the cost of Mayfair Medical, which is now the recipient of all sorts of grant money, and Ash's Last Will and Testament will be observed with complete honor by Mayfair and Mayfair, have no doubt."

"And you think you owe me this explanation?" I asked.

"In a way, yes," he said. "You did rescue the Taltos. And of course you can tell all this to Mona when the subject arises. And I trust it will."

I nodded.

"While we're on the subject," he said, "might I ask, how do you live yourself?"

"On blood," I said.

"No, but I mean the financial part of it."

"Stirling, look to the Chronicles and your own Talamasca files. Hand to mouth immortals are the stuff of B movies. I have more wealth than I know what to do with. It's managed in Paris and in New York for me by mortals who know me by voice. When I do become ragged, it's a matter of moral disposition, nothing more."

"Fascinating," he replied.

"Go on with what's been happening," I said.

"Well, Rowan is so busy in the laboratory with the two bodies, she's scarcely looked at the letters. Michael is reading through them now. He'll show them to me later.

"Of course, the Talamasca has turned over all the computers from the morning raid to the Mayfair family. The computers are the property of Michael and Rowan by force of Ash's will. We had no choice but to do it. Perhaps they'll allow us to study the material later on."

"Has Mayfair and Mayfair taken any action about the island itself, to keep off the drug people?"

"They've contacted every form of authority policing that part of the World, I believe, but I gather that it's rather complicated. We offered to send back the soldiers of fortune. They may take us up on it. A private security force of some type has been sent there. Also some kind of cleanup crew. Apparently the cabin cruiser, the plane—these things were Ash's property. This Rodrigo whom you so obligingly destroyed was a major DEA target. This was made known to the family when they asked for protection for the island. The family has not cooperated with the DEA or invited them in. It's all being handled privately."

"Hmmm. . . ." I felt uneasy about the island. All that jungle. I wish I had taken the time to walk through that jungle. "Where are the Taltos?"

"You want the short answer, or the story?"

"You kidding?"

"Well, Miravelle and Oberon spent the morning and early afternoon at the First Street house in the company of Dolly Jean and Tante Oscar," said Stirling. "It was quite amazing. At times, I thought I was hallucinating. Apparently Tante Oscar has not left her French Quarter apartment in years. You remember, she wears three and four dresses at a time?"

"Yes indeed I remember," I said. "She spreads evil rumors about me. I'd set her right, but if she's really over a hundred years old, I might give her a heart attack."

"Good point. When Dolly Jean called her on the famous refrigerated telephone, she agreed to come to First Street if the car were sent, and she spent the afternoon with Dolly Jean and Michael regaling 'the Walking Babies' with stories, or with Miravelle or Oberon regaling them, I'm not quite sure which, but all of it has been recorded for posterity by me and by Michael. Miravelle was shocked by a great deal that the two old women had to say, but Oberon was in hysterics. He thought them the funniest human beings he'd ever met, and he was stomping his foot and slamming the table.

"Naturally I was enthralled merely watching this entire collection of beings, including Tante Oscar." He drew on his cigarette. "She was indeed wearing some three or four dresses under her maroon fox trimmed coat, and a black hat with roses on it and a little face veil, and she does have eyes like eggs. She entered the house making the Sign of the Cross over and over again, rosary beads running through her right hand, a battalion of exquisite twelve-year-old boys accompanying her up the marble steps and into the dining room. The boys soon discovered the swimming pool and were invited to swim and went to it with gusto. They might be still swimming now. Apparently they'd never been swimming in their lives before."

Stirling stopped.

The Dazzling Duo had appeared. Both were tricked out in safari jackets and khaki slacks, Quinn with an open shirt, Mona with an olive green turtleneck—a startling contrast to the formal clothes they'd always worn before.

They were both pale and a little gaunt. They had no need to feed, thanks to last night's repast, but apparently the dark adventure had taken their energy. Quinn appeared to be fasting. Mona looked wounded and frail.

Just for a moment, I saw in her the gaunt dying girl she'd been when I first laid eyes on her. It frightened me.

Kisses and hugs for Stirling, who rose to his feet to receive them.

I clasped her hand and she bent low to kiss me on the mouth. I felt a fever in her, as though her body were consuming her past dreams. And an ashen sadness clouded her vision.

She came right to the point, even before she flopped into a wicker chair and put her feet up on the table.

"Rowan has to know whether they're alive or dead by now," she said.

"Darling, they're dead," said Stirling, "there's no question. They've been brought up to a temperature of perhaps forty degrees, and connected to every sort of monitor known to Rowan. There's no life in them whatsoever. Only a gold mine of tissue and blood and bone which Rowan wants to examine."

"Oh, yeah, oh of course," said Mona in a low fast-running voice. She closed her eyes. She seemed so lost. "So the Mad Scientist must be overjoyed."

"What about the poison?" I asked. "Oberon said that Ash and Morrigan had been slowly poisoned by the rebel children."

Stirling nodded. "There were several compounds in their blood and tissue. Apparently they'd been given arsenic, Coumadin and some other rare chemical that strikes at the musculature. The doses would have been fatal to human beings. But it's a tricky matter. There might have been other poisons which didn't survive in the bodies. There were also huge amounts of benzodiazepines."

"Evil Silas," whispered Mona.

"Has either Miravelle or Oberon said any more about the life of the Secret People?" Quinn asked. "I think the more Mona hears about that the better she will feel."

"To Hell with it," said Mona in a low voice.

Stirling went on gently.

"Yes, they've both talked a lot. So did some of the New York lawyers who represented Ash. Their life was very good, and it lasted some four years before this villainous Rodrigo took over the island. Oberon enjoys describing their trips and their studies very much. Miravelle has reverted more and more to a childlike state. Oberon becomes impatient with her."

"Where are they now?" asked Quinn.

"At Mayfair Medical. Rowan had them both admitted for tests earlier this evening."

"Oh, splendid, and they agreed to it!" Mona said. "How could I not know that? The two dead ones are not enough! Lorkyn isn't enough. She has to have the live ones immediately as well! That's Rowan. Did she say the poor children looked a bit peaked? Or did she just shoot something into their veins and then throw them on the stretchers? I wish I could mount a conscientious opposition, but I haven't the spirit for it. So let them disappear into the laboratories and secret rooms of Mayfair Medical. Good-bye, sweet Miravelle! Will I ever lay eyes on you again? Farewell, oh, acid-tongued Oberon, may you not alienate too many of the nurses with your withering wit, for they can make your life miserable. And who am I, the Blood Child, to seek such a privilege as to see these odd, out-of-time beings, except perhaps to turn them loose into the workaday world where they'd undoubtedly fall victim to some insidious human equivalent to Rodrigo the Drug Lord!"

"Mona, Miravelle and Oberon won't be kept there," Quinn said. "We can see to it ourselves. Rowan won't make them prisoners. You're making Rowan the enemy again for no reason. We can go to Mayfair Medical now and see them, very likely, if you wish. Nobody can prevent us."

"Listen to you!" Mona said, with a faint affectionate smile. "You think you know Rowan, and you don't know Rowan. And Beloved Boss here has fallen under her dark spell same as Ash Templeton apparently, who forswore her for his species and failed to save them for Morrigan's jealousy of her, Oh, Darkness, Oh, Piteous Darkness; Lestat, how can you find her glacial heart!"

"You're using Rowan as a lightning rod," said Quinn calmly. "What's the excuse now for hating Rowan? Because she pronounced Ash and Morrigan dead? Lestat told you they were dead. Let it go. Let it all go."

Mona shook her head, words rushing. "Where's the wake? Where's the funeral? Where are the flowers? Where is the family with everyone kissing? Will they put Ash and Morrigan in the family tomb?"

I reached over and took her hand. "Ophelia," I said softly, "what need have they for flowers now, or kissing? 'Is't possible a young maid's wits should be as mortal as an old man's life?' Be still, my beauty."

She answered me with Shakespeare:

" 'Thought and affliction, passion, hell itself, She turns to favour and to prettiness.' "

"No, come back. Hold on."

She shut her eyes. The silence lengthened. I felt her draw breath.

"Stirling, tell her how it went," I said cautiously. "Tell her the comic parts."

"If I may say so," Stirling said, "after an afternoon with Tante Oscar and Dolly Jean, and all their stories of Walking Babies in the swamps, Miravelle and Oberon were ready for a hospital suite. And very likely Michael Curry was glad to see them go."

"Did they never try to escape the house?" asked Mona.

"Guards all around it," conceded Stirling. "But Mona, how can anyone let these two go unshepherded into a human world? Yes, the Secret People endured for some five years, it seems, and Oberon and Miravelle told the most wondrous tales of their life with Father and Mother, but the basic concept was falling apart from the start. The Silas Rebellion lasted two years. Rodrigo's takeover another two, and that's the story we have at this point."

"Well, what's going to happen to them?" Mona demanded.

"Oberon's placed his fate entirely in Rowan's hands, and after meeting Michael and wandering about the First Street property, and his high comic rounds with Tante Oscar and Dolly Jean, I think he's insisting that Miravelle do the same. You might say that Oberon committed himself to Mayfair Medical and committed his sister. That's where things stand."

"Any word on Lorkyn?" I asked.

"No," said Stirling. "None at all. Only Rowan knows what's happening with Lorkyn. Michael didn't have a clue."

"Ah, that's marvelous!" said Mona bitterly, her lip quivering. "I wonder if she will cut her up alive."

"Stop it," I said softly. "Lorkyn's filthy with the blood of others. She was the cohort of Rodrigo. Rodrigo slew Ash and Morrigan! Let it be."

"Amen," said Quinn. "I've seldom seen a more frightening creature than Lorkyn. What is Rowan supposed to do with her? Pass her over to the Drug Enforcement people? You think she wouldn't give them the slip? Rowan has a jurisdiction beyond the law, as we do."

Mona shook her head. She was becoming ever more fragile by the minute.

"And what about Michael?" she asked, with a note of hysteria in her voice, her face still pallid and her eyes hard with pain. "What's happening to my beloved Michael in all of this? Does he guess that Rowan's enchanted with the great Lestat behind his back!"

"Oh, so that's it," said Quinn gravely. "And you, the child that bedded him and bore Morrigan, are now coming down upon Rowan for a bevy of kisses. Mona, bear up!"

She shot him a deadly glance. "You've never said a mean thing to me, Quinn!" she whispered.

Stirling was quite taken aback by all this.

I spoke not one word.

"You sell the love of Michael and Rowan short and you know you do," said Stirling with a bit of harshness. "Would that I could break all the confidences bestowed on me. I can't. Suffice to say Rowan loves Michael with her entire soul. Yes, there were moments of extreme temptation in New York with Ash Templeton. She, no longer able to bear, and this wise immortal, who could so well understand her . . . but she never yielded. And she won't break the foundations of her life for anyone else now."

"That's the truth," I said quietly.

Quinn reached over and kissed Mona. She yielded to it forgivingly.

"Where is Michael now?" she asked, avoiding my glance.

"Sleeping," said Stirling. "After Rowan rushed in and took Oberon and Miravelle away, a bit dramatically perhaps, Michael collapsed on his bed upstairs and fell into a deep slumber. I don't think it helped his peace of mind one bit that Tante Oscar had looked deep into his eyes before she left and declared him 'the father of doomed progeny.' "

Mona was immediately furious. (But it was better than being insane.) Her eyes were moist and rimmed in red. "That's just what Michael needs! How dare this creature come making such predictions! I'll bet Dolly Jean latched on to that too. Dolly Jean would never let an opportunity like that slip through her crafty little fingers."

"Yes, indeed," said Stirling. "She told Michael he had best sprinkle yellow powder all around his bed. I think that was the last straw for him."

"You know," said Mona, her hysteria cresting, her words racing again, "in my glory as Designée of the Mayfair Legacy, when I was going around in a cowboy hat and shorts and big-sleeve shirts, riding in the company plane, worth billions of dollars and eating all the ice cream I ever desired, I wanted to purchase a radio station. And one of my dreams was to give Dolly Jean her own show so that people could call in and chat with her about country ways and country wisdom. I was going to give Ancient Evelyn her own show—

"—you know Ancient Evelyn, don't you, Stirling?

"—Lestat, Ancient Evelyn just whispers and whispers—

"—and I was going to give a prize to anyone who could actually understand her. I figured whisperers would call in, you know, who would whisper right back to her the way she whispered to them. We'd have an hour of whispering. I'd give them prizes too, Hell, why not? Then there would have been the Michael Curry Hour, when people could have called up with stories of the Irish Channel or Irish songs, and Michael and the callers could have sung them together. And of course I was going to have my own show, all about the world economy and world trends in architecture and art—(sigh). I had designs for every kook in the family. Never got to do that, got too sick. But Dolly Jean's still jiving. And Michael—Michael's wife cheating on him with you, and he's got no one to defend him."

"Oh, Mona let it go," said Quinn.

My pain was no one's concern but my own.

She collapsed back into a pale, glazed-eyed trance, but only for a moment:

"And you know the damnedest thing," she said, squinting as though she couldn't quite recall her theme. "Oh yeah, vampires, I mean, real vampires, they don't have any websites."

"Let's keep it that way," said Quinn. "They shouldn't have any websites."

"It's time for you to hunt," I said. "You're both thirsting. Make a night of it. Head up north. Hit the beer joints along the roads. Beat the hours down with hunting. By tomorrow, it's my guess Rowan will be ready to let us see the remains of Ash and Morrigan. And we can see Miravelle and Oberon too."

She gave me a dazed look. "Yeah, that sounds great," she whispered. "A regular sideshow. There's a part of me that never wants to see Rowan or Michael again. There's a part of me that never wants to see Miravelle and Oberon ever again. As for Morrigan—."

"Come on, my precious Ophelia," said Quinn. "We're going to take to the air, baby, we're going to do what the Beloved Boss said. I know that jukebox, pool table route. We go for the Little Drink with the truckers and the cowboys, and maybe we stop to dance to the Dixie Chicks now and then, and along comes some guy with a conscience full of pure coal and we lure him out to where the parking lot falls into the trees and we fight over him."

She laughed in spite of herself. "Sounds brutal and basic," she sighed.

He pulled her up out of the chair. She turned, and reached down to give me a warm hug and a kiss.

I was happily surprised. I held her tight. "My pixie," I said. "You've only begun on the Devil's Road. You have such wonders yet to discover. Be clever. Be swift."

"But how do real vampires connect on the World Wide Web?" she asked with painful seriousness.

"Beats me, sweetheart," I said. "I've never sufficiently recovered from my first sight of a steam locomotive. I almost got run over. What makes you think real vampires want to connect?"

"Stop putting me on," she said dreamily. "But you don't want me to create my own web page?"

"Absolutely not," I said somberly.

"But you published the Chronicles!" she protested. "Now what about that?" She put her hands on her hips. "How do you defend that, I'd like to know?"

"An age-old form of public confession," I said, "sacrosanct. Goes back to ancient Egypt. A book goes forth quietly into the world, labeled fiction, to be perused, pondered, passed from one to another, perhaps put aside for the future, to perish if unwanted, to endure if valued, to work its way into trunks and vaults and junk heaps, who knows? I don't defend myself to anybody anyway. Stay off the World Wide Web!"

"Sounds positively dusty to me," she said. "But I love you just the same. Now think about this radio station idea. Maybe it's not too late. You could have your own show."

"AAAAAAHHHHH!" I cried. "I can't bear it! You think Black-wood Farm's the World. It's not, Mona! There's just Blackwood Farm, and all the rest is Sugar Devil Swamp, trust me. And how long do you think we'll have Blackwood Farm, you, me or Quinn? My Lord, you've got a direct connection to the one who told you where to find the Secret People, you're E-mailing Wisdom Central, and you're carry-ing on about websites! Be gone from me, now! Save thyself from my wrath!"

I think I scared her just a little. She was so tired and gaunt that she fell back from the sound of my voice. "We're not finished with this dis-cussion, Beloved Boss," she said. "Trouble with you is you get too emotional. I question anything and you just blow your stack."

Quinn picked her up and carried her off, making huge circles on the terrace as he went, singing to her, and so they disappeared from sight and her laughter rang out in the softly purring evening.

A warm breeze came to fill the silence. The distant trees were doing their subtle dance. My heart was suddenly beating too hard and a cold anxiety crept over me. I picked up the statue of Saint Juan Diego from the flagstones and set him properly on the table where he belonged. I said nothing about him. Ah, tacky little dude with thy paper roses, thou art surely destined for better representations.

I was in the depths. The pulsing night sang to me of the nothing-ness. The stars spread out to prove the horror of our universe—bits and pieces of the body of no one flying at monstrous speed away from the meaningless, uncomprehending source.

Saint Juan Diego, make it go away. Work another miracle!

"What is it?" Stirling asked softly.

I sighed. In the distance the white fence of the pasture looked pretty, and the smell of the grass was good.

"I've failed at something here," I said, "and it's a major failure." I studied the man to whom I'd just spoken.

Patient Stirling, the English scholar, the Talamasca saint. The man who got down with monsters. Starved for sleep yet ever attentive.

He turned to look at me. Clever, quick eyes.

"What do you mean?" he asked. "What failure?"

"I cannot impress upon her a sense of the gravity of her transformation."

"Oh, she knows," he said.

"You surprise me," I answered. "Surely you don't forget who I am. You don't buy this facade. There's some reservoir of goodness and wisdom in you that never lets you forget what's behind this mask. And now you think you know her better than I do?"

"She's reeling from one shock after another," he said calmly. "How can it be helped? What did you expect of her? You know she worships you. And what if she teases you with outrageous propositions? It was always her way. I feel no fear when I'm near her, no instinctive wariness of an undisciplined power. In fact, quite to the contrary. I sense that there may come a moment when you look back and realize that somewhere along the line her innocence was lost and you can't even remember when it happened."

I thought of the massacre last night, the ruthless elimination of Lord Rodrigo and his soldiers. I thought of the bodies heaved into the everlasting sea. I thought of nothing.

"Innocence is not our stock-in-trade, my friend," I said. "We don't cultivate it in one another. Honor, I think we can have, more than you may know, and principles, yes, and virtue as well. I've taught her that, and every now and then we can behave magnificently. Even heroically. But innocence? It's not to our advantage."

He drew back to think on this, with just a little nod. I sensed that there were questions he wanted to ask me, but he didn't dare. Was it propriety or fear? I couldn't tell.

We were interrupted and perhaps it was for the best.

Jasmine came across the lawn with another carafe of coffee for Stirling. She was in a sharp tight red dress and high-heel shoes. She was singing loudly:

"Gloria! Gloria! In Excelsis Deo!"

"Where'd you pick up that hymn?" I asked. "Is everybody around here committed to driving me to madness?"

"Well, of course not," she said. "What would make you say a thing like that? That's a Catholic hymn, don't you know that? Grandma's been singing it in the kitchen all day. Says it's from the Latin Mass in the old days. Says she saw Patsy in a dream singing that hymn. Patsy all dressed in pink cowboy clothes, with a guitar."

"*Mon Dieu!*" A shiver passed through me. No wonder Julien was leaving me alone tonight. Why not?

She poured two cups of the steaming coffee. She set down the carafe. Then she kissed me on top of my head.

"You know what Aunt Queen said to me last night in my sleep?" she asked in a cheery voice, her hand on my shoulder. I kissed her satin cheek.

"No, what?" I asked. "But please break it to me gently. I teeter on the brink."

"She said she was tickled you were sleeping in her bed, said she always wanted a man handsome as you in her bed. She laughed and laughed and laughed. Grandma says when the dead come laughing and laughing in your dreams that means they're in Heaven."

"I think it does mean that," said Stirling very sincerely. "This coffee is perfection. How do you do this?"

"Drink up," I said. "You have that powerful little MG TD with you, don't you?"

"I certainly do," he said. "You could see it right out there in front of the house if you had eyes in the back of your head."

"I want you to take me for a ride in that thing. I have to deliver this saint here to Oberon."

"Can you hold this carafe and this cup for me while I drive? Jasmine, you mind if I borrow them?"

"Don't you want the saucer? That's Royal Antoinette, the saucer's the prettiest part. Just look at it. Come in a big package from Julien Mayfair, this pattern, service for twelve, present for '*La Famille.*'"

Zap. "No," I said. "Not from Julien Mayfair."

"Oh, yes, it did!" she said. "I have the letter. Keep forgetting to give it to Quinn. Was Julien Mayfair at the wake? I never met a Julien Mayfair."

"When did this package arrive?" I asked.

"I don't know. Two days ago?" she shrugged. "Right after Mona Mayfair came to join the menagerie. Which one is Julien Mayfair? Julien Mayfair been out here?"

"What did the letter say?" I asked.

"Oh, something about if he was going to be visiting Blackwood

Farm all the time, he wanted to see his favorite pattern of china. What's the matter with you? That china's beautiful!"

I hadn't the slightest intention of explaining to her that Julien Mayfair was a spirit, and that this very pattern had figured years ago in a spell created by Julien in which he'd entertained an unsuspecting and all too human Quinn with hot chocolate and cookies and a long tale of how he, Julien, had coupled with Quinn's great-grandmother. Damn the infernal spirit.

"You don't like it?" Jasmine said. "I just really do think it's a lovely pattern. Aunt Queen would have been thrilled with it. This is Aunt Queen's style, these roses. You know that."

Stirling was concentrating on me too steadily. Of course Stirling knew Julien Mayfair was a ghost. Or dead. Why was I concealing the activities of this demon? What was I ashamed of?

"Yes, it's very quaint," I said. "Has an old-fashioned delicacy to it. Stirling, what about you drink all you want and then we take a ride?"

"I'm quite fine," Stirling said. He was on his feet.

So was I.

I clutched Jasmine to me with reckless abandon and kissed her madly. She shrieked. I held her face in my hands, looking into her pale eyes. "You're a lovely woman," I said softly.

"What are you so sad about?" she asked. "Why you look so miserable?"

"Do I? I don't know. Maybe because Blackwood Farm is a moment in time. Just a moment. And it will pass. . . ."

"Not in my lifetime," she said smiling. "Oh, I know Quinn's going to marry Mona Mayfair and she can't have any children. We all know that. But Jerome's growing up here. That's my boy, and he's Quinn's son, and Quinn has put his name on the birth certificate. I never asked Quinn to do that. Tommy's growing up here. And he's Tommy Blackwood. And Nash Penfield will grow old taking care this place, he loves it so much. And then there's Terry Sue, Tommy's mother. I don't know if you ever reckoned on Terry Sue, but if ever there was a sow's ear beaten into a purse of silk it's Terry Sue, that's Aunt Queen's little miracle, I'm telling you, and Terry Sue'll be giving the tours on the weekends soon, and so will her daughter Brittany. That's Tommy's sister now. Now that's a lovely girl, a polite girl. And she's going off to a good school, thanks to Quinn, all of it thanks to Quinn. And Aunt Queen. You don't know what all Aunt Queen taught Brittany. Blackwood Farm's just fine. You should have that faith. How can you help Patsy's ghost across the bridge and not know the future?"

"Nobody really knows the future," I said. "But you're right. You know all kinds of things I don't know. It figures." I picked up Saint Juan Diego.

"It's you and Quinn and Mona that'll move on," she said. "I feel your restlessness. But Blackwood Farm? It will outlast all of us."

She gave me one more quick kiss. Then off she went, hips swaying beautifully in the tight red dress, pencil heels making her legs fine, her tightly cropped blond head high—the lady with the keys, and the future.

I went with Stirling.

We climbed into the low-slung car, delicious smell of leather, Stirling slipping on a pair of handsome beige driving gloves, and we roared down the drive, rattling over every rock and pebble.

"Now this is a sports car!" I declared.

Stirling flashed his lighter in front of his cigarette, then threw the car into high gear. "Yes, baby!" he shouted over the wind, sloughing off twenty years of his life, "and when you want to stub out your cigarette, you can do it right on the road," he said. "It's a beauty."

We went roaring on into the swampland.

We didn't leave the paths of speed and recklessness for Mayfair Medical until about three hours before dawn.

For a long time I walked the corridors, marveling at the murals and the benches and seating areas for the patients' families, and the finery of the waiting rooms with their warm furniture and paintings. And the lobbies with their grand sculptures and sparkling marble floors.

And then I penetrated the halls of the laboratories and research areas, and lost myself in a labyrinth of secret places where white-coated individuals who passed me nodded, assuming I knew where I was going carrying the statue of a saint close to my chest.

Enormous, more than my mind could contain, this monument to a family and to one woman. Affecting the lives of so many thousands. A great garden with so many seeds carefully planted to grow into a forest of self-perpetuating splendor.

What was I doing on the Sacred Mountain of the One Who Walks with God?

Find Oberon in the velvety quiet.

Oberon was standing at the window, in white scrubs, looking out at the lighted arcs of the two river bridges. Soft crystalline glow of down-town buildings. He spun around when I entered the room.

"Saint Juan Diego," I said, as I put the saint on the table by the bed.

"Oh, thank you," he said warmly, without a trace of the old disdain. "Now I'll be able to sleep."

"Are you unhappy?" I asked.

"No," he said softly. "Only wondering. In my cell I told myself that all beauty was contained in the ever changing waves of the sea. I had to believe it. But oh, the great world is such a wilderness of marvels. I am very happy. And my soul is not on guard for Miravelle, my sweet fool-ish Miravelle! I am safe. And so is she. And I am free."

28

THE ROOM WAS MAINTAINED at about 40 degrees. Even I was cold. Rowan's lips were blue. But she stood, uncomplaining, right inside the door, her arms folded, her back to the wall, allowing for us to take as much time as we wanted. She was wearing her white coat, even her name tag, and white pants. Her shoes were black, simple. Her hair was brushed back from her face. She didn't look at me. I was glad.

The walls were white. So was the tile floor. There was all kinds of equipment in the room, monitors, wires, tubing, tanks, but it was shut off and retired to the sidelines and into the corners. The windows were covered with white metal blinds, shutting out the colorful night.

Miravelle, dressed primly in a long pink cotton nightgown, cried quietly. Oberon, in white silk pajamas and robe, merely observed with those half-mast gleaming eyes.

Mona stood silent, the wanderer in safari clothes, her left hand against Miravelle's back, her right arm holding a huge bunch of random flowers. Mona's eyes were dry and she looked cold and careworn.

Quinn remained against the door with me. Quinn held the bouquet which Mona had asked him to carry for her.

The perfume of the flowers filled the room. There were daisies and zinnias and lilies and roses and gladiolus, and other flowers I didn't know, lots of different colors.

The bodies were lying on separate gurneys. The limbs looked pliant, the flesh greenish, the faces slightly sunken. Morrigan's full red hair had been brushed out as though she was lying in water. Did that make Mona think even more of Ophelia? Ash had eyelashes which were extremely long, and his fingers were long. He must have been seven feet tall. He had full black hair, almost to his shoulders, with lots of white above his ears. A beautiful mouth. Morrigan looked very much like Mona. The pair quite lovely to behold.

Their heads were positioned on pillows. The sheets were clean beneath them.

They wore fresh clothes, plain white cotton pants and V-neck shirts, much like the simple clothes they'd been wearing when we found them, which seemed an eon ago.

Their naked feet looked very dead. I wasn't sure why. Perhaps they were more discolored, or even a little misshapen.

I wanted to see Ashlar's eyes. I wanted to know if that was possible, to lift the eyelid and see an eye. But I didn't want to speak, or to ask for anything.

Miravelle finally moved to put her right hand around Ash's face. She bent to kiss his lips. When she found they were soft, she closed her eyes, and the kiss was long and fervent. With her left hand she reached out, and Mona gave her half of the flowers.

Miravelle took these and distributed them all over Ash, moving up and down, until she had partially covered him. Then Mona gave her the rest, and she finished, leaving only Ash's face. Before she withdrew, she kissed his forehead.

It was Morrigan who drew the sobs from her. "Mother," she said. Mona, who cleaved to her, didn't say a word. But she laid her own hand on Morrigan's hand, and, finding it flexible, she curled her own fingers around Morrigan's fingers.

Quinn brought the flowers to Mona. Mona gave half to Miravelle. Together they laid them on the body of Morrigan.

Oberon observed everything in silence, but tears formed in his eyes. Tears wetted his cheeks. A slight frown marred his forehead.

Miravelle's broken ragged sobs finally died away. Mona motioned her slowly towards the door. Then Mona looked back.

"Good-bye, Morrigan," she whispered.

We all filed out of the room and followed Rowan down a short thickly carpeted corridor.

We entered a rather spectacular conference room. Michael was there, and so was Stirling, both in dark suits. That's how I was dressed, and same with Quinn.

The chairs in this surprising room were genuine Chippendale, around a finely buffed oval table. The walls were a cool lavender and there were wonderful paintings on them, paintings by expressionists, full of rich and throbbing color. I wanted to steal them for my flat. The windows were open to the flickering burning night. There was a marble-top bar against the inside wall, and glittering glasses and decanters.

Michael was drinking bourbon in heavy gulps. Stirling had a glass of Scotch.

Miravelle tried to dry her eyes but with little success. Rowan poured a small glass of sherry for her, and Miravelle laughed as she held up the delicate stem in the light, and then she sipped the sherry. She was laughing and crying at the same time very softly. Her pink nightgown looked very soft.

Oberon waved away any suggestion of a drink. He stared past the assembly out into the night. He didn't bother to wipe away his tears. Only now did I notice he had cleaned his fingernails of all polish.

Mona said:

"What will you do with them?"

Rowan sat back. She considered for a long time, then she answered: "What would you do with them if you were me?"

"I can't imagine being you," said Mona simply.

Rowan shrugged. But her face was sad. She didn't disguise it.

Oberon spoke up:

"Do whatever you want with them, Rowan," he said, with a touch of the old disdain. "Hell, Father told Rodrigo to save the bodies for you, didn't he? It's plain enough. Rodrigo wasn't knowledgeable or reflective enough to imagine such a speech or such an intention. Father wanted something accomplished. The bodies are yours by the wish of Father. No more needs to be said."

"All that is very true," said Miravelle with a simple nod. "Rowan, Father loved you. He really did. You do what Father wanted, please."

Rowan didn't answer. She sat there staring off as was her custom and then she pressed a button under the table.

Within seconds the door opened, and Lorkyn came into the room.

I was once more utterly shocked by this creature's appearance, not only because she was unaccompanied but because she wore the white pants and coat of a doctor, along with the name tag, stating her name as Lorkyn Mayfair, and her face was as unreadable as it had been when we first confronted each other on the Secret Isle.

That kitten sweetness—small upturned nose, rosy mouth, big eyes—was, if anything, enhanced by the purity of the white clothes, and she had her hair swept up on top of her head again and pouring down her back, red as Mona's, and her eyes were just as green.

She took her place at the table freely, across from me and from Oberon and Miravelle.

Mona stared coldly at her. And Oberon was on full alert. Miravelle merely looked at her as though she was a curiosity. Only Rowan seemed to know why she was here.

It was Lorkyn who explained.

"I'll say this once for you, Oberon, and Miravelle. I do not intend to be mercilessly questioned. It's my intention to be heard."

"It better be sensational, darling," said Oberon bitterly.

"It is," said Rowan. "Please listen to what Lorkyn has to say."

"I was shifting money from Rodrigo to numbered accounts for us," said Lorkyn. "I was also tipping off the authorities in Miami Beach as to his activities there, getting rid of his contacts as quickly as I could. Keep in mind, I never would have had a line out or recourse to the financial info if I hadn't played the proper role for Rodrigo. I was also trying desperately to find out who Father and Mother were legally, who owned the Secret Isle legally. But I couldn't do it. I didn't have Father's last name. Years ago, when Father first suspected trouble from Silas, he destroyed every scrap of paper that would have enabled Silas to get control of his finances. Father's lawyers came in by plane and left with everything in their briefcases.

"If I'd had the names Templeton and Lost Paradise, I could have connected us to Father's lawyers in New York.

"As for Rodrigo, I had no opportunity to kill him. Wherever we went there were dozens of armed men with us. That held true until the night he died, when this blond-haired archangel managed to slaughter every one of his gunsels before killing him. I never had that kind of power or advantage.

"But I was biding my time for it, and accumulating the money and figuring how to get both Rodrigo and his mother, and free you, Oberon, and you too Miravelle, and get clear of the island and safely to Mayfair Medical where we could find help."

Oberon was silent. It seemed that he wanted to believe Lorkyn but that he couldn't quite accept all that she said.

Lorkyn continued:

"In my spare time, which was plentiful, I did a great deal of research on Mayfair Medical. Since Father had told us about it, and told us about Rowan Mayfair, I wanted to know what this was all about. I wasn't going to call for help until I was sure that it was the wise thing to do. I scoured the Internet for information on Rowan Mayfair and Mayfair Medical. I read everything I could get my hands on. Nowhere could I find any real assurance that Rowan Mayfair had the power, the experience or the means to free us from Rodrigo and his crime family. It seemed to me that I had to take care of Rodrigo. And then I could get us off the island and we would contact Rowan from there. Now if you two don't believe me on this score, I have no way of proving it to you. My suggestion is you use your heads."

"Why in Hell didn't you simply contact the authorities," said Oberon fiercely. "Why didn't you E-mail the evidence you had to the Drug Enforcement Agency?"

"And if I had done that, just where do you think you would be right now?"

The anger vanished from Oberon's face, yet he held her gaze steadily, then:

"I don't know," he replied.

"Well neither do I," said Lorkyn. "Do you think they would have believed you were innocent? Do you think they would have believed the story of the Secret People? Do you think they would have locked you up as a material witness? Do you think Rodrigo's enemies couldn't have gotten to you before there was a trial?"

"I see your point," he said with an air of boredom.

"Do you really see it!" she demanded. She was at her most dramatic, though still relatively low-key. "Rowan Mayfair knows what the Taltos are."

"So what were you looking for?" Mona asked.

"I was looking for a haven," said Lorkyn. "Possibly the only haven that exists. And only after I arrived here, after I spent eight solid hours talking to Rowan, did the last of my suspicions drop away."

"Probably a little too soon," said Mona.

Lorkyn looked at Mona. Lorkyn raised her eyebrows. "Oh?"

Mona didn't respond.

Rowan said nothing. She didn't even look at Mona.

"Please excuse Mona," said Quinn quietly.

"Go on, Lorkyn," I said. "You spent eight hours straight talking to Rowan. So what gives?"

"This is a place where the Taltos can stay," said Lorkyn.

"What, to be studied?" said Mona. "You're going to be put in cages in a lab. You call that a haven? The woman knocks you out with a syringe on the tarmac next to her jet plane and you place all your trust in her?"

Lorkyn stared at Mona. It was a curious moment, the tall long-necked Taltos completely bewildered by Mona's behavior. Then she drew back and went on:

"You're misunderstanding me, Mona," said Lorkyn with soft confidence. "I'm talking of this place as an environment, a community, a world in which we can live and function and be protected and thrive. I myself have studied a great deal in medicine. You knew this when you went into my computer on the island. You brought the hard drive to Rowan. You gave it to her. You gave her proof of my studies. I've given her oral proof of my studies. I want to continue my studies. I want to become a doctor. That's my wish and Rowan has accepted me as a pupil here. I've found favor with Rowan. And there are opportunities for fruitful work here for Oberon and for Miravelle, and this is a self-contained universe in which the Taltos can be supervised without conspicuous constraints and be protected effortlessly and be at peace."

"Ah, wondrously clever," said Stirling. "I never thought of it."

"Oh, I think it's a lovely idea!" said Miravelle. "And we can wear nightgowns all the time, or at least I can. I love nightgowns."

"There are, as you may know," Lorkyn continued, her eyes fixed hard on Mona, "many apartments connected to this hospital, which are provided for the visiting families of the sick, and we can live in those apartments as we study here and as we work. We need never leave this compound, except when we have a preordained goal."

Lorkyn turned her focus from Mona. She looked at Oberon.

"My progress was slow," she said, "and my success incomplete. But Rowan has the evidence of my efforts. And Mona, you saw them. And you, Lestat, you saw them as well. Oberon, do you accept what I'm saying?"

Oberon was trying. I couldn't penetrate his thoughts. But I could tell by his expression.

"Why did you never during the entire two years come to me?" he asked.

"You were Lucia's lover," Lorkyn said. "I heard you howling with pleasure in the night. What was I to say to you? How did I know what you might say to her?"

"You could have let me know you were alive."

"You knew I was alive. You saw me. Besides, my movements were circumscribed. My real freedom was on the computer. I studied. I had to find a safe place not only for us to go, but for us to stay."

"You're cold," said Oberon disgustedly. "You always were."

"Perhaps," said Lorkyn, "but now I can learn to be warm. Rowan Mayfair will teach me."

"Oh, that's rich!" said Mona. "Oberon and Miravelle, you had better order your winter furs."

Michael roused himself from his quiet reflections. "Mona, honey, please try to trust in what we're trying to do."

"If you say so, Uncle Michael," said Mona.

"Don't you agree, both of you?" asked Lorkyn, looking at Oberon and Miravelle, "that we need a haven? We cannot simply go out into the world."

"No, no, I don't want to go out into the world," said Miravelle.

Oberon thought for a long moment, the fabulous eyelids lowering and then rising.

"You're right, of course you are. Where else but here can we discover some contraceptive that allows us to couple without hatching another immediately? Of course. It's brilliant. Very well." He gave one of his languid graceful shrugs. "But do we have money from the accounts you managed to transfer?" he asked.

"We have wealth from Father," said Lorkyn. "Great wealth. The Mayfair family discovered it. That's no longer a problem. You need not feel beholden. We're quite free."

"No, never feel beholden," said Rowan softly.

"Very well. I feel this discussion has come to an end," said Lorkyn.

She rose. She looked at Rowan and something silent passed between the two women, some exchange of approval and confidence and belief.

Oberon rose to his feet and took Miravelle by the hand.

"Come, my blessed little idiot," he said to Miravelle, "we'll go back to my suite and continue watching *The Lord of the Rings*. By now they'll have the white chocolate candy for us and the cold cold milk."

"Oh, everyone's so good to us," said Miravelle, "I love you all, I want you to know. And I'm so glad all the bad men died and Rodrigo fell off the balcony. It was just the best of luck."

"Isn't it uplifting, the way she describes it?" asked Oberon archly. "And to think I get to listen to this eighteen hours a day. What about you, Lorkyn? You ever going to drop in to see your brother and sister and indulge in a little intelligent discourse about your medical studies? I might go simply mad if I don't speak to someone from time to time who can use four-syllable words."

"Yes, Oberon," she said. "I'll come to you more than you might think."

She came round the table and stood before him. A great relaxation came over him, and he took Lorkyn in his arms. There was an ardent kiss and a slow moving away, with reverence and a locking of thin delicate fingers.

"Oh, I am so happy," said Miravelle. She kissed Lorkyn on the cheek.

Oberon and Miravelle left.

Lorkyn gave formal nods to all the company, gesturing for the men to take their seats again, and she too went out the door.

The room fell quiet.

Then Rowan spoke: "She's incomparably brilliant," she said.

"I understand," I responded.

No one else spoke.

Mona sat there still for a long time, her eyes every so often engaging Rowan.

Then very softly, Mona said, "It's over."

Rowan didn't answer.

Mona stood up, and so did Quinn. Finally I did also. Michael rose out of courtesy, and Rowan remained in her chair, thoughtful, remote.

For a moment it seemed Mona was going to leave without another word, but just as she reached the door, she looked back, and she said to Rowan:

"I don't think you'll see me much anymore."

"I understand," said Rowan.

"I love you, sweetheart," said Michael.

Mona stopped, her head bowed. She didn't turn around.

"I'll never forget you," she said.

I was stunned. I was caught completely off guard.

Michael's face crumpled as though he'd been hit by a heavy blow. But he said nothing.

"Farewell, my beauteous mortal friends," I said. "You need me, you know how to find me."

Indescribable expression on Rowan's face as she turned and looked up at me.

And so I realized it. It came over me slowly. It was like a chill.

The cause that had bound us together was no more. It wasn't only Mona's turning away. We had no more reason to come to one another. No more mystery to justify our intimacy. And honor and virtue, of which I'd spoken so surely, demanded we cease to interfere with one another, cease to learn about each other. We couldn't walk the same paths.

The Taltos had been discovered, recovered and would be safe within Mayfair Medical. Lorkyn's speech had been the epilogue.

We had to withdraw.

Why had I not seen it? Why had I not felt the entirety of it? Mona had known last night, and the night before, when she'd stood on the island looking out to sea.

But I had not known. Not known at all.

I turned and followed my companions.

Down we went through the Sacred Mountain of Mayfair Medical in the shining glass elevator and through the wondrous lobby with its mystifying modern sculptures and richly tiled floors, out into the warm air.

Clem ready with the limousine door.

"You sure you wanna go to *that* part of town?"

"Just drop us off, we're expected."

Silence in the car as we move steadily on, as if we are not with one another.

We are not Taltos. We are not innocent. We do not belong on God's Holy Mountain. We are not protected and redeemed by those whom we have served. They cannot thank us with grace, can they? They cannot open the doors of the tabernacle.

Give us the underbelly of the city, let us spread out, where the cheapest killers come to us in the wild tangled thickets of the empty lots, ready to sink a blade for a twenty-dollar bill, and the corpses rot for weeks in the weeds amid the charred wood and the heaps of brick, and I was ravenous.

Rampant moonflower, chimney stack tall as a tree, didn't they make this place for me? Whiff of evil. Crunch of broken boards. Morthadie. Cohorts behind the jagged wall. Whisper in my ear: "Ya'll lookin for a good time?" You couldn't have said it better.

29

I WOKE with a start. The sun had set a long while ago. I'd been so comfortable in Aunt Queen's bed. I'd even done the strangest thing before retiring. I'd yielded to Jasmine's lectures about my fine linen suit, and hung up all my clothes, and put on a long flannel nightshirt.

What was this mad pretense? I, who had slept in velvet and lace when coffined in the dirt, yielding to these encumbering pleasures? I'd fled the sun into the raw earth itself. I'd bedded down once in the crypt beneath a church altar.

Julien sat at the table. He packed a small thin black cigarette on his gold case, then lighted it. Flash on his cool elegant face. Perfume of smoke.

"Ah, now that is something."

"So you're drawing more and more energy from me, I see," I said. "Do you draw it from me even when I sleep?"

"You're stone-cold dead by the light of day," he remarked. "However, you've dreamed a pretty dream in the past hour. I rather like your dream."

"I know what I dreamt. What can I give you to make you go away, forever?"

"I thought you were fond of me. Was that all banter?"

"And so you failed," I said. "You aided Mona to couple with Michael, and the birth of Morrigan destroyed her. How could you have known? And as to Merrick Mayfair becoming one of us, that wasn't your fault. You merely entrusted her to the Talamasca. Don't you see you have to go on? You can't keep meddling and making mistakes.

Lasher's dead. Morrigan's dead. You have to let them go, your adorable Mayfairs. You're playing at being a saint. It isn't gentlemanly."

"And will *you* let them go?" he asked. "Oh, I don't speak of my treasure, my Mona. She's lost. I concede that. You know what concerns me now." His voice was thick with emotion. "Is not the destiny of the entire clan at stake?"

"What are you talking about?" I said.

"Hasn't the one you covet redeemed the family's unseemly wealth? Hasn't she sanctified the family's incalculable power?"

"What do the angels tell you?" I replied. "Pray to Saint Juan Diego for your answer."

"Answer me!" he pressed.

"What answer can I give that you'll accept?" I asked. "Go to Tante Oscar, she'll know who you are. Or seek out Fr. Kevin Mayfair in his rectory. Put your questions to them. But go away from me."

"I beg you!" he said.

We stared at each other. He was amazed at his own words. So was I.

"What if I beg you," I asked, "to interfere no more! To leave them to conscience and fortune?"

"Do we strike a bargain then?" he asked.

I turned away from him. The chills had me. *Do we strike a bargain then?*

"Damn you!"

I got up, pulled off the nightshirt and put on my clothes. Too many buttons to a three-piece suit. I straightened my purple tie. I combed out my hair. And then there were my boots, outside the door, of course.

There was a master switch for the lights. I hit it. I turned around. He was gone. The little table was untouched. But the smoke lingered. And the perfume of the cigarette with it.

I beg you!

As soon as I slipped on the boots, I left the house by the rear door, walking fast over the wet grass, along the edge of the swamp. I knew where I had to go.

It was the city.

It was the downtown streets.

Just walking, walking and thinking, on the bum, walking. Forget the blood. Blood forget me.

And from downtown I walked uptown, faster and faster, beating the pavements, until it loomed before me on the outskirts of the city, Mayfair Medical, sprawling grid of lights against the close clouded nighttime sky.

What was I doing?

This was the Patients' Garden, wasn't it?

Empty at this hour of the night, a wilderness of ligustrum and roses and gravel paths. Harmless to wander here. No hope of seeing anyone in particular. No hope of mischief. No hope of—.

It was Julien before me, blocking the way.

"Ah, you devil!" I said.

"Now what are you up to? What goes on in your crafty mind?" he demanded. "Finding her in her midnight laboratory and offering her your blood again? Asking her to analyze it beneath her microscope, you trickster devil? Any cheap excuse to draw close?"

"Will you never understand? You can't sway me, man! Seek the Light. Your curses betray your origin. Now take my curse from me!"

I reached for him—I shut my eyes. I saw the spirit in me, the goading vampiric spirit that animated my flesh, that craved the blood that kept me alive, the spirit in my two hands as I caught him by the throat, and the spirit in him, the animus that sought to project the image of the man that was no man, and I opened my mouth over his, as I had done to Patsy, and I sent the wind into him, the fierce wind of rejection, not love, of renunciation, of repudiation.

Be gone from me, you evil thing, be gone, you twisted, worldly spirit, be gone to whatever realm in which you belong. If I can free you from the Earth, I will it.

He blazed before me, solid, in a fury. I struck him with the full strength of my arm, shattering him, sending him so far from me, I couldn't see him anymore, and an anguished cry rang out from him that seemed to fill the night.

I was alone.

I gazed up at the huge facade of the Medical Center. I turned around and I walked, and the night was simple and noisy and warm around me.

I walked all the way back downtown.

I sang a little song to myself:

"You have the whole world. You have till the end of time. You have everything you could ever want. Mona and Quinn are with you. And there are so many others in the Blood who love you. It is truly complete now, and you must go your way. . . .

"Yes, you must go your way and return to the fold of those whom you cannot harm. . . ."

30

I T WAS AN HOUR before dawn when I returned to Blackwood Farm, a weary soul for my bloodless wanderings, and bound for bed. The Kitchen Committee, as Quinn calls it, was already having coffee and setting the dough to rise.

I had missed Tommy's departure. He had left me a note—very kind and somewhat unique—thanking me for helping Patsy's spirit go into the Light. Ah, yes.

I at once sat down at the haunted desk, and, finding the central drawer to contain Blackwood Farm notepaper as I knew it would now that the key was lost, I wrote a note to Tommy saying that I thought he would become an extraordinary man and do great things that would make everyone proud of him.

"Beware of ordinary life," I wrote. "Reach for something finer, greater. I believe that is the message of Blackwood Farm."

Jasmine, who was already fully dressed at that hour, with a white apron over her blue suit and silk blouse, went into ecstasies over my handwriting. Where did I get all these curlicues, these flourishes and this swift perfect use of the pen?

Why was I too tired to answer? Tired as the night that Patsy had crossed over? Was Julien really gone for good?

She took the note, slid it into an envelope and said it would go out with the first package of fudge which they were already cooking for Tommy.

"You know Quinn and Mona won't be back for a week," she said. "You and Nash are the only two in this great big house, and you won't touch a morsel of food we cook, you're so particular, and if you leave, there's just going be Nash and I'll cry my eyes out."

"What?" I asked. "Where did Mona and Quinn go?"

"Who am I that I should know?" she asked with exaggerated gestures. "They didn't even tell us good-bye. It was another gentleman came here to tell us they'd be gone for a while. And he was the strangest man I've ever seen in my life, skin so white it looked like a mask. Hair jet black and long to his shoulders, and such a smile. It almost gave me a fright. Check in Aunt Queen's room when you go to bed. He left a note in there on the table for you."

"That man's name is Khayman. He's kindly. I know where they went." I sighed. "You going to let me stay in Aunt Queen's room while they're gone?"

"Oh, bite your tongue," she said. "It's where you belong. You think I'm bubbling over with joy that Miss Mona is raiding Aunt Queen's closets like the Queen of Sheba, just leaving fox furs and rhinestone shoes all over the floor? I am not. Never mind, I straightened it all up. You go on to bed."

We went back the hallway together. I went into the room, found it softly lighted with only the dressing-table lamps, and stood there for a moment, just breathing in the perfume and wondering how long I could play out this spectacular hand.

The bed was already turned down for me. And a fresh flannel nightshirt was laid out, and sure enough, as they say on Blackwood Farm, there was a letter on the little table.

I sat down, tore open the parchment envelope and discovered the letter printed in a graceful cursive font.

My dearest rebel,

Your darlings want badly to be received by me and so I have granted their request. It is highly unusual, as you know, for me to bring ones so young to my compound. But there are excellent reasons for both Quinn and Mona spending some time here with me, acquainting themselves with the archives, meeting some of the others who go and come, and perhaps gaining some perspective on the gifts which they have been given and the existence which lies before them.

It is my strong feeling that their entrenchment in mortal life is not altogether wise, and this visit with me, this retreat among the immortals, will serve to insulate them against the shocks which may come. You are right in fearing that Mona does not grasp the full sacramental power of the Blood. But Quinn does not either, having been made against his will. Another reason for my bringing them here is simply that I have become quite real to Mona and Quinn, as the result of our communication regarding the Taltos, and I want to dispel any harmful mythmaking which might surround my person in their young minds.

Here they will come to know me as I am. They will perhaps appreciate that at the root of our lineage there exists not a great goddess but a fairly simple personality, honed by time, and linked to her own mortal visions and desires.

Both children seem to be exceptionally gifted, and I am in awe of your accomplishments with them, as well as your patience.

I know what you are suffering at present. Only too well, I understand. But I have every confidence that you will behave according to the highest standards which you have set for yourself. Your moral evolution simply doesn't allow for anything else.

Let me assure you that you are welcome here. And I could easily have arranged for you to be brought to me with Quinn and Mona. But I know that you don't want to come.

You are now free to spend weeks in mortal peace, lying in Aunt Queen's bed, reading the novels of Dickens over again. You are entitled to that rest.

Maharet

There it was, the evidence of my failure with Quinn and Mona, and the revelation of Maharet's marvelous generosity in bringing them to herself. What finer teacher could they have in all the wide world than Maharet?

I'd given Mona and Quinn all I could in my own fashion. And that wasn't enough. No, it simply wasn't enough. The problem was probably what Maharet had called my "moral evolution." But I wasn't so sure.

I'd wanted to make "the perfect vampire" in Mona. But my plan had been quickly swallowed by forces which had taught me more than I could ever teach anybody else.

And Maharet was so right that I did not want to be taken to her famous jungle compound. No, not for me that fabled place of stone rooms and screened enclosures, where she the ancient lady who looked more like a statue in alabaster than a living thing held quiet court with her mute twin sister. And as for the legendary archives with their ancient tablets, scrolls and codices of unimaginable revelations, I could wait forever for those treasures as well. What can't be revealed to the world of men and women can't be revealed to me. I had no taste or patience for it.

I was going in quite the other direction—caught in the thrall of Blackwood Farm—this lost corner of the South where things more mundane were far more precious to me.

I was at peace with it. I was also weak in my soul, without doubt. And it was from my battle with Julien, and sure enough, he was nowhere about.

I folded the letter.

I got undressed.

I put all my clothes properly on hangers like a decent mortal individual, put on the flannel nightshirt, pulled out the copy of "Little Nell" from under the pillow and read until the sun came creeping over the horizon and over my consciousness, locking me down into emptiness and peace.

31

T HIS BOOK'S FINISHED. You know it. I know it. After all, what more is there to say? So why am I still writing? Read on and find out.

How many nights passed? I don't know. I don't count well. I get numbers and ages wrong. But I feel time. I feel it the way I feel the evening air when I walk outside, the way I feel the roots of the oak tree under my foot.

Nothing could have made me leave Blackwood Farm. So long as I was on the property, I was safe. I even put off Stirling for a while. Just can't talk about the Taltos now, though it is a most interesting subject, of course, but you see, she's wrapped up in it, she's at the core of it—.

So when I wasn't reading "Little Nell" or *David Copperfield*, I went walking on the property, down along the swamp where I'd encountered Patsy, or through the little cemetery, or over the broad lawns to admire the flower beds that were still tended so faithfully even though Pops, the man who planted them all, is gone.

I had no predictable path, but I did have a predictable time. I usually went out about three hours before dawn.

If I had a favorite place it was the cemetery. All those nameless graves, and the four oaks that surrounded it, and the swamp so perilously close.

They'd cleaned away all the soot from the grave on which Merrick Mayfair had built her pyre. One would never know there had been such a blaze there. And the leaves were raked regularly, and the little chapel, quite a building, was swept clean every day.

It had no real door; its windows had no glass. It was a Gothic piece of work, all pointed arches. And inside there was a bench where one could sit and meditate.

But that wasn't my favorite spot.

My favorite spot was to sit at the foot of the biggest of the oak trees, the one that had a limb that lay on the ground above the cemetery, a limb that stretched into the swamp.

I headed there with my head down. I wasn't thinking of much of anything, except perhaps that I had seldom been this happy or this miserable in my life. I didn't need blood but I wanted it. I craved it unbearably at times. Especially on these walks. I dreamt of the prowl and of the murder. I dreamt of the soiled intimacy—the needle of my hunger plunged into heated hatefulness. But I didn't have the stamina for it just now.

The boundaries of Blackwood Farm were the boundaries of my soul.

I headed to my oak. I was going to sit there and look over the cemetery, look at the little iron lace fence with its ornate pickets, look at the graves, and the rising hulk of the chapel. And who knows? Maybe there would be a mist coming off the swamp. And the sky would turn the familiar and oh, so essential, purple before the sun came.

That was my intent.

I live in the past, the present, the future. And I was remembering that once, very near here, under the other oak tree, the one closer to the gate of the cemetery, I had met Quinn, all alone, after he had killed Patsy, and I had given him my blood to drink.

I've never in all my long wandering years been hated by anyone the way Quinn was hated by Patsy. Patsy had attached to him all the hate her soul could tender. Who can judge such a thing? Ah. My own mother, given the Blood by me, is simply uninterested in me, and more or less always was. A very different thing from hate. But what was I going to say?

Yes. That I had met Quinn, and I had given him to drink my own blood. An intimate moment. A sad and thrilling moment. And a conveying of power from me to Quinn. He'd belonged to me in that little while. I had seen his complex and trusting soul and how the Dark Trick had stolen it, and how there had emerged from the theft a bold and unyielding survivor of Quinn Blackwood, determined to make sense of what had occurred.

Our irrepressible creative power.

I loved him. Sweet, easy. No kindling of possessiveness or fierce want. No concomitant emptiness. And then to witness his fulfillment in Mona, that was finer than blood lust.

I thought of that as I approached my oak tree, as I was dreaming, and weaving into my dreams bits of poetry, poetry I stole and broke and wove into my desires: *You have ravished my heart, my sister, my spouse . . . how fair is my love.* Can I not envision? Can I not dream? *Set me as a seal upon thine heart.*

What is it to me that I catch the scent of a mortal? Blackwood Farm is a citadel of mortals. What does it matter to anyone that Lestat is walking, whom they've all made so welcome? So one of them now comes to cross my path. I close my mind. My mind collapses in upon itself and its poetry: *Thou art all fair, my love, there is no spot in thee.*

I found my tree and my hand found the trunk of it.

She was sitting there, sitting on the thick roots, looking up at me. Her white coat was spattered with dried blood, her name tag askew, her face drawn, her eyes huge and hungry. She rose up into my waiting arms.

I held her, this supple, feverish creature, and my soul opened. "Love you, love you as I've never loved, love you above wisdom, above courage, above the glamor of evil, above all riches and the Blood itself, love you with my humble heart which I never knew I had, my gray-eyed one, my brilliant one, my mystic of the medical magic, my dreaming one, oh, let me just surround you with my arms, I don't dare to kiss you, I don't dare—."

She rose on tiptoe and pushed her tongue between my lips. *Want you, want you with my whole soul. Do you hear me, do you know what gulf I've crossed to come to you? There is no god in my soul but you. I've belonged to greedy spirits, I've belonged to monsters made of my own flesh, I've belonged to ideas and formulae and dreams and designs of magnificence, but now I belong to you, I'm yours.*

We lay down on the grass together, on the slope above the cemetery, under the canopy of the oak tree where the stars couldn't see us.

My hands wanted all of her, her flesh beneath the stiff cotton, the small full curve of her hips, her breasts, her pale neck, her lips, her privy parts, so wet and ready for my fingers, my lips grazing her throat, not daring to do more than feel the blood beneath the skin as my fingers brought her up to the climax, as she moaned against me, as her limbs went stiff with the finish, as she lay limp against my chest.

The blood thudded in my ears. It raced through my brain. It said *I want her.* But I lay still.

My lips were pressed to her forehead. The blood threaded through me turned to pain. The pain peaked, as her passion had peaked. And in the softness of her cheek and her lips, I knew a measure of sweetness and quiet, and the morning was still dark and the stars fought to flicker in the canopy of leaves above.

Her hand moved over my shoulder, over my chest.

"You know what I want of you," she said in that deep lustrous voice, her words underscored with pain and determination. "I want it from you, and I want you. I've told myself all the noble reasons to turn away from it, I've told myself all the moral arguments, my mind has been a confessional, a pulpit, a place beneath the porch where the philosophers gather. My mind has been a forum. In the emergency room I worked day after day until I could hardly stand any longer. Lorkyn's learned from me and me from Lorkyn, and programs of study have been designed for Oberon and Miravelle, and we have talked the nights through with formulations and proposals in which they are enshrined and encapsulated, and their collective well-being has been institutionalized, and good will surrounds them and stimulates them—and my soul, my soul has remained steadfast. My soul craves *this* miracle! My soul craves your face, you! My soul has been always with you." She sighed. "My love. . . ."

Silence. The songs of the swamp. The songs of those birds who always begin before morning. And the sound of the water moving, and the leaves all around us listing to a faint and uncertain breeze.

"This is something I never expected to feel again," she whispered. "I thought it would never come to me again," I felt her trembling. "That those parts of me had been forever burnt out," she said. "Yes, I love Michael and will forever, but what that love demands of me is that I set Michael free. Michael languishes in my shadow. Michael wants and should possess a simple woman who can bear him a wholesome child. And we've lived together in mourning for what might have been had monsters not possessed us and ruined us. We've whispered our Requiems for too long.

"And then this fire is born. Oh, not because of what you are! What you are could terrify. What you are could repel! But because of who you are, the soul inside you, the words you speak, the expression on your face, the certain witness of eternity I read in you! My world collapses when I'm near you. My values, my ambitions, my plans, my dreams. I see them as the scaffolding of hysteria. And this love has taken root, this savage love which knows no fear of you, and only wants to be with you, wants the Blood, yes, because it's your blood, and all else melts away."

I waited. I listened to the rhythm of her heart. I listened to the blood inside her. I listened to her sweet breath. I held myself back—the raging animal that had so many times shattered the cage and taken the object of its desire. I wrapped her so close!

For an age it seemed I held her.

Then I found myself letting her go, folding her limbs against her own breast, and rising and leaving her, refusing her outstretched hands, refusing them with kisses, but leaving her and walking to the edge of the swamp alone, my body growing cold, so cold it was as if some northern winter had found me in the gentle heat and driven its teeth into me.

I stood alone, so very alone, looking into the gnawing unformed morass of the swamp, and thinking only of her and letting my imagination run rampant with the undisciplined glory of loving her, of having her. The world reborn in love, and common things overlayered with common despair leapt into colors brilliant and irresistible. What was this point in time to me? What was this place called Blackwood Farm that I couldn't take her with me and shake its dust from off my feet and soar with her to other lands of certain enchantment?

Oh yes, and what has this to do with pure love, Lestat? What is the luster of pure love? What is the luster of that most uncommon one who lies there waiting?

I don't know how long I stood there, apart from her. My rosy dreams of palaces, of wanderings, of bowers and realms of love were vaporous and great and small and vanishing.

And she was there, patient, wise—condemned by her own lips, wasn't she?

A sadness came to me, as pure as pure love, and then a pain, a pain as true as the pain I'd heard in her unhurried voice, her deep and total commitment.

At last I turned and I made my way back to her.

I lay beside her. Her arms were waiting for me. Her lips were waiting.

"And you believe this can happen?" I asked, speaking slowly. "You believe you can walk away from everyone who looks to you for a future they couldn't envisage without you?"

She said nothing. Then, "Let me fall into eternity," she sighed. "I am tired."

Oh, I understand, I do, and you have done so much!

I waited, then I spoke with careful words.

"You believe the ongoing world will know what to make of Lorkyn and Oberon and Miravelle without your wisdom and your insight?" I asked. "You believe that ego-driven science can truly take custody of something so delicate, so explosive, so fine?"

No answer.

"You believe the Medical Center will reach its full perfection without your guidance?" I asked. I spoke the words as lovingly as I could. "There are plans yet in your heart, magnificent plans, and bold visions yet uncommitted to record. Who will pick up the scepter? Who has the courage? Who has the Mayfair billions coupled with the discrete power? Who passes from the operating table to the laboratory to the swarm of the architects and the scientists with the fierceness of a Gamma Knife? Who? Who can go beyond the daring already accomplished in the Medical Center? Who can double its size? Perhaps even triple it? And you have those years to give it. You know it. I know it. You have them chaste and pure and driven by compulsive virtue. Are you ready to turn your back on that?"

No response. I waited. I held her close, as if someone were going to steal her from me. As if the night was full of menace. As if the menace didn't come from me.

"And Michael," I said. "Yes, he has to be released, but is this the time to do it? Will he survive your coming to me? He's still snared in horrors. His heart's been broken by Mona's fate. Can you really slip away on Michael? Can you write the cryptic note? Can you say the dark farewell?"

For the longest time she didn't answer. I felt I could say no more. My heart ached as much as it had ever ached. We lay so near to one another, so bound in one another's limbs, so warm and belonging to each other that the night had gone quiet of all its random sounds for us.

At last she stirred ever so faintly, ever so tenderly.

"I know," she whispered. "I know." And then again, "I know."

"This can't happen," I said. "Never have I wanted anything so much, but it can't happen. You know that it can't."

"You don't really mean that," she said. "Surely you don't. You can't refuse me! You think I'd come to you like this if I didn't know how you really feel?"

"Know how I feel?" I said, holding her against me, clasping her tight to me. "Yes, you know how much I love you. Yes, you know how much I want you, and to slip away with you, away from anyone who could divide us, yes, you know. What are mortal lives to me after all? But don't you see, Rowan, you've made your mortal life magnificent. You turned your soul inside out to do it. And that simply cannot be ignored."

Her arms continued to hold me. She pressed her face against mine. I stroked her hair.

"Yes," she said. "I tried. It was my dream."

"It is your dream," I said. "Even now."

"Yes," she said.

I felt such hurt in me I couldn't speak for a little while.

Again, I let myself imagine we were in a dark bed, she and I together, and that nothing could part us, and in each other we had found sublime meaning, and all the cosmic troubles were gone from us like so many veils torn away.

But that was fantasy, and weak as it was beautiful.

She broke the silence.

"And so I make another sacrifice," she said, "or you make it for me, a sacrifice so great I hardly grasp it! Good God—."

"No," I answered. "You make the sacrifice, Rowan. You've come to the brink but you move back from it. You've got to go back, you, yourself."

Her fingers moved against my back, as though trying to find some human softness in it. Her head nestled against me. Her breath came choked as if in sobs.

"Rowan," I said. "It's not the time."

She looked up at me.

"The time will come," I said. "I'll wait and I'll be there."

"You mean this?" she asked.

"I mean it," I said. "You haven't lost what I have to give, Rowan. It's just not the time."

A soft mauve light had come into the sky; the leaves were burning in my eyes. I hated it.

Lifting her gently with me, I sat up and helped her to sit beside me. Bits of grass clung to her, and her hair was prettily disheveled and her eyes glistened in the growing light.

"Of course a thousand things may happen," I said. "We both know it. But I'll be watching. I'll be watching, and waiting. And when the time comes, when you can really draw back from all of it, then I'll come."

She looked down, and then up at me again. Her face was pensive and soft. "And will I lose all sight of you now?" she asked. "Will you go away beyond my reach?"

"From time to time, perhaps," I answered. "But never for very long. I'll be guarding you, Rowan. You can count on it. And the night will come when we'll share the Blood. I promise you. The Dark Gift will be yours."

I rose to my feet. I took her hand and helped her to stand.

"I have to go now, beloved. The light's my mortal enemy. I wish I could watch the sunrise with you. But I can't."

I clasped her to me suddenly, violently, kissing her as hungrily as I ever had. "I love you, Rowan Mayfair," I said. "I belong to you. I'll always belong to you. I'll never never be far away."

"Good-bye, my love," she whispered. A faint smile appeared on her face. "You really do love me, don't you?" she whispered.

"Oh, yes, with my whole heart," I said.

She turned from me quickly, as though that was the only way to do it, and she walked up the rise of the lawn and to the front drive. I heard the motor of her car, and then I went slowly back around to the rear door of the house, and into my room.

I was so utterly unhappy that I hardly knew what I was doing. And at one point it struck me that what I'd just done was mad. Then it hit me that it just couldn't have happened. A selfish fiend like me just would not have let her go!

Who said all those noble words!

She'd given me the moment, perhaps the only moment. And I'd tried to be Saint Lestat! I'd tried to be heroic. Dear God, what had I done! Now her wisdom and her strength would carry her far away from me. Age would only enlarge her soul and dwindle for her the glow of my enchantment. I had forfeited her forever. Oh, Lestat, how I do hate thee!

There was plenty enough time for the nightshirt ritual, and as I finished with it, torn with thirst and torn with grief for what I'd just refused and might lose forever, I realized I wasn't alone.

Ghosts again, I thought. *Mon Dieu.* I looked quite deliberately at the small table.

What a sight.

It was a grown woman, perhaps twenty, twenty-five. Glossy black hair in marcel waves. Flapper dress of layered silk, long string of pearls. Legs crossed, fancy heels.

Stella!

It seemed monstrous, like the little girl I knew stretched and pulled and blown up; cigarette in a holder, poised in her left hand.

"Ducky, don't be so silly!" she said. "Of course it's me! Oncle Julien's so frightened of you now, he won't come near you. But he just had to send the message: 'That was superb!' "

She vanished before I could throw one of my boots at her. But I wouldn't have done that anyway.

What did it matter? Let them come and go. After all, this was Blackwood Farm, wasn't it, and Blackwood Farm has always opened its portals to ghosts.

And now I lay me down to sleep, and the book comes to a close.

Against the deep down pillow, I realized something. Even in grief and loss, I possessed Rowan. She was a presence within me forever. My loneliness would never again be as bitter. Over the years she might drift away from me, she might come to condemn the point of passion that had brought her to my arms. She might be lost to me in some other mundane fashion that would wring tears from me all my nights.

But I'd never really lose her. Because I wouldn't lose the lesson of love I'd learned through her. And this she had given me as I had tried to give it to her.

And so the morning dew covered the grass on that day at Blackwood Farm like any other, and I dreamt before the sun rose that:

I wanna be a saint, I wanna save souls by the millions, I wanna look like an angel, but I don't wanna talk like a gangster, I don't want to do bad things even to bad guys, I wanna be Saint Juan Diego. . . .

. . . But you know me, and come sunset, maybe it will be time to hunt the back roads, and those little out-of-the-way beer joints, sure enough, smell the malt and the sawdust, and yeah, right on, dance to the Dixie Chicks on the jukebox, and maybe crush a couple of heavy-duty Evil Doers, guys who are just waiting for me, and when I'm flush with blood, and sick of the smack and roll of the pool balls and that warm light on the green felt, who knows, yeah, who knows just how glorious the firmament with all its breaking clouds and lost little stars will appear as I rise above this Earth and spread out my arms as though there was no want in me for anything warm or good.

Be gone from me, oh mortals who are pure of heart. Be gone from my thoughts, oh souls that dream great dreams. Be gone from me, all hymns of glory. I am the magnet for the damned. At least for a little while. And then my heart cries out, my heart will not be still, my heart will not give up, my heart will not give in—

—the blood that teaches life will not teach lies, and love becomes again my reprimand, my goad, my song.

THE END

Anne Rice
October 5, 2002
New Orleans

A NOTE ON THE TYPE

This book was set in Janson, a typeface long thought to have been made by the Dutchman Anton Janson, who was a practicing type-founder in Leipzig during the years 1668–1687. However, it has been conclusively demonstrated that these types are actually the work of Nicholas Kis (1650–1702), a Hungarian, who most probably learned his trade from the master Dutch typefounder Dirk Voskens. The type is an excellent example of the influential and sturdy Dutch types that prevailed in England up to the time William Caslon (1692–1766) developed his own incomparable designs from them.

Composed by Creative Graphics,
Allentown, Pennsylvania
Printed and bound by Berryville Graphics,
Berryville, Virginia
Designed by Virginia Tan